BLOODBORN

A NOISE FROM behind her brought her head around – the scuff of shoe leather on brick. There was lantern light coming from another tunnel on the far side of the intersection. A silhouetted figure in a long coat and broad-brimmed hat appeared at its mouth, as tall and straight as the little man had been hunched and squat. It held a torch and a pistol in its gauntleted hands.

'Halt, bloodsucker!' it cried in stentorian tones. 'My bullets are silvered!'

A WARHAMMER NOVEL

ULRIKA THE VAMPIRE
BLOODBORN

NATHAN LONG

BLACK LIBRARY

To Rob Clark, who bled for this.

A BLACK LIBRARY PUBLICATION

First published in Great Britain in 2010 by
The Black Library,
Games Workshop Ltd.,
Willow Road, Nottingham,
NG7 2WS, UK.

10 9 8 7 6 5 4 3 2 1

Cover illustration by Winona Nelson.

A CIP record for this book is available from the British Library.

ISBN13: 978 1 84416 825 5

Distributed in the US by Simon & Schuster
1230 Avenue of the Americas, New York, NY 10020, US.

See the Black Library on the internet at
www.blacklibrary.com

Find out more about Games Workshop
and the world of Warhammer 40,000 at
www.games-workshop.com

Printed and bound in the US.

THIS IS A dark age, a bloody age, an age of daemons
and of sorcery. It is an age of battle and death, and of the
world's ending. Amidst all of the fire, flame and fury
it is a time, too, of mighty heroes, of bold deeds
and great courage.

At the heart of the Old World sprawls the Empire, the
largest and most powerful of the human realms. Known
for its engineers, sorcerers, traders and soldiers, it is
a land of great mountains, mighty rivers, dark forests
and vast cities. And from his throne in Altdorf reigns
the Emperor Karl Franz, sacred descendant of the
founder of these lands, Sigmar, and wielder
of his magical warhammer.

But these are far from civilised times. Across the length
and breadth of the Old World, from the knightly palaces
of Bretonnia to ice-bound Kislev in the far north, come
rumblings of war. In the towering Worlds Edge Mountains,
the orc tribes are gathering for another assault. Bandits and
renegades harry the wild southern lands of
the Border Princes. There are rumours of rat-things, the
skaven, emerging from the sewers and swamps across the
land. And from the northern wildernesses there is the
ever-present threat of Chaos, of daemons and beastmen
corrupted by the foul powers of the Dark Gods.
As the time of battle draws ever nearer,
the Empire needs heroes
like never before.

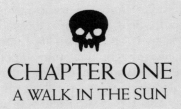

CHAPTER ONE
A WALK IN THE SUN

THE SCENT OF blood was in her nose – blood not yet
shed, blood still in the vein. She could hear the rush
of it too, the frantic, frightened pulse throbbing in her
ears like a lover's moans. Her eyes saw the world in red
and black, in looming shadows and ember-gleaming
heart-fires – fires that would warm her and stave off
the ever-encroaching cold of death.

The scent grew stronger, the throbbing louder, mad-
dening her, driving all thought from her until there
was nothing inside except hunger, a roaring emptiness
that demanded to be fed. It told her she would die if
it wasn't sated, and that death would be no release
from pain. It told her that nothing else mattered
except feeding – not loyalty, not honour, not compassion. All that mattered was clinging to life, even unlife,
for as long as she could.

She could hear the weeping of her prey now as she
bounded naked after it through the winter woods.
She could hear its feeble bleatings to its uncaring

gods. Its heart pounded like a rabbit's, and the stink of its fear-sweat was heady enough to make her drunk. Only a few more paces and her fangs would be in its neck, drinking deep, feeding the hollow blackness, basking in the glow of the heart-fire.

The man broke from the trees, racing across a snowy, moonlit field towards a miserable thatch-roofed shack, as if he expected its flimsy walls to protect him. She thought for a moment of letting him reach it, just to toy with him, to let him have one last false hope before she ripped the door off its hinges, but her need was too great. There was no time for games. Her hunger would not wait.

With a last lithe leap she hit him high in the back and brought him down in a rolling jumble through the powdery snow. He flailed, shrieking with fear, and tried to scramble away, but he was weak and she was strong. She pinned his limbs, scissoring them between her naked legs, then grabbed his chin, forcing it back and exposing the dirty neck under his scruffy beard. His carotid artery twitched beneath his skin like a mouse trapped under a sheet. Well, she would free it.

As her head shot forwards, something thudded into the ground beside her, kicking up a spray of snow – a crossbow bolt. She looked up, snarling, fangs bared. Who dared interrupt her while she fed?

Galloping across the moon-bright snow on horseback were a woman and a man, heavy sable cloaks billowing behind them. The woman was raven-haired and coldly beautiful in blood-red velvet under her furs, the man a hulking, golden-maned epitome of knightly strength clad in steel breastplate and high boots. A gilded crossbow glinted in his right hand, and he was already winching it back for another shot.

She barked angrily and returned to her prey, desperate now to feed before they stopped her, but as her fangs touched the peasant's throat, the woman's voice rang out over the field, freezing her before she bit.

'No, Ulrika! You will not!'

Ulrika growled low in her throat, then bent forwards again. The blood was so close. She could think of nothing else. They would not keep her from it.

'Stand, child!' called the woman. 'Obey me!'

Ulrika strained, but the words were like a chain, holding her from her prey. She could not go against them. She crouched over the peasant, trembling with frustration, and glared as the woman and the golden-haired knight thudded up on their horses and stopped before her.

'Up,' said the woman. 'Let him go.'

'I'm *hungry*,' Ulrika whined.

'And you shall feed,' the woman said, holding out a beringed hand. 'But not here. Not like this. Not like a beast. Now stand.'

The urge to throw herself at her tormentor was overpowering, but Ulrika knew she couldn't, and wouldn't survive if she did. With a petulant grunt she pushed herself to her feet, her bare limbs shaking from hunger and suppressed violence, and raised her chin defiantly before the woman and the knight as the peasant mewled pathetically at her feet.

The knight's lip curled in disgust as he looked her up and down. The woman's face was as calm and cold as a statue's.

'You must learn control, dear one,' she said. 'Did I not promise your friends I would teach you to do no harm?'

Flashes of her former companions' faces flitted through Ulrika's mind – the poet, the wizard, the dwarf. What would they think if they could see her now, naked and savage, clawed and fanged like a wolf? She didn't care. They were only meat after all.

'*I* didn't promise,' she growled.

'But *I* did,' said the woman. 'And I do not break a pledge lightly, so you will refrain. Am I clear?'

Ulrika remained glaring for a long moment, then lowered her head. 'Aye,' she said. 'I will refrain.'

The woman smiled sweetly. 'Good. Then come, climb up behind me and we will return to Nachthafen.'

Ulrika stepped reluctantly from the cowering peasant, then hopped onto the rump of the woman's horse in a single bound. As they turned towards the dirt track that ran past the snow field, Ulrika saw a group of huddled figures standing before the entrance to the shack – an old man, a young woman and two dirty children, all dressed in meagre night shirts. They bowed low to the woman as she rode past and touched their forelocks respectfully, then hurried to help the peasant who still lay whimpering where Ulrika had left him.

Ulrika had died two weeks before.

Adolphus Krieger, an ambitious vampire who had come to the besieged city of Praag searching for a relic of great power, had taken her hostage there in order to escape the end her friends Max Schreiber, Felix Jaeger,

Gotrek Gurnisson and Snorri Nosebiter, had meant for him. Though initially Krieger had intended to dispose of her as soon as he won clear of Praag, he had taken a liking to her, and that affection had sealed her doom.

Travelling alone with the vampire for hundreds of miles as his coach hurried through the winter snows towards Sylvania, she had fought against his unnatural charisma, but eventually she had succumbed, and allowed him to drink from her. After that, her will was not her own, and when they had reached Drakenhof Castle, where he intended to raise an all-conquering army of the undead, she had not resisted when he told her that he would make her his queen and gave her the blood kiss – the ritual that had killed her and brought her back to life as a vampire.

Unfortunately for Krieger, her friends had not given up the chase, and had arrived at Drakenhof shortly thereafter in the company of one Countess Gabriella, the vampire who had long ago given Krieger the blood kiss, and who was now bent on frustrating his ambitions. Together, the two men, the two dwarfs and the vampiress had succeeded in killing Krieger, and in making Ulrika an orphan.

Gotrek had wanted to kill her as well, saying she had become an irredeemable creature of darkness, but the countess promised him and the others that she would see to Ulrika's education and teach her to do no harm, and the Slayer had reluctantly relented and allowed Gabriella to take her away.

When she had brought Ulrika to Nachthafen Castle that first night, the countess had told her that there had been a Countess von Nachthafen living there for more than two hundred years. Sometimes she had been the wife of the count, sometimes the daughter, sometimes a cousin or a long-lost niece, but no matter her name, and no matter if she were dark or fair, young or old, stern or sweet, it had always been herself, a woman whose true name and place of birth had been hidden behind so many false guises and biographies that she had almost forgotten them, they had been so long ago.

In her current incarnation she called herself Countess Gabriella von Nachthafen, a well-travelled socialite, raised and schooled in Altdorf, who had inherited the castle from her aunt, tragically killed in a hunting accident ten years before. In the castle and the town below it, which shared its name, the countess was absolute mistress, kind and fair, but demanding of unquestioning obedience from her serfs and servants, all of whom knew precisely who and what she was, whatever name and face she might wear at the moment. That the countess seemed to think that she was absolute mistress of Ulrika as well, and demanded the same unquestioning obedience from her, Ulrika was having difficulty accepting.

'You may not order me!' she snarled as she paced naked around the dark, richly-appointed tower room Gabriella had given her. 'I am no servant! I am a boyar's daughter. I have commanded a hundred Kossars! I can trace my name back a thousand years!'

'And I can *remember* back a thousand years,' said the countess calmly, from where she sat in her crimson velvet in a high-backed mahogany chair. 'Do you think your lineage means anything to me, who can trace her blood back to the royalty of Nehekhara?

Your people are barbaric children, barely crawling from the crib. And *you* are an infant, little more than twenty when that fool Krieger turned you, and less than two weeks dead today.'

'I am my own woman!' shouted Ulrika, stamping a bare foot on the thick rug that covered the stone floor. 'I still have free will!'

'You do not,' said Gabriella, and though she did not raise her voice, it suddenly had an air of command that made Ulrika tense as if expecting a blow. 'Had I allowed Krieger to live, it would have been his responsibility to see to your education, but as he is dead, that responsibility lies now with me.' She toyed with a gold and crystal hourglass that sat on the velvet-draped table beside her. 'I could have just as easily killed you, and saved myself a lot of bother, but as Krieger was my get, and you were his, I felt some familial obligation to you. I hope I do not live to regret it.'

'I need no education,' growled Ulrika. 'I know how to feed.'

Gabriella laughed. 'Like tonight? Child, a babe knows how to suckle at the teat, but you can't take one to table.' She stood and stepped towards Ulrika, who paused from her pacing and shrank back. 'Every vampire has an obligation to every other vampire to be discreet – to feed covertly, to live privately – for when one is discovered, it riles the sheep and endangers us all. If I were to let you rage through the countryside, slaughtering indiscriminately, the witch hunters wouldn't just come for you. They would begin to wonder who else might have hidden fangs. They would prowl about, asking questions and bringing lanterns and silvered blades into crypts. I can't allow that, and so you must be taught. You must learn *not* to feed. You must learn to control your hunger lest it control you, exposing you – and me – to the cattle's ignorant wrath.'

The countess turned from Ulrika and clapped her hands twice. The door to the circular room opened and a handsome young man in homespun doublet and breeches stepped in, bowing low, then waited, head lowered, his hands clasped nervously at his waist.

'Now,' said Gabriella, turning to the table. 'Johannes here is eager to receive your kiss. But he is the youngest of my flock, and you must be gentle with him. You must also be patient.' She picked up the hourglass. 'To learn restraint, I would have you wait until these sands run out before tasting him, and when you do, you must do so without passion or violence – or slaughter.' She turned the glass over and crossed to the door. 'I will return when you have finished. Farewell.'

Ulrika barely heard the door close behind the countess. She could only stare at the silvery grains trickling down into the empty lower chamber of the glass. They went so slowly, like drifting snowflakes. Her eyes slid to Johannes, who remained quaking at the door. His pulse was as hard and loud as a marching drum in her ears as he bowed to her. She could smell his fear, and also his arousal. The two smells boiled up from him like the fragrance of some jungle flower, rank and fleshy, but intoxicating. Her fangs and claws extended of their own accord as she inhaled it. She forced them to retract. It took every ounce of willpower she possessed.

'Mistress–' he began.

'Shut up!' Ulrika snapped. 'Don't speak.'

She cursed and looked away from him. How was she to do this? She had fed correctly before, but never after so long a wait. For the first few nights after her rescue from Krieger, the countess had let her feed almost hourly, but always under the closest supervision, and always upon victims for whom she had no regard – the last tattered remnants of Krieger's hangers-on, hunted down across the Sylvanian countryside. But since returning to Nachthafen, Gabriella had been increasing the time between feedings, and only letting her sip where once she had guzzled. Ulrika had not felt sated once. The hunger had never released her, and now it was killing her with its grip.

This last gap had been the longest and worst. She had not fed for over two nights. Of course she had made it worse for herself by escaping. The countess would have no doubt let her feed earlier this evening but, in her blood-madness, Ulrika had broken out of her tower room as soon as the sun had dipped below the trees and gone charging naked through the forest after the scent of human blood. That and being caught and dragged back and lectured to had taken time, and now she was hungrier than ever before.

She turned back to the hourglass. Ursun's teeth! The sand must have stopped! Hardly any had piled on the bottom of the chamber. This was intolerable.

She faced Johannes again. His pulse pounded in her ears like it was her own. He shrank back against the panelled door, whimpering, and Ulrika realised that she had advanced on him without meaning to. She forced herself away again, taking her embroidered robe from her canopied bed and pulling it on as she looked up at the arched window from which she had earlier that night smashed the diamond panes and torn the iron bars with her bare hands. It was shuttered now, in preparation for the coming of morning, but it would be nothing to tear away the shutters like she had the bars. She could flee again, but she knew she would only be dragged back and chastised once more.

A tremor of hunger went through her and she clenched her hands to her sides, fighting it. She must be strong. Was she not the daughter of a boyar? Had she not endured pitiless winters and terrible pain? Had she not lived through loss and sickness and privation? She had the iron will of the Kossars in her. She was a Kislevite, born with ice in her veins.

But that was before – before Krieger had killed her and resurrected her in his own image, before he had turned her into a monster, before he had weakened her spirit with his corrupting whispers and bloody lips. After his kiss, she had been reborn, this time with nothing in her veins. Their emptiness hurt worse than winter, worse than the death of loved ones, or the loss of honour. They needed to be filled.

She shot a glance at the hourglass. Not even a quarter full. Without turning she could feel the blood heat of young Johannes radiating against her back like the warmth of a hearth. She wanted to be nearer to it. She wanted to warm her hands in it. The cold of winter might not harm her any more, but the void within her empty heart ached like it had been plunged into a frozen lake.

'Mistress, what are you doing? An hour is not yet passed.'

Ulrika found she was approaching the boy again, though she couldn't remember turning towards him. She tried to speak, to say something reassuring, but her fangs got in the way and her words became a guttural snarl. He pressed himself against the door, eyes wide. His fear-smell maddened her. She snatched at him, claws lengthening.

With a yelp he turned and scrabbled the door open. She kicked it shut, catching his right hand in it, then jerked him away from it and threw him into the table, upsetting it and knocking the hourglass to the floor. His fingers remained in the door.

He shrieked on the floor, staring at the crimson stumps of his digitless hand. She grabbed his shirt front and hauled him up, his feet dangling above the ground. He continued to scream.

'Shut up!' Ulrika cried. 'Stop that noise!'

He would not.

She snapped her head forward and tore out his throat with her fangs.

He was silent at last.

ULRIKA WAS ON all fours, puking up black gobbets of heart meat, when Countess Gabriella opened the door a while later. She shook her head and sighed as she surveyed the carnage. Young Johannes's disparate parts were strewn across the tower room's stone floor like grisly islands in a red sea.

'This will not do,' she said. 'This will not do at all.'

Ulrika glared up at Countess Gabriella, opening her mouth to curse her, but another convulsion rocked her and she spewed a stream of undigested organ bits onto the flagstones. She had never felt so sick in her life – or her death. She was full, her belly bloated like an over-full wineskin, and was woozy and nauseated as if with hangover, one worse than she had ever had after drinking kvas with her father's troopers.

Worse was the sickness of her soul. She was horrified by what she had done – disgusted by her savagery. In life she had never shied from bloodshed, but neither had she killed an innocent. She had never torn apart a defenceless boy with her bare hands. She buried her face in her arms, sobbing though no tears would come.

Gabriella called down the tower stairs for servants to come and clean up the mess, then raised her floor-length skirts and stepped fastidiously through the maze of Johannes's limbs to sit again at the chair by the smashed table. She picked up the cracked hour-glass from the ruins. The lower chamber was less than a quarter full of sand.

'I apologise, Ulrika,' she said. 'I have tested you too severely. I have forgotten how hard it is at first.'

Ulrika pounded the flagstones with her fists, splashing herself with gore. 'Why did you not just kill me?' she screamed. 'I don't want this! I've become an animal!'

'It won't always be like this, child,' said Gabriella. 'Restraint will come. You must have patience.'

'I don't want restraint! I want to die!'

Gabriella looked at her levelly for a moment, then stood and crossed to the window. She opened the shutters, being careful to avoid the knife-edge of morning light that stabbed in and highlighted the table, and the red flecks of blood that dotted its legs.

She turned to Ulrika, gesturing with her hand like a butler inviting a visitor into a great house. 'You may walk in the sun any time you like, beloved.'

Ulrika looked with desperate longing at the rosy dawn that glowed above the distant snow-capped hills. All she had to do was leap – a jump to the window and a jump to oblivion as the sun tore the flesh from her bones and ripped her soul from the cage of dark magic that held it there. Nothing but an empty, blackened skeleton would hit the rocks at the base of the castle wall if she leapt. She tried to force her limbs to move, to give up their selfish desire for existence and finish the job Krieger had started.

She crouched there, trembling with tension for a full minute, but she couldn't do it. She was weak. Her will to live was stronger than her loathing for what she had become.

She lowered her head to the bloody flagstones and shut her eyes. 'Close it,' she said. 'I don't want to see it.'

AFTER THE SERVANTS had carried away Johannes's remains, mopped up the blood and taken the rug for cleaning, Ulrika retired to her bed for the rest of the day. She lay awake for a long time, finding it hard to summon the trance-state that vampires call sleep. Her thoughts would not settle. She remained disgusted with herself, even more so now that she had proved again that she was a coward as well as an animal.

She wished she could cry for the release of it, but that was a thing vampires could not do. They shed no tears. Perhaps that was why her grief expressed itself in rage and violence, since it had no other outlet. If only she could talk to Max Schreiber, the wizard with whom she had travelled on her adventures in Kislev and the Worlds Edge Mountains, and whom she had come to love after he had saved her from the terrible illness that had nearly killed her in Praag. Max was wise. He would tell her what was best to do. He would comfort her. Perhaps he could even cure her.

She longed to see her old lover Felix Jaeger, too. She and the poet had drifted apart, but he had never turned his back on her when it mattered. He was a good man, no matter how annoying he could sometimes be, and lying in his arms had always given her great comfort. She fell asleep at last wishing that she could be folded within them again, and hear him whispering foolish rhymes in her ear as they lay in bed.

CHAPTER TWO
BY ORDER OF THE QUEEN

'How DOTH MY lover love me?' whispered Felix as he held Ulrika in his arms. 'Doth she pine for me by moonlight? Doth she sing sad songs of my departure? Doth–'

'What does "doth" mean?' Ulrika interrupted, laughing.

'Ah, it's an old-fashioned way of saying "does", said Felix. 'Certainly you could understand that from the context.'

'Yes, but why use it? Is it an old poem?'

'No. I wrote it myself.'

'Then why write it that way?' Ulrika insisted. 'You don't say "doth".'

Felix squirmed. 'I… I wanted to evoke an earlier, more romantic era. A time of grand passion and–'

Ulrika raised an eyebrow. 'Are you saying that romance and grand passion no longer exist? Should I be insulted?'

'No, I...' Felix stopped, then sighed, exasperated. 'You are a very difficult young woman to recite a poem to. Do you even want to hear the rest?'

'By all means,' said Ulrika, then smiled slyly and kissed his naked chest. 'Unless, that is, you would rather learn better how thy lover doth love thee.' She kissed his collarbone. 'Perhaps you could add a few more stanzas to your poem.'

Felix grunted with renewed lust and pulled her close for a long, deep kiss. Their bodies moved against each other. She ran her hands down his hard back, desire beginning to glow brighter within her like the embers of a stirred fire.

As they began to move together, the fire flared to a roaring blaze and she rolled on top of him, nipping at his shoulder while they caressed and grappled and gasped. He was so warm and strong and full of life.

Their tempo increased. Her lips pressed against Felix's neck. His touch was enflaming. His scent was intoxicating. His taste made her weak. She could hold back no longer. With a wild animal cry, Ulrika crushed herself against him and tore his throat out with her fangs.

ULRIKA JERKED AWAKE, gasping, the taste of Felix's blood on her lips and the smell of his sweat on her skin. The dream faded slowly as she lay back, shaking and staring unseeing at the ceiling. Was that what she would do if she saw Felix again? Or Max? Was her passion to be like her grief, transmuted into nothing but rage and violence? Was bloodletting the only release left to her? She closed her eyes and made a silent prayer to the gods who would no longer receive her that she would never see her old friends again.

At least it wasn't likely to happen. When she and Countess Gabriella had parted ways with the four adventurers, they had been heading back to Kislev to help defend Praag against the spring return of the Chaos hordes. It was doubtful any of them would survive this second siege. Praag itself was unlikely to survive, and knowing Felix, Max, Gotrek and Snorri as she did, she was sure they would die fighting before they let it be overrun.

She wondered if they were already back at the White Boar, drinking and brawling and waiting for the real battles to start. Probably not. Little more than two weeks had passed since they left. They would be on the road still, bickering and joking and complaining about the weather.

Suddenly, despite her previous prayer, she wanted to be with them more than anything in the world, trading quips with Felix, listening to Max go on about all and sundry, smiling at Snorri's forthright ignorance and Gotrek's hardheaded certainty. But no, they had let her live – letting her travel with them was something else altogether. She was a monster now. They killed monsters. And she killed humans. It was impossible for them to continue to be companions.

After brooding a while longer on her old life and her new, she rose from her bed and donned a silk robe. It was evening, and she could hear sounds of activity in the castle below. The noises grew louder as she descended the narrow stone spiral of the tower, and as she stepped into the dark upper corridor she was nearly knocked down by two servants hurrying by with a great, brass-bound trunk. Another servant swerved past with a stack of hat boxes.

In the vast stone entry hall, looming gargoyles looked down on more confusion. Trunks and wardrobes were being piled by the front door, and maids and footmen were covering ornamental suits of armour and heavy, carved furniture with white sheets. Near the doors to the music room, Countess Gabriella, in a forest-green bodice and dress, was in conference with Lady Grau, her sober chatelaine, ticking off things in a giant ledger that the golden-haired knight Rodrik, Gabriella's champion, held open before them.

Ulrika padded barefoot down the sweeping stone steps and crossed to them. 'Mistress,' she said. 'What is happening?'

Gabriella looked up, distracted. 'I must leave for Nuln. Tonight.' She returned to the ledger, tapping a finger on some entry. 'No. There will be no need of groomsmen while I am gone. Rodrik, select two to travel with us, then dismiss the rest.'

'As you wish, m'lady,' intoned the knight.

A thrill of anxiety went through Ulrika. Was the countess leaving her alone? Could she survive without her? Could she control herself? 'How… how long will you be gone?'

Gabriella's eyes flashed up at her again. 'I don't know! Now, I have quite a lot of details to attend to before I go, and–' She paused, her brow furrowing. 'And you are one of them, aren't you?'

Gabriella took the ledger from Rodrik and gave it to Lady Grau. 'You may finish the arrangements yourself. You know what I wish. The bare minimum that will keep the house in order until I return.'

Lady Grau curtseyed. 'Yes, countess.'

As she withdrew, Gabriella beckoned Ulrika and Rodrik into the music room, then closed the door behind them, shutting out the noise in the entry hall.

'There has been trouble among my sisters in Nuln,' she said, facing Ulrika. 'And I am commanded by my queen – *our* queen, the Lady of the Silver Mountain – to go there and assist them in the crisis. I must of course obey, but the order comes at an inconvenient time – at least as far as you are concerned.'

'You do not wish to leave me alone,' said Ulrika.

'I dare not,' said the countess. 'And yet, to bring you into Nuln–'

'M'lady, you cannot,' said Rodrik, appalled. 'I saw what she left of the boy. She is not ready.'

'But to leave her is to doom her,' said Gabriella. 'Without guidance she will become the animal she thinks she is now.'

'Have I no say in this?' asked Ulrika, stiffening. They spoke of her as they would a dog.

'None whatsoever,' said the countess, then shrugged her shoulders and turned to Rodrik. 'She will come. Have her things packed. No, wait. I will show her first. Go.'

Rodrik didn't appear to like it, but he only bowed. 'As you wish, m'lady.'

As he turned and stepped into the hall, Gabriella smiled at Ulrika, as warm now as she had been cold only a moment before. 'I have a surprise for you. Come.'

The countess took Ulrika's hand and led her through the castle to the library, a high, arch-ceilinged room, lined with books, which served her as both study and office. Ulrika froze for a moment on the threshold as Gabriella threw open the doors and drew her in, for it seemed at first that there were five head-less noblewomen waiting at attention for her in the centre of the room. Then she saw they were dress-maker's dummies, clothed in beautiful floor-length gowns and dresses, and she was just as puzzled.

'What is this?' she asked, staring at the mannequins.

Gabriella laughed and danced through them, spreading her hands. 'Why, they're for you!' she said. 'That clown Krieger brought you from Kislev to Sylva-nia in one set of riding clothes, and provided you with no replacement when you got here. I had these altered from some things of mine – as tall as you are they wouldn't have fit otherwise – and I think they came out fine, don't you? Here, look.'

She led Ulrika forward, flitting from one outfit to the other as if she were a girl of eighteen instead of a thousand-year-old undead aristocrat. 'This black one is for formal affairs, meeting dignitaries, that sort of thing. This is a simpler one, for day to day.' She laughed. 'Or night to night, I should say. And this, with the red and the lace, is for grand balls and par-ties. Aren't they lovely?'

'Yes,' said Ulrika, fondling the velvets and satins with distracted fingers. 'Lovely.'

'And look at this,' continued Gabriella, turning to a long wig of glossy black hair on a wig stand on a table. 'A wig made from the hair of virgins from Cathay, to cover that unruly corn-thatch you wear on your head.'

Ulrika barely heard her. The dresses were indeed lovely, more beautiful than any she had ever owned in cold, hard Kislev, and though she was more used to breeches than skirts, they stirred an almost forgotten girlishness in her. At the same time, she was trying to imagine the creature she had been the night before, the red-eyed, red-fanged monster that had torn a boy limb from limb then vomited up his organs, wearing one of the exquisite things. She couldn't see it. And there was something else.

She turned and bowed respectfully to Gabriella. 'Thank you. They... they are more beautiful than I deserve, and I will wear them with pride, but...'

Gabriella raised an arched brow, a dangerous glint appearing in her eyes. 'But?'

Ulrika bowed again. 'Forgive me. But what will I fight in?'

Gabriella drew herself up, stiff. 'You will not fight,' she said. 'Fighting is not the Lahmian way.' She started for the library door, all her earlier effervescence gone, then paused and looked back over her shoulder. 'And you will learn to curtsey, not bow. Only men bow.'

Embarrassment prickled Ulrika's skin. She didn't know how to curtsey. She'd never done it in her life.

THEY SET OFF from Nachthafen a few hours before dawn – a luxurious enclosed coach with louvred windows and heavy curtains for the countess and Ulrika and Lotte, the countess's plump, red-headed maid, a pony cart for their luggage, an escort of six knights led by Rodrik, two grooms, two drivers and eight extra horses. The plan was to ride through the morning until noon, stay the afternoon at a coaching inn, then continue on as soon as the sun set. They would be eight nights on the road to Eicheshatten, where they would board a riverboat that would take them down the River Aver to Nuln in six more days. The countess did not care to travel by river, but the situation in Nuln was apparently desperate, and so speed was of the essence.

'I only hope we are quick enough,' she sighed as she drew off her hat and veil and set them on the padded leather bench beside her.

'What is the trouble there?' asked Ulrika. 'You didn't say before.'

Gabriella pursed her lips. '"What is the trouble there, *mistress*," you should say, child. I am your mistress, and you must learn to address me as such.'

Ulrika raised her chin. 'A countess is not superior to a boyarina,' she said.

Gabriella chuckled. 'The titles we show to the outside world mean nothing within our sisterhood, darling Ulrika. I was not born a countess, and you are no longer a boyarina. The only rank that has any true meaning to you now is your rank within our society, and at this moment you are on the bottom rung. In fact, you are lower than that, for you were not born of a sister. You are an adopted stray, and you will have to prove your usefulness and loyalty before you are fully accepted into our sorority.'

Ulrika grew hot at this and her fists clenched.

The countess saw this and smiled sadly. 'I mean you no offence, beloved. I only tell you the truth. I see great potential in you, and you may rise high with us, but you start at a disadvantage, and you should know that from the beginning.'

Ulrika nodded, curt. 'And how far up the ladder are you?'

Gabriella shot her a sharp look and Ulrika lowered her head, glaring at the floor.

'How far up the ladder are you, *mistress*?' she repeated through her teeth.

'Much better,' said Gabriella. 'I am little more than halfway up. It has been my duty, for the last two hundred years, to watch Sylvania for my queen. To make sure that lunatics like Krieger and others of his ilk do not try to bring back the time of the von Carsteins. But I have been seconded to other places during that time, as now, when situations have arisen.'

'And the situation in Nuln?' asked Ulrika, then caught herself. 'Mistress?'

'Very good,' said Gabriella, then turned and looked out through the louvres into the winter night. 'Nuln is troubling. We have six sisters there. Two of them have been killed in the last two weeks, torn apart by an unknown assailant. Worse, they were exposed as vampires – their corpses left to be seen by the cattle, their fangs and claws extended. This has of course led to panic in the streets. The two sisters were prominent figures in Nuln society. One was Lady Rosamund von Andress, mistress to a prominent general. The other was Karlotta Herzog, who posed as a Shallyan abbess. They were also the most senior Lahmians in Nuln, which makes their deaths doubly suspicious.'

'You suspect a coup?' asked Ulrika. She had experienced enough of Kislevite politics to know what a purge looked like.

'Not by another Lahmian,' said Gabriella. 'With the exposure of Rosamund and Karlotta, the witch hunters will have begun to suspect every powerful woman in Nuln of being a vampire. No Lahmian would bring that on themselves.' She shook her head. 'The queen has ordered me to help our sisters discover the murderer, stop him and defuse the situation somehow, so that the cattle will again forget we exist.'

'Have you any idea how you will do this, mistress?' asked Ulrika.

Gabriella closed her eyes. 'No. It would not be easy even if I could expect complete and cordial cooperation from my sisters there, but I doubt that will happen.'

'Why not?'

Gabriella sighed. 'With Lady Rosamund and Sister Karlotta dead, the senior Lahmian in Nuln is Lady Hermione von Auerbach. We… we have a history.'

Ulrika waited for the countess to continue, but she did not.

'A history, mistress?'

Gabriella opened her eyes and smiled wryly. 'There are only so many positions available in the hierarchy of the Lahmian sisterhood, my dear, only so many of us who can live in one city without risking detection. Lady Hermione and I were turned at roughly the same time, and have, throughout our unlife, vied for many of the plum posts – Altdorf, Nuln, Miragliano, Couronne. Sometimes I won, and sometimes it was her, but unlike me, she has never considered it a friendly game.' The countess's smile began to show more teeth. 'It was she who reminded the queen that Krieger was my get, and had me assigned to that dreary Sylvanian backwater Nachthafen to watch him.'

She shrugged and the smile faded. 'I bear her no ill-will for that. Krieger was indeed my fault, and I accepted my punishment. And the post was an important one. I have kept more than just Krieger from achieving their mad goals in my time there. But Hermione reflects everyone through the mirror of her own jealous mind, and so will not be happy to see me. She will think that I manipulated the queen somehow, in order to get her to send me to Nuln. She will think I have returned for revenge. She will think I want her position, or mean to destroy her in some way.'

'And do you, mistress?'

The countess lowered her eyelids and stared coolly out of the dark window. 'Not unless she tries to destroy me first.'

THE COUNTESS DID not let Ulrika feed that day, saying it was too soon after Johannes, but the next morning, when they had stopped at a second coaching inn, she brought Quentin, the youngest and fairest of her knights, to Ulrika's room. She also brought the hour-glass.,

'We will try again,' she said as Ulrika stood before her in one of her new dresses. 'Again, you will wait the length of the glass, and then feed with restraint and delicacy. Am I understood?'

'Yes, mistress,' said Ulrika, attempting a curtsey. But she was far from sure if it would matter if she understood or not. She was famished. Though she had drunk Johannes dry two nights previously, she had vomited up most of his blood along with the inedible meat she had eaten, and this past day had been an aching misery of need. She was trembling with hunger now, and could hardly keep her eyes off Quentin's throat, which pulsed rapidly above the rich blue broadcloth of his collar.

Rodrik, hovering at the door, was also uneasy. 'Is this wise, m'lady?' he asked. 'Quentin is a seasoned man, not some pot-boy like the last. Let her take one of the grooms.'

'The grooms have not been blooded,' said Gabriella. 'Quentin knows what to expect.'

'But we are at an inn, m'lady,' said Rodrik, trying another tack. 'If she makes a repeat of–'

'She will not!' snapped the countess. 'She will succeed in controlling herself, or perhaps it will be time for us to part company. I will not be embarrassed in Nuln.'

Ulrika's eyes widened at this. 'You would leave me behind, mistress?'

Gabriella raised hard eyes to her, and it was a moment before she spoke. 'No,' she said at last. 'No, I would not. I made that mistake with Krieger. I dismissed him when he displeased me, and you see what occurred. This time, I will leave no loose ends.'

Fear constricted Ulrika's chest. Did the countess mean she would kill her rather than abandon her? Did her life depend on how well she controlled herself with Quentin?

Before she could ask the questions, Gabriella turned the hourglass and set it down sharply on a table by the bed, then turned and strode out the door without a backwards glance. Rodrik stepped aside to let her pass, then looked back in and gave Ulrika a black look. She glared back sullenly, but he turned his gaze to Quentin, who stood at attention in the centre of the room.

'Courage, lad,' he said.

'Thank you, sir,' said Quentin, his voice shaking.

Rodrik closed the door. Ulrika could smell the boy's terror. It was nothing compared to her own.

CHAPTER THREE
THE LAHMIAN WAY

ULRIKA PRESSED HER extended claws into the palms of her hands, fighting down with difficulty the urge to leap on the young knight then and there. She could not fail this time. She must not!

When she had regained some measure of control, she turned from him and stepped to the table with the hourglass.

'Stand away from me,' she said. 'As far as you can. By the fire.'

'Yes, mistress,' said the knight.

'And don't speak. Don't make a sound. I want to forget you're here.'

'May… may I sit?'

'Yes, yes,' said Ulrika. 'Just be silent.'

She heard him draw up a stool beside the fire as she took a chair at the table facing away from him. She picked up the book Gabriella had given her, *The Nehekharan Diaspora*, a vampire-written history of the times of Neferata and Nagash, opened it to the place where she had left off and tried to read.

It was no use, of course, the strange foreign names – W'soran, Abhorash, Ushoran – jumbled senselessly in her head, and she found she was reading the same sentence over and over again. And it made no difference how silent Quentin was. She could still smell him, and hear his blood beating in his veins like a hawk's wings. Her eyes continued looking blankly at the pages of the book, but all her other senses were focused behind her, noting every change in the youth's breathing or the tempo of his pulse.

How was she going to resist as she must? She had no illusion that the countess would not follow through on her threat to destroy her if she failed. Gabriella seemed to have some affection for her, but she had seemed to have some affection for Johannes as well, and she had left him to be torn to pieces without a second thought. Ulrika was certain that if she disappointed her here, the countess would have no compunction about 'taking care of loose ends'. She even understood the necessity of it. If all one's children had the potential to become Kriegers, abandoning them to their own devices was foolishness. They would have to be controlled or killed.

This put Ulrika very close to death. If she failed to control herself with Quentin, she was finished. Of course, there was another option. The windows of the room were not locked or barred. She could run again, and this time she could hide, find shelter in the forests and never have to worry about control again.

Her eyes slid to the windows. The thought was terrifyingly appealing. What a glorious feeling to just let herself go, to surrender completely to the animal within her and hunt like a wolf in the night. What a joy to run and howl, to bring down her prey at a sprint and drink it dry as it thrashed beneath her.

But there was another side to that savage freedom – the hunters, the men with torches. Ulrika remembered a time from her youth when her father had roused his lancers and they had gone in search of something in the woods, something that had been dragging off the peasants in the night. She hadn't known what it was then, and he had never said, but she knew now. That was what she could expect if she lived like an animal – to die like an animal, to be hounded at every turn, to hide and starve and never know peace.

And there was another thing, perhaps more important than all that. A wolf had its pack. A fox had its mate. Would there be others of her kind to run with out in the wild? Ulrika had never been entirely comfortable alone. At home she had enjoyed the company of her father's men and the camaraderie of patrol and watch. Even when she had left for the south as her father's envoy she had always found someone to travel with – Felix, Max and others before them. And now, in this new existence, where nothing was familiar, and she knew none of the rules, she felt even more unwilling to be alone. She hardly knew the countess – Gabriella had plucked her from the haunted ruins of Drakenhof little more than two weeks before – but the thought of leaving her, of being without her guidance and wisdom, was paralysing. She would be lost without it. She might have her wild run in the night, but it would be short. Too soon the hunters would come, and she would die alone – alone and damned.

Quentin shifted on his stool behind her. Ulrika glanced at the hourglass. The bottom chamber was a quarter full. Her heart leapt. She was doing better. Johannes had already been dead by this time. Not that bettering a complete failure was anything to crow about.

She cursed as a fresh wave of hunger rolled over her. She had distracted herself with her thoughts for a few moments, but now the craving had returned, stronger than ever. The room was perfumed with the scent of the young knight's blood. It throbbed with it. Red visions of carnage shot through Ulrika's mind as she inhaled it. She saw herself in mid-leap, she saw Quentin's stool smashing to kindling, the youth slamming to the floor, her claws tearing his doublet, her fangs sinking into his neck.

With a hiss of effort she forced herself to remain in her chair, closing her eyes and clamping her hands around the armrests until they creaked. Frozen there, as flexed as a drawn bow, she let her mind play out the rest of the scene – the guzzling, the rending, the gorging, the bloated stomach, the pounding head, the nausea, the puking, the shivering in the puddle of red vomit and undigested meat – the shame.

The shame. That was the most painful part – worse than all the physical agony. How could she, the daughter of a boyar, with all the strength of a Kislev winter bred into her bones, with the iron will of a warrior of the marches – how could a woman with such a heritage have let herself become a mindless beast, a thing that rolled in its own sick, a monster with no control over its hungers and urges? It was beneath her. It was beneath her dignity and her heritage.

Had not her father and all his march warden forbearers stood for ten generations at the very edge of the Chaos Wastes, that desert of madness and mutation, and remained untouched by it? Had they not kept their sanity and humanity when all else around them had surrendered to the siren call of carnage and corruption? Could she allow herself to dishonour their memory? Could she allow herself to give in to savagery and slaughter when they had not?

Ulrika knew then that she would be able to last the rest of the hour, or two hours if that was what the countess wished. She had found the key that would give her the will to maintain control, a key more powerful even than Gabriella's threat of death if she failed. All she had to do was call up the image of herself naked and quaking on all fours, heaving out her guts, and her veins filled with cold Kislev ice. She would never let that happen again.

WHEN THE LAST grains of sand trickled through the neck of the glass, Ulrika stood and turned to Quentin, perfectly composed.

'It is time,' she said.

'Yes, mistress. Thank you, mistress.' The knight stood and undid the points of his collar, then bared his oftscarred neck and tipped his head as she crossed to him. He showed no fear now, only arousal – his breathing quick and sweat on his lip. It was clear he had done this many times before, and relished it. He stretched out his arms to her, hands trembling. 'Please, mistress.'

She stepped into his embrace and pulled him close, lowering her head to his neck to inhale him. Now it was her turn to tremble. The blood was so close, and she was so hungry. She would wait no more. With a snort she shot out her fangs. Quentin flinched, frightened again. She snarled and clamped her hands tight around his arms. He shoved away from her, panic giving him strength, and stumbled back.

'Please, mistress!'

She leapt on him with a growl and slammed him down onto the bed. He thrashed under her.

'Please, mistress, don't kill me!'

Ulrika twisted his head aside and opened her mouth, then froze as thought finally caught up with instinct. She cursed. After just promising herself that she would not give in to the beast, she had nearly done it again at the smallest of provocations. A single frightened flinch had roused the animal within her, and drove her to an inch of tearing Quentin's throat out.

She sighed and relaxed her grip on him. 'I am sorry, Quentin. Here, I will do it properly. Only, lie still. It is difficult to resist playing cat if you act like a mouse.'

The young knight nodded. 'Yes, mistress.' And he lay still, arms at his sides, as rigid as a corpse. She lay down beside him, draping an arm across his heaving chest, and nestled against his neck. The urge to rend and tear was still there, but she forced it back and let out her fangs slowly, then kissed his neck. It was salty with panic sweat. She bared her teeth, bit gently, not yet piercing the skin.

Quentin groaned and some of the tension went out of him. She found the vein in his neck and bit harder. Her knife-sharp fangs pierced it smoothly as Quentin gasped, and rich red blood welled up into her mouth.

A shiver of pleasure went through her, and with it another surge of bestial frenzy. She had to force herself not to bite and pull, not to dig her claws into his chest. Instead she only pulled him tighter and drank deeper, letting the warmth of his heart-fire spill down her throat and spread from her stomach through her aching empty veins. The feeling was delicious, intoxicating, stronger than kvas, sweeter than brandy, more comforting than hot broth on a cold Kislev night.

Quentin moaned beneath her and she caressed him absently as she closed her eyes and lost herself in a salty sea of sensation, a soft pulsing susurrus of sound and rapturous fulfilment.

'Mistress,' murmured Quentin. 'Mistress, stop.'

She didn't understand the words – hardly heard them. They were only faint discordant notes hidden behind a soaring crimson melody.

'Mistress…'

A loud noise behind her brought Ulrika's head up with a snarl. She looked around. Countess Gabriella stood in the door, Rodrik at her shoulder.

'That is enough,' she said.

Ulrika stifled a growl and looked down at Quentin. He was deathly pale, except for a stain of red at his neck, and glazed with sweat. He barely had the strength to open his eyes.

'You did well restraining your more savage instincts,' said the countess as she entered the room. 'And I applaud you for it. Now you must learn moderation.'

Rodrik crossed to the bed and swore under his breath as he looked down at the boy. 'Blast her, he won't recover for days!'

Gabriella ignored him and held out a hand to Ulrika, then raised her from the bed. 'Congratulations, child. You are well on your way.'

Ulrika swayed slightly, drunk from the blood, then curtseyed. 'Thank you, mistress. Though I fear I nearly failed again.'

'You are learning,' said Gabriella. 'I am proud of you.'

Ulrika's chest swelled. She was proud of herself too. Though it had been strong, she had conquered the beast within her. She had proven that her will was stronger than her nature. But another glance at Quentin twisted her stomach and made her feel unclean. Was it right to be proud of doing that to a man?

His eyes fluttered and he reached up to clutch at her hand with weak fingers. 'Mistress,' he whispered. 'I am yours, always.'

She turned away, sickened, and withdrew her hand. It was offensive to her to see a strong man so weakened and enthralled – and *she* had done it to him. She suddenly felt nothing but contempt for him, and for herself. Or perhaps she had only drunk too much blood.

'And if this same duke were to grab your bosom?' asked Countess Gabriella. 'Or pinch your behind?'

'I would slap his face,' said Ulrika. 'If he did it again I would challenge him to a duel.'

The countess sighed. 'No, my dear. You would not. You would at most slap his hand with your fan, but you would do it while smiling and looking at him from beneath lowered lashes.'

'Ursun's teeth, I'll be damned if I would!' said Ulrika. 'I don't even have a fan.'

She and the countess were again travelling in the shuttered coach as it raced through the snow-covered countryside. They sat together on one bench while Lotte tended to the prostrate Quentin on the opposite bench and fed him hearty soup. It was the night after their daylight stay at the inn. They were to pass out of Sylvania and into Stirland sometime after moonrise, then continue on their way to Eicheshatten to meet the riverboat that would carry them down the Aver to Nuln.

'Then you must learn to wield one,' said the countess, 'and as deftly as ever you wielded a sword.' She snapped open her own fan as if to illustrate her point, and fluttered it before her. 'A noblewoman you may be, but the manners of a daughter of a Troll Country boyar are a far cry from those of a courtier at the court of Countess Emanuelle von Liebwitz, the ruler of Nuln. You must learn to flirt and flatter, to listen while making small talk, to kill with a compliment, and to earn trust while trusting no one. In short, you must learn to be a woman.'

Ulrika made a face. 'I despise all that nonsense.'

Gabriella pursed her lips. 'That is unfortunate, for such nonsense is the way of the Lahmians. Our strength lies in appearing to be weak. We get our way by appearing to acquiesce, and win with a smile what cannot be won with a sword.'

Ulrika sighed and looked away. 'Then perhaps I'm not a Lahmian.'

The countess was silent at that for a long moment, and Ulrika was afraid she had said something to anger her, but when she looked up, Gabriella's eyes were far-away.

'You are not,' she said at last. 'Not entirely. None of us are, really, except the very first.'

Ulrika frowned at that. 'I don't understand. The book you gave me explained how the five branches of vampire-kind descended from the court of Neferata and–'

Gabriella waved her silent. 'The book is useful as a history, but many of the things it says about the bloodlines, and what they mean... Well, let us just say that the vampire who wrote it had his own reasons for wanting the rest of us to believe that his blood was pure and his claim to rulership unimpeachable. The truth is... cloudier – like our blood.'

'What do you mean, mistress?'

Gabriella leaned back against the padded bench, folding her hands across her torso. 'It is the common conception, even among our own kind, that the founders of the five bloodlines somehow left their stamp upon their blood, and that any who receive it will share their personalities and predilections – they of the blood of Abhorash will become mighty warriors, the daughters of Neferata will be seductresses, the descendants of W'soran will wield powerful sorcery, the get of Ushoran will be mindless beasts and the sons of Vashanesh will burn with unbridled ambition – and to a certain extent, this is true. But it is not that simple.'

'How so?' asked Ulrika.

'The mysteries of our forebears' blood and the elixir that gave it its fell power cannot be charted out like some alchemist's formula. There is no precise "if A is added to B then C will occur". The blood affects each who receive it in different ways, and who they were in life has as much to do with who they become in undeath as whose blood they inherited.' She raised a gloved finger. 'Also, there are very few vampires existing today whose blood comes entirely from one line.'

Ulrika frowned. This seemed to go against everything she had read in *The Nehekharan Diaspora*. 'But how is that possible? Vampires do not breed. Their children are not the result of two parents, but only one. How could the blood become mixed?'

Gabriella smiled. 'We do not breed, no,' she said. 'But we do sometimes mate. And we do not always find love within our own families. Sometimes a son of Vashanesh will fall for a daughter of Neferata. Sometimes a daughter of Abhorash will lose herself in the wild animal embrace of a son of Ushoran. And when they do, blood is exchanged – and mixed – and any progeny that either of them birth may have the traits of one or both.' She tapped her breast. 'I am a blood-daughter of a woman who had the blood of both Vashanesh and Neferata within her veins. It was one of the reasons I was asked to be my queen's eyes in Sylvania, for I could pass as a von Carstein. It is also the reason that my "son" – your blood-father, Adolphus Krieger – joined Mannfred's cause and hoped to bring back the Golden Age. It was in his blood. He was as much a son of Vashanesh as he was of Neferata – perhaps more so in the end, for Mannfred surely blooded him at some point, if only to ensure his loyalty.'

'So...' said Ulrika slowly as she tried to work it all out. 'So, I am both Lahmian and von Carstein?'

Gabriella shrugged. 'And probably much more besides. But as I said before, who you were in life has as much to do with who you become in undeath as whose blood you happened to inherit. What aspect of yourself you choose to allow to dominate is up to you.' She raised her head and looked Ulrika in the eye. 'I hope you choose wisely.'

Ulrika nodded, more than a little overwhelmed. She hoped so too.

Just then there was a loud bang and a shout from outside, and Ulrika and the countess were thrown forwards as the coach slowed sharply, slewing left and right. Lotte shrieked and clutched at Quentin. The coach juddered to a stop with the neighing of horses, the cursing of drivers and the angry cries of Rodrik and his knights. Then a commanding voice rose over all.

'Stand and deliver, gentles, and y'won't be hurt!'

'Back off, dogs!' growled Rodrik's voice. 'Dare you attack a noble lady? You'll lose your heads for this!'

'Not before y'lose yers, sir knight,' said the commanding voice. 'I have ten guns pointed at ye and yer men. It would be a shame t'ruin all that fine filigreed plate to stop ye, but I'll do it if I must.'

Countess Gabriella cursed in a most unladylike fashion as she resumed her seat. 'We must be out of Sylvania,' she said. 'Sylvanian bandits know better than to stop a black coach.'

She began weaving her hands in a complicated pattern while muttering strange foreign words under her breath. Ulrika edged back as curls of shadow began licking around the countess's fingers like black worms.

'Fire, then,' Rodrik was shouting. 'Your bullets won't stop me before I ride you down.'

Ulrika opened the louvres of her window and looked out into the night. Even with the ability to see in the dark that Krieger's gift of blood had granted her, she could see little. There was a bright glare off the snow on the ground, but the trees were too thick on either side of the road to see into. There might have been no one within them. There might have been an army. She wanted to leap out and hunt them down, however many there were.

'Restrain yourself,' said Gabriella. 'Rodrik and I will handle the situation.'

Ulrika turned back. The countess's hands were now hidden in a ball of writhing shadows.

'But they will shoot him,' she said.

'They will not,' said Gabriella, and then flung her arms apart. The sphere of shadows shredded into darting tatters of black that wiggled out through the cracks in the doors of the coach and vanished.

'Ye asked for it!' said the commanding voice. 'All right, lads! Ready? Fire!'

A second later the night was filled with hissing and soft pops – but no explosions.

'Fire, I said!' cried the commanding voice.

'My powder's fizzled,' came a second voice.

'Something wrong with my gun,' said a third.

The countess smiled. 'So unreliable, these modern weapons.'

'Charge!' roared Rodrik, and Ulrika listened, her hands gripping the bench, to the sounds of thundering hooves and clashing steel and the hoarse cries of combat.

She turned to the countess, pleading. 'Please, mistress. Let me defend you!'

Gabriella chuckled. 'You care not a whit to defend me. You only want to get your claws wet.' She shook her head. 'No. I have said you must learn the Lahmian way, and this is not it. We are ladies. We let the men do the heavy work.'

'But–'

'It is precisely because it calls to you that you must fight it,' Gabriella interrupted. 'You will not succeed in our society if you give in to violence.'

Ulrika threw herself back on the bench and crossed her arms angrily. 'I am a warrior. I was bred to fight.'

'You *were* a warrior,' said the countess.

Ulrika listened with rising anger and bloodlust as the sounds of battle raged all around the coach. Curses and cries and the thud of weapons biting flesh filled her ears as the smells of fear and anger and freshly-spilled blood filled her nose. She glared at Gabriella, who sat primly beside her, apparently unconcerned. Did she feel nothing? Did the song of battle touch her not at all? Or was her control that much greater than Ulrika's own?

But then the countess did react. A grunt and a low curse that sounded like it came from Rodrik reached them, and she looked up.

Another knight's voice rang out. 'Sir, are you hurt?' then, 'Defend him!'

The countess swore in what sounded like Bretonnian.

Ulrika turned to her again. 'Mistress, please. Let me help him. Please!'

Gabriella chewed her lip for a moment as the shouts of the knights grew more desperate, then nodded her head stiffly. 'Very well.'

Ulrika let out a cry of relief and spun to the door.

'But you must kill without passion,' called the countess from behind her. 'And do not feed!'

'Yes, mistress,' said Ulrika, then threw open the door and leapt out into the night.

Outside, all was carnage. The scent of blood hit Ulrika like a blast of forge heat. Scrawny corpses in battered leather jerkins littered the snow, and one of the baggage cart ponies was dead, as was the driver. The knights on their horses were clustered at the front of Gabriella's coach, guarding a fallen figure, dead bandits surrounding them in a ring. They faced no living opponents, but all had their shields up, pin-cushioned with crossbow bolts and arrows.

The commanding voice came from the woods. 'Lay down yer arms, gentles, or we shoot the horses next.'

Ulrika could still not see the bandits through the thick cover, but she could smell them, and hear their shifting. She darted for the trees and dived into the brush, then cursed as the long skirts of her beautiful dress caught on twigs and branches. No wonder ladies didn't fight. They were too encumbered.

She gathered her skirts around her as best she could and weaved through the closely set trees towards the scent and sound of the hidden bandits.

'I shall give ye to three to put yer weapons down, gentles,' came the voice again. 'Then ye'll be walking to town, and dragging yer coach besides.'

'Though we'll make it lighter for ye!' laughed another voice.

Ulrika circled a dense patch of brambles and ducked a branch. She could see one of them now, a scruffy crossbowman, crouched behind a screen of shrubs. She padded towards his back.

'One!' called the commanding voice.

Ulrika caught the man under the chin with one hand and gashed his throat with the claws of the other. She spied an archer hiding behind a tree to her left as she let him drop.

'Two!'

Ulrika snatched the bow from the archer and garrotted him with the string before he could make a sound. The rest of them were just on the far side of a fallen tree, hidden by its branches.

'Three!'

Ulrika vaulted the dead tree and leapt amongst them just as they were about to fire. There were five of them left – a tall man with a staff and a cocked hat, and four ragged archers. She attacked the archers first, knocking them down and tearing their bows from their hands.

They bellowed in surprise, drawing knives and rusty swords as they recovered themselves. She sprang at the first as his sword cleared its sheath, pinning his arm and tearing his throat out, then hurling him at the others as they dodged away. His sword fell at her feet and she snatched it up.

Two of them charged her, howling. She knocked their blades from their hands with two flicks of the sword, then ran the first through while the other shied away. It felt glorious to be fighting again. She was so fast, so strong, quicker and more aware than she had ever been alive. She had all at once achieved the level of prowessof which she'd always dreamed. She could see every intention in her opponent's eye, seemingly before they knew themselves what they meant to do, and she reacted so fast to those intentions that they appeared to be standing still. Her blade, clumsy rusting thing that it was, still slipped around theirs with ease and tore bellies and throats and groins before they even knew she had attacked. She hacked the arm off one as he fell, then decapitated another, the scent of blood turning the world red around her. She wanted to bathe in it.

Something hard cracked her across the back. She turned. It was the last man, the leader, backing away into the brush, his quarterstaff held out before him, his air of command lost to a quaking, mewling terror.

'Ranald save me,' he whimpered. 'What are you? Leave us be!'

Ulrika laughed and tore the staff from his hands then grabbed him by the throat and lifted him off the snow-covered ground with one hand, though he was twice her weight.

She bared her fangs. 'I shall leave you dry.'

'Ulrika!' came a voice from behind her.

Ulrika froze, cringing, and looked over her shoulder.

Countess Gabriella stood just outside the tree line, looking in at her coldly. 'What did I say?'

Ulrika shrank from the countess's displeasure and glanced at the ground around her. She cringed with embarrassment at what she saw. The bandits were hacked to pieces. She had not killed without passion. She had ripped them apart, and she had been about to feed on the man she held in the air.

Ulrika hung her head. 'I… I'm sorry, mistress,' she mumbled, then lowered the leader to the ground and snapped his neck. She picked her way awkwardly back to the countess as the man toppled amongst his comrades behind her. 'I was carried away.' She looked down at her dress. It was torn and muddy and drenched in blood. 'And I have ruined your lovely dress.'

'The dress is the least of my worries,' sniffed the countess. 'Do you see why I feared to bring you with me? It is one thing to maintain restraint in controlled circumstances. It is another when one is out in the world. Even in my defence you must be discreet. Had this slaughter happened in the city, it would not have gone unnoticed. We go to quiet a crisis, not to enflame one, do you understand?'

'Yes, mistress,' said Ulrika, staring at the ground. She wanted to be mad at the countess for scolding her, but there was no denying she had lost control – and after she had promised herself that she would not. 'I apologise. It will not happen again.'

'Be sure that it doesn't.'

Rodrik pushed through his knights, glaring at Ulrika and cradling his right arm. A crossbow bolt jutted through the armour above the elbow. 'She should have stayed in the coach, mistress. We did not require her help.'

Gabriella gave his wound a look. 'It was clear to me that you did.'

He grunted. 'Well, we would not have, had she not bled poor Quentin near to death. At full strength we would have bested them.'

'Of course you would have, Rodrik,' said Gabriella, patting his cheek as she passed him. 'My champion never fails me.'

Rodrik looked sullen at that and shot Ulrika a venomous look as she followed the countess into the coach.

CHAPTER FOUR
LADY HERMIONE

THE REST OF the trip passed without incident – indeed, there was so little incident that Ulrika nearly went mad. She had never made a journey like it. They passed into the Moot on their way to Eicheshatten, where she and Gabriella, Rodrik and Lotte boarded the riverboat, the *Aver Queen*, while the rest of Gabriella's knights and drivers turned around and went back home to Nachthafen. Then Ulrika and the countess remained within her stateroom for six days and nights as the boat made its way down the River Aver to Nuln. They travelled a distance of more than three hundred miles, and Ulrika saw none of it!

Things may have been happening outside – she heard fellow travellers passing them all the time, and often the distant howling of wolves and stranger cries, but in the coach, with the louvres closed during the day, she had seen nothing, and by night there had been nothing to look at but snow and black trees. In the stateroom of the riverboat there were no windows at all, only four panelled walls. On more than one occasion, Ulrika had the strange fantasy that they were going around and around in circles and would emerge from their room at the same place they left from. There was certainly nothing to tell her otherwise.

How could one travel like this? Trapped in boxes with no wind on one's face, and no idea of what was going on in the world outside the walls. She had grown up riding across the vastness of the northern oblast, and had been a traveller ever since. She liked seeing the scenery change, and the passing of the clouds. She liked the smells of earth and air and water. She liked the rain and the snow. To hide from them like this seemed almost a blasphemy.

It was, therefore, a great relief when they at last berthed at the docks of Nuln, and stepped down onto the warped grey wood of the wharf just as the sun vanished behind the belching black smokestacks that rose from the Imperial forges to the south of the river.

Ulrika knew Nuln's reputation as the iron heart of the Empire, and she had had many reasons to thank its cannon makers and forge tenders in the past, when the magnificent field pieces and long guns they made had helped defend the cities of Praag and Kislev, and even her own father's estates, but she had never visited the city before, and as she waited with Gabriella on the quayside while Rodrik hired a wagon and a coach – another coach! – to carry them to their final destination, her first impressions were that it was dark, ugly and sooty, and smelled much too strongly of hot iron, burning coal and unwashed peasants. Even the snow was black! Still, it was not the inside of a stateroom, and therefore she welcomed it, turning her face to the pungent wet breeze that licked up off the wide river and looking with delight at the crowds of stevedores, sailors and fishwives who moved to and fro along the wharf. She had not realised how strongly she missed the hustle and bustle of human life.

When Rodrik returned with the hired coach and wagon and they started through the city, Ulrika couldn't stop herself from opening the window and continuing to drink in the passing parade. The smell of living blood was everywhere. The throb of a thousand pulses rang like a symphony in her ears. Everywhere she looked there was meat on the hoof – soldiers and priests and lawyers, butchers and drivers and shopkeeps, all going about their business wrapped in their scarves and cloaks, utterly unaware of the predators that travelled through their midst.

Actually, that wasn't entirely true. The sheep might not sense her looking at them, or know Gabriella for what she was at a glance, but Ulrika could smell fear in the air along with the rest of the overwhelming bouquet of scents, and the broadsheet sellers were crying its name.

'Vampire seen in the Halbinsel!' cried one, holding aloft a gazette with a garish woodcut of a thing with foot-long fangs printed on it.

'Daughter of councillor tested with garlic!' called another. 'A pfennig to know the story!'

'Sisters of Shallya held in the Iron Tower!' bellowed a third. 'Disappearances in Shantytown! Whole family goes missing!'

A woman at a makeshift stall was selling high leather collars that rose all the way to the ears. 'Don't fear the night, lords and ladies! Protect yourself with a witch hunter's collar!'

A woman beside the first hawked silver hammer pendants on ribbon chokers. 'Repel the fiends with the symbol of Sigmar's power and grace!'

The people who moved through the slushy streets did so at a scurry, looking over their shoulders before entering their houses, and eyeing dark alleys with suspicion.

The countess sighed as she listened to it all. 'It is as bad as I feared. Panic in the streets, and a full-fledged hunt. This must be stopped.'

Ulrika nodded, but continued looking out the window. They had turned onto a quieter, more prosperous street now, and the noise of the crowd had faded, but the few people abroad still hurried from place to place like frightened rabbits. She had to quash the thought of bolting after them like a greyhound.

'Dear one,' said Gabriella.

Ulrika cringed and turned. Had the countess read her thoughts? But no, she didn't look angry. In fact she looked positively pensive, her hands pressed together in her lap and her lips pursed. What had made her so nervous?

'Yes, mistress?' she asked.

'Sit by Lotte and let her put your wig on and comb it out for you,' she said, fluttering a hand. 'We want to look our best.'

'Yes, mistress,' said Ulrika, and moved to the other bench as the maid took the long dark wig out of its box. Ulrika didn't like the thing. It was hot and itchy, and made her feel like a little girl playing dress up, but she understood that her scissor-cropped hair would not do for polite society.

Gabriella smiled weakly at her as Lotte draped the wig over her head and tugged it into place. 'I... I wish to remind you that you must be on your best behaviour at Lady Hermione's. You are my ward – my child almost – and as such, whatever you do, whatever you say, reflects on me and how well I have taught you. I would have wished for another year at the least before I introduced you into society, but it can't be helped. So I command you, no, I beg you, not to embarrass me. Particularly not in front of Hermione, who, as I have mentioned, does not care for me much, and would use any excuse to belittle me.'

Ulrika stiffened. 'I may be new to your sisterhood, mistress, but I am not a rube. I–'

Gabriella waved her down. 'Yes, yes, I know. You are the daughter of a boyar, and a lady born. But, as you have shown in the recent past, the difference between being a lady and acting like one can be vast indeed.'

Ulrika inclined her now bewigged head, as rigid as a rapier. 'I shall endeavour not to disappoint you, mistress.'

LADY HERMIONE LIVED in a grand three-storey townhouse in the Aldig Quarter, the richest neighbourhood of the city, home of the nobles that frequented Countess Emanuelle von Liebwitz's court. The house was in the Tilean style, with twisting columns flanking the front door, and snow-capped plaster curlicues topping every window. A liveried footman trotted out to open the coach door for Countess Gabriella and Ulrika, and another came to

take the reins of the wagon from Rodrik. Ulrika noted
that theirs was not the only coach in the curving drive.
A plain black rig stood near the gate, its driver watching them intently.

Gabriella paid the other coach no mind, and started
up the curved steps. As Ulrika and Rodrik followed
her, the carved front door opened and a handsome
woman in a severe black dress curtseyed deeply to
them. Her dark hair was pulled back in a tight bun,
and her manner was as starched as her ruff collar.

'Welcome, countess,' said the woman in reverential
tones. 'We have awaited your arrival. Your rooms are
ready. Please come in.'

'Thank you, Otilia,' said Gabriella, stepping through
the door and handing her cloak to a waiting maid. 'It
is good to be back in Nuln. Is Lady Hermione receiv-
ing?'

Otilia, who Ulrika guessed must be some sort of
housekeeper, pursed her lips and glanced over her
shoulder towards the parlour doors. 'You have come
at an inconvenient moment, m'lady,' she said. 'Lady
Hermione is just now entertaining Captain Meinhart
Schenk, of the witch hunters.'

Gabriella paused at that, and looked to the parlour
doors uneasily. Ulrika could certainly understand
why. Even in Kislev she had heard tales of the crazed
fervour of the Imperial witch hunters. It was said they
burned whole villages to kill a single witch, and
strung men up for the merest suspicion of congress
with the dark powers. They were a law unto themselves, and acted with impunity. No matter how
barbaric their measures, none dared raise their voice
in complaint, lest theyfind themselves next to be

branded witch. If the witch hunters were here, Lady Hermione might be in dire trouble. The murmur of voices from behind the doors seemed to confirm that. It did not sound like a pleasant conversation.

'I see,' said Gabriella. 'Perhaps the drawing room then, until she is finished. That has a connecting door, does it not?'

'Yes, m'lady,' said Otilia, taking up a taper. 'Very good, m'lady. This way.'

The maid collected cloaks from Ulrika and Rodrik and then they followed Gabriella as Otilia led her through the entry way to a pair of doors further down the hall. As Ulrika passed the parlour doors voices came through them loud and clear.

'Do you say that you did not know Lady von Andress and Sister Karlotta?' asked a man's voice.

'You put words in my mouth, captain,' said a woman's voice. 'I said I knew them as well as any other noble woman in Nuln knew them. They were confidantes of Countess von Liebwitz, as am I. It would have been impossible for me not to know them, but was I particular friends with them? No. I...'

The words faded out as they continued down the corridor, then got louder again as Otilia ushered them into a large, elegant room with a harpsichord in one corner and clusters of delicate Bretonnian furniture neatly arranged across an enormous Araby rug woven in shades of blue, yellow and white. The walls and ceiling kept to the colour scheme, with sky-blue panels bordered in white moulding and a gold and crystal chandelier hanging from the ceiling. Choosing the colours of the day seemed to Ulrika an incongruous choice for a vampire's abode, but perhaps that was the point. Perhaps the theme had been chosen to allay suspicions. If so, it didn't appear to be working – not if the angry words that seeped through the set of doors that led to the other room were any indication.

The housekeeper stepped up to the lamps with the taper, but Gabriella waved her away.

'Leave it dark,' she whispered, then stepped closer to the double doors.

Otilia curtseyed and withdrew, taking the taper with her.

Ulrika joined the countess at the doors while Rodrik waited a discreet distance away. The voices in the other room continued to rise with emotion.

'I find your denials confusing, m'lady,' the man was saying. 'I have it from several other women of the court that you and Lady Rosamund were intimates, and that you visited her house regularly. Do these women lie?'

'They make something of nothing,' came a sharp reply. 'Nuln is not as large as Altdorf, and the social circle is small. We are all in each others' houses all the time. I visited Lady Rosamund no more and no less than any of the others.'

'Ah, but you did go to her house, and often, it seems.'

'Well…'

'You did say "all the time", did you not?'

'Yes, but…'

Ulrika saw Countess Gabriella's fists tightening.

The man continued. 'But you say that on such intimate acquaintance you did not notice that she cast no reflection? Or that she ate and drank nothing? Come now, I find it hard to credit.'

'She was not an intimate acquaintance! Did I not just deny it?'

'You deny it and belie it at the same time, m'lady. It confuses me. I also note that you have no mirrors here.'

There was a short pause, then the woman's voice came again, as cold as ice. 'I am neither vain nor vulgar, captain. I do not need to look at myself at every opportunity. I have a glass on my vanity. It suffices.'

'Ah. Perhaps you could show it to me.'

'You dare, sirrah?' cried the woman. 'I am not accustomed to inviting strange men into my boudoir. That I am forced to let such as you as far as my parlour is insult enough. If you have an accusation to make, make it! Otherwise, get out. I have lost my patience with you!'

Gabriella shook her head and growled under her breath. 'Foolish woman.'

'No accusations, m'lady,' said the man. 'Only a request. If you would look into this mirror I carry here, I will be on my–'

'I will not!' snapped the woman. 'I will not be subject to your demeaning little tests. I am not some peasant heretic who trembles before your authority. I am the widow of Lord von Auerbach, the hero of Wissenburg! I am a friend of Countess von Liebwitz!'

Gabriella stepped to the doors and put her hands on the latches, her face grim.

'Not even the countess is above Sigmar's justice, m'lady,' said the man.

'Go show your glass to her, then!' said the woman. 'If she consents to look in it, then I will too, but not before!'

'I am sorry, m'lady,' continued the man in level tones. 'But I am afraid I must insist.'

'No! I refuse! I–'

With a hiss, Countess Gabriella thrust open the doors to the parlour and strode in, smiling and spreading her arms.

'Cousin! Hermione!' she cried, fluttering forwards to enfold a slim young woman in her arms. 'How delicious to see you!'

The woman looked at her for a moment with alarmed eyes, but then played along. 'Cousin Gabriella, I… I did not expect you so soon. Welcome.'

Ulrika looked the woman up and down as she followed the countess into the room. From what Gabriella had said of her, she had expected Lady Hermione to look older. In her mind she had imagined some bitter, pinched dame with suspicious eyes, but nothing could have been further from the truth. Lady Hermione appeared young – younger than Ulrika even – and as fresh-faced and wide-eyed as a new bride. Her hair was a rich chocolate-brown, her skin a healthy pink, and her figure, beneath her embroidered powder-blue bodice and skirts, was shapely but still girlish.

Countess Gabriella stepped back and held her at arm's length. 'I declare you grow more beautiful every time I see you, my dear, and–' She broke off as if noticing the others in the room for the first time. 'Oh! Pray forgive me, cousin. Otilia did not tell me you were entertaining. Who are these handsome gentlemen?'

Ulrika turned her attention to the men. There were four of them and, in calling them handsome,

Gabriella was stretching the truth to the point of breaking. Their leader, a grey-haired man in sober but well-cut clothes under a heavy leather coat, might charitably have been called ruggedly attractive, with his stone-cut brow and square, close-shaved jaw, but the three men lined up at his back were downright gruesome – hard, scarred, lank-haired men in leather armour with pistol-butts and rapier hilts sticking out from under their cloaks at all angles.

Lady Hermione sniffed as she indicated them. 'This is Captain Meinhart Schenk, cousin,' she said. 'And he appears to be here to arrest me.'

Gabriella laughed like a glissando of silver bells. 'Arrest you? Oh, my dear, have you been dallying where you shouldn't? The shame, the shame!' She curtseyed in front of Schenk. 'Captain, I am honoured to make your acquaintance.'

Schenk looked like an angry stuffed frog, but bowed politely. 'The pleasure is mine, m'lady.'

'And do you truly want to arrest my beloved cousin? Could you be so cruel?'

'I only wish her to look into this mirror, m'lady,' said Schenk, sternly.

Gabriella laughed again and turned to Hermione. 'Look into a mirror, cousin? Why, surely that is no hardship for you, is it. You do it hourly, do you not?'

'He believes me to be a vampire, cousin,' said Hermione, her lips tight.

Gabriella stifled another laugh and looked from Schenk to Hermione, wide-eyed. 'You, cousin? With that complexion? I would believe a milkmaid, or a goose girl, but a vampire?' She turned to Schenk. 'Surely you jest, sir.'

'It is no jest, m'lady,' said the witch hunter, inclining his head. 'There have been two noble ladies revealed as vampires within the past weeks, and we are ordered to speak to anyone, regardless of rank, who knew them well.'

Gabriella rolled her eyes. 'Ridiculous, but if you must. Here.' She held out her hand. 'Let me see this mirror of yours. My cousin will certainly not refuse me.'

Captain Schenk hesitated, then withdrew a small rectangular mirror from between the pages of a leather-bound book and handed it over.

'Thank you, captain,' said Gabriella, then took his arm. 'Come, let us see what monsters lurk in the glass, eh?'

Lady Hermione stepped back, wary, as the countess led the captain forwards. Gabriella smiled at her. 'Fear not, cousin, the captain will only see your beauty doubled. Now then…'

She angled the little glass so that she and Schenk could see where Hermione stood. Schenk peered intently, then blinked.

Gabriella gasped, making Ulrika jump. 'Oh!' she cried. 'Cousin, you have a spot!' She relaxed. 'No, no, it is only a crumb. Here, I have it.' She brushed Gabriella's cheek as if she were her mother, then turned to Schenk. 'There you are, captain, are you satisfied?'

'Er,' said the captain. 'It seems–'

'Would you like to test me as well?' Gabriella asked and, still holding his arm, she turned the mirror so that it faced them both. 'Are we not handsome to look on?'

Ulrika stared, for though she was at the correct angle, she could only see Schenk in the glass, while the witch hunter could clearly see more. Had Gabriella magicked the glass, or his eyes?

'No need, m'lady,' he said, stepping from her and bowing abruptly. 'You have proven your point. It seems I have been in error. It was only the lady's refusals that caused me to–'

'There is no need to apologise,' said Gabriella, steering him to the door with a gentle hand and lowering her voice to speak in his ear as his men lumbered awkwardly behind. 'Ladies of noble birth are sometimes high-strung, and unused to being questioned. My cousin is only a little more high-strung than most.'

'I see,' said Schenk. 'Thank you for interceding.'

'Not at all.' Gabriella opened the door and snapped her fingers. 'Otilia, see the gentlemen out.'

And after another brief exchange, the captain and his grim-faced lieutenants followed Otilia down the hall and Gabriella closed the door behind them with a deep sigh of relief. Ulrika relaxed as well. She had been holding herself ready to fight since they had entered the house.

Lady Hermione, however, did not seem to share in the general mood. She turned on Gabriella with a snarl. 'Interfering witch!' she said. 'How dare you pretend to save me!'

Gabriella raised an eyebrow. 'Pretend?'

'I had the situation well in hand,' cried Hermione. 'I would have looked in his glass and done your measly trick, but I would not be properly noble if I did not protest the impertinence of peasants first.'

'Ah, of course,' said Gabriella. 'I see it all now. I apologise, sister. I will refrain from helping next time.'

Hermione sniffed, apparently unappeased. 'You do not begin your visit well, Gabriella. I pray you serve me better from here on.'

'I am here to serve our queen, sister,' said Gabriella. 'If serving you serves her, then I will do the best I can.'

Before Hermione could respond, Otilia returned through the door from the hall.

'Their coach is gone, m'lady,' she said, curtseying. 'I have asked Gustaf to make sure they have left no spies.'

'Thank you, Otilia,' said Hermione. 'You did well.'

Otilia made to withdraw, then pursed her lips and paused. 'M'lady, are you certain you will not consider retiring to the country until all this has blown over? We would be much safer from prying eyes at Mondthaus.'

Hermione sighed. 'Much as I'd like to, Otilia, I cannot,' she said. 'The queen would see it as dereliction of duty, but thank you for your concern.'

'Of course, m'lady,' said the housekeeper.

She stepped back again but, before she had closed the doors, a handful of exquisite dandies pushed them open again and strolled through around her. They were all graceful, handsome young men, all in the latest court fashions, and all with perfectly trimmed beards and moustaches. Their leader was as dark as a Tilean, but with piercing blue eyes.

'They would not have left this house alive had they exposed you, m'lady,' he said, putting a hand to the hilt of his bejewelled rapier.

Ulrika heard Rodrik snort from the drawing room door. 'Lapdogs,' he muttered.

A third door opened – a cleverly concealed panel in the left wall – and a timid golden-haired head looked out. 'Have they gone?'

'Beloved!' Hermione's pinched expression melted and she crossed to the secret door to lead out the most beautiful girl Ulrika had ever seen. She wasn't a lush, dark beauty like Countess Gabriella, nor a pouty, sweet-faced seducer like Lady Hermione. She was tall and thin, with fair skin and straight golden hair that hung to the flaring skirts of her dark green dress, and the stately beauty of a queen. It was only as Hermione drew her to the centre of the room that the regal illusion was broken, for the girl walked with a coltish clumsiness and downcast eyes that made Ulrika wonder how old she was.

Hermione turned to Gabriella with a smug look. 'Well, since you are here, I suppose I must introduce you to my household.' She indicated the swaggering dandy and his men. 'Lord Bertholt von Zechlin, my champion, and his men – the finest blades in the Empire.'

'Your servant, madam,' said von Zechlin, bowing and making a leg.

Rodrik rumbled something about 'not being the finest blades in the room', but Ulrika didn't think the men heard him.

Hermione then turned to the housekeeper. 'My chatelaine, Otilia Krohner, you already know, and…' She put a hand on the blonde girl's elbow and urged her forwards. 'And this is Fraulein Famke Leibrandt, my… protégée.'

The girl smiled at Gabriella and Ulrika shyly, then, lifting her skirts, curtseyed deeply. 'I am at your service, mistresses,' she said. 'Welcome to our humble home.'

Ulrika frowned. Lady Hermione was showing the girl off like a prize calf. Was she some favoured blood-swain? No. She had called her her protégée. She was a vampire! She was to Hermione what Ulrika was to Gabriella. But why so smug? Did Hermione mean to imply that she had made a better choice of apprentice than Gabriella had? The thought made Ulrika growl in her throat.

Gabriella returned the curtsey and gestured to Rodrik and Ulrika. 'And allow me to introduce Rodrik von Waldenhof, heir to the Waldenschlosse, my champion, and a knight without peer, and Boyarina Ulrika Magdova Straghov of Kislev, *my* protégée.'

Rodrik executed a smart bow, clicking his heels together in martial fashion, but Ulrika, flummoxed by the thought that she was somehow on display, and confused by all the bowing and curtseying, first tried one, then the other, and failed at both, stumbling awkwardly on her petticoats.

As she recovered, Ulrika saw that Hermione's smile had turned into a sneer, and she almost sneered back, but then she caught Gabriella glaring at her, and lowered her head respectfully, letting the long tresses of her wig hide her anger.

'Your friends are obviously tired from their journey,' Hermione said smoothly. 'Let us repair to the drawing room where they can rest comfortably while we talk.'

Gabriella betrayed not the slightest notice of the subtle dig. 'Of course, sister. After you.'

As they moved to follow their mistresses into the next room, Ulrika caught Famke looking at her. The girl was trying to stifle a grin and, failing miserably, her eyes twinkled with silent merriment. Ulrika wanted to feel indignant that the girl was laughing at her, but she couldn't. She found she was grinning too, and they went into the drawing room shoulder to shoulder, friends in a single instant.

AFTER LAMPS WERE lit and the fire built up, Countess Gabriella and Lady Hermione sat near the carved marble hearth on delicate gilded chairs, while Ulrika and Famke waited in attendance behind them, and Rodrik and Hermione's gentlemen eyed each other sullenly from opposite ends of the room.

'Well then,' said Gabriella. 'Tell me all. How did it start? And where do we stand now?'

'We stand well equipped to deal with the difficulty ourselves,' said Hermione coldly.

Gabriella sighed. 'Sister, I would not have come had I not been so ordered. I do the bidding of the queen. No more. I promise you I will leave when the business is finished. I have no ambitions here. Now, please. The quicker we begin, the quicker I am away again.'

Hermione stared into the fire for a moment, then nodded. 'Very well. I will tell you. It started a month ago. Lady Rosamund went to the theatre with her lover, a blood-swain named General Steffan von Odintaal, who is one of Countess von Liebwitz's advisors on military matters and, through Rosamund, one of *ours*. They parted after the play, he to his club, and she for home.' Hermione's hands clasped convulsively. 'On the way home she was attacked, by what I know not, except that it was strong enough to defeat her and tear her flesh horribly.'

'There were no witnesses?' asked Gabriella.

'None that we could discover,' said von Zechlin, from the corner of the room.

Gabriella nodded, though her expression made it clear that she doubted Hermione's champion had looked very hard. 'Go on,' she said.

'Rosamund was found hung from the Deutz Elm in the Reik Platz a few hours before dawn,' continued Hermione. 'Her fangs and claws were extended as if she had died in the midst of blood frenzy. Unfortunately she was taken down before daylight and brought to the cellars of the Iron Tower, so she did not burn in the sun. Her face was recognisable, and she was identified.'

'What followed?' asked Gabriella.

'She was very well known,' said Hermione. 'One of the premier ladies of Countess von Liebwitz's court. There was an immediate scandal. The witch hunters arrested the general, her lover.'

Gabriella looked up. 'Did he talk?'

Hermione shook her head. 'We have a friend among the jailors. He died of poison before they put him to the question.'

Gabriella looked relieved. 'And then?'

'Panic,' said Hermione. 'The broadsheets cried the tale. Everyone at court began to suspect everyone else of being a vampire. Ladies took to carrying mirrors and meeting in daylight. And if that wasn't bad enough, people started vanishing, all over town – rich, poor, all kinds. Vampires were of course blamed.'

'And *were* they to blame?' asked Gabriella. 'Were these victims bled?'

'None have been found,' said Hermione. 'Though the witch hunters have searched the town from top to bottom.' She shuddered. 'It all became so unbearable that I retired to my country place, Mondthaus, and feigned illness.'

'Did you inform the queen?'

'Karlotta did,' said Hermione. She seemed to Ulrika much less the grand lady now, and more just a frightened woman, though still every inch a beauty. 'After which, she called a meeting at the Silver Lily, Madam Dagmar's brothel, so that we remaining sisters could confirm her as our new leader, and to discuss what was to be done.'

Gabriella held up a hand. 'Who are these remaining sisters?'

Hermione looked annoyed that her tale had been interrupted, but then shrugged. 'Besides myself, there is Lady Alfina, married to a guildmaster, a blood-swain who is our ear in the Nuln guilds; Madam Dagmar, who runs the Silver Lily, an invaluable tool for gathering rumour and blackmail, and lastly…' She made a face. 'Mistress Mathilda, an uncouth hoyden who runs a tavern in the slums south of the river, and gathers information among the unwashed.'

Gabriella nodded. 'New blood, then. I have met none of them. Pray continue. You were saying that Mistress Karlotta had called a meeting?'

'Yes,' said Hermione. 'It was a grim affair. None of us had any clue as to why Rosamund had been killed, or by whom – or what. Had it been random? Had it been an assassination? Were the disappearances connected? Once we acknowledged her as our new leader, Karlotta instructed us to send our flocks to scour the city for witnesses or information, but...' She paused and licked her lips. 'But soon after, Karlotta was dead too. Found staked out on the altar of Shallya in the convent where she posed as the abbess, again with teeth and claws bared, and again horribly torn and maimed.'

Gabriella grimaced, Famke shivered.

'The panic grew even worse after that,' Hermione continued dully. 'The entire convent was arrested, women have been burned by mobs in the street, and the witch hunters began questioning every lady in high society and among the clergy. It has been nerve-wracking.'

'No doubt,' said Gabriella.

Hermione hung her head. 'With Karlotta's death it became clear that these were not random attacks. Karlotta had been second to Rosamund, and was second to die. Whoever is behind this, knows who our leaders are, and...'

Gabriella finished Hermione's thought for her. 'And you are now leader.'

Hermione swallowed, then nodded. 'Yes – and next on the gallows.' She rose and began to pace. 'I returned from my country place to give the situation my full attention, and have ordered our remaining sisters in Nuln to stay in their houses and double their guards, as I have done. They will remain so until the assassin is found. There will be no more murders! I will not disappoint my queen!'

The doors to the hallway creaked open and everyone looked up. Otilia, the housekeeper, stood between them, her face as pale as moonlight. 'M'lady,' she said, curtseying. 'Madam Dagmar is below stairs. She has asked to see you.'

'What!' cried Hermione angrily. 'Did I not tell her to stay in her house? What is she doing here?'

Otilia hesitated, her stoic features working with emotion, then spoke. 'There has been another murder. Mistress Alfina is dead.'

Lady Hermione and Famke gasped. Gabriella cursed. Von Zechlin and his men jumped to their feet, as did Rodrik.

Hermione rose from her chair, arms trembling. 'The… the same way?'

'Yes, mistress,' said Otilia.

'Was Alfina discovered?' Hermione asked. 'Do the witch hunters know?'

'I know not, mistress,' said Otilia. 'But they do not have her body. It is in the kitchen.'

CHAPTER FIVE
A JOB FOR A SPY

Ulrika followed Gabriella and the others down the stairs to the house's low-ceilinged subterranean kitchen, and joined them around a wide preparation table at one side of the room. A tablecloth had been spread upon it, and laid across it was the corpse of a woman – Mistress Alfina, Ulrika presumed – in the expensive cloak and dress of a well-to-do merchant's wife, all terribly torn and bloodied. Hermione gasped when she saw the body. Gabriella remained silent, but clenched her fists and jaw.

A woman in a gaudy, low-cut, plum-coloured dress huddled at the end of the table, leaning miserably against the wall, her flame-red hair and voluptuous form half-hidden under a long shawl she wore draped over her head. Ulrika surmised that this must be Madam Dagmar, who ran the Lahmian brothel, though she seemed at the moment unable to conjure any of a madam's traditional bawdy cheer.

'Mistress,' she whimpered, holding out trembling hands to Hermione. 'I... I am sorry for leaving the Lily, but... but...'

'Never mind that, sister,' said Hermione, tight-lipped. 'What happened? Where did you find her?'

Ulrika thought it fairly obvious what had happened. She stared at the corpse of the dead vampire with morbid fascination. That is what I shall look like when I die, she thought. She saw Famke staring uneasily at the corpse as well, and wondered if she was thinking similar thoughts.

The late Mistress Alfina may have once been an attractive woman, but it was difficult to determine that from the broken remains that lay before Ulrika. Her fangs and claws were extended in the way Hermione had described the other corpses being discovered, while her limbs were locked in an attitude of furious attack and her face frozen in a hideous snarl of rage.

But it seemed that neither claws nor fangs nor rage had been enough to protect her. Her well-cut clothes had been torn to shreds, as had the flesh beneath them, and a wooden stake had been driven through her heart – so deeply that it came out her back. None of these things, however, was as fascinating, and at the same time repelling, as the quality of her skin. Alfina must have looked young in life, no more than thirty, but now her skin looked a hundred years old. It was as dry and powdery as a parched riverbed, and had sunk in against her bones as if the meat had withered and shrunk within it. She might have been dead for centuries, which, as Ulrika came to think about it, was most likely true.

Ulrika inhaled deeply as a strange mix of smells came to her from the body. Beneath the usual Lahmian scent of musk and spice and dusty corruption was another, a faint putrid odour rising from the body – foul and earthy, like a battlefield full of corpses after a week in the rain.

'She...' began the red-haired woman, then shivered and began again. 'She was hung up on the iron fence outside the brothel. Hung by the stake.'

Famke winced.

Hermione cursed. 'Did anyone see her? The witch hunters?'

Madam Dagmar shook her head. 'I do not think so. My doorman, Groff, found her when he went out to get a carriage for one of our gentlemen. He and the grooms brought her in as quick as they could. But... but who could have done this? Mistress, there are three of us dead now! Three!'

Hermione grabbed Dagmar and shook her. 'Be quiet, curse you! Answer my questions! No one saw her before Groff brought her in? Are you certain?'

Dagmar pulled away from her and covered her face with her shawl. 'I don't know! I don't know! No one said anything! The witch hunters didn't come!'

Hermione breathed a sigh of relief and Ulrika saw that Gabriella shared it.

'Then at least we can cover it up,' said Hermione. 'Good.'

'It still leaves us with the question of who did it,' said Gabriella.

'A beast,' said Famke.

'Aye,' said Rodrik angrily. 'A savage beast.'

'Beasts don't wield wooden stakes,' said Ulrika. 'Or hang women from fences.'

Rodrik glared at her, but Gabriella patted her arm. 'Very true,' she said. 'No, this was not as mindless an attack as it appears. It was clearly meant to kill two birds with one stone.'

Hermione and the others looked at her curiously.

Gabriella held up a finger. 'One, it was to expose poor Alfina as a vampire, as Rosamund and Karlotta had been exposed before her.' She raised a second finger. 'And two, it was to cast suspicions onto Madam Dagmar's brothel.'

'They mean to ruin us!' snarled Hermione.

'Indeed,' said Gabriella. 'Whoever "they" are.'

Otilia coughed politely from the stairs. 'Pardon, mistresses. If I might suggest?'

Hermione turned to her. 'Yes, Otilia?'

The housekeeper smoothed her dresses nervously, then spoke. 'Perhaps a trip to the brothel? Perhaps traces left by the murderer could be found there.'

Gabriella nodded approvingly. 'Very good, Otilia. You are the smartest of us all.'

The housekeeper looked down to hide a blush at the compliment.

'My men and I will go,' said von Zechlin, stepping forwards. 'And kill the murderer if he still haunts the scene.'

Rodrik snorted at this.

'I will go as well,' said Gabriella. 'And as quickly as possible.' She motioned to Ulrika and Rodrik and started for the stairs. 'Come. We will–'

'No,' said Hermione, cutting her off. 'Bertholt will see to it.'

Gabriella turned on her, suppressing a scowl. 'Sister,' she said mildly. 'I was summoned here for this purpose. I must go.'

Hermione lifted her chin. 'You were summoned here to assist me. And I have other work for you.'

'Other work?' asked Gabriella. 'I am to help with the crisis. Not–'

'And you will be,' said Hermione. 'The husband of Alfina, Guildmaster Aldrich, is a blood-swain, but he does not love the rest of us as he did her. He will make a fuss when he learns Alfina is dead. He might rave in public, or go to the witch hunters. He must be quieted. Go to him and comfort him.' She smiled primly. 'In fact, it would be best if you took up residence there instead of here. I still need an ear in the guild halls.' She waved a dismissive hand. 'Otilia will give you the address.'

Gabriella stiffened, and seemed about to argue, but then nodded curtly. 'Very well. I see that this is necessary. I will do it, but I will be your frequent visitor.' She turned again to the stairs. 'Come, my dears. There is work to do.'

As Ulrika and Rodrik followed, Ulrika passed Famke, who gave her a sympathetic goodbye glance. Ulrika returned it with a shrug and a wry smile. It was a shame she and the girl seemed to be on opposite sides of a bitter rivalry.

'DAMN THE LITTLE Estalian bitch!' hissed Gabriella once she, Ulrika, Rodrik and Lotte were safely in the coach and away. 'She means to keep me out of everything!'

She slapped the bench in frustration. 'Would that Hermione had died instead of any of the others. She is the least suited to lead of all of them – so concerned with shining in the queen's eyes, and making sure that I do not, that she will ruin everything.'

Ulrika had to agree with the assessment. The pretty little snob didn't seem capable of leading a sing-along, let alone a secret sisterhood, but she was clever enough to get her enemies out of the way. Ulrika looked at the address that the housekeeper, Otilia, had written on the back of a visiting card. Babysitting a guildmaster? There would be no excitement in that.

'And her pack of boudoir pimps won't find a thing at this brothel,' sneered Rodrik from where he sat beside the maid. 'They'll be too busy keeping their boots clean.' He leaned forwards. 'Let me go, mistress. My wound is near healed. I am fit. If there is something to find, I will find it.'

Gabriella looked at him for a moment, then patted his arm. 'It is a good thought, Rodrik. Someone must go, but you are not the man for the job.'

Rodrik looked affronted. 'Why not? I am your champion. Who better?'

'That you are my champion is the difficulty,' said Gabriella. 'Hermione's gentlemen may see you and know that I disobey their mistress's orders. I need not a knight, but a spy. Someone they do not know.'

Ulrika's heart leapt with sudden hope. 'Mistress,' she said.

Gabriella turned to her. 'Yes, child?'

Ulrika reached up and pulled off her dark-haired wig, revealing her thatch of short straw-coloured hair. 'They know your long-haired protégée, but they do not know me.'

Gabriella's eyes widened and a smile cracked her lips, but then it faded. 'No, I cannot,' she said. 'You are still not ready. Faced with danger, you may make a bigger mess than the killer.'

'Mistress, I promise you–' Ulrika pleaded.

'You have promised before,' said Rodrik. 'And still finished soaked in blood.'

Gabriella shot him a hard glance. 'She is mine to chastise, sir, not yours.'

Rodrik bowed his head sulkily. 'Aye, mistress.'

Ulrika glared at the knight, but did not retort. She didn't want to ruin her chances by making Gabriella angrier.

The countess sat in silence for a long moment, staring out the window into the night. Finally she sighed. 'But I must know. There's nothing for it.' She turned to Ulrika. 'Very well, you shall go.'

Rodrik grunted.

Ulrika suppressed a grin of excitement. 'Thank you, mistress. You will not regret this!'

'Quiet, girl,' snapped Gabriella. 'You shall go, but you will follow my rules to the letter, do you understand me? You will keep yourself hidden at all times. You will not fight. Not anyone. Not even the killer, should you find him, unless you are in danger for your life. You will not feed. You will speak to no one unless it is absolutely unavoidable, and when you have seen what there is to be seen, you will return to me immediately. This is not an invitation to explore Nuln, nor to play at hero. Am I clear?'

Ulrika nodded respectfully. 'Yes, mistress. Very clear. I will not disappoint you.'

'I trust you will not,' said Gabriella, then her face fell. 'But wait. This may not work after all. You cannot do this in dresses, and you would drown in Rodrik's clothes. What am I to send you out in?'

Ulrika smiled. 'Not to worry, mistress. I packed my old things.'

As THEY NEARED the house of Guildmaster Eggert Aldrich, Gabriella signalled the coach to stop, then turned to Rodrik and Lotte. 'You must leave us here. Take the baggage wagon and find a nearby inn. I will contact you again tomorrow night once I know the lay of the land at this new place.'

'But, mistress,' said Rodrik. 'I am your champion. I must not leave your side.'

'And who will dress you, m'lady?' asked Lotte.

'I'm sorry, Rodrik,' said Gabriella. 'My job is to woo this Aldrich and win my way into his heart and home. Until I have done that it would not do to seem to have a rival for his affections. And Ulrika will act as maid, at least for now, Lotte. For I need a spy more than I need a dresser at the moment. Now go, both of you. I will send for you soon.'

Rodrik shot a dark look at Ulrika, then thrust through the coach door with more force than necessary. Lotte ducked her head sadly and followed.

On the snowy street, Rodrik bowed coldly to Gabriella. 'I pray for your safety, mistress.' Then he closed the door.

Gabriella laughed and shook her head. 'As faithful as a dog, and as stupid.' She rapped on the wall of the coach. 'Drive on!'

* * *

THE COACH STOPPED in front of a sturdy, prosperous-looking townhouse in the Kaufman District, where all the houses were sturdy and prosperous-looking, and a bit dull. As the countess and Ulrika stepped down onto the drive and approached the white panelled door, Ulrika thought she had never seen a cleaner, more well-kept street, or one with so little character.

Gabriella knocked, and a few moments later, a thick-set butler in regal black opened the door and looked down his nose at them. 'Yes?'

'Herr Aldrich, please,' said Gabriella. 'It is about his wife.'

'I shall inquire,' said the butler, then closed and locked the door again.

After another short wait, the sound of hurried footsteps could be heard within, then the locks turned and the door flew open to reveal a wild-eyed and panting fat man staring at them, his breeches hastily pulled on under his night shirt.

'What do you know of my wife!' he cried. 'Where is she?'

'I cannot tell you on the street, Herr Aldrich,' said Gabriella. 'Will you invite me in?'

Aldrich's round face collapsed as he looked at Gabriella, and he staggered back. 'You… you're one of her sisters. Oh, Sigmar, it's bad, isn't it? Something's happened.'

'It is bad,' said Gabriella. 'May I come in?'

The guildmaster sobbed and motioned them in, then led them to a dark parlour. When the butler had lit the lamps and withdrawn, he turned to Gabriella with pleading eyes.

'Tell me,' he said.

'She is dead, mein herr,' said Gabriella. 'I am sorry.'

Aldrich closed his eyes and sagged into a stout wooden armchair. 'Dead. I knew it. Somehow I knew it.' He raised his head. 'But how? What happened?'

'The thing which killed her sisters,' said Gabriella. 'It has struck again.'

Now Aldrich wept in earnest, sobs shaking his big frame as he mopped at his eyes with the tailing cuffs of his nightshirt. Gabriella shifted with impatience, then sat down in the chair next to his and put a comforting hand on his arm. 'Mein herr, I am truly–'

Aldrich flung her off. 'Don't touch me, leech! This is all your fault! You and your filthy coven with your filthy intrigues. You killed her, as sure as you had wielded the knife yourselves!'

'Mein herr, I assure you–' started Gabriella, but Aldrich wasn't finished.

'Alfina wasn't like you!' he cried. 'She was no black-hearted witch! She was good and pure, and only took blood because she had been trapped into becoming something she despised by a cruel trick. She wanted nothing to do with your plots and back-stabbings, but now she has died of them, and you still live! I hate you! Leave me alone!'

He buried his face in his hands and Gabriella rolled her eyes at Ulrika. Ulrika frowned at the countess's contempt. The man was a fool, certainly, to believe such a story, but pitiable nonetheless.

Gabriella tried again, this time putting her hand on Aldrich's wide neck. 'Mein herr, I understand your anger, and you are right. Some intrigue has killed Alfina. I came to Nuln to stop the killing, and I am sorry to the bottom of my heart that I was not in time to save her.'

'Have you a heart?' Aldrich sneered.

'You know Alfina did,' said Gabriella.

Aldrich sobbed anew. 'She did. She did.'

Gabriella lifted his head and turned it so that she could look into his eyes. 'I will be honest with you, mein herr. Lady Hermione sent me to quiet you. To seduce you so that you will not go rushing rashly to the witch hunters or the watch.'

Aldrich blinked, stunned. His mouth dropped open.

Gabriella smiled sadly. 'You see. The truth. But I am not so cynical as my sisters. I know that I could never replace Alfina in your heart. I know true love when I see it. I will not try to cozen you. Instead I will respect your grief if you will return the favour and respect our secrets.'

'I… I don't understand you,' said the guildmaster.

Gabriella looked uncomfortable. 'I must stay here and pretend to beglamour you, for I cannot flout Lady Hermione's orders, but I will leave you alone to mourn your dear Alfina if you will promise me that you will keep the nature of her death a secret, and not reveal us to the authorities.'

'But, I do not want you here!' moaned Aldrich. 'I want Alfina!'

'I assure you, I don't wish to be here either,' said Gabriella. 'But as neither of us has a choice in the matter, I would make our enforced cohabitation as painless as possible.' She moved her hand to his shoulder. 'Here. I will make you a promise. You will see me as rarely as I see the sun. Now, do I have *your* promise?'

Aldrich shook his head sadly. 'It seems I must. You have my promise. But… but what am I to say about Alfina? And your presence here?'

Gabriella let out an almost inaudible sigh of relief. 'We will work all that out on the morrow. Now, if you will have your servants bring my things to Alfina's rooms, I will leave you to your grief.'

THERE WAS MORE weeping upstairs, for Alfina had left behind a maid as well as a husband, but Gabriella silenced the girl, whose name was Imma. There was no time to waste in sweet-talking her like she had Herr Aldrich.

'Do not cry, child,' Gabriella said, patting her hand as Ulrika quickly changed into her riding clothes on the far side of the room. 'We will bleed you just as your mistress did. Have no fear. But now you must tell me, why did Alfina leave the house when Hermione ordered her not to? Did someone come to her? Was a note left?'

'I… I don't know, mistress. None that I saw.'

'And she said nothing before she left?'

The maid shook her head. 'She fed very strongly on me this evening. I woke only a little while ago. I didn't know she… she had gone.' The girl burst into tears again.

Hermione gripped Imma's arm so hard she cried out. 'Enough of that. Listen to me. Do you know where Madam Dagmar's brothel is? Can you tell Ulrika how to get there?'

The girl sniffed and wiped her nose on a handkerchief. 'I know not, but Uwe, Herr Aldrich's coachman, was also a blood-swain to my mistress. He took her everywhere.'

'Very good,' said Gabriella. 'Then we will rouse him.' She turned to Ulrika, who was just strapping on her old cavalry sabre. 'Do not fail me here, beloved,' she said. 'And do not lose control. For if you are caught, I cannot protect you. I have not the influence here that I do at home.'

Ulrika bowed like a Kossar, sharp and correct. 'I will not fail.'

As she followed Imma down the back stairs towards the stables, she could hardly keep herself from whooping with excitement. Action and freedom at last!

CHAPTER SIX
THE STENCH OF DEATH

HERR ALDRICH'S COACHMAN took Ulrika through the Altestadt Gate into the Universitat, where the Imperial Gunnery School and the College of Engineering rose like brooding black giants over the roofs of lesser structures, then south to the middle-class commercial district known as the Handelbezirk. This was where most of the business of Nuln occurred, and the walls of the tall, stone and half-timbered buildings that she passed were hung with the signs and plaques of trading companies, exchanges, guild associations and solicitors.

This deep into the evening, the broadsheet sellers and charm hawkers had gone home and the area was quiet, with only the occasional furtive figure hurrying out of sight, or a patrol of the city watch making its rounds, squelching through the mud and slush with long staffs and lanterns in their hands. It became even quieter as Ulrika's coach turned off the main streets.

Here the buildings were private homes, not as nice or solid as those in the Kaufman District, but still respectable, with glass in the windows and fresh paint on the doors. If this is the neighbourhood of the Silver Lily, thought Ulrika, it must be quite a discreet and high-class establishment.

A few streets on and the coachman pulled the coach to a stop.

'Just around the corner, lady,' he said.

Grinning with pent-up excitement, Ulrika rose and opened the door, then looked cautiously up and down the street. It was dark and quiet. The burghers and their wives were all abed and asleep at this hour. She stepped out and started for the corner.

'Shall I wait, mistress?' whispered the coachman. 'You will have difficulty getting back into the Altestadt on foot.'

Ulrika looked back, then paused. It would be wiser to ask him to stay, but she was sick of coaches, just as she was sick of dresses and wigs and curtseys. It would be much more exciting to find her own way back. 'You may go,' she said. 'I don't know how long I will be.'

'As you wish, mistress,' he said, and began to turn the coach about.

Ulrika stepped to the intersection, feeling freer already. She edged her head around the corner to look down the street on which the Silver Lily had its door, then pulled back quickly as she saw men milling about in front of a nondescript townhouse in the middle of the street. There was no sign above the door, nor red lamps in the windows, yet Ulrika was certain it was the brothel – firstly because every one of its windows was brightly lit, and secondly, because the men before it were Lord von Zechlin and his exquisite gentlemen.

She was surprised to see them still at the scene of the crime, for it was almost two hours after she and the countess had left Hermione's house, but there they were. In fact, it looked like they had only recently arrived.

She smiled to herself as she crouched at the corner to observe. Hermione's brave heroes had seemed so full of righteous fire when von Zechlin had promised her they would look into the murder, but it appeared they must have stopped at some watering-hole along the way, and were now full of something else entirely. In fact, one of them was being sick on the iron railing in front of the brothel – the same iron railing, Ulrika was certain, upon which Mistress Alfina had been found.

Von Zechlin was at the door of the Lily, talking to a man in servant's livery, who was gesturing up and down the street, while the others prowled the snow-rimed cobbled street like drunken scholars looking for a pair of lost spectacles. Ulrika grunted, annoyed, for whatever traces the killer might have left behind, they were no doubt grinding them into the slush under their high-heeled Estalian boots.

Then one of them gave a great shout and nearly fell over. Von Zechlin and the others ignored him, most likely thinking it drunken clumsiness, but then the gentleman found words to go with his excitement and beckoned them all over, pointing animatedly at the ground.

His comrades gathered around him in a swaying circle, all jabbering at once until von Zechlin waded through them, pushing them aside, and squatted down in their centre. After a second he called for a lantern, and one of his men fetched one from the brothel and came back.

Ulrika wondered what they had found. She supposed she should have been wishing them success, as catching the killer was the reason she and her mistress had come to Nuln, but really she hoped it was nothing, so that she would have a chance to find a real clue and give the glory to her mistress. Lady Hermione and her perfumed gentlemen had so far not impressed her in the least.

A moment later von Zechlin stood, lantern in his left hand, examining something in his right that Ulrika could not make out. Seemingly satisfied, he handed the lantern to one of his men, took out his handkerchief and laid the invisible thing in it and folded it up.

'Back to the house!' he called, and strode off down the street in the direction of the Altestadt. His men swaggered loosely after him, taking the brothel's lantern with them, without so much as a thank you or a goodbye.

Ulrika waited until they were out of sight around the corner, and until the Lily's servant had closed the front door, then she hurried forwards to where the men had been squatting. The spot was a wide oval mud hole where the cobbles had come up, half pooled with icy water from the melting snow. Ulrika knelt beside it and peered into it. With her night vision, she needed no lantern to see immediately what the men must have been looking at.

A set of large paw prints was pressed into the mud, made either by a big dog or perhaps a wolf, and also, matted in the muck, big tufts of black fur. Ulrika looked at the surrounding cobbles and saw more tufts there, as if they had been pulled out during a fight. It must have been one of these that von Zechlin had folded into his handkerchief.

Ulrika chewed her lip. Finding the fur was strange. She had been certain that the killer had not been a beast, as it had used a stake. Perhaps the murderer had a dog that did his killing for him? She picked up a tuft of fur and inhaled. It smelled, unsurprisingly, of animal, but also, oddly, of cloves. She looked at the position of the paw prints and determined that the dog might have come from an alley opposite the brothel. She hunched towards it, almost on hands and knees, sniffing but, strangely, the animal scent vanished almost immediately. Had the dog leapt? Flown? And why had she not smelled its scent on Alfina's body? She paused and looked back at the fence where Alfina had been hung by the stake through her torso. Perhaps she would smell it there.

She tucked the tuft of fur into her belt pouch and crossed to the fence. A few wooden splinters on the ground were all the visual evidence that remained of any unpleasantness happening there that night. The brothel had cleaned up everything else. Blood on the fence was undoubtedly bad for business. But there were still some lingering smells. The most overpowering came from the puddle of vomit von Zechlin's man had contributed, but under that sour stench there were others. She could smell various human signatures, and the distinctive Lahmian musk of Mistress Alfina, and again, stronger here, the rotting, earthy scent that had also been on her body – but she did not smell the dog scent. With each new inhalation the picture of what happened changed in her head, like a drawing as an artist erased and redrew different elements – a man with a dog, then a man alone, then the man erased and replaced with something inhuman, possibly undead, or at least something that had lain recently with corpses. But, then, what of the dog?

She shook her head. She couldn't hold one picture in her mind. She couldn't see it. There were too many elements. She turned back to the alley across the street, thinking she might scent something there. A shape ducked back into the shadows, then around a corner. Ulrika's hair bristled on the back of her neck. Someone had been watching her!

She started quickly forwards, drawing her sabre. Her night vision had shown her a man's face, but indistinct, hidden under a deep hood. She had not recognised it. As she entered the alley she heard swift footsteps receding away from her. The prey was fleeing. Her blood-born hunting instinct welled up in her and she plunged down the alley and took the corner, skidding in the snow and dodging mounds of rubbish, her claws and fangs extending unconsciously.

Thirty paces ahead of her was a further intersection of alleys, but the man was already out of sight. She sprinted for the junction, not slowing to wonder which way he had turned. She knew. He had left footprints in the slush, and a trail of stench like the tail of a comet – not the rotten, earthy odour, though that was present too – but an ordinary human stink; a mix of sweat, food and fear – and also cloves!

She banked round the corner, jumping a slumbering beggar, and saw him, a scrambling, puffing little man, with too much belly to be running so hard. She loped after him easily, her long legs and inhuman strength easily closing the gap between them.

He took another corner, this time onto a street. She laughed as she bounded on. Poor little mouse. His attempts at escape were pathetic.

She rounded onto the street and skidded to a stop. The mouse was gone – vanished as if he had never been. Then she saw a sewer grating that had been pulled aside, revealing a square black opening in the gutter. The mouse had found a hole.

She ran towards it, then paused at the lip. Was it a trap? Surely the little man could not have lifted the grate himself. He must have had accomplices. She inhaled. The death reek was strong here, overpowering the little man's stink of sweat and cloves. Had some undead monster moved the grate? Was it still down there?

She looked down into the hole. She could see nothing but brickwork and an iron ladder and the greasy glint of sewage moving through the sewer channel below. Furtive assailants could be hiding just out of sight. She might be dropping into an ambush.

She sneered. Good. Her blood was up. After so much sitting and talking, she wanted a fight. And when she was done she would drag the mouse back to Gabriella and let her play with him.

With a snarl she leapt into the hole, her hands and feet barely touching the rungs of the ladder as she flashed down it, then landed on guard on the slick narrow ledge that flanked the sewage channel. There was no ambush. She was alone, and the overpowering stench of sewage hid the man's subtler scent. She looked left and right. The curve of the arched brick tunnel hid the distance, but to her left she heard the slapping of flat feet echoing away. She turned and sped silently after them.

As she rounded the curve, her night vision picked out the little man's paunchy form fleeing into the underground murk. He was limping now, as if he had a stitch in his side, and she could hear him wheezing like a bellows. She grinned, baring her fangs. Little mouse, she thought, you have only trapped yourself in a smaller maze.

He crossed a narrow bridge over the muck and staggered on towards an intersection of six tunnels, a great arched hexagon surrounding a wide basin of sludge more than twenty paces across. She raced after him. The little man looked back, then started waving his hands and arms as he stumbled on. Ulrika wondered if he was having some sort of seizure, and ran faster, hoping he wouldn't die, or worse, collapse into the lake of sewage. She wanted to question him, and didn't want to have to pull him out of the stew to do it.

He stumbled into the junction only ten paces ahead of her, but then, rather than take another corner in a vain attempt to elude her, he stopped, drew a great ragged breath and shouted a strange phrase.

Ulrika shielded her eyes as an explosion of blinding red light erupted into being around him. She skidded to a stop at the very edge of a ledge and went on guard, afraid it was some sort of attack, but nothing happened. She felt no magical sting, no tearing at her mind or soul.

She blinked and squinted as the light faded, looking around, then cursed. The mouse had gone. But where? She rose from her crouch and peered at the lake of muck, wondering if he had dived in, but she could see no bubbles or ripples. She crept to the intersection, sniffing and listening.

Again, the sewer stink hid his smell, but she thought she heard the tread of stealthy feet down the next tunnel to the left. She stepped to the mouth of it to look and listen. She had been right, there were definitely limping footsteps receding down it, but she could not see the man. She paused. It wasn't the darkness. She could see a hundred yards down the tunnel, and it appeared empty, but the footsteps were closer than that. Had he turned himself invisible? There seemed no other explanation. She growled in her throat. So he was going to make it difficult. No matter. She still had her ears. And they heard better than any human's.

A noise from behind her brought her head around – the scuff of shoe leather on brick. There was lantern light coming from another tunnel on the far side of the intersection. A silhouetted figure in a long coat and broad-brimmed hat appeared at its mouth, as tall and straight as the little man had been hunched and squat. It held a torch and a pistol in its gauntleted hands.

'Halt, bloodsucker!' it cried in stentorian tones. 'My bullets are silvered!'

CHAPTER SEVEN
HUNTERS IN THE DARK

ULRIKA EDGED BACK against the wall. The man was peering across the lake of muck, holding his lantern high and aiming his pistol at her. A shiver of fear shot up her spine. A witch hunter! And he knew what she was!

'Stay where you are, monster!'

Her first instinct was to flee, for she didn't want to lose her invisible quarry, but she also didn't want to get a silvered pistol ball in the back. Her second instinct was to kill him and kick him into the sludge, or better yet, drain him, then kill him and kick him into the sludge – for the thrill of the hunt had stirred her hunger, and she was aching to feed.

Then she remembered Countess Gabriella's admonition not to kill unless she was in mortal danger, and not to feed until she returned home. It would also not be very wise to drain and kill a witch hunter when the city was in the middle of a vampire panic. Even if he weren't found, he would be missed, and suspicions raised. No. She could not kill him, and she could not flee. But what else was there? If he already knew she was a vampire, he could not be allowed to live.

But did he?

The man was making his way slowly across the narrow bridges that arched over the channels at the mouth of each tunnel, holding out the lantern to guide his steps. If he could barely see to walk, could he truly have identified her for what she was? Perhaps he was only making a guess.

With an effort, Ulrika forced her animal instincts down and retracted her claws and fangs. Perhaps this was an occasion where Countess Gabriella's beguiling tactics would work better, where she could attempt to do things the Lahmian way. She winced, imagining herself cooing and showing her cleavage like some harlot. She had never won a lover like that. It was not in her nature. Why, hadn't she wooed Felix with swordplay and forthright words?

The witch hunter crossed the last bridge and held up his lantern to look at her, all the while keeping his pistol trained on her heart. 'A woman!' he cried, then glared suspiciously. 'Or a female fiend. Show me your teeth, wretch!'

'Sir, I assure you–' Ulrika began, but he aimed his pistol at her head.

'Your teeth!'

With a sigh, Ulrika smiled as wide as she was able, showing her retracted canines. 'Are… are you a vampire hunter, sir?' she asked through her teeth.

'I will ask the questions!' he snapped, leaning in to squint into her mouth.

Close up, Ulrika could see that he was young – only a year or two past twenty at the most – and handsome in a hard, stern way, with fierce grey eyes and a strong, square jaw. Six rowan-wood stakes and a hammer were slung through his broad, brass-buckled belt, as well as another pistol and a heavy, basket-hilted sword, while bandoliers hung with glass vials of she-knew-not-what criss-crossed his broad chest and a silver hammer of Sigmar glittered on a chain at his throat.

'What do you do here in the sewers?' he asked. 'And without a lamp? Do you see in the dark, then, fiend?'

Ulrika, swallowed, thinking fast. The lack of a light was indeed damning. What story could she tell? She thought back to the wooing of Felix. Swordplay and forthright words. It was worth a try.

'I think we are here for the same purpose, sir,' she said, showing him her drawn sabre. 'I hunt a vampire too. Indeed, I was just now grappling with him. Did you see a bright light?'

'Aye,' said the witch hunter cautiously.

'My lantern. It fell into the channel as we struggled. I thought I was next to fall, but your words and the light from your torch sent the monster fleeing. I thank you for it. You likely saved my life.' She looked down the tunnel that the little man had disappeared into. 'We may still catch him if you help me.' She started towards the tunnel, beckoning behind her. 'Come. Hurry.'

'Stand where you are!' the witch hunter barked. 'Face me.'

Ulrika froze, then turned slowly. The witch hunter stepped closer to her, examining her from head to foot, his lip curled.

'A female vampire hunter?' he said. 'I have never heard of such a thing. Why do you wear men's clothes? How do you come to this profession?'

'Sir, our quarry is slipping away,' Ulrika said. 'Perhaps we could talk on the way–'

'Answer the question!'

Ulrika sighed, buying time to craft a reply, then spoke. 'I wear men's clothing because hunting is impossible in skirts, and I did not choose this profession, it chose me. I hunt because...' She paused, as if choked up and, truth to tell, an unexpected surge of emotion did well up in her as she imagined a tale that was almost but not quite her own. 'Because my sister was seduced by a vampire, and given the curse of unlife against her will. The thing stole her from the man she loved, from the country she adored, from her friends and father, then made her into a monster and abandoned her in a cold, evil place.' She raised her chin. 'I have sworn vengeance upon all his kind ever since.'

The witch hunter's face lost some of its anger as he listened to her story, becoming sad and cold. 'And did you kill your sister?' he asked.

Ulrika swallowed, remembering Countess Gabriella pointing through the open window of her tower room to the bright dawn beyond and telling her that she might walk in the sun at any time. She hung her head. 'I had a chance once. I failed to take it.' Then she bared her teeth. 'But the vampire who turned her is dead.'

The witch hunter hesitated, then lowered his pistol. 'You should not have flinched,' he said. 'Sparing your sister was a false mercy. She was already dead and her soul long lost. You would only have put her out of her misery.'

'Aye,' she said, hiding a wince. 'I know.' She wished now she had told a different story, one that had not reminded her of her cowardice. At least it seemed to have convinced him. She had achieved a Lahmian victory. It hadn't been nearly as enjoyable as a fight.

She looked up, trying to think of some way to bid him adieu and hurry after the little man, but she couldn't think of a way to explain how she could continue hunting without a lamp in the dark. 'Will you help me now? I have no light, and the fiend is escaping while we talk.'

The witch hunter frowned at her, considering. 'I dislike leading a woman into such a business.'

'But if you take me back to the surface you will never find him again.'

'Aye,' he said, then grunted unhappily. 'Very well, but stay back.'

'Yes, sir,' said Ulrika, grinding her teeth. She pointed down the correct tunnel. 'He went that way.'

The witch hunter nodded and started into the tunnel, his spurs ringing as he stomped ahead in heavy riding boots. Ulrika followed, cursing his plodding speed. They would never catch the little man at this rate, but perhaps they could at least follow his trail to his lair. His footprints showed clear enough in the slime that filmed the ledge.

'What is your name, fraulein?' the witch hunter asked as they trotted along.

'Ulrika Straghov of Kislev,' she said without thinking, and then immediately wondered if she should have given a false name. It was too late now. 'And yours, mein herr?'

'Templar Friedrich Holmann,' he said, bowing curtly. 'A witch hunter of the Holy Order of Sigmar.'

'I am honoured,' said Ulrika, though terrified was closer to the truth. She seemed to have won his trust for the moment, but she knew that the slightest slip of the tongue or lapse in her masquerade would bring his suspicious witch hunter nature to the fore again. She felt she was treading on eggshells every moment she was at his side.

They jogged on in silence for a moment, then Holmann coughed. 'I know how difficult it is to be strong in the face of corruption, fraulein,' he said. 'Particularly when you discover it within your own family, but it must be done. I killed my own parents when I discovered they were mutants.'

Ulrika looked up at him, aghast. In a single sentence, he had proven all the tales she had heard of his kind correct. They would indeed sink to any depths to show their devotion to their faith. And yet...

And yet, she did not see the light of fanaticism blazing from the young man's grey eyes. Nor did she hear the hectoring tone of boastful righteousness, only a grave, faraway sadness. He was not proud of what he had done.

'It hurts to this day,' he continued. 'But I find strength in Sigmar, and you would be wise to do the same. In his teachings I have learned that I gave them release from their suffering.'

'I pray you are right, mein herr,' said Ulrika, and smiled sadly to herself. In his grim, ham-fisted way, the witch hunter was trying to comfort her, to give her courage for an unpleasant task. It was touching.

She remembered her father giving her a similar talk when she had been a little girl and hadn't understood why he had taken her older brother out on a hunting trip one day, and not come back with him. It had been a hard thing for a child to hear, but on the northern marches, so close to the Chaos Wastes that their glow could be seen behind the mountains to the north every night, it was something to be learned and accepted young, for mutation there was terrifyingly common. There had been many others throughout the years – cousins, uncles, aunts, any number of peasants – some of which she had dispatched herself. It had been part of her duties as the boyar's surviving heir – a difficult, painful task, but she had made herself believe, as Templar Holmann believed, that she was practising mercy. She wondered if one day she would have the courage to practise it on herself.

They came to another intersection in the tunnels and Holmann held the lantern close to the ground, trying to determine which way the little man had gone. Ulrika pointed to the footprints she saw going over one of the narrow bridges. 'There. He's gone straight on.'

Holmann gave her a look. 'You have sharp eyes.'

Ulrika swallowed as he started off again. She had to be more cautious. She had forgotten how much better her inhuman eyesight was than his. 'I inherited them from my father,' she said.

As they ran on, her mind finally settled enough for her to wonder about things other than her own survival and catching the little man. For instance, why was Templar Holmann down in the sewers hunting vampires in the first place? Had he seen something? Had Mistress Alfina's corpse been noted after all? Or had the witch hunter seen her killer?

'What led you down here, Herr Templar?' she asked at last. 'Do we hunt the same vampire?'

Holmann shrugged. 'I know not,' he said. 'A man came to my comrades and I while we were investigating a disappearance earlier, claiming to have seen a vampire climbing a fence near the Silver Lily.'

Ulrika stifled a groan. They *had* seen Alfina!

'He was drunk,' Holmann continued. 'But a Templar of Sigmar must investigate even the most unlikely rumour of evil, so the captain dispatched me and Jentz to follow him back. We found nothing at the brothel, and Jentz berated the drunk for wasting our time.'

Ulrika breathed a silent sigh of relief. They *hadn't* seen Alfina. Good.

'Jentz wanted to return to the captain,' said Holmann. 'But I had a…' He shrugged. 'A feeling, I suppose, and wanted to look around a bit more. I sent him back, then scouted the area. A few streets away I found an open sewer grate, and went down to investigate.' He looked back at Ulrika. 'I had just given up searching when I heard shouting and saw your light.'

'And thank Ursun you did,' said Ulrika, though, in reality, she was cursing the god for the mischance that had led to their meeting. 'Or I might be drowned in filth now.'

She glanced down to be sure of the little man's tracks and stared. They were gone. She stopped and looked back. They had just passed a ladder.

'Wait,' she said, and padded back. 'What is it?' asked Holmann.

Ulrika looked at the rungs of the ladder. Yes. Someone had gone up them recently, and she could smell the little man's distinctive clove scent on them. She glanced up through the circular chimney to the grate. It had been pulled aside, just like the one she had entered earlier. She was about to tell Templar Holmann that their quarry had gone above ground again when she realised that the sky showing through the grate had a faint grey tinge. She froze, frightened. Dawn was coming. What should she do?

She could not follow the little man's trail through the city during the day. She would burn like a match. But if she stayed in the sewers any longer she would have to wait down there a whole day before she could return to Gabriella at Guildmaster Aldrich's house. She couldn't wait. She had to go back immediately and tell Countess Gabriella what she had discovered. But what excuse was she to give to Holmann for their parting that wouldn't make him suspicious? She couldn't just run off in the middle of the hunt after telling him she was a vampire hunter. Of course, she could just kill him. But she had promised not to kill. She needed a believable reason for splitting up.

Ah! She had it.

'It seems he went up this ladder,' she said, turning to Holmann. 'But I think it might have been a feint to throw us off the trail. Look here.' She stepped past him and pointed to the ledge further along the tunnel. There were no footprints there except their own, but Holmann hadn't the eyesight to know that. 'You see. It looks like he continues down the tunnel too.'

Holmann nodded as if he could see the prints. 'Clever. So he continues down the tunnel?'

'I don't know,' said Ulrika. She stood up beside him, then shivered at the proximity. This close she could smell the blood in him, and hear it pounding, and the urge to feed grew like a fire in a hay loft within her. She fought it down with difficulty. She had to get away, as soon as possible. 'We'll… we'll have to split up. You have the lantern. You follow the tunnel. I'll go look in the street.'

Holmann nodded. 'Very well. But how will we find each other again?'

Hopefully we won't, thought Ulrika. I might not be able to resist temptation again. 'Name the place,' she said. 'I'll wait for you there.'

The witch hunter scratched his square chin. 'The Armoury, in the Halbinsel. It is a tavern. You know it?'

'I'll find it,' said Ulrika, and put a foot on the ladder. 'Good hunting, Templar Holmann.'

And with that she scrambled up into the pearl-grey pre-dawn and ran, racing the sun and fleeing her hunger.

ULRIKA CURSED HERSELF as she ran through the waking city. Why had she dismissed Aldrich's coach? With it there would have been no trouble going home as the sun came up. Now it was going to be a race, and one with deadly consequences if she lost. She kept one eye always on the east, to watch the progress of the dawn. At first, there was almost no distinguishing the houses from the sky behind them, but as she wound through the Handelbezirk, where shopkeeps put out the morning's wares and watchmen dragged off last night's drunks, their silhouettes began to stand out against the brightening horizon, and as she reached the wall between the Neuestadt and the Altestadt, the sky had turned from grey to pink.

It had been nothing to pass through that wall in the coach of a wealthy merchant. The guards at the High Gate had saluted, and not bothered to look within. But as the coachman had warned, going back through alone in the early hours of the morning, dressed in patched male riding gear and speaking with a Kislevite accent, was going to be more difficult.

Ulrika paused at the last intersection before the gate, watching the bored guardsmen pace back and forth before it. She could try invoking Guildmaster Aldrich's name to gain passage, but it might not work, and worse, it might draw suspicion to his house, something of which Countess Gabriella would most definitely disapprove.

She glanced again at the eastern sky. It was blushing brighter now, and beginning to hurt her eyes. It looked like it was going to be a cold, bright day, without a cloud in the sky. There was no time to hesitate, but what did she do? The sewers must go under the wall, but they were a maze. She might never find her way. Could she go over? She had heard of vampires who could turn themselves into bats or mist, but she had not so far noticed any of these abilities manifesting in herself.

Perhaps she didn't need them. Hadn't she made leaps and jumps that would have shamed a cricket? Hadn't she broken out of the tower at Castle Nachthafen and climbed safely to the ground? She backed around the corner, out of sight of the gate, then wound through the neighbourhood until she came to the street which paralleled the wall. She looked up and down it. The architects of Nuln had built with security firmly in mind. There were no buildings on the wall side of the street, just the sheer face of the fortification itself, with every now and then a square watch tower dotted along its length. It was in these, strangely, that she saw an opportunity.

Where the square shape of the tower jutted from the wall was a right angle, which would make for an easier climb than a flat surface. She hurried to the shadow of the nearest and sighted up it. The wall looked to be about five times her height, and the stonework tightly mortared, with almost no gaps between blocks. But the stone itself was roughly quarried, with lots of easy places to grip and pull – easy, that is, for hands that could tear a man limb from limb.

She started up, using the angle of the walls to brace against, and climbed fluidly. This close she was hidden from the eyes of any guards patrolling above by the overhanging lip of the battlements that ran along the top of the wall. But that benefit turned into a problem when she reached it. The underside of the lip was smoother stone, and there was no place for her to grab onto.

She leaned back as far as she dared, her claws gripping the wall so hard that she gouged white scars in it. Craning her neck, she could just see past the lip, and up the crenellated stone of the battlement. At first she saw no secure handholds, just smooth granite blocks, but then she noticed that spaced out along the bottom of the battlement were small rectangular holes, drainage holes, also no doubt meant to pour boiling oil down on any besiegers who made it this far into the city. There were only a few of them, and none directly above her, but they would have to do.

She drew her head back in, then crabbed sideways across the face of the wall – a harder trick than the climb, because she didn't have the angle of the other wall to brace against – until she thought she was under one of the holes. She stretched her neck again, her claws slipping unnervingly. Yes! There was a hole directly above her. The only difficulty was that it was too high to reach without letting go with both hands, and if she did that she would fall.

She looked down between her wide-braced legs. With her newfound strength and vitality the fall would be unlikely to kill her, but it might hurt her badly enough that she would be unable to find shelter from the sun. It didn't matter. She had to risk it. There was no longer any time to attempt a new plan.

She bunched herself as close as she could to the wall, finding the firmest, deepest holds for her feet, then tensed like a crouching spider and leapt up and out.

She flew out from under the shadow of the battlements as she arced up, watching for the narrow slot of the drainage hole. There it was. She shot an arm up and caught it. The edges were slimy with algae and snow run-off. Her fingers slipped, but she dug her claws in and they stopped her, her body swinging back and forth slightly as she hung beneath the battlements with nothing below her but air.

Dangling there one-handed, she marvelled once again at the new-found abilities Krieger's kiss had given her. She could certainly feel her weight pulling at her muscles, but her arms and hands were nowhere close to the limits of their endurance, and she felt no fear of falling. She was nearly as comfortable here as she would have been on the ground.

She listened above her for guards. There were voices and footsteps far to her right, but none above her, and she sensed no nearby pulse or heart-fire. Now was the time.

Pulling herself up one-handed, she stretched up with her free hand and grabbed at the deep crenellation above her, then swung herself easily up and over the wall and onto the catwalk. She crouched there, motionless, looking and listening. The voices to the right were getting closer and she saw two spearmen in the black uniforms of the garrison of Nuln walking slowly towards her along the circuit of the wall.

She crept to the inner edge of the wall and saw that the defensive measures outside the wall were not enforced inside the wall. The buildings of the Kaufmann District – all domed banks and marble-columned arcades – butted up almost directly against the wall, with only the narrowest of alleys between them, and their snow-covered roofs rising more than halfway up the height of the wall.

Ulrika smiled. That was good enough for her. With a frog-like kick of her legs she leapt off the catwalk and dropped down to a tall building, landing as lightly as she could on the snowy slanting shingles of its roof.

She still made quite a clatter, and the voices of the guards were raised above her.

'What was that?' said one.

'A cat?' said the other.

Ulrika scrabbled up the slick slope and rolled behind a fat brick chimney, then held still as their footsteps thudded closer.

'There was never a cat so big,' said the first guard. 'Did you hear the noise it made? And look at the snow on that roof! Something's been climbing on it.'

'Aye, but where's it gone, then?' asked the second. 'I don't see it.'

'Nor do I, but we better report it,' said the first. 'I'll feel like a fool if it's nothing, but I'll feel like a worse fool if isn't.'

'Aye,' said the second. 'Come on then.'

They hurried off to the left and Ulrika let out a breath, then grinned. 'A fool either way, then,' she said, then sprang from her hiding place and jumped to the next roof.

It felt so glorious to fly through the air that she laughed with the delight of it, and vaulted to another roof, and then another, spraying clouds of snow with every impact. What a feeling! She had never felt anything like it before in her life. Indeed, in her life, she couldn't have done it. It was her undead strength that allowed her this impossible grace and agility. She wished suddenly that she could run and leap and dance across the rooftops forever. What a joy it was to use her strength this way. What a joy to bound and spring like a cat, to skip across the skyline of the city as if in a weightless dream, to look down on the poor earth-bound mortals below and know that you were stronger and faster and deadlier than any of them, to know that you could reach down like a razored shadow and pluck away their lives without them ever knowing you were there. Was this what it was like to be a goddess? She licked her lips as she imagined dropping down on some poor unsuspecting fool of a banker. The goddess was hungry. Who would deny her hunger?

The merest sliver of the sun broke above the shoulder of Countess von Liebwitz's palace and stabbed her in the face. She hissed and crashed to the shingles of a steep roof as blisters boiled up on her cheeks and forehead, steam hissing from her bubbling skin. The agony was incredible, and she scrambled, half-blind and entirely panicked, for a patch of shade. She found a deep V between two gables, and rolled into it, gasping and shaking in the cool hidden lee.

Fool, she thought, cradling her head in her arms. Dreaming of godhood when you cannot even face the sun!

She crawled to the edge of the roof then dropped down by balcony and corbel and crossbeam to the still-dark street, then scurried from shadow to shadow like a skulking rat, seared head covered by her riding jacket, all the way back to Guildmaster Aldrich's house.

Countess Gabriella stood as Ulrika stumbled through the door to her private apartments.

'Child!' she cried, clutching her robe about her. 'You're back! I thought you had been caught. Or worse.'

Ulrika collapsed in a chair and raised her head, hardly able to see through eyes almost swollen shut. '…was caught,' she mumbled. 'By the sun.'

The countess gasped and crossed to her, folding her in her arms. 'Oh, your face! Your poor face! I should not have let you go.' She turned and snapped her fingers. 'Imma, quick! Bare your neck. Mistress Ulrika must feed, immediately.'

The maid curtseyed and came forwards, unfastening the high collar of her uniform. 'Yes, mistress.'

Ulrika whimpered, shivering and clutching at Gabriella's robe. 'Yes,' she murmured. 'Hungry. Hungry.'

Imma knelt beside Ulrika's chair and pulled aside the lace at her neck, revealing her scarred throat. The smell and sound of her blood as it rushed through her veins called to Ulrika like a lover. She could wait no longer. Her fangs thrust out. She grabbed the girl and pulled her roughly into her lap. Imma squealed with surprise. Ulrika paid her no mind. She sank her fangs into the tender white flesh and drank deeply, the sweet blood flowing through her like a soothing balm, easing all hurts.

'Ulrika!' came a voice from far away. 'Be gentle! Ulrika!'

The words meant nothing to her. She sucked harder, swooning with bliss as a red ocean of warmth and comfort wrapped her in its soft surging embrace.

'Ulrika!'

CHAPTER EIGHT
COUNCIL OF WAR

'ULRIKA!'

Ulrika woke with a start as something cracked her across the cheek. She blinked and struggled to stand, but could not. Her limbs were weak and constrained and her mind befuddled.

Another crack.

She hissed and cringed back, then squinted up at her attacker. Countess Gabriella stood above her, dressed to go out, glaring at her.

'Get up, girl,' she snapped. 'Will you sleep the night away too?'

Ulrika looked around her, head throbbing, limbs feeling like lead. She was in Gabriella's bed, still in her riding clothes, and the light seeping in around the curtained windows was the colour of sunset. She groaned. She hadn't felt this sick since... A horrible thought struck her as memory flooded painfully back into her mind. She looked around again.

'The maid! Imma,' she said. 'Did I–?' She let out a breath when she saw the girl lying unconscious on the chaise on the far side of the room, wrapped in blankets. 'She lives, then?'

The countess turned away, pulling on a pair of long gloves. 'Not through any mercy of yours.' She sniffed and crossed to the girl. 'Had I not been there you would have another soul on your conscience.' She smoothed the maid's hair. 'As it was, I nearly tore the girl's throat out trying to get you to withdraw your fangs.'

Ulrika closed her eyes, ashamed. The world spun sickeningly behind her eyelids. 'I – I am sorry, mistress,' she said, lowering her head. 'My lack of control is unacceptable. I promised you I would not do this again, and–'

Gabriella sighed and turned back to her. 'You were wounded. Sun sick. I can make an allowance for that – this time. But as I said before, there is *no* time when it is safe to be out of control. Our lives are a never-ending test of restraint, and it is when we fail that test that we die the true death. Even when our pain is over-whelming, we must not give in to the beast.'

'I understand, mistress,' said Ulrika. 'And I thank you for your forgiveness.'

Gabriella waved a hand. 'Forget it. Now get dressed. We have been summoned by Lady Hermione. She says she has discovered who the killer is.'

'What!' Ulrika fought her way out of the sheets and rose from the bed, her blood-sodden brain sloshing around inside her skull like a bag of porridge. 'Has she found the little man, then?'

Gabriella raised an eyebrow. 'What little man?'

Ulrika began taking off her riding clothes. 'I saw a little man in a hood and cloak watching me when I went to the brothel to investigate. I chased him, but–' She paused, suddenly not sure she wanted to tell Gabriella about the young witch hunter, Friedrich Holmann. 'But he cast some spell and vanished and I wasn't able to follow him.'

'A warlock?' said Gabriella. 'You believe he had something to do with Mistress Alfina's death? Was he the killer?'

Ulrika pulled off her breeches and stepped naked up to the wash basin. 'I don't think so. Or if so, he was not alone.' She poured water into the basin and began to wash her hands, still grimy from clambering over rooftops and sooty walls. 'I smelled the same smell outside the brothel that I smelled on Mistress Alfina's corpse. A rank, rotting corpse smell. The little man did not smell like that. He smelled of cloves. And then there was the dog.'

'The dog?' asked Gabriella.

'I found black fur at the site,' Ulrika said. 'And paw prints. Von Zechlin and his men found them too, and seemed to think they had meaning, but I'm not so sure. I did not smell the dog scent on Alfina's corpse, or on the fence where she was hung.'

'Rotting corpses, a warlock who smells of cloves and a dog,' said Gabriella thoughtfully. 'What a jumble. Does any of it have to do with the killings, I wonder?'

Ulrika soaped her hands and began to wash her face, then paused, probing her cheeks and brow. She could feel no blisters or cracks. Out of old habit, she looked up into the mirror on the wall, but could of course see nothing. She turned to Gabriella.

'Mistress,' she said. 'My face. Is it–?'

Gabriella smiled. 'You are unmarked,' she said. 'The blood heals us, unless the wound is very great.' She waved an impatient hand. 'Now hurry. Perhaps Hermione has solved the mystery for us and we can return home to Sylvania and peace and quiet.'

ULRIKA LIFTED HER skirts and avoided a puddle as she stepped down from the countess's coach before the inn in which Rodrik had taken up residence, a respectable-looking establishment called the Sow's Ear. The snow of the previous night had melted during the day, and the streets were now muddy rivers of run-off. She paused to smooth her black wig, then stepped through the low-lintelled door into a genteel tap room, a cosy place with a warm fire and fat, prosperous merchants murmuring quietly to each other in the corners. Ulrika was about to cross to the landlord and ask him to send someone up to Rodrik's room, when she saw him. He sat in a high-backed chair near the fire, his legs stretched out so that the heels of his knee-high riding boots were almost in the fire.

Ulrika threaded her way through the room, trying to ignore the appraising stares of the men she passed. In her usual attire she received her fair share of looks, but they weren't the leers and lingering glances she got now. All this bother for a dress and a wig. Did men always look at the wrapping, and never see what was inside?

Rodrik raised his leonine blond head and glowered at her as she approached. She saw he had a glass of wine in his hand, and a nearly empty bottle on the table beside him.

'If it isn't the stray,' he said. 'What do you want?'

Ulrika ignored the slight. 'We are summoned to Lady Hermione's,' she said. 'The countess awaits you outside.'

He snorted and put down his glass with exaggerated care. 'So spying has failed her and she has need of a knight again?'

'A wise leader makes use of both the right hand and the left,' said Ulrika, politely. After her embarrassment with Imma she was not going to get in any more trouble by antagonising Gabriella's favourite.

Rodrik sneered as he levered himself out of his chair and pointed an unsteady finger at her. 'Try no honeyed words with me, alley cat. You aren't Lahmian enough to know the trick of it.'

Ulrika looked around to see if anyone had heard him. Fortunately, it seemed no one had. 'Is this how a knight protects his lady?' she hissed. 'Spilling her secrets in public?'

Rodrik drew himself up, then strode past her towards the door without a word. She followed, glaring at his back. A single spring and a slash across the throat and he would trouble her no more, but she mustn't. Restraint in all things – that was the Lahmian way.

Rodrik ducked out through the door, then climbed up into the coach, and bowed low over the countess's hand.

'My lady, I am overjoyed to be recalled to your side,' he said, then dropped into his seat with a thump.

Gabriella made a face. 'Rodrik, you're drunk,' she said as Ulrika took her seat beside her and closed the door.

'Forgive me, countess,' said the knight, with mock contrition. 'As we have been separated, I did not know when you would require me.'

The coach started forwards and he swayed in his seat.

'Ah,' said Gabriella. 'So it is my fault, then.'

Rodrik shook his head and slid his eyes over to Ulrika. 'Not at all, mistress. Not at all.'

Ulrika turned away from him, disgusted, as they rode on. What petty, pitiful things men were, filled with jealously, lust and rage. It made her almost glad that she was no longer human.

LADY HERMIONE WAS pacing impatiently as Otilia ushered Gabriella, Ulrika and Rodrik into her drawing room, and glanced up sharply as they entered.

'There you are!' she said. 'You certainly took your time.' She was dressed in yellow this time.

'We came as soon as the sun set, sister,' said Gabriella, then nodded politely to the others assembled in the room – Madam Dagmar of the Silver Lily, Famke, and von Zechlin and his men. 'And we are eager to hear your news.'

Ulrika exchanged a smile with Famke as Hermione beckoned them all to gather around the harpsichord, then looked around at the others. Lady Dagmar, wearing a modest, high-necked burgundy dress that still managed to emphasise her abundant figure, was looking more composed than she had in Hermione's kitchen, though still a bit ashen, and von Zechlin and his men were their usual impeccable selves – apparently none the worse for their drunkenness of the night before.

'Look, then,' said Hermione. 'And see how unnecessary it was for you to come and "help" us.' She took a
folded handkerchief from her sleeve and set it on the
broad top of the harpsichord. 'My dear Bertholt found
this last night in front of the Silver Lily. Indisputable
proof of the killer's identity!'

Hermione unfolded the handkerchief, revealing
what Ulrika expected to see, a few tufts of black fur.
Everyone stared at it. Gabriella raised an eyebrow,
apparently underwhelmed.

'What is it?' asked Dagmar.

'Has your dear Bertholt torn out his hair?' asked
Gabriella.

Hermione glared at them, exasperated. 'It is the fur
of a wolf!' she said. 'And Bertholt found paw prints
there as well.'

Gabriella frowned, as if this was the first she'd heard
of it, though Ulrika had told her of it earlier. 'You are
suggesting Mistress Alfina was attacked by a wolf?' she
asked. 'In the middle of a city?'

Von Zechlin snorted at this, and Hermione rolled
her eyes.

'My dear countess,' she said. 'It is clear you are not as
knowledgeable as you should be about your sisters
here in Nuln. I mentioned to you earlier that vulgar
slut Mathilda?'

'She who presides over the slums south of the river?'
said Gabriella. 'Yes, I remember.'

'Well,' continued Hermione. 'Mathilda is so lost
within her animal nature that she is capable of
becoming a great black she-wolf when her blood is up
– a she-wolf with a vampire's strength, powerful
enough to tear any of us to shreds with ease.'

Dagmar gasped. 'Sister, do you mean to say–?'

Hermione nodded and pointed to the curls of fur. 'It can be no one else. Mathilda has murdered Rosamund and Karlotta and Alfina. She is trying to take Nuln for herself. We must stop her before she completes her coup. We must kill her before it is our throats that are torn out.'

Ulrika was fairly bursting to speak, wanting to mention the little warlock who had run from the scene, and the fact that the wolf smell had been absent from Mistress Alfina's body – that she had in fact smelled it nowhere except near the mud where the paw prints had been found – but she dared not open her mouth. To do so would reveal that Gabriella had sent her out to investigate the crime against Hermione's direct orders.

Gabriella's brow furrowed deeper. 'This is a bold charge, sister,' she said. 'Are you entirely certain it was her? There are other skin changers in the world.'

'But with a grudge against us?' asked Hermione, her eyes flashing. 'No, the wolf-kin and bear-kin stay in the forests with their cousins. They care nothing for us. Mathilda, however, has ample reason to be covetous of her fairer sisters. We have beauty and breeding while she has neither. We live in fine houses while she lives in a filthy hovel. We mix with the cream of society, while she feeds on the dregs.' Her pretty face twisted with hate. 'It is her, I know it!'

'That may be so,' said Gabriella calmly. 'But I still find it hard to credit. As I said before, no Lahmian would expose other Lahmians for fear the witch hunt that followed would expose her as well.'

'Yes, Hermione,' said Dagmar timidly. 'Would even Mathilda dare so much?'

'The witch hunters do not look among the poor!' cried Hermione. 'Not for us at least! Do you not see how clever she is being? Mathilda kills Rosamund and Karlotta and the witch hunters do the rest of her work for her. Soon all of her rich sisters north of the river will be exposed and staked and she will be the last Lahmian in Nuln. The queen will have no choice but to name her leader here!' She shivered with disgust. 'She will move into my house! She will soil my sheets! She will befoul my beautiful clothes!'

A faint smile played around Countess Gabriella's lips. 'The horror,' she murmured.

Hermione folded up the handkerchief with the tuft of fur in it, then tucked it back into her sleeve. 'I will not wait for her to attack,' she said, lifting her chin. 'We must strike first. We will go tonight, all of us, and kill her in her lair – her and her barbarous flock.'

Dagmar stared and stepped back from the harpsichord. 'You want us to fight? To kill?'

Hermione sneered at her. 'Will you not defend yourself, sister? You have fought before.'

'Not for centuries,' Dagmar said. 'Not since my rebirth. I have always used... other weapons to win my battles.'

Hermione smirked, looking Dagmar's hourglass figure up and down. 'Those won't prove effective against Mathilda, I don't think,' she said. 'You will have to sharpen your claws.' She turned to her housekeeper, who waited discreetly by the door. 'Otilia, have the coaches brought around. We will be leaving immediately.'

'Hermione, please,' said Gabriella, as Otilia curtseyed and withdrew. 'Let us not be rash. The queen will not like this. Her law has always been that we do not make war upon each other.'

'And Mathilda has broken that law!' snarled Hermione.

'But should we not send word to the queen first?' Gabriella pleaded. 'I would feel much easier if this murder were given her blessing.'

'Would you have another of us fall while we wait for her reply?' asked Hermione. 'No. I will not risk my sisters' lives so needlessly. We go. Come.' She turned on her heel and started for the door.

Ulrika saw Gabriella clench her fists and stifle some outburst, then follow smoothly after her. 'Then, sister,' she said, 'may I at least beg for a trial before execution? Can we not hear what this Mathilda has to say in her defence before we condemn her?'

'Oh, yes!' said Dagmar, her eyes lighting up at the thought of postponing the fight. 'That is the right thing to do. Let us hear her first.'

'Hear her?' asked Hermione, without slowing. 'For what reason? She will only lie.'

'So that we may say to the queen that we have done it,' said Gabriella. 'You know as well as I do that no matter how justified this killing may be, there will be questions from the mountain. I for one would wish to be as prepared as possible for their coming.'

This gave Hermione pause. She stopped at the door and turned to look at Gabriella, her eyes suddenly uncertain. 'I hadn't thought of that. There will be a reckoning.'

The countess nodded. 'There will indeed. And it would behove us to cover ourselves as best we can, don't you think?'

Hermione bit her lip, then nodded. 'Very well,' she said at last. 'We will let her speak. It will give her the opportunity to hang herself.'

CHAPTER NINE
MADAM MATHILDA

ULRIKA HAD HOPED to speak more with Gabriella of her doubts about Hermione's she-wolf theory, but Gabriella had insisted they all travel together in the same coach so she could continue her attempt to get Hermione to listen to reason. Ulrika was therefore denied the chance to talk to the countess alone. Instead, she sat beside Famke while, on the opposite bench, their mistresses argued back and forth about what they should do and say once they got to Mathilda's.

It seemed a foregone conclusion to Ulrika, for Hermione had armed her party for war. Just outside the coach doors, Rodrik and von Zechlin stood on guard on the running boards, wearing breastplates and strapped with swords and pistols, while the other coaches followed behind – Madam Dagmar and her guards in her own, and the rest of Hermione's gentlemen armed to the teeth in a third.

In Ulrika's experience, if one went into a negotiation with loaded guns, they were almost sure to go off. Hermione would kill this wolf-woman, though it was unlikely she was the culprit, and then Ulrika and the countess would get down to the business of finding the real killer. It wasn't fair or right, but there didn't seem to be any way to stop it, and so Ulrika found Hermione and Gabriella's arguing pointless and annoying, and turned away from it, looking out the window of the coach to watch the sights and sounds of the city roll by.

The charm hawkers and broadsheet sellers were still out in force, screaming about vampires and disappearances and guaranteed protections against them. On one corner, a woman was selling bells on strings.

'Put 'em round your babies' necks!' she cried. 'And ye'll hear if the fiends try t'snatch 'em from their cradles!'

On another corner, a fellow in a broad hat and a pathetic attempt at a witch hunter's costume was doing a brisk business testing women for vampirism on the spot.

'One prick of my silver knife, gentles,' he shouted, 'and ye'll know for certain. Test yer wife! Test yer maid! Test yer daughter! Only a pfennig a prick!'

Outside a tavern opposite, two rude fellows were offering passing ladies *two* pricks for a pfennig, though they had no silver knives.

As the coach crossed the Great Bridge over the River Reik, Ulrika marvelled again at the bustling forges and foundries along the south bank. Did they never stop? It was hours after sunset, and still the air rang with their clanging, and the orange glow of their fires reflected in the black surface of the water like so many flickering daemon eyes.

As the coaches rolled off the end of the bridge they passed between a pair of looming gun works, their towering smokestacks belching black smoke that blotted out the stars. They seemed grim sentinels guarding the entrance to the vast dreary neighbourhood beyond them – a shabby warren of muddy, unpaved streets, tottering tenements and seedy taverns, of ramshackle tanneries and shuttered slaughterhouses, known as the Faulestadt.

The people who hurried through the streets were as tattered and begrimed as their world – soot-faced foundry men just getting off shift, gaunt-cheeked fish-wives, trundling their barrows home after a day flogging their wares north of the river, filthy children crouching in doorways like feral cats, pimps and harlots and pickpockets eyeing the rest of the crowd appraisingly. But though their lives seemed bleak, there was rude vitality to these peasants Ulrika found attractive, a stubborn determination to survive that gave them an intoxicating energy. She closed her eyes and inhaled. The scent of their blood, wafting into the coach, smelled as strong and raw as cheap kvas, and would no doubt be as invigorating to taste.

She also smelled fear. The vampire hysteria that gripped the rest of Nuln was here as well. The charm sellers and street-corner shouters did booming business, and even the poorest beggars huddling in the gutters wore the sign of Sigmar's hammer or Ulric's wolfshead as a protection against the night, even if it was only daubed upon their flesh in mud.

Gabriella was right. The tide of panic must be made to recede before it rose up and drowned them all.

'How long have you been a sister?' whispered a voice in her ear.

Ulrika started and turned. Famke was smiling at her, only inches from her face, a merry glint in her pale green eyes.

'I?' said Ulrika, slightly unnerved. 'Uh, only a few weeks.'

Famke's eyes widened. 'A few weeks? You are a baby! I am older than you!'

Ulrika snorted. How could such a gawky young thing be older than her? 'How old are you, then?' she asked.

'Lady Hermione turned me in the autumn of last year,' she said, then grinned. 'So I have five months on you.'

Ulrika smiled back. It seemed impossible to be annoyed with the girl. 'That *is* ancient,' she said. 'I am humbled that someone so wise and worldly would deign to acknowledge an infant as lowly as myself.'

Famke stifled a laugh with a long-fingered hand, then shot a look at their mistresses, still arguing on the opposite side of the coach. She leaned in again towards Ulrika. 'Fair enough,' she said. 'Then we shall be babies together. And who were you before the countess turned you?'

Ulrika's smile faltered. 'I was a boyar's daughter, from the north of Kislev, but the countess did not turn me,' she said quietly. 'I… I am a stray. I was turned by a villain named Adolphus Krieger, against my will. The countess was good enough to rescue me from myself when he was killed.'

Famke's face fell and she touched Ulrika's arm. 'I am sorry,' she said. 'I did not know. It must be a frightening thing to receive the kiss without one's consent.'

Ulrika could only nod, for her voice would have shook if she had spoken. 'So,' she said after a moment. 'You welcomed it, then?'

'Oh yes,' said Famke. 'With all my heart. You see, Lady Hermione rescued me as well. My father…' The girl paused, and Ulrika could see that she was mastering some emotion, just as she herself had done. 'My father, though no vampire, was a villain nonetheless. He saw… *opportunity* in my beauty.' She clenched her fists. 'Just as he had in my mother's.'

Ulrika growled in her throat. She did not like to hear such things. She covered Famke's hand with her own. 'I am sorry too.'

Famke shrugged, as if divesting herself of a weight, then smiled brightly. 'No matter. Lady Hermione saw opportunity in my beauty as well, but told me she would make me mistress of it, instead of its slave. She would show me how to make all men grovel before me, instead of me cringing before them. I… I could not wait for her kiss.'

Ulrika looked at Famke, unnerved again. There was an anger under the girl's sweet nature that was frightening. 'I hope you find what you seek,' she said at last.

Famke grinned, her eyes flashing. 'I already have. As soon as I was able after Lady Hermione turned me, I returned to my father's house.'

Ulrika blinked as the girl's meaning became clear. 'Ah,' she said. 'I see.'

'Did you kill your tormentor as well?' Famke asked, as if enquiring about the weather.

Ulrika shook her head. 'No. I was still lost in my birth pangs then. I could not think. My old companions killed him – a pair of dwarf trollslayers, and two men of my acquaintance – a poet and a mage. Good men and good friends. They crossed all of Kislev and Sylvania to rescue me.'

The girl curled her lip and turned away, vanishing into herself as abruptly as she had started the conversation. 'There are no good men,' she said.

Ulrika looked for a long moment at Famke's beautiful profile, now as cold and hard as a statue's, and wished she could dig up and breathe life into the corpse of the girl's father, just so she could kill him all over again.

THE COACHES STOPPED in the very heart of the Faulestadt. A sprawling, sway-roofed tavern slouched at the corner of a block of tinder-box tenements, a red lantern hanging from a hook over the door. Its crimson light illuminated the sign of the place, a stuffed wolf's head mounted to a plaque, patchy and dull from the weather, and missing one of its glass eyes.

Though she saw no guards as they approached the place, it was obvious to Ulrika that they had been observed, for a lanky villain with an iron-shod cudgel over his shoulder swaggered out and held up a hand before they were able to pull into the yard.

'Tain't a place for swells, yer worships,' he drawled as he stepped up to Hermione's coach window. 'Best do yer slummin' somewhere else.'

'We are here to see Madam Mathilda,' sniffed Hermione. 'We are her "sisters".' She sounded loath to admit it.

The villain looked closer at Hermione, then behind her to Gabriella and Dagmar. He swallowed, nervous, then touched his forelock, suddenly respectful. 'Sorry, mistress. Didn't recognise ye.' He pointed down the street. 'Take the first alley and come round the back. More private, like, there.'

'Thank you, my good man,' said Hermione, then drew back into the coach and signalled the coachman to drive on.

As they trundled on, Ulrika heard the swaggering guard whistle shrilly behind her.

'Dirk!' he cried. 'Tell her nibs there's company comin'!'

Gabriella looked out the window as the coach turned into the narrow alley and the dark walls closed in on either side of them. 'Are we sticking our heads into a trap from which it will be difficult to withdraw?' she asked.

Hermione waved a hand. 'Mathilda's trulls are nothing but alley bashers. Bertholt alone could fight his way out of this cheese box.'

Gabriella frowned but said nothing. Ulrika knew how she felt. If this Mathilda was behind the killings of the other Lahmians, and it did come to a fight, they would not have an easy time of it. She looked down at her beautiful dress, and wished the countess had let her wear her hunting clothes tonight.

The coach slowed suddenly, and the coachman's voice came from above. 'There's a dead end ahead, mistress,' he said. 'I don't know–'

A rattling and screeching drowned out his words, and Ulrika and the others went on guard. Was it some sort of attack? Ulrika looked out the window and to the front. What had seemed to be a solid wall was swinging back to reveal a square muddy yard surrounded by the backs of a ring of tenements. It appeared that Mathilda's domain was more than just the tavern on the corner of the street. The thought did not ease her mind.

'Come ahead, yer worships,' called a harsh female voice.

The coaches started forwards again then, once they had all passed through it, the secret gate shut behind them again with the same rattling and screeching.

'The teeth close,' muttered Gabriella.

As the coaches stopped in the centre of the yard, Ulrika saw scruffy bravos with long guns and crossbows watching from the windows of the tenements, and a dozen more stepping out from the back door of the tavern, the sloping roofs of which rose in the far corner of the yard. These men surrounded the coaches with swords drawn. Ulrika tried to imagine von Zechlin fighting his way through them all in his high-heeled boots, and found she couldn't. Perhaps he had hidden depths.

Hermione looked at the ring of bashers and hesitated as von Zechlin opened her door from the outside. Gabriella smiled flatly behind her.

'Having second thoughts about baiting the she-wolf in her den?' she asked.

Hermione assembled a sneer. 'Bah!' she said. 'They are nothing. Once Mathilda is dead they will fight to kiss our hems.' She threw back her shoulders and stepped down to the slushy ground as if she owned the place. Gabriella followed, and Ulrika and Famke filed out after her, Rodrik and von Zechlin handing them down one at a time as Dagmar and the rest of Hermione's guard exited their coaches and joined them.

Out to greet them all strolled a scrawny young woman with hennaed hair and terrible spots. She wore a red dress and had a boat hook tucked into the wide leather belt that cinched her waist. 'Hoy,' she said, by way of greeting. 'To what does my mistress owe th' pleasure?'

Hermione looked down her nose at the woman. 'That is a private matter between Madam Mathilda and myself.'

The hennaed woman grinned around at the rest of the group, showing snaggled yellow teeth. 'If it were private, why'd y'bring so many?'

The bravos in the yard laughed, and Ulrika saw that the men in the windows were aiming their weapons at them.

'You tell 'em, Red,' said one.

'Enough of your impertinence, trull,' snapped Hermione. 'Just fetch your mistress.'

'She's already waitin',' said the woman. 'But she won't see all of ye. Just the ladies. Yer guard dogs'll have to wait here.'

Hermione looked anxiously to Gabriella.

Gabriella shrugged. 'What did you expect?' she murmured.

Hermione fumed, then turned back to the woman in red. 'I will not enter this place without at least one escort. The rest can stay.'

'I will take a guard too,' said Gabriella.

Red frowned, then turned to an enormous man in a leather apron who waited at the back door of the tavern. He gave an almost imperceptible nod and the woman turned back.

'Two bravos, then,' she said. 'But no more. Now come on.'

She beckoned them across the yard, then into the back door of the tavern. Rodrik and von Zechlin went first, like the champions they were, but Gabriella drew Ulrika close and kept her there.

'You are my secret weapon in this, if aught goes ill,' she whispered. 'My bodice dagger, you understand me?'

'Aye, mistress,' said Ulrika. A thrill went up her spine. One part of her hoped that her mistress would face no danger, another part prayed for it.

And it seemed at first, as if her prayers had been instantly answered. She had expected to come into some kitchen or back room when they entered the tavern, but as Red led them through the low door under the cold gaze of the huge man in the leather apron, they found themselves in a dark corridor almost too narrow to turn around in, and much too narrow to fight in. Ulrika eyed the walls and ceiling warily. There were odd openings in them that reminded her too much of the murder holes one found in the entrances of castles.

As they went deeper in, Ulrika could hear the sounds of rowdy merrymaking and smell the stink of sour beer, vomit and unwashed bodies filtering through the walls. Above her, she could hear merrymaking of a different sort, and smelled a miasma of unsubtle perfume.

'A veritable cornucopia of vice,' murmured Gabriella.

Red heard her and smiled. 'An island of pleasure in an ocean of misery, her nibs calls it,' she said, gesturing around. 'Girls upstairs – boys too, if that's yer fancy – drinkin' and dancin' in the tavern, then cards and dice downstairs, and poppy and pipeweed below that. Something for everyone.'

'It sounds... profitable,' said Gabriella politely.

'We get by,' said the woman.

They turned into a close-walled stair and wound down into the bowels of the building, and with each flight Ulrika could hear and smell evidence of the woman's words – the rattle of dice and cries of dismay at the first floor below ground, the sickly-sweet reek of narcotic smoke at the second. But the stair didn't stop there. As they descended past a third level, she heard pitiful moans and weary pleading.

Gabriella shot their guide another look.

Red grinned again. 'The black hotel,' she said. 'A little service we provide to the, ah, *professional* classes. A place to hide for them what's on the lam, and a place to stash kidnapped marks while the blackmail is sorted out.'

'Good rent in that, I'll wager,' Gabriella said.

'Good enough,' said the woman, then continued on.

They descended another three flights, with Ulrika feeling the weight of all the floors above pressing down on her more strongly with every step.

'Illusion all around,' murmured Gabriella in her ear. 'We have taken three branching stairs as we have sunken into this hell, though it seems we have been on only one. One without witch sight would never get out again.'

Ulrika swallowed and looked around her. She
hadn't noticed a thing. She concentrated hard, trying
to see with her mind and not her eyes, and for a brief
second she thought she saw doors and other stairs
splitting off from theirs, but then the vision was gone
again.

'I shall stay at your side then, mistress,' she said.

Gabriella patted her arm.

'Here we are,' Red called, then pushed past Rodrik
and von Zechlin as the stairs ended in a square little
room that appeared to have no doors, but which was
once again riddled with little holes in the walls, ceiling and floor. She crossed to the opposite wall and
rapped on it as the others gathered warily in the centre of the death box.

'Visitors fer madam,' she called.

A door appeared in the wall as Red stepped back.
Ulrika blinked, for it didn't pop into being like something out of a magician's trick, but was just there, as if
she hadn't noticed it, and had forgotten to look in
that spot before.

Red opened the door and curtseyed with exaggerated courtesy. 'Enter, yer worships.'

Hermione reassembled her haughty dignity, which
had crumbled somewhat during their unnerving
decent, and strode into the room, chin held high,
looking like a miniature galleon at full sail. Von Zechlin followed close behind her, then Famke, Rodrik,
Gabriella and Ulrika.

The room beyond the hidden door was like the
harem of some Araby caliph, if decorated by a mad rag
and bone man. At first glance it looked obscenely opu-
lent, a glittering cave of treasure that winked red, gold

and purple in the light of a hundred fat candles. Velvet divans and low gilded tables surrounded a carved fireplace, and the floor was a layered patchwork of eastern carpets, from which rose a clutter of ornate lamps, vases and statuettes. But on closer examination, the furniture was scarred and patched, the carpets threadbare, and all the décor rescued from the rubbish. The glitter was glass and the gold was brass, and dented brass at that.

In the midst of this shabby excess, a curious tableau greeted the Lahmians' eyes. On the divan closest to the fire, a black-haired woman in red petticoats lay face down, clutching a pillow, while a plump, sweating girl in a ragged maid's outfit hunched over her, a knee in the small of her back, pulling mightily upon the stays of a whalebone corset.

'Harder, y'slut!' cried the woman. 'I didn't tear out them nether ribs for nothing. I want to be able to circle my waist with my hands when yer finished!'

'Yes, mistress,' said the girl, and hauled again.

The woman on the couch looked up at her visitors with a leering smile. 'Just a minute, dearies,' she said. 'You catch me at my toilette. Make yerselves at home.'

Neither Hermione nor Gabriella nor Dagmar accepted her offer, but instead stood uneasily in the centre of the room while the maid huffed and puffed over the final stays.

While they waited, Ulrika examined the woman, who she presumed must be Madam Mathilda. A creature less like the other Lahmian sisters she could not have imagined. Coarse-featured and thick-lipped, with an unruly mane of jet hair that spilled down her back and hung in her face, she was certainly not beautiful, and yet despite that, and the deep scar that pulled up the left corner of her mouth into a permanent leer, she was disturbingly attractive. A crude magnetism radiated from her onyx eyes, promising rough and rowdy delights. Her body, as her maid at last finished her monumental task and Mathilda stood to greet her visitors, promised the same, in abundance. She had curves to rival the figurehead of a Tilean galley, and a sultry saunter that knew how to display them. She put the prodigious Madam Dagmar to shame.

'Now then, sisters,' she said as her maid helped her on with her bodice and sleeves. 'This is right neighbourly of ye. I don't believe we've had the pleasure of yer company south of the river before. Or the acquaintance of yer friends.'

'Save the oil for your customers, Mathilda,' snipped Hermione. 'You know very well why we've come.'

Mathilda's eyes opened wide. 'Not I, lady. I've been keeping to home as you directed. Haven't left this room in days.'

'No,' said Hermione, curling her lip. 'But the nights are another matter, I'll warrant.'

Gabriella stepped forwards and curtseyed respectfully before Mathilda could reply. 'I am Countess Gabriella von Nachthafen,' she said. 'Sent by our queen to help Lady Hermione put an end to the murders of our sisters. It was about this that we wished to speak with you.'

Madam Mathilda returned Gabriella's curtsey with a nod, and a more appraising glance. 'Luck to you, then,' she said. 'Her ladyship certainly ain't been makin' much of it.'

'I beg to differ!' said Hermione stiffly. 'In fact, with the help of my champion here, Lord von Zechlin, I have discovered the culprit!'

'Oh?' Mathilda raised her painted-on eyebrows. 'Who's that then?'

Hermione levelled a beringed finger at the madam. 'You.'

Mathilda's eyes widened again, and this time Ulrika thought the reaction might be genuine.

'Me?' Mathilda laughed explosively, then lay back on the divan, displaying her preposterous curves to best advantage. 'And why would I kill Rosamund and Karlotta, who never done harm to me?'

'You're forgetting Lady Alfina, she-wolf,' said von Zechlin.

Mathilda turned from him to Hermione. 'Alfina's dead too? By the queen, that's bad! In the same way?'

Hermione sneered. 'Your shock is almost as artfully constructed as your illusions, sister. And just as false.' She tugged the handkerchief from her sleeve and threw it on the table. 'Look there,' she said. 'Open it!'

Mathilda gave her a glare, then rose and sauntered to the table to unfold the kerchief, revealing the black curl within. She looked up at Hermione, frowning. 'From yer hairbrush?' she asked.

'From your pelt!' snapped Hermione. 'Wolf's fur. Bertholt discovered it at the scene of Alfina's murder, next to a trail of paw prints.'

Mathilda goggled at her for a moment, then bellowed out a laugh. 'This is your proof? A few tufts of hair?'

'From the beast that slew our sisters?' said Hermione. 'It is enough. Who else among us can become a wolf? Who else could tear a vampire limb from limb?'

'But why would I want to?' asked Mathilda, advancing angrily. 'I told ye. They done nothing to me.'

As she came forwards, her perfume came with her, a cheap rosewater reek. Ulrika inhaled it, searching for what it hid. Beneath it she found dirt and mildew and the usual dry Lahmian musk, but not the smells she hunted for.

'Ah, but they *have* done,' Hermione snarled at the madam. 'They have lived well. Something that must wound you to your core, stuck here in this flea-bitten hovel. You mean to kill us all and take our places! To steal what you aren't entitled to.'

Mathilda barked out another laugh. 'You think I want that?' she asked. 'Having to ponce around and put on airs all the time? Having to watch my step every second of every day? No thank you! This is my place. I rule here more completely than you rule the neighbourhoods you hide in, and that's the truth.'

Ulrika inhaled again, deeper this time. There was indeed an animal scent there, as if even in human form the madam could not entirely hide her nature, but it was not the smell from the fur she had found in the mud. It was a wilder scent, more wolf than dog, and of the battlefield corpse stench she found no sign at all. She edged to Gabriella as Hermione and Mathilda continued to shout at each other.

'Mistress,' she murmured. 'I do not smell on Madam Mathilda the stench I found on Mistress Alfina's corpse and outside the Silver Lily.'

Gabriella shot her a sharp look out of the corner of her eye. 'It wasn't her, then?'

Ulrika shrugged. 'She could be hiding the scent, but the scraps of fur do not smell like her either. And her scent was nowhere at the scene.'

Gabriella nodded, then shot a grim look at Hermione. 'Thank you.'

'It is a lie!' Hermione was saying. 'Who could want to live here? You couldn't possibly–'

Gabriella took a deep breath and stepped forwards. 'Lady Hermione, wait. I fear we have come here in error.'

Hermione spun around, eyes flashing. 'What do you say?'

'You have tracked the wrong wolf,' Gabriella said. 'The fur Lord von Zechlin collected is not that of Madam Mathilda. The scent is not her scent, and her scent was not present outside the Silver Lily or on Alfina's corpse.'

Mathilda grinned. 'There y'are. Y'see?'

Hermione stared at Gabriella. 'What is this nonsense? Are you trying some trick?'

'No trick, sister,' said Gabriella. 'Surely you remember when we all stood around Lady Alfina's corpse in your kitchen. Did you smell Mathilda's scent on her? I did not.'

'I don't go around sniffing corpses,' said Hermione. 'It's disgusting. And–' She frowned suddenly, then narrowed her eyes. 'And how do you know that her scent wasn't present outside the Lily? Did I not forbid you to go there? Did you disobey me?'

Gabriella hesitated the barest moment, then spoke. 'I did not go there, sister. I did as you commanded and established myself at the house of Guildmaster Aldrich, but you gave no such order to my protégée.'

Ulrika hid a smile as Hermione hissed.

'Conniver!' she cried. 'The order was for your household!'

'I apologise, sister,' said Gabriella. 'I must have misinterpreted it. Nonetheless, Ulrika was the only vampire to examine the scene, and she sensed things that Lord von Zechlin – only human for all his astuteness – was incapable of noticing. And she swears to me that Madam Mathilda's scent was not there.'

'Then she masked it!' said Hermione. 'Or has changed it now! She's covered her tracks!'

Gabriella nodded. 'That is indeed possible, but not certain, and to accuse a sister of killing another sister, one must be certain. The queen would accept nothing less. We must find more proof.'

Hermione looked around at them all, her dainty fists balled in frustration. 'This is madness! I remember no smell! And I have only your word that there ever was one!' A light dawned in her eyes. 'I know what this is! You want to be the one to find the proof! You want to be the one who wins the queen's favour, so you pretend that my proof has no merit! Well I won't fall for it!' She pointed a finger at Mathilda. 'As head of the Lahmians in Nuln, I order you to execute this murdering wolf-bitch.'

CHAPTER TEN
ALFINA'S FOLLY

'Hoy!' said Mathilda, stepping back. 'Hang on!'

'Hermione,' said Gabriella. 'Listen to me—'

'No!' Hermione cried, and Ulrika could see the fear in her eyes behind the rage. 'There are three of us dead! Will you allow the slaughter to continue? We must end this, now! Kill her!'

Mathilda snarled, her fangs shooting out and, on that signal, hidden doors all around the room slammed open, spilling a mob of bravos and bashers that surrounded them all, swords and cudgels at the ready. Rodrik and von Zechlin whipped their blades from their scabbards and faced them as Ulrika went on guard, her claws extending. Beside her, Famke and Dagmar and Hermione did the same. Only Countess Gabriella kept her talons sheathed.

'No,' she said into the tense silence. 'I'm sorry, Hermione. I will not support you. If you wish to fight, you do it on your own.'

Hermione turned on Gabriella, furious. 'You are disobeying your orders from the queen! You were to help me!'

Gabriella drew herself up. 'My orders were to find the killer and put an end to the killings, not to follow you blindly. I am not convinced Mathilda is the culprit.'

Hermione sneered. 'Not until you can find a way to claim credit for it, you mean.' She turned to Famke and Dagmar. 'Sisters, you will obey me! Kill the she-wolf while I subdue this treacherous countess! Come, we fight for our very lives!'

Famke dutifully lined up behind her mistress, though Ulrika could see questions in her eyes, but Dagmar bit her lip, piercing it with an extended fang and looking around at the enemies ranked against her. Ulrika remembered what she had said about not having been in a fight for centuries, and didn't wonder at her hesitation.

'Do not act rashly, sister,' Gabriella said to Hermione. 'Are you prepared to face the queen's displeasure if you are wrong?'

That seemed to decide Dagmar. She turned to Hermione, lowering her head meekly. 'I'm sorry, mistress,' she said. 'I do not wish to make a mistake.'

'Foolish cow!' Hermione snarled, then glared around at them all. 'You all conspire against me! It is mutiny!' She turned, and turned again, like a cornered rat, then blew out an angry breath and turned on Mathilda. 'Let me out of this filthy hole! I will not stay to have my authority flouted.' And with that she started across the room, her nose in the air, with Famke and von Zechlin trailing uneasily behind her.

Mathilda raised an eyebrow, then chuckled. 'Y'think yer walking out after all that?' she called after Hermione. 'My back's not safe with ye walkin' around.' She snapped her fingers and her bashers closed ranks in front of the main door.

Countess Gabriella stepped in front of Madam Mathilda. 'Have a care, sister. The queen's wrath will fall just as heavily on you if you kill her without provocation.'

Mathilda laughed. 'She told ye to kill me! Y'don't call that provocation?'

'No blow was struck,' said Gabriella. She put a hand on the bigger woman's arm. 'I promise you, if you are innocent, no harm will come to you. We will find the true killer and that will be an end to it.'

'Will it?' asked Mathilda. 'She seems set on having my head, no matter who the killer is.'

Gabriella shot a glance over at Hermione, who was fuming near the door while Famke attempted to comfort her and von Zechlin turned in wary circles. 'She will see reason. I will calm her.'

Mathilda hesitated, then sighed. 'See you do, then,' she said. 'I'll not start anything, but if she comes after me, I'll finish it.'

'That's fair enough,' said Gabriella, nodding. 'Now let us out. We've a killer to catch.'

HERMIONE STORMED AHEAD with Famke and von Zechlin, and was already in her coach by the time the rest of them climbed the rickety stairs and stepped out into the yard. As they crossed the muddy court under the watchful eyes of Mathilda's bullies, Dagmar edged close to Gabriella.

'Countess,' she whispered. 'I fear for my place here, now I have gone against Lady Hermione. You will speak to the queen? You will say that I did the right thing?'

Gabriella patted her hand. 'I will. And fear not. I am the primary object of Hermione's wrath. When the killer is caught and I leave again, all will return to normal.'

'I hope so, sister,' said Dagmar. 'I hope so. I do not like trouble.'

'None of us does,' said Gabriella, and gave her a smile. 'Now, go home and stay in. You will hear from Hermione when all is well again.'

Dagmar curtseyed, then turned and mounted the step of her coach. Gabriella and Ulrika continued towards Hermione's coach with Rodrik following behind as rear guard.

'Things would be so much easier,' Gabriella muttered, 'if I could just tear Hermione's head off.'

Ulrika smirked as the countess climbed into the coach. She had been thinking the same thing.

ULRIKA AND FAMKE sat side by side in uncomfortable silence as the three coaches rode back out of the Faulestadt slums and rumbled across the wide bridge towards the north side of the city, listening to Gabriella and Hermione continue their argument.

'Six Lahmians ruled in Nuln before this horror began,' Gabriella was saying. 'Now there are three. You, Dagmar and Mathilda. If you go to war, there will be two, or less. Don't you see? No matter what happens, fighting among yourselves will weaken the Lahmian hold over Nuln for a long time to come. You can't allow this to happen.'

'Well, I didn't start it,' said Hermione, pouting. 'It was that she-wolf, no matter what you say.'

Gabriella sighed. 'If there is one single iota of doubt about her guilt, we cannot go forwards. The queen will have both our heads if she is innocent.'

'And if she isn't innocent? She knows we suspect her now. She will strike while we wait to find your precious proof!'

'You can't blame me if you played your hand prematurely,' said Gabriella.

As they reached the end of the bridge and rattled onto the cobbles of the Neuestadt District, Ulrika thought she saw a flash of black streak past out of the corner of her eye, and turned to look out the window, holding her breath. She let it out again when she saw that it was only Madam Dagmar's coach splitting off from theirs as she headed home to the Silver Lily. She laughed to herself. A vampire jumping at shadows. For shame. But after their visit to Mathilda's domain, perhaps it wasn't an unreasonable reaction.

A few minutes later they rolled through the gate into the Altestadt and then came to Hermione's house. As they stepped down to the drive, Gabriella turned to Hermione one last time.

'I do not ask that you do nothing,' she said. 'If you suspect Mathilda, by all means, spy on her, follow her, bribe her acquaintances, gather what proof you may. Just don't attack. Not until I am able to present our case to the queen. Have I your word on that?'

Hermione looked sullen, but at last nodded. 'Very well, sister, but I am certain that we will find that we should have acted when I said.'

'If that it the case,' said Gabriella. 'Then I will humbly beg your forgiveness.'

As she and Rodrik and Ulrika turned to enter their own coach, Ulrika found Famke looking at her. The girl gave her a sad smile, then turned and followed her mistress into her house.

As THEY NEARED Guildmaster Aldrich's house, Gabriella once again rapped on the roof of the coach and called for the driver to stop.

'You must return to your inn,' she said, turning to Rodrik.

The knight did not move. 'The situation grows more dangerous, m'lady. The killer is still at large, and you have made an enemy of Lady Hermione. I must be at your side to protect you.'

'I wish that you could be, Rodrik, truly,' said Gabriella, 'but I am still not well enough established in this fat fool's house. He only barely accepts me. If I were to tell him that you were joining his household he would rebel and go to the witch hunters. Fear not. It will be soon, I promise you.'

Rodrik still looked obdurate, but at last he stood and stepped to the door. 'I pray that it is, mistress. For a fat fool cannot keep you safe as I can.' He pushed open the door and stepped down, then bowed in Ulrika's direction. 'Nor can an alley cat.'

Ulrika rose in her seat, growling, but Gabriella shoved her back down. 'Enough!' she said. 'The feuds within the sisterhood are bad enough. I will not have my children at each other's throats as well. You will apologise to each other.'

Ulrika glared at Rodrik through the door, then snorted and lowered her head. 'Forgive me, sir knight,' she said. 'I am sorry for my anger.'

Rodrik looked like he would rather spit on her, but he too bowed. 'Forgive me, fraulein,' he said. 'I should not have insulted you. I too am sorry.'

Though it was clear neither of them meant it, Gabriella chose to accept their statements as contrition. She nodded. 'Very good. I hope you can remain as civil in the future. Good night, Rodrik. Uwe! Drive on!'

Ulrika looked back as the coach trundled away. Rodrik followed it with angry eyes before turning and striding towards the inn.

PROOF THAT GABRIELLA had been right about Herr Aldrich's state of mind was apparent as soon as the coachman let them off in the townhouse's carriage yard. The guildmaster barrelled out of the back door of the town house in a robe, slippers and nightcap, his round face red in the light of the lantern he carried.

'Where have you been?' he barked. 'Where did you take my coach?'

'On business with the sisterhood, mein herr,' said Gabriella coolly. 'It is no concern of yours.'

'Is it not?' cried Aldrich, spewing spittle. 'Is it not? Do I not have neighbours? What will they think when my coach comes and goes at all hours of the night?'

'Why they will think you have a mistress,' said Gabriella, smiling as she crossed to him. 'Like every respectable merchant prince.'

Aldrich was not so easily put off. 'You must be more discreet,' he said. 'Alfina did not come and go like this.

Only when it was absolutely necessary, and always only after informing me.'

Gabriella tried to go around him to the door, but he stepped in her way. Ulrika saw he was trembling, and there was perspiration on his brow.

'I have allowed you to stay here,' he said, scratching his neck. 'But I will not allow you to trample over me without a by-your-leave.'

Gabriella raised an eyebrow. 'I thought you wanted to see me as little as possible,' she said. 'I thought you wanted me to leave you to mourn your dear Alfina.'

'I do,' he said. 'But... but you cannot leave me in the dark. You cannot make of my house a... a way-station without... without...' He scratched his neck again as he searched for words.

Gabriella smiled sweetly and reached forwards to pull his hand away from his neck. There were old scars there. 'I think I understand, mein herr. And there is no shame in seeking solace in the depths of heartbreak.'

He looked up at her, and the shame in his eyes made Ulrika turn away. 'It isn't that I've forgotten her,' he said. 'It isn't that–'

'Of course it isn't,' said Gabriella. 'Who could, once they had looked in her eyes.' She took his hand and led him towards the house. 'Now come, let me comfort you. I will put you to bed and tuck you in.'

As they reached the door, Gabriella looked back at Ulrika and gave her an exasperated grimace, then put her arm around Aldrich's slumped shoulders and led him inside.

Ulrika twitched, overcome by a quiver of disgust, though she wasn't sure if it was for Aldrich, Gabriella or herself.

She followed them inside.

As ULRIKA PULLED off her wig and unlaced her bodice in Gabriella's apartments, she thought back over the evening's events and marvelled that the countess had successfully kept Hermione and Mathilda from killing one another. Ulrika had been resigned to the fact that the meeting would end in bloodshed and murder, but by keeping her cool and standing her ground, the countess had defused the situation and bought herself some time.

Growing up her father's child, Ulrika had always admired martial prowess and good generalship – had she not fallen for Felix because of his skilful sword and quick mind? But she had never thought of language and argument as a martial art. Scholars and politicians who split hairs and talked to hear their own voices bored and disgusted her, but Gabriella's display of diplomacy this night had been masterful. Ambushed, outnumbered, backed to the wall and with her allies mutinying, she had still managed to win free without a life lost, and all with words, all without lifting a hand in violence.

Ulrika knew she could not have done the same. She was a fighter, not a talker – if she had been a better talker she probably wouldn't have lost Felix. But she knew mastery when she saw it, and Gabriella had it. She hoped she could one day do half as well.

All this made her think of the other Lahmians she had so far met, and she laughed to herself. She had certainly had the luck of the draw when it came to mistresses, hadn't she? Mathilda was friendly enough in her coarse fashion – at least when she wasn't being threatened – but her life of pimps and thieves and blackmailers, and her willingness to wallow in filth and live by the degradation of others, did not appeal. Dagmar was a quivering non-entity, a follower, not a leader, and Hermione was just a horror, a snapping little shrew who could not tell friend from foe, and who lashed out at the hands that tried to help her.

Yes, Ulrika had been lucky. Gabriella was a woman to look up to, a woman of honour and resource, who did her best for her queen and her sisters, with little thought of personal glory. Ulrika could not have chosen better, and she was proud to serve under her. She suddenly felt pity for poor Famke, bound to a bad mistress and subject to her rages and fevered whims. How would she grow wise, learning at the knee of such a witless, frightened harridan?

Ulrika donned a robe of embroidered Cathay silk and went to warm herself by the fire. Gabriella had told her early on that as a vampire she no longer needed heat to live, but she still felt the cold. Indeed, since she had risen from her deathbed, she had never truly been warm unless she was feeding.

She curled herself in a high-backed leather chair beside the hearth, her thoughts still worrying at the conflict between her new 'sisters'. It seemed inevitable to her that, left to their own devices, Hermione and Mathilda would soon go to war, and one or both of them would die, while the true killer of the Lahmians remained at large. Personally, Ulrika didn't care much one way or the other. She was too new to this strange midnight society to have developed any loyalty to Queen Neferata, or any sense of belonging to her sisterhood. These were not her people. Not yet, at any rate.

Gabriella, however, was another matter, and if she wanted to keep her sisters alive and find the murderer, then Ulrika did too, and would do what she could to help. The question was, what? She could certainly do no more than Gabriella already had to make peace between the two women. Really, the only way to patch things up would be to find the real killer. But how was she to do that? She could return to the sewer grate where the little man had left the tunnels and sniff around, but his footsteps and his scent had undoubtedly been obliterated by a day's worth of Nuln traffic, so she would likely not be able to follow it. What other leads did she and Gabriella have? Would they have to wait for the killer to strike again? That would only make things worse between the sisters.

Then a thought came to her and she turned to the day-bed where Imma the maid slept, still recovering from the rough feeding Ulrika had subjected her to the morning before. She was reluctant to wake her. The poor girl was no doubt terrified of her now, but she was the only one who knew any details of Alfina's last days. Of course, Gabriella had already questioned her, but perhaps she had missed something.

Ulrika stood and crossed hesitantly to the day-bed, then sat on the edge. She put a hand out and shook the maid gently. 'Imma, wake up,' she whispered. 'I must speak with you.'

The girl moaned and mumbled, but did not wake.

Ulrika shook her again. 'Imma.'

Slowly the maid opened her eyes, then blinked around her stupidly for a moment, before discovering Ulrika leaning over her. She gasped, her eyes wide.

Ulrika put a hand on her shoulder. 'Do not be afraid, Imma,' she said. 'I won't hurt you.'

The maid covered Ulrika's hand with her own, then pulled it to her lips. 'Oh, mistress,' she said, kissing her fingers. 'Oh, mistress, do you wish to feed again? Please say you do.'

Ulrika pulled her hand away, aghast. 'But... but I nearly killed you.'

'I care not,' said the maid. She looked up into Ulrika's eyes, pleading. 'I would die a hundred times to be yours again, mistress. You are so strong. So...' She trailed off and turned her head to expose her neck. The wound Ulrika had given her was still raw.

Ulrika stood abruptly, fighting to keep her face from betraying her nausea and contempt. It was the same reaction the young knight Quentin had had, and it made her sick. She had attacked the girl, nearly killed her, and the little fool loved her for it. Had they no self-respect? Were they all so weak? Or was it the feeding that weakened them?

Her mind flashed back to her time with Krieger, as they had travelled from Kislev to Sylvania. She too had weakened. She too had let him feed. She too had come to long for it, to melt in the bliss of powerlessness. Unfortunately, the reminder that she had also been weak did not make her feel any less contempt for the maid, only more for herself.

'No, Imma,' she said at last. 'It is too soon. You must regain your strength first. I require something else of you.'

'Name it, mistress,' said the maid. 'It is yours.'

Ulrika ground her teeth and sat again, out of reach. 'I only want you to think. That is all. Countess Gabriella asked you before if Mistress Alfina received any letters or visitors before she was killed, and you said no. I want you to think on it again. Are you certain of this? Did she behave in any peculiar way on that last day? Did she do anything unusual?'

The maid seemed disappointed to be turning the conversation away from more intimate subjects, but dutifully put her mind to it, folding her hands across her breast and lying back to stare at the ceiling.

At last she shook her head. 'I remember no visitor or note, mistress, although she might have received one without my knowing. I usually brought up her correspondence in the evening when she awoke, but sometimes if I was on an errand, or laundering her clothes, the butler would bring things up.' She shrugged. 'And as I said before, she fed strongly from me that last night, so strongly that I did not know that she was gone until I woke later. I suppose that was unusual. She usually bled me very lightly, for she was long-lived and did not require much.' She sighed and looked doe-eyed at Ulrika again. 'Sometimes it was absolutely ages between feedings.'

Ulrika coughed. 'Do you think she bled you so strongly so that you wouldn't know she had left?'

Imma frowned at that. 'Maybe so, mistress. If she was disobeying Lady Hermione's orders by going out, then she mightn't have wanted me to know. I would never have betrayed her by telling, but the ladies are suspicious sometimes, and don't like to take chances with secrets.'

Ulrika nodded, lost in thought. So Alfina went out of her own accord, and tried to cover her tracks. Why? What had drawn her out? She must have received some message or been under some obligation. Did she have a secret lover? Had she been a traitor to some other vampire house?

Ulrika turned back to Imma. 'Where did Mistress Alfina keep her private correspondence? Things she did not want you or Herr Aldrich to read?'

The maid hesitated, biting her lip.

'She is dead, Imma,' Ulrika said impatiently. 'She has no more need of secrecy.'

Imma nodded, then pointed to an ornate wardrobe near Alfina's bed. 'There is a false bottom in that. It is magicked shut, so that only Lady Alfina could open it.' She blushed. 'Not that I ever tried.'

Ulrika smiled and stood. 'Of course you didn't.'

She crossed to the wardrobe and opened it. It was stuffed with beautiful dresses, coats and cloaks, while the floor of it was heaped with delicate little shoes. Ulrika swept these aside and looked at the wood panel beneath. It had neither seam nor latch. It looked entirely solid. She rapped on it. It even felt solid. She tried to extend her new senses and feel for the illusion that masked the lock, but could only see a few black shimmerings that vanished as soon as she looked at them. She didn't yet have enough control over her witch sight to see through such things.

She sighed and looked towards the door. She could wait for the countess to return from *comforting* Herr Aldrich, but she was too impatient. She wanted to know now.

With a grunt she raised her hand, then struck down sharply with the heel of it. The panel cracked lengthwise. She struck it again and broke it in two. She pulled up the pieces and looked below it. In a shallow drawer lay a pile of letters, journals and jewellery. Ulrika was going to sift through them when she saw, right on the top, a small folded piece of vellum with 'Frau Alfina Aldrich' written upon it in a neat, clerky hand. She picked it up and unfolded it. Inside, in the same hand, was written a short note.

Five hundred gold crowns to the house with the black door near the corner of Messingstrasse and Hoff by midnight tomorrow, or you shall be revealed, just as your sisters were.

Ulrika stared at the note. Who would be stupid enough to attempt to blackmail a vampire? The answer came quickly. One who had the power to rip them limb from limb if they refused to pay. Another question followed. Why? Why would someone with such power stoop to simple blackmail?

Just then, Ulrika heard footsteps in the hall outside. She stood and closed the wardrobe. The door to the hall opened and Gabriella stepped in, then shut it behind her and stood there for a moment, her eyes closed.

'Are you all right, mistress?' asked Ulrika.

Gabriella shivered, then smiled wanly. 'It was at least mercifully short, and I believe our position here is now secure.' She squared her shoulders and stepped further into the room, tugging at her lacings. 'And you, my dear? Are you recovered from the excitement of the evening?'

'I am fine, thank you,' said Ulrika. 'But look, I've found something.' She crossed eagerly to Gabriella and held out the note. 'It was in the wardrobe.'

Gabriella took it and read it, then pursed her lips. 'Blackmail? I would not have thought that likely. Still, it gives us something to go on.' She looked up at Ulrika and smiled. 'You have done well. Tomorrow, you shall go to this address and see what you can find. But for now–' She sighed and turned away to continue undressing. 'If you would be kind enough to draw some hot water, I am in desperate need of a bath.'

CHAPTER ELEVEN
BEHIND THE BLACK DOOR

ULRIKA WAS DONNING her riding clothes the next night, in preparation for finding the address of the blackmail note, when there was a knock on the door to the countess's apartments. Little Imma, up and around at last, answered it. It was the butler.

'Inform your mistress that there is a Lord von Waldenhof to see her in the parlour,' he said. His impassive face looked no different than it ever had, but still seemed to register disapproval.

Gabriella, who was writing at Alfina's old writing desk, looked up sharply. She stood and crossed to the door, waving Imma away.

'Is Herr Aldrich in?' she asked.

'No, m'lady,' said the butler. 'He is out on guild business.'

'Then tell the gentleman I will come down,' she said.

The butler's lip twitched at that, but he merely bowed. 'Yes, m'lady.'

Gabriella waited until Imma had closed the door before she cursed. 'Damned idiot! What does he think he's up to?' She turned to Ulrika. 'Finish dressing. I'll need a chaperone to keep things proper.'

Ulrika hesitated. 'Should I change into my dresses?'

Gabriella shook her head. 'There is no time. I must get him out as quickly as possible. Fool!'

Ulrika quickly pulled on her doublet and belted on her sabre as Gabriella paced and muttered under her breath. At last she was ready and she and Gabriella exited the apartments and descended through the dark house.

RODRIK ROSE UNSTEADILY from an armchair as Gabriella and Ulrika entered the parlour, a tastefully dull room with heavy woodwork and dour portraits of wealthy guildmasters glaring from the walls.

'Mistress,' Rodrik said, and bowed stiffly to Gabriella. Ulrika could smell the wine on him from the door.

'This had better be of the utmost importance, sir knight,' said Gabriella, stopping before him. 'For I can think of no other reason why you would come to this place without being called for.'

Rodrik drew himself up and threw back his mane of blond hair. 'It is indeed important, mistress,' he said. 'I have come to request that you move to other lodgings.'

Gabriella's eyes widened. 'That?' she said. 'You came to say only that? You endanger my standing here to make the same whining demand you have made too many times before? How dare you!'

'I am your champion, m'lady!' Rodrik said through closed teeth. 'I am sworn to protect you! How may I do it if we are separated? If you are unable to find a way to bring me into this house, then you must find some other situation where I may be at your side!"

'Must?' snapped Gabriella. 'You say to me *must*? Am I sworn to obey you, sir, or are you sworn to obey me? Answer me!'

Rodrik flushed as he realised he had gone too far. 'Forgive me, mistress, it is only an excess of concern that compels me to say these things.'

Gabriella glared at him for a moment, then sighed. 'You are forgiven, but you must go, and quickly. I believe I have brought him around, but if you are discovered here before I speak of you to him, our host will baulk, thinking I plot behind his back. Wait only a little longer and all will be well.'

'Tonight, then?' asked Rodrik, sullen. 'Tomorrow?'

Gabriella exploded. 'When I say! At my will, and not a moment before! By the queen, I begin to wonder if it is not an excess of jealousy that compels you! Now, go! Leave us!'

Rodrik's face turned crimson at this, but he only bowed. 'Your servant, mistress,' he said.

He started for the parlour door, but then Gabriella looked up and stepped after him. 'Wait,' she said.

He turned, his face pathetically hopeful. 'Mistress?'

'As you are here, I have orders for you,' she said.

'I am yours to command,' Rodrik replied, bowing.

'I am gratified to hear it,' said Gabriella. 'Go then to Hermione and tell her we have found proof that Mathilda is not behind the slaying of our sisters. A blackmail note was found, threatening to expose

Alfina as a vampire if she didn't pay a ransom. I am sending Ulrika to the address to see what she can find. Tell Hermione I hope to have news before morning.'

Rodrik stiffened. 'You make me a messenger, and send this... girl-child to do a man's work? Mistress, I am your knight! I should be finding this killer!'

Gabriella's jaw clenched. 'Did you not just say that you were mine to command?' she asked.

'Yes, mistress, but–'

'But, what?' the countess insisted. 'Either you are, or you are not. Which is it?'

Rodrik hung his head, glaring at the floor and saying nothing. Ulrika looked on him with loathing. For all his knightly bearing, he was nothing but a petulant child. But was it his fault? It was Gabriella's feeding that had made him this way. He was no different than Imma or Quentin. Drawing their blood made needy infants of them all.

Gabriella stepped up to Rodrik, laying a hand on his arm. 'Dearest Rodrik. I understand your wish to serve me, but as before, the night's work is not... knight's work.' She laughed lightly at her pun. 'It is scout's work, hunting and sniffing out trails. And for that, Ulrika is a better choice.' She nudged him playfully. 'You don't have her nose, now do you?'

Rodrik remained looking at the floor, refusing to rise to her humour, but at last he nodded. 'I... I will go to Lady Hermione, mistress. Forgive me.'

And with that he strode to the door without a backwards glance.

Gabriella stared after him, pensive, then turned to Ulrika. 'Take this as a lesson for when you have swains of your own,' she said. 'Their love turns quickly sour if they are too long denied a chance to prove their devotion.' She frowned. 'I shall have to give Rodrik a battle soon, to soothe his wounded pride.' She beckoned for Ulrika to follow her. 'Come. It is time you were going, too.'

Ulrika followed her through the house to the carriage yard door, then paused as Gabriella opened it for her.

'Mistress,' she said, troubled. 'The blackmail note is not proof of Mathilda's innocence. It might have been her who wrote it.'

Gabriella smiled and patted Ulrika's cheek. 'I know that. But I must tell Hermione something that will keep her claws in. I only hope she is not as smart as you.' She pushed her towards the door. 'Now go. And bring back some real proof.'

Ulrika bowed. 'I will do my best, mistress.'

THE INTERSECTION ULRIKA was looking for was somewhere within the neighbourhood the locals called Shantytown. Ulrika remembered from stories Felix had told her that parts of the area had been burned to the ground during the skaven invasion that he and Gotrek had helped fight a few years previously. The scars were still visible. All around her as she walked through the narrow muddy streets, she saw houses and tenements that still bore telltale black smudges above their windows and doors, while other places were makeshift patchworks of new construction and old – brick layered below plaster layered below raw planks. Some buildings were hardly more than tents, flapping canvas stretched between the charred timbers of a collapsed front wall to try to keep out the bitter winter wind, and some were nothing but piles of blackened spars, untouched since the burning.

She found Messingstrasse first, and followed its winding course deeper into the grubby neighbourhood. It was a dirty dog-run of a street, heaped with rubbish and crawling with rats, and lined on both sides with disreputable-looking businesses and dingy taverns, from which spilled laughter and vulgar songs and the sad stench of impoverished humanity. A few streets on, she was surprised to find that she recognised some of the buildings and streets, though she would have sworn she'd never been there before. Then she remembered – her headlong flight across the city the morning she had raced the sun back to Aldrich's house – it had started near here. The open sewer grate had been somewhere close by!

A thrill went up her spine. The sewer grate and the blackmail address in the same vicinity? Things were coming together.

Only two streets later, Messingstrasse crossed Hoff in a knee-deep mud-pit of an intersection, and she slowed her pace. Four- and five-storey tenements were jammed together shoulder to shoulder above the streets like gawkers crowding around an accident. It was dark below them, even though both moons were in the sky, for they rose so high the light could not find the ground.

Ulrika welcomed the dark. It would keep spying eyes from seeing her as she crept around looking for the building with the black door – unless, of course, they were eyes like her own, which was not impossible. Despite Mathilda's protestations, the she-wolf could still be the killer, or could have sent some undead servant to do her dirty work. It could even, she supposed, be Madam Dagmar, hiding a savage, devious nature beneath her demure, deferential exterior, though somehow she doubted it.

Ulrika tilted her head at a door, trying to determine if it was black or grey or dark red. Though she could see perfectly well in the dark, night colours remained as muddy as they had when she had lived. She sighed and turned to look across the street. There it was! The door to the building two down from the intersection on Hoff was unquestionably black – shades darker than any other nearby. It also had a white 'X' painted on it.

Plague. The X was the sign of the plague. Ulrika shrank back instinctively, but then caught herself. What did she have to fear from human sickness? She was already dead. She started forwards, then paused again. Plague might be the least danger of the place. Best to have a look all around before walking straight in through the front door. She turned her steps and went down Messingstrasse until she came to the alley that ran behind the buildings that faced Hoff. These were all tenements, and had no yards, so the alley was a mere slot, with walls that rose up four storeys on either side, and blacker even than the intersection out front.

Ulrika crept down it as quietly as she could, eyes wide and ears cocked. She could hear voices and sense heartbeats all around her, and smell stale cooking and staler bodies. It was early evening, and the people inside the buildings were still at their leisure – singing, fighting, weeping and making love. But as she reached the back of the building with the black door the human sounds and smells faded into the distance.

She looked at the back door. It too was painted black with a white X, and the windows above it were all boarded up. She could smell the sickness that had been there, and the reek of bodies long ago dead and desiccated, as well as that of the vermin that had fed on them, but nothing else. The place was desolate, abandoned to disease and never reoccupied. She stepped to the door and put an ear to it, then froze. Not quite desolate. From somewhere within she could hear the sound of cautious movement, and a single beating heart.

She paused. She had little to fear from one living man, but still she should be cautious. It might be the fat little warlock again. He might vanish before she could grab him, or hurl some spell at her. She examined the door closely. The lock had been torn out, and it had been done recently. The splintered wood around the hole was still white and fresh. She pressed against it. It swung open, creaking on its hinges. She stopped it, then slipped through the gap and eased it shut behind her.

Her foot touched something as she turned to look around, and she found she was standing amidst a loose pile of withered corpses, all clustered around the door as if they had died clawing at it to get out. The poor beggars, she thought. Locked in to die.

She was in a narrow corridor that ran straight to the front of the building. It had several doors on either side and a stairwell halfway down on the left. At the far end, around the front door, she could see another clump of corpses, no more successful in escaping than their comrades at the back. She could also see fresh footprints in the years-thick layer of dust that lay over everything. There were several sets. Some in boots, some barefoot, and one that sent a thrill up her spine – a woman's print, neat and small, with a pointed toe.

A rustle from above reminded her that one of those sets of prints was very fresh indeed. Whoever it was, they were one floor up, and moving cautiously. Ulrika listened harder. The steps, though stealthy, were heavy, and had the dull thud of boots. A man, then, and not small. She drew her sabre and crept forwards as lightly as she could. The boards creaked anyway, but only faintly. The sounds and the heartbeat above her did not signal any alarm.

The doors she passed on her way to the stairs were open, and revealed the final purpose of the house. Each small room was lined with rows of low cots, and on every cot, wrapped in dirty sheets, lay a body that was now more skeleton than corpse. Between the cots, and collapsed on top of them, were other bodies, wearing the white robes of sisters of Shallya, who had apparently succumbed to the plague while still at their duties. Ulrika wondered if they had volunteered to be locked in with their patients, or had fallen ill while treating others and been abandoned like the rest. She didn't know, but found herself touched by the nobility of women who would continue to help others after they had been condemned to the same death.

She turned into the stairwell and looked up towards the first floor. Yellow light and moving shadows on the walls told her that the person above had a lantern. Then the light cut off sharply and the footsteps grew muffled. The person had entered a room. Good.

Ulrika cat-footed it swiftly up the stairs, keeping close to the wall where the treads would creak least, and gained the landing. A door led into the first-floor corridor, while the stairs continued to zigzag up to further floors. She crouched at the corridor door, listening.

The footsteps were getting louder again, and the corridor getting brighter. Her quarry was exiting the room he had gone into. She edged back into the darkness of the stairwell, waiting for him to go into another room, but he did not. The light swung closer. He was coming down the corridor.

She edged back further, stepping up onto the first step of the flight that rose to the next floor, and gripped her sabre tightly, prepared to spring.

The light and the footsteps paused just outside the stairwell, and Ulrika could hear the man turning this way and that, as if weighing options. She inhaled as his scent came to her, then froze as she recognised it. The templar witch hunter! The one from the sewers!

She took an involuntary step back. What should she do? Should she flee? Should she kill him? Should she question him?

The witch hunter stepped into the stairwell, raising his lantern to start up the next flight, then stopped dead, staring at Ulrika, who crouched upon them.

'You,' he said.

Ulrika swallowed. 'Templar Holmann,' she said. 'We meet again.'

CHAPTER TWELVE
THE RAVEN AND THE ROSE

HOLMANN STEPPED BACK warily, a frown furrowing his forehead. 'What are you doing here, Fraulein Magdova?' he asked.

Ulrika stood and lowered her sword. It seemed she wasn't going to kill him. 'The same as you, I would think,' she said. 'Following up on our hunt from the other night.'

He continued frowning. 'I find you once again in the dark without a lantern,' he said. 'It is most strange.'

Ulrika's hand clenched around her sabre. 'I… I had a candle, but I snuffed it when I saw your light. I thought you might be a villain, and didn't want to give away my position.' She smiled. 'I… I was about to jump you just now.'

'Mmmm,' he said, still stiff. 'You did not come to the Armoury. I waited.'

Ulrika almost laughed. Was he suspicious, or hurt? 'I was kept away,' she said. 'Family business. And I'm afraid I lost the trail that morning. It seems you had more success?'

Holmann lowered his lantern, his expression softening somewhat, though still wary. He shook his head. 'I found nothing in the sewer. And I had to return home to sleep afterwards. My duties with the witch hunters are at night.'

'Then how did you find this place?' Ulrika asked. It seemed best to keep him talking about himself instead of asking uncomfortable questions about her.

'I returned to this neighbourhood after my rounds the next night and spoke to the men of the local watch,' said Holmann. 'They said several citizens had reported hearing a loud fight near this intersection, but the watch found nothing. I wanted to question the locals, but it was by then too late. They were all abed.'

Ulrika smiled. 'So you shirked your duties to come again tonight at a more reasonable hour?'

Holmann looked shocked. 'Certainly not. I asked my captain leave to investigate the incident. My request was granted.'

Ulrika turned her head nervously, listening for other men. Could she have missed them? 'You're not alone this time?'

He shook his head. 'No others could be spared. We are still questioning the acquaintances of the women who were revealed to be fiends.'

'Ah,' said Ulrika, relieved. 'Of course.'

'Tonight I spoke to several persons near here who had heard the fight,' he continued. 'And was able to more closely pinpoint the source.' He spread his free hand. 'This was the only unoccupied house in the vicinity, and the only one the watch had not checked.'

'And no wonder,' said Ulrika, wrinkling her nose. 'You're a brave man, entering a plague house.'

Holmann touched the hammer pendant at his neck. 'Sigmar protects his servants. You are brave as well.'

'Ursun protects too,' she answered. 'Have you found anything?'

'Footprints,' he said. 'So far that is all.'

Ulrika gestured up the stairs. 'Shall we continue, then?'

Holmann glared at her. 'One day your bravery will be your undoing,' he said. 'I understand your reasons for pursuing this life, fraulein, but it is still unseemly for a woman to be in a place like this, with a sabre and breeches and...' He trailed off, embarrassed.

Ulrika was tempted to tell him she thought she looked a damned sight more seemly in breeches than he did, and likely fought better with a sabre as well, but knew it wouldn't do. Instead she lowered her head meekly. 'I wish it were otherwise, templar,' she said. 'But I have made a vow to wipe out the things that corrupted my sister. I would lose Ursun's favour if I renounced it, and bring shame upon my family name.'

That seemed to be the right line to take, for Holmann nodded curtly and looked like he had swallowed a lemon. 'Vows to one's gods must be upheld,' he said. 'You are an honourable woman.' He stepped ahead of her and lifted the lantern. 'Come. I shall light the way.'

The second floor was the same as the first, room after room of dry corpses lying on low cots, and nothing else – no sign of a fight and no sign that Alfina had been there.

'The authorities must have brought every afflicted person in the neighbourhood to this place,' Ulrika said as they turned from the door of the last room and started up to the top floor.

The witch hunter nodded. 'I was here during the trouble. There were houses like this all over the city. It was the only way.'

'Do you think it made a difference?' Ulrika asked.

Holmann shrugged. 'Nuln still stands.'

The layout of the top floor was different from the others – three large rooms instead of many small ones. The first they entered was lined like all the others with neat rows of corpses and cots. The second had corpses too, but they were no longer neat.

'Sigmar's hammer,' murmured Holmann as he took in the destruction. 'What battle happened here?'

Ulrika knew instantly, but didn't answer. Looking around she was certain this was the place Mistress Alfina had been killed. It had been a sick ward like all the others, but the dozens of corpses that had filled it had been tossed about like straw in a hurricane, and were scattered all over the room, limbs askew or snapped off entirely. Ulrika saw a parchment-skinned skull lost under an overturned cot, and near it, a pair of skeletons thrown together as if they were making love.

And there were other signs of violence. A boarded-up window had been broken open, the timbers split and smashed, and great gouges had been dug into the walls and floor as if by mighty claws. Black blood was spattered across the boards in dust-furred splashes and streaks.

And then there was the stench, so strong even Holmann could smell it.

'Sigmar's blood,' he said, coughing. 'That comes from no ancient plague corpse. It smells like a drowned body in the sun.'

'Aye,' said Ulrika. And more than that, it was the same stench she had first smelled on Alfina's corpse, and again outside the Silver Lily, only now it was overpowering, like being buried in rotting carcasses. It raised her hackles and made her want to vomit, but at the same time she relished it. This was the scent of the killer, she could be certain of it now. If she could follow it back to its source, she would find what was attacking the Lahmians, and she could put an end to the terror, and hopefully to Hermione and Mathilda's feud. But where had it gone, and how?

'What did this?' said Holmann, examining the gouges in one wall.

Ulrika stepped back out into the hall, ignoring him, and inhaled deeply. The smell did not come out this far. It faded out quickly at the door of the room, and she had certainly not smelled it on any of the other floors as she came up. What did this mean? Did the thing change form like Mathilda, and only smell like a corpse in one form? Perhaps, but–

Suddenly she had it. She pushed past Holmann back into the room, then crossed to the smashed-open window. Yes. Claw marks on the sill and the sides, and the revolting rotten corpse smell on every surface, so powerful it made her wince.

'It came in through here,' she said. 'And went out again the same way.'

Holmann joined her and looked out into the night. 'Then it must be able to fly,' he said.

Ulrika followed his gaze. The window looked out over the intersection. The closest building was across the street, perhaps ten yards away. 'Or leap,' she said, remembering her rapturous rooftop gallop of two nights previous.

'A prodigious leap,' he said.

'Aye,' said Ulrika, already lost in thought again. If she was going to track it to its lair, she would have to go to the other building and sniff around there, then try to follow the thing's progress from roof to roof, guessing at directions all the while. It would be a difficult task, and if it *did* fly, it would be impossible.

She turned back to the room. There had to be another way – an easier way. She frowned at the floor. There had been others here besides the killer and Mistress Alfina. There were footprints all over the room. Perhaps she could track them instead.

'But what did this flying monster fight?' asked Holmann as she began pacing the room, looking at the tracks. 'It must have been something as strong and ferocious as itself, or this would have been a massacre, not a battle.'

Ulrika remembered Mistress Alfina's face, frozen in a snarling mask of rage, and the horrible wounds she had survived before someone had plunged a stake through her heart. 'Aye,' she said. 'Strong and desperate.' She kicked a black rag aside and squatted over a palimpsest of footprints. 'Men with boots,' she muttered. 'Men with bare feet. At least five. Were they accomplices? Where did they go? Where did they come from?'

'You may be a great tracker, fraulein,' said Holmann behind her. 'But you must learn not to overlook the obvious.'

Ulrika turned. Holmann was picking up the black rag she had kicked away.

He shook it out and held it up. 'The robe of a priest of Morr,' he said. 'Or part of one, anyway.' He showed her the breast of the garment, where a hollow square containing a rose had been embroidered upon it in black thread. 'You see the sign of Morr's portal?' He grimaced and looked at his hand, which was sticky and red where it had touched the cloth. 'Recently shed blood.'

Ulrika frowned, confused, and looked around the room again. Her mental picture of what had happened here shifted and became cloudy again. 'So the monster was fighting a priest or priests of Morr?' But what of Alfina?

'It is their job to settle the restless dead,' said Holmann.

New possibilities whirled up in Ulrika's head like leaves in a wind. Could it be that her theory that an undead monster had killed the Lahmians was wrong? Could the killers have been priests of Morr instead? An image of some impossibly strong templar of Morr smashing through the window and attacking Mistress Alfina in a holy frenzy flashed behind her eyes. But could any human hero, no matter how great, make a leap like that, or claw marks like that? And what of the smell of rotting flesh? What of the little man in the sewers? Had she been mistaken about him? Had he been a priest, not a necromancer? She felt suddenly more lost than when she had begun.

'But if priests of Morr are exposing these vampires,' she said at last, 'wouldn't they speak up about it?' She turned to Holmann. 'Your fellow witch hunters have certainly not kept their investigation quiet.'

Holmann nodded, looking at the cloth. 'True. Perhaps we should talk to a priest.'

Ulrika shrugged. It sounded more feasible than attempting to follow the smell of rotting flesh across the rooftops of Nuln. 'Lead on, mein herr.'

THE NEAREST TEMPLE of Morr was by the docks on the south edge of Shantytown, a small place devoted to augury rather than burial, and Ulrika began to have misgivings about pursuing their chosen course of inquiry as soon as she saw its open stone door.

In her life before Krieger's kiss she had heard the same stories everyone had, that vampires were repelled by the symbols of Sigmar and Ursun and the other gods, but she had not so far noticed this repulsion in herself. In her journey with Countess Gabriella from Sylvania to Nuln their coach had passed any number of temples and roadside shrines, and she had come face to face with many priests and knights of various orders in the inns in which they had stayed, and no otherworldly fear had overcome her in their presence, just the reasonable wariness that all prey has for its predator.

She still couldn't call what she felt as she and Holmann approached the door fear, only a profound nervousness. Morr was the protector of the dead, and his priests, as the witch hunter had pointed out, were dedicated to putting to rest the undead. Could they also somehow sense them? She felt that if she stepped over the temple's threshold all eyes would instantly turn towards her, and all hands would be raised against her. She feared she would be attracting the scrutiny of the god himself, and that was not a risk she wished to face. What if she was struck down on the spot?

As Holmann started up the black stone steps, she paused. He looked back at her, an eyebrow raised.

'Perhaps you should go in alone,' she said. 'I am but a woman from Kislev. I have no official sanction to be asking questions. You are a templar – a servant of Sigmar. They will answer you.'

Holmann smirked. 'My authority will not be diminished by your presence, fraulein. Come. A vampire hunter has nothing to fear in this place.'

But a hunting vampire might, thought Ulrika. She swallowed, and considered fleeing, but then decided she could not. The torn robe was the only real lead she had. She did not want to go back to Gabriella and say she had not followed it out of a lack of courage.

'Very well,' she said. 'Let us go.'

Ulrika followed Holmann up the steps, her shoulders tensing as she walked between the two pillars, one white, one black, that flanked the open door. Holmann went into the temple without difficulty but, for Ulrika, there was a pressure at the threshold, like the tension on the surface of water. It pushed back against her, trying to deny her entry, and her mind was suddenly filled with an almost overwhelming fear of Morr and his servants, a dread of their ability to end her unlife and snuff out her tenuous existence.

She fought forwards, both physically and mentally. She was not some mindless thing escaped from the grave. She was still Ulrika Magdova Straghov. She still had Ulrika's joys and sadnesses, her dreams and longings. She had not yet surrendered herself completely to the night.

The barrier weakened the more she thought on her humanity, and with a last effort she stumbled into the temple and continued after Holmann, feeling weak and diminished.

He looked back at her.

'Sorry,' she said. 'Tripped.'

He nodded, then turned as, out of the darkness of the temple's simple stone interior, drifted a tall, gaunt priest in long black robes, his hood thrown back on his narrow shoulders.

'Welcome, children,' he murmured, surveying them with heavy-lidded eyes. 'Have you questions for the god of portals and dreams? Do you seek to know which path is most propitious?' He sounded like he was talking in his sleep.

Ulrika hung back, eyeing the priest warily. Would he recognise her for what she was? Had he the power to strike her down? He looked like a doddering old sleepwalker, but one never knew with priests.

'A more prosaic question, father,' said Holmann, crossing to him and taking the bloodied black robe from where he had tucked it through his belt. 'We found this during the investigation of the vampire menace. Have you heard of any of your brethren fighting these fiends, or of any being wounded in pursuance of their duties?'

The priest's eyes widened, and he was suddenly much more awake. He reached out and took the robe, then examined it closely. 'That is a lot of blood,' he said.

'Aye, father,' said Holmann patiently. 'And I seek the fiend that inflicted the wound. Have you heard aught of it? Was the unfortunate who wore this of your temple?'

The priest shook his head. 'I have heard of nothing like this. And we have lost no brothers here. But this…' He touched a spindly finger to the breast of the shredded garment. 'This is not our symbol. We are a temple of augury. Our symbol is the raven, you see?' He pointed to the breast of his own robe, upon which was stitched the outline of a black bird. 'This rose – it is the symbol of Morr's garden. Our brothers who tend the cemetery wear it.'

Templar Holmann inclined his head. 'Then we will inquire there, father,' he said, 'and trouble you no further.'

He took back the robe and turned for the door. Ulrika followed him, and breathed a great sigh of relief when they stepped once again through the open door and out into the cold night air.

ULRIKA FOUND IT interesting to walk with a witch hunter. She might be a creature of the night and an enemy of all mankind, but it was Holmann who the people feared. As they strode through the Neuestadt on their way to the Garden of Morr, street-corner demagogues stopped their tirades and vanished down alleys. Student agitators dispersed into their colleges. Harlots and beggars and swaggering bravos turned about on their strolls and found that they had business elsewhere. Even staid, respectable burghers blanched and found it difficult to know where to look when Holmann passed them by.

Ulrika hid a smile at each new tremor and stumble. No wonder witch hunters suspected everyone. Everyone looked guilty when they met them. It was also no wonder they were so often solitary men. Who could relax enough around them to be friends with them?

Only once did anyone approach them, a middle-aged woman in apron and mob-cap, wailing with grief, her arms outstretched.

'Witch hunter!' she cried. 'Find my son! The vampires have taken him! You must save him!'

Ulrika's heart leapt with hope as Holmann steadied the woman. Had the monster struck? Were they in time to catch it? That would be a stroke of luck.

'When did this happen, mein frau?' the templar asked. 'Did you see the fiends?'

'It happened last night,' she moaned. 'Jan went out and didn't come home. He's been taken, like all the others! I'm sure of it!'

Ulrika sighed, disappointed. It didn't sound like a disappearance to her.

Holmann seemed to think the same, for his face hardened. 'How old is your son?' he asked. 'What is his profession?'

The woman blinked, surprised by the questions. 'He is nineteen, a student at the university,' she said. 'He–'

'A student missing for a day hasn't been taken by vampires,' rasped Holmann, cutting her off. 'He is drunk in some brothel, sleeping it off.'

'Oh no,' gasped the woman. 'Not my Jan! He is a pious boy. He–'

'If he is still missing four days from now,' interrupted Holmann again, 'report his disappearance at the Iron Tower and we will investigate. Until then, wait and pray to Sigmar for his safe return. Now excuse me. I have more pressing matters.'

And with that he strode past the woman, leaving her weeping behind him.

'Fool,' he growled under his breath as Ulrika caught up to him. 'It is always the same. For every one true disappearance, there are reports of ten. Our work is hard enough without ignorant house-fraus leading us on wild goose chases.'

Ulrika nodded, her thoughts elsewhere. 'Aye, but do you think she's right? Are the disappearances connected to what we seek?'

Holmann shrugged. 'There are always disappearances. People only take notice of them when something else stirs their fear – vampires, cultists, mutants – but they never cease.'

After that, they had walked quietly for a while, each deep in their own thoughts, when Holmann raised his head and looked at her.

'You never spoke of how you came to be chasing the vampire in the sewers,' he said.

Ulrika coughed, caught off guard. This was precisely what she had meant about the difficulty of being friends with a witch hunter – a companionable walk, some casual talk, and then, out of the blue, dangerous questions. She quickly thought back to their earlier conversation, struggling to remember what lies she had told him so she wouldn't contradict herself now.

'I... I have been hunting my sister since that moment when I was not able to go through with killing her,' she said at last. 'I realised, as you said, that it was a false mercy to spare her, and have been determined to rectify my error.'

Holmann nodded approvingly.

'I came to Nuln,' she continued, 'thinking she might have something to do with these women who have been exposed as vampires.'

'You believe she is spreading her corruption?' the templar asked.

Ulrika shrugged. 'I know not.' She paused then went on. 'I was on the hunt that night when I heard, as you did, of some monster outside the Silver Lily. I too found nothing, but saw a man – or what I thought was a man – watching me from the shadows across the way. He fled when I approached him, and I chased him into the sewers. The rest you know.'

Holmann nodded again and they continued in silence. Ulrika hoped he was done asking questions. The less she talked about the dead Lahmians in his presence the better. She didn't want to give anything away by accident, or add to what he already knew. But when the witch hunter spoke next, it was not a question.

'You... you are a most unusual woman, fraulein,' he said, looking at her sidelong.

More than you know, Ulrika thought, but only said, 'In what way?'

He barked a harsh laugh. 'In every way!' He waved a gloved hand at her. 'Your mannish clothes, your hair, your manner. It goes against all convention and all seemliness, and yet... and yet with you it seems normal and right.'

Ulrika smiled. 'I grew up in the far north of Kislev,' she said. 'The daughter of a Troll Country march warden. There, this dress *is* normal and right, for it is so dangerous a place that even the women must learn to fight and ride.'

Holmann nodded. 'Aye. A hard land breeds hard folk,' he said. 'I am from Ostermark. It too is harsh country. But...' He paused, then went on. 'But there is more to you than that. I have known bold hoydens before – hard-drinking, hard-fighting women. They haven't your gravity, nor your sense of purpose. And I have known pious women before, devoted to their god, and the destruction of the Ruinous Powers. They haven't your...'

He stopped, seemingly at a loss for words, and Ulrika could hear his blood suddenly begin rushing through his veins. The heat from his heart-fire was suddenly like a blazing hearth. The warmth of it made her dizzy. She looked up at him, blinking in surprise. What was this? He turned away, flushed, and gripped the pommel of his sword.

Ulrika stifled a smile and did her best to keep any laughter out of her voice. The dour templar found her attractive! 'I thank you, sir,' she said. 'I take it as a great compliment, coming from a man of your virtue.'

Holmann shrugged as if his collar irritated him. 'It is only that I... I have never before met a woman who... who has lost what I have lost, and faced what I have faced, and come away stronger for it.' His face grew dark, as if at some memory, and his eyes far away.

Ulrika's smile fell. She had been ready to laugh at him for a fool who could not admit simple lust and must cloak it in high-sounding words, who was trying to convince himself that what he felt had some noble basis, but the ache of pain and loneliness in his last words was not amusing at all. Where did a man so driven find companionship? Where did a templar find a woman who would understand what he faced every day? They were few and far between, and those that would not only understand, but also share his lot in all its harshness and horror, rarer still. He must be very lonely.

She looked at him out of the corner of her eye as they continued on. She had never had any use for grim-faced fanatics, so sure of their own righteousness that they were willing to pass sentence on their fellow man, and she had at first taken Templar Holmann to be one of these. But though he was clearly a religious man, and zealous in the execution of his duties, there was yet humanity in his eyes and his heart. He was not the flint-hearted witch hunter of popular legend. He was certainly striving towards that ideal, but he was still young, and had not achieved it – not yet.

She remembered his story of killing his parents, and realised that he had come to his profession in nearly the same way she had come to her inhuman state. He had been forced into it. Had Krieger not taken her, Ulrika would never have chosen the life of a vampire. Had mutation not taken Holmann's parents, he would never have chosen the witch hunter's life. They were both children of misfortune.

She understood his loneliness too. She felt trapped between two worlds, and not entirely part of either. The human world was closed to her now, and the vampire world foreign and strange, and she dared not confide even to Gabriella her myriad fears and confusions, for fear of appearing weak or foolish.

Who had Templar Holmann to confide in? To whom could he admit weakness or doubt? The unbending demagogues who were his fellows? His priest? They would cast him out as heretic and coward. They might even burn him. Nor could he tell some wife who could have no understanding of the horrors he faced down every day. She might comfort him, but she could never empathise.

A sudden fondness for Holmann tightened her chest. A witch hunter and a vampire should be natural enemies, but she liked the templar. He was a good man, and she found herself wishing she could be the woman he thought she was, a comrade and confidante that would fight by his side in battle and comfort him body and soul afterwards. But thoughts of intimacy brought stirrings of another kind. His blood was still pumping strongly in his veins, and the smell of it was intoxicating. Entering the temple of Morr and piercing its wards had drained her, and left her hungry. She found she could not think of Holmann without thinking of drinking from him. She cursed silently. It was infuriating. Would physical desire and bloodlust always be conflated in her mind? Was even just walking with a human to be a forbidden pleasure?

If she grew any hungrier she would have to leave him, or she might have difficulty controlling herself. She didn't want to attack him, not at this late date. She could only imagine the look of betrayal on his face. The thought made her cringe. Foolish though it was, she wanted him to continue liking her. She was pleased to have won his respect, and didn't want to lose that to revulsion and rage.

Of course, if she fed on him, his rage would melt away, wouldn't it? He would become like the other swains. He would love her too much to betray her to his zealot companions. Her heart leapt at the idea. Why not? She would no longer have to keep her secret from him. He would no longer have to be alone. They could be comrades, prowling the midnight world in search of the common enemies of vampire and man, and spending the days in shadowed embrace.

The image of Quentin staring up at her doe-eyed as blood flowed down his neck flashed across her mind and the dream popped like a bubble. Such a relationship with Holmann would not be as she longed for it to be. They would not be friends. They would not be comrades. They would be mistress and servant. Once fed upon, a swain lost his will and his self, and became only a devoted slave to she who drank from him. She had seen it in Quentin, and in Imma – that sick, dog-like worshipfulness that had nauseated her so. She didn't want Holmann to become like that. She liked him for his hardness, for his deeply held beliefs, for his honour and grim humour.

All that would be lost if she bled him. No matter how martial a man he seemed afterwards, he would be hollow on the inside, a weak, needy thing like Rodrik, consumed with jealousies and insecurities, a lap-dog masquerading as a mastiff. She would have possessed the shell, but lost the pearl within. It was this, she realised suddenly, more than any other aspect of her new life, that she despised. The hunt, the blood frenzy, she could appreciate. They thrilled her. Even killing a victim, as long as it was the right victim, she had little trouble with. But taking someone's will, that sickened her. She knew then and there that she would never take the blood of anyone she respected, for doing so would destroy the very thing that had won her admiration. She did not want slaves. She wanted friends. She wondered if it would ever be possible.

CHAPTER THIRTEEN
EATERS OF THE DEAD

'WHAT BUSINESS HAVE ye in the Garden of Morr,' asked a hooded, heavy-cloaked priest through the spiked iron gates of the Cemetery of Nuln.

'Sigmar's business, initiate,' said Holmann, showing his chain of office. 'Open up.'

The priest peered peevishly out through the bars, holding up his lantern and revealing an ugly, wart-studded face, then sighed and took out a jingling iron ring of keys. 'I don't know what ye want with our lot, witch hunter,' he sneered. 'They don't respond to torture.'

'It isn't your charges I wish to speak with,' Holmann growled.

Ulrika smirked as the priest paled and hurried more quickly with the lock, his gloved hands shaking with fright. They had had less trouble getting through the Altestadt wall than winning entry into the cemetery. The guards at the High Gate had waved them through without a second glance – a much easier entry than her previous attempt. She might be able to climb walls, but a witch hunter could pass through them with nothing but a glare and a wide-brimmed hat.

She had walked to the cemetery with Templar Holmann through the spire-hemmed streets of the temple quarter, and though she had feared the journey, had felt not a twinge of fear or pain. The sight of the icons and statues of the gods that ringed the marble walls had seemed to have no effect on her. Perhaps it was because they were not her gods. Perhaps things would be different in Kislev. She hoped she never had cause to find out.

'Welcome, herr witch hunter,' said the priest, bowing obsequiously as he swung open the creaking iron gate and let them through. 'Shall I fetch the senior priest?'

Ulrika tensed as she stepped onto the cemetery grounds, fearing to again come up against the enervating force that had tried to deny her entry into the temple of Morr, but there was nothing. Whatever holy influence had protected the other place was absent here. She breathed a sigh of relief.

'That won't be necessary, sexton,' said Holmann. 'Unless you fail to answer me fully.'

The wart-faced priest trembled and ducked his head. 'I shall do my best, templar,' he said.

Holmann took out the torn and bloodied black robe and showed it to him. 'We found these robes while hunting vampires this night. Have your brothers fought any of these fiends recently? Have you lost any of your number?'

The priest held his lantern close to the black cloth, then grimaced. 'I'll ask Father Taubenberger, but I haven't heard of anything like that. We leave the fighting to you lot, and the Black Guard.'

'Of course you do,' said Holmann, sneering. 'And no one has disappeared, or reported sick, or had an "accident"?'

The priest scratched a wart thoughtfully, then shook his head. 'Not that I can remember. Not recently.'

Holmann sighed. 'Fetch your superior, then,' he said. 'He may know more.'

'Aye, mein herr,' said the priest, then turned and limped away towards the low black stone temple that rose some thirty paces from the gate. He hadn't taken more than three steps when he paused and turned back. 'We have had some robes gone missing, though,' he said. 'And a grave disturbed. Would that be important?'

Holmann shot a glance at Ulrika. She raised her eyebrows. This sounded promising.

'Yes,' said Holmann, turning back to the priest. 'That may be important. Tell me more of it. Who took the robes? How many were taken? In what way were the graves "disturbed"?'

'Six robes have been reported missing,' said the priest. 'Don't know who took 'em. Resurrection men, most likely. They pose as priests of Morr to steal bodies, then sell 'em to "scholars" for "medical research" if you get my meaning.'

'I know the practice,' growled Holmann.

'That's likely why the grave was dug up, too,' said the priest. 'They stole the coffin and left the body. Most likely using it to collect fresh corpses.'

Or to transport mangled Lahmians, Ulrika thought, a vision of a group of robed figures carrying a coffin through the streets of Nuln from Shantytown to the Silver Lily flashing through her mind. Is that how they'd done it?

'Did you or your brothers see these grave robbers at their work?' Holmann asked. 'Have they returned?'

The priest shook his head. 'Nobody saw 'em,' he said. 'But some of the brothers have been whispering since then about seeing shadows off in the distance at night when there shouldn't ought to be anybody there.'

'And you have hunted down these shadows?'

The priest swallowed. 'Well, we've gone out during the day, but haven't seen no sign.'

Holmann glared at him. 'Sexton, is it not the sacred duty of the priests of Morr to make sure that the dead remain undisturbed? This is consecrated ground! You must protect it!'

The priest shrank inside his robes. 'We do, mein herr,' he said. 'We do. At least most of it we do.' He gestured around him. 'This bit around the temple, and the noble mausoleums, and the merchant quarter – we patrol them and make our prayers all the time, but...'

'But what?' snapped Holmann.

'Well, mein herr,' said the priest, leaning in to whisper. 'There's parts of the old place nobody goes any more, not since the trouble.'

Holmann frowned. 'Trouble? What trouble?'

'The plague, mein herr,' murmured the priest. 'You remember. And the... the rats.'

The witch hunter drew himself up, shocked. 'Since the great fire? You mean to say that there are places in this garden that haven't been visited for three years?'

'We daren't,' pleaded the priest. 'We daren't. The

sickness still lingers. It isn't safe.'

Holmann sneered. 'You don't fear the plague. You fear old wives' tales. Rats that walk like men. Fah! Do you know it is heresy to believe in them?'

'I don't! I swear I don't!' cried the priest.

Ulrika did. She had in fact defended her father's estate against them once, but she thought it was probably wisest to keep that to herself just now.

'Never mind,' said Holmann. 'Where is this place that priests of Morr fear to tread? I want to see it.'

'I won't take you there!' the little priest wailed. 'I don't want to get sick!'

'You have only to point out the direction,' said Holmann through his teeth. 'I wouldn't have you along anyway.' He nodded towards Ulrika. 'I prefer braver companions.'

Ulrika ducked her head in thanks and hid a smile. Templar Holmann really was rather fetching when he was putting on his 'Wrath of Sigmar' act.

ONCE OUT OF sight of the main gate and the central temple, the Garden of Morr was an endless ocean of the dead. Low hills covered in black rose bushes undulated off into the mist-shrouded darkness like storm-swollen waves floating with solemn debris. Jutting up from the brittle, snow-patched grass at precarious angles were grave markers of all kinds, from simple headstones to massive monoliths and towering skull-faced saints. A few black and bare-limbed trees loomed above it all like ships half-sunk, while from their branches came the mournful hooting of owls and the heavy flapping of unseen wings.

Despite being gifted with eyes that could pierce the

dark, Ulrika could still see no further than ten paces, for glowing sheets of freezing fog drifted through the graves like ghostly sails, obscuring the distance.

Their journey took them through neighbourhoods and quarters of the dead, much like those in which the interred had once lived. First there were long avenues of dead merchants, neat rows of tall marble monuments, each competing with its neighbour for ostentation and ornament. Then came the mansions of departed nobility, mausoleums and crypts larger by far and better constructed than the quarters of most of Nuln's living inhabitants. After that there were the slums, tiny plots, all crowded together, with monuments that were little more than kerbstones, and sometimes less than that.

Then at last they came to the place they sought – a part of the cemetery that had been old when the Deutz Elm was a sapling, a place of worn-away names and crumbling tombs, of overgrown obelisks and faceless, weathered statues entwined in dagger-thorned rose vines like martyrs bound for the fire.

Templar Holmann looked around him, his jaw tight as something howled in the distance. 'The neglect here goes back longer than three years. These priests are cowards.' He made the sign of the hammer on his chest. 'Anything might be breeding here. Anything.'

Ulrika nodded, her eyes down, scouring the ground for footprints or other signs. She saw little. The snow of a few days ago was mostly melted, and the graveyard grass was coarse and long and did not betray passage. They moved on, the ground mist wrapping around their legs like an overly affectionate cat.

Then, at the top of a low rise, she smelled it, faint

but unmistakable – the bloated corpse stench of the killer. She looked around. There was nothing to see but more graves and more hills half-hidden in the mist. She crouched and sniffed the ground.

'You have seen something?' asked Holmann.

Ulrika paused. She wasn't going to make the mistake of revealing her superior senses again. 'I... I don't know,' she said. 'More a feeling. Let's try over this way.'

'Lead on,' said Holmann, motioning her ahead. 'I have grown to trust these feelings. Sigmar guides his servants.'

Ulrika smiled at that. She would rather trust her nose. Sigmar was not likely to favour a woman of her nature with any guidance in the near future.

The corpse reek grew stronger as they continued west through a tree-choked dell, and then up another low hill and through a line of overgrown cypress trees that overlooked a bowl-shaped valley. Here the smell hit Ulrika square in the face, and even Holmann jerked his head back. It seemed to be all around them, denser than the fog.

'Sigmar's mercy,' he murmured. 'The stench again.'

'Aye,' said Ulrika, grimacing. 'I think we have found the place.'

They looked down into the fog-wreathed valley, the sides of which were ringed with cracked and crooked monuments like the sharp teeth that filled the maw of a remora. At the bottom – the throat – a cluster of derelict mausoleums surrounded a long-dry fountain with a headless statue of Ulric the Wolf God rising from its centre.

The templar pointed with his lantern. 'One of those tombs, I'll warrant you, houses more than its rightful occupants.'

'Aye,' said Ulrika. 'I believe you're right.'

Holmann started down into the valley, drawing his basket-hilted long sword. 'Then come. Let us evict them.'

Ulrika paused. She was not at all sure this was a good idea. Unlike the witch hunter, she had seen what the monster who had killed the Lahmians was capable of. It had torn vampires with centuries of experience to shreds. She knew she was a skilled fighter, and her new powers gave her great strength, but she wasn't so confident that she was willing to go up against such a thing alone. And she would be alone. Holmann was brave and true, but no human, not even a Templar of Sigmar, would have the necessary strength to fight it.

'Herr templar, wait,' she whispered, hurrying after him and unsheathing her sabre. 'We may face overwhelming odds. Let us reconnoitre and see if we should come back with reinforcements.'

Holmann turned, his brows lowered, but then he softened. 'Your pardon, fraulein,' he said. 'I take you into danger without a by-your-leave.' He smiled. 'You make such a brave show that I momentarily forgot that you are still but a–'

Ulrika silenced him with a gesture. She had heard a noise. She turned and looked behind her. There was a movement in the mist at the top of the hill. 'Something above us,' she hissed.

Holmann raised his lantern and peered down the hill. 'Below us too,' he said.

She turned to look, but saw nothing. Then a movement to the left caught her eye. A dark shape had slipped behind a shattered monument. She looked right. More shapes were advancing – vanishing behind graves and statues the moment she spied them.

'More to either side,' she murmured.

Holmann set his lantern on a cracked marble plaque and drew a heavy pistol. 'We are surrounded.'

Ulrika extended her senses. The death reek she had come to associate with the killer was wafting from the hidden figures. They were ripe with it but, to her surprise, they did not seem to be dead themselves. She could hear their hoarse breathing and their feverishly beating hearts. 'Aye,' she said. 'But by what?'

'I will inquire,' said Holmann, then strode forwards and stood tall. 'Reveal yourselves, ye skulking creepers!' he barked as Ulrika cringed. 'Be ye man, beast or fiend, step into the light in Sigmar's name!'

Ulrika shook her head, bemused. That was one way to do it.

There was no reply to his command but the echo of his voice ringing back from the far side of the valley and the whispering patter of stealthy feet coming ever closer. Ulrika counted the low-burning heart-fires that swarmed around them – ten, fifteen, twenty – like fireflies drawn to a torch. She stepped back and bumped into Holmann, who was looking out into the darkness in the opposite direction.

He looked over his shoulder at her. 'My lady,' he said. 'I am shamed that I have led one so fair to so foul an end, and I hope you can forgive me.'

Ulrika warmed at his words, and she fought down an urge to kiss him, then bite him. 'Let us not speak of endings and death, templar,' she said. 'Let us instead fight and win, so that you may compliment me again another day.'

Holmann's stony face split into a grin. 'With a will,

fraulein,' he said. 'May Sigmar watch over us both.'

Then, with ear-piercing shrieks, the lurking shadows attacked. Bounding from behind gravestones and trees and leaping over fallen columns and faceless statues came a hideous horde of hunched, loping naked things – men once, but men no longer. Their limbs were white and gnarled, their hands hook-clawed talons, their cadaverous heads bald and criss-crossed with scars and lesions. Teeth filed to points flashed in their howling mouths, and eyes lit with mindless madness blazed in their sunken sockets.

Holmann's pistol cracked and one went down, spindle limbs flailing, then he threw aside the gun and tore one of the glass vials from his bandolier. A creature fell screaming as he hurled it at its face and it shattered, splashing the thing with blessed water that ate the flesh from its bones.

Ulrika spit another on her sabre. It did not even try to block, but as she fought to pull the point free, three more were on her, pummelling her. Only her inhuman speed and strength saved her, allowing her to dodge one while shoving another into the third. She cleared her blade at last and gutted the other two, then gashed out the throat of the other with the claws of her free hand.

Only as she drove back the next wave did she remember what company she kept, and drew back her claws with a painful effort. Her fangs had extended too. She retracted them and glanced over her shoulder to see if Holmann had noticed. He was too busy keeping half a dozen of the things at bay with his sword and more vials of blessed water. What a foolish predicament. She would have to fight with sabre alone, and remember not to show too much of her strength.

More monsters came in from every side. She drew her dagger and fought Tilean-style, blocking her opponents' claws with the short blade while running them through under their raised arms with her sabre. The fiends fell back screaming with each impalement, but half got up again, so lost to bloodlust that their wounds seemed only to goad them.

'With the power of Sigmar, I cleanse thee from his land!' roared Holmann. He hurled another vial and two more ghouls fell back, screaming, as their flesh bubbled.

'What are these things?' Ulrika called, gagging at their stench as she cut them down.

'Ghouls,' said Holmann. 'Fallen men. Eaters of the dead.'

Ulrika was embarrassed. A human telling a vampire about the children of the night? And yet, was it so strange? Krieger's knowledge had not been poured into her with his blood – only his hunger. She had not risen from her deathbed instantly wise in all the things a vampire should know. She knew more of these filthy scavengers from the battlefield stories of her father's soldiers than she had yet learned from Countess Gabriella. Haunters of graveyards, cannibals, feral servants of vampires and necromancers, they were the lowest a living man could go, lower even than mutants, who at least kept their intelligence.

She decapitated one and turned to face two more, but there was a sudden tearing pain in her right calf. She looked down. A ghoul she thought she had killed had its filed teeth deep in her leg. Cursing, she hacked down at it, cleaving its skull. The other two leapt. She brought up her sabre, but too late. They slammed her down and the three of them bounced down the hill in a jumble, with more bounding after her.

'Fraulein!' cried Holmann.

She slammed to a halt against a granite grave marker with stunning force, and saw through the tangled limbs of her opponents the witch hunter fighting through five of the monsters to come to her rescue.

'No! Protect yourself!' she shouted, but he didn't hear her.

A ghoul raked him from behind and he staggered forwards, lashing around him desperately. Another grabbed his wrist as he was about to throw another glass vial. A third bit his shoulder.

'No!' Ulrika shrieked.

She surged to her feet, claws and fangs shooting out, and threw the ghouls who held her aside like they were children. More leapt at her, ripping her clothes and flesh. She gutted one and tore the arm off another as she rushed up the hill.

Holmann was down, clubbing in all directions with the butt of a wooden stake and trying to free his sword from a ghoul's abdomen as three more tore at him.

'Get off him!' Ulrika screamed.

She hacked off a ghoul's head and leapt over two more to land behind the one on Holmann's chest. She tore its throat out with her claws and threw it over her shoulder, then slashed left and right with her sabre. The other ghouls scattered and she hauled Holmann up. He was staring at her through half-conscious eyes. Had he seen?

'Can you fight?' she asked.

He only stared, his mouth hanging slack. His clothes were in tatters and he had bite and claw marks all over his body.

A ghoul slashed Ulrika's arm. She turned and fanned it away. The others were closing, snarling, still more than a dozen. She lashed out and the ones in front of her danced back, but those behind attacked Holmann. She spun to fend them off, and more came in from another angle. It was impossible. She couldn't fight them all, not and keep Holmann alive.

With a curse, she tucked her left shoulder against the templar's belt buckle and heaved him up off his feet so that his head and torso hung down over her back.

'Away, filth!' she shouted, then flailed out at the ghouls and ran up the hill. Even with her unnatural strength, Holmann was heavy – taller than her and twice as broad – but she would not slow. She would not leave him to such a death.

She ran through the line of cypresses and turned east, towards the stone wall that separated the cemetery from the temple quarter. Unencumbered, the ghouls paced her easily, but she kept her sword flashing around her and they did not close. Like wolves chasing an elk, they were content to wait and let her tire, then pounce when she stumbled.

And she would stumble soon, she knew, for the fight and the wounds she had taken had weakened her. Already her legs were buckling under Holmann's weight. She looked ahead for the wall, but could only see more hills and graves before her, receding into the mist. She would not make it.

Then salvation appeared – an old mausoleum,

weathered but intact, except for the door, which was missing. She turned her steps for the yawning black rectangle, finding new strength with her renewed hope. The ghouls saw what she intended and tried to get ahead of her, but she hacked at them savagely and they fell back.

With a final burst of speed she ran down a grassy bank and shoved through the mausoleum's open door, the ghouls baying at her heels like albino hounds. She dumped Holmann roughly on the leaf-strewn floor then turned to face them. Some had already made it inside, but these she cut down swiftly and stepped into the door, kicking more back and blocking it.

'Come and die!' she snarled.

They did just that, but it didn't matter how many came at her now. In the narrow confines of the door they could no longer flank her, and they could not avoid her flashing sabre. One after the other they fell back, missing fingers, arms and eyes, and dying of wounds that bled from both the chest and the back. Finally, after a few furious moments, they had had enough, and ran howling with rage and fear back the way they had come, leaving their dead and dying behind.

Ulrika stepped out and finished off the last of these, then made sure her fangs and claws were retracted, and went back into the mausoleum to see how badly Holmann was hurt.

He was standing, leaning against the crypt's central sarcophagus, his broad-brimmed hat lost and his head bare, and stared at her with wild grey eyes.

She stopped, cold dread filling her chest. 'Templar Holmann,' she said, as evenly as she could. 'Are... are you well?'

Holmann shoved away from the sarcophagus and stepped forwards into a shaft of moonlight that streamed down through a hole in the ceiling of the tomb. He raised his sword and pointed it at her. 'You are one of them!' he cried. 'You are a vampire!'

CHAPTER FOURTEEN
CLAWS IN THE NIGHT

ULRIKA STEPPED BACK. 'You are mistaken, mein herr. In the excitement you must have imagined–'

'I know what I saw!' he shouted, then pointed again, his sword trembling. 'Look! Your hands still drip with their blood! And no mortal woman could have carried me so!'

Ulrika retreated again, her heart sinking. 'Templar Holmann, Friedrich, please.'

'Call me not by my name, whore of darkness!' He roared. 'I see your ways now! You have seduced me with your soft words and foul sorcery! You have tricked me into believing that–' He choked on the words. 'Into betraying my oaths! You have tainted me with your corruption!'

It tortured her to see his pain. This was exactly what she hadn't wanted to happen. 'Templar, please,' Ulrika pleaded. 'Let me explain.'

'There is nothing to explain!' Holmann bellowed, raising his sword and pulling one of the glass vials from his bandolier. 'You are fiend in female shape! An enemy of the Empire and humanity itself! In Sigmar's name, I shall destroy you!'

He threw the vial and lurched at her, stabbing clumsily, hampered by his wounds and his rage.

She dodged both attacks easily. 'But I saved you!'

'Another seduction!' he snarled, stabbing again. 'You save me to falsely win my loyalty! You mean to make a pawn of me. A besotted spy that would do your bidding against my masters!'

'I don't,' said Ulrika, but she knew it was no use. He was a Templar of Sigmar. His beliefs were too strongly held. He would never see her as anything other than a monster. Again the temptation to feed on him came to her, but she cast it away. She would not be what he called her.

Of course, that left killing him. There was no question that was what she should do. He knew her secret. He knew she was in some way connected to the vampire women that had so recently been exposed. He knew everything she knew about the murder in the plague house and the secret in the cemetery. He had to die, and he would be easy to kill. He could barely lift his sword or throw his glass grenades. He was limping and slow. She had only to knock aside his blade and thrust him through the heart with her sabre and it would be over.

He came forwards once more, throwing another vial and flailing wildly. She knocked the vial out of the air with her sabre and sidestepped his attack. He stumbled and caught himself against the wall. His neck was exposed. A swift chop and he would be dead. Her hand clenched her hilt, but for some reason she could not force her arm to move, instead she only stood there and watched him recover.

'I'm sorry to have disappointed you, Templar Holmann,' she said, then turned and fled out of the mausoleum and into the cold black night.

ULRIKA CURSED HERSELF as she ran. Was there ever a bigger fool? She should have killed Holmann when she first met him in the sewer. Failing that, she should have killed him in the plague house. What possessed her to try to befriend a witch hunter of all people? She could say that it was to gain knowledge and use him to get her into places she would have found it hard to enter, but that was little more than a rationalisation. Was it because she was lonely for company other than Gabriella? Was it because she missed Felix? And why hadn't she killed him just now when she'd had a perfect opportunity? Was it because she liked him, or was it only pride? Had she spared him only to prove him wrong?

At least she had given him no clues to follow. He could not follow her back to Aldrich's house. She would never have to see him again.

And why would she want to, she thought peevishly? He had tried to kill her only moments after she had saved his life. Of course, she knew his reasons. She had revealed herself to be a monster, by his reckoning, but he hadn't shown even a moment's regret before he attacked, only blind, savage rage. He had fought the ghouls with less passion.

Of course she knew the reason for that too. The ghouls hadn't pretended to be anything other than what they were. They hadn't won his heart.

THREE HOUSES FROM Guildmaster Aldrich's home, Ulrika knew there was something wrong. Faint screams reached her sensitive ears as she trotted down the wet cobbled street, screams she recognised – Imma, and Gabriella, frightened and enraged, then a splintering crash and an animal roar.

She sprinted ahead, drawing her sabre. Something was attacking her mistress! She must protect her!

From the front, the rich house appeared quiet. The door was closed and the drive empty, but shrieks and crashes came from the upper floors, and as she ran up the front steps, she saw a smear of blood on the threshold.

She tried the door. It was locked tight. She stepped back and kicked it near the latch, using all her inhuman strength. It flew inwards, wood splintering, lock parts flying, and she launched herself through it, sword at the ready.

Aldrich's disapproving butler was dead in the foyer, slumped against the wall with his throat torn out. She cursed and leapt up the stairs four at a time. At the first-floor landing she found Aldrich himself, his nightshirt and his belly ripped asunder and his intestines spilling out across the carpet. He had a sword in his limp hand. It didn't appear that he'd had time to use it.

She pounded down the hall towards the screams and the sounds of violence, then slammed through Countess Gabriella's door into…

Blackness.

Not since before Krieger's kiss had she been so blind. She could see nothing, not the room, not her sabre held in front of her, not the open door behind her. She froze for an instant, frightened and disorientated. Her night vision was no help. It was as if someone had thrown a sack over her head. Her other senses still worked, however. She could hear shrieks and roars and furniture smashing all around her, and she could smell – blood, smoke, Imma's fear, Gabriella, and over all of those, like a filthy, choking blanket, the smell of a battlefield full of corpses after a week in the rain. The killer. The killer was here!

She leapt at the stench, swinging blindly with her sabre, and connected with something that roared. A club or a fist hit her in the face and sent her flying back into a jumble of broken furniture, stars exploding in the darkness behind her open eyes.

She sat up, head ringing, and heard lighter feet dancing away from her – and another scent she recognised. The smell of cloves! The fat little man from the sewers.

'You!' she snarled, and lashed out at him with her sabre.

The hidden man laughed and kicked her in the temple, then skipped back out of the way again as she covered up. He can see, she thought.

'Ulrika!' came Gabriella's voice. 'Are you here?'

'Aye, mistress,' Ulrika gasped.

'Get away!' Gabriella cried. 'Go to Hermione! Go–'

A smack like clay hitting stone, and the countess's voice cut off with a gasp.

Ulrika surged up and leapt towards the source of the stench again, stabbing this time. An invisible foot tripped her and she went down flat on her stomach. She whipped the sabre at the retreating steps and was rewarded by a hiss of pain and an eye-blink dissipation of the blackness before it closed in again.

In that eye-blink she saw the fat little warlock hobbling back, clutching his leg through his all-enveloping robe, and the shadow of something huge and hunched looming on the wall, raising massive, clawed fists over its misshapen head. Then all was dark again.

Ulrika rolled up. There was no time to go after the little man. She spun and swung where she hoped the thing that had cast the shadow was, and chopped into something meaty. Another animal howl, and the whistle and breeze of something moving through the air. This time she ducked, almost in time. Claws raked the top of her head and her ear, but at least she wasn't knocked across the room again. She stabbed in front of her, and scored a glancing hit, tearing flesh and cloth.

A strike like a hammer knocked her sabre away, and a hand as big and hard as a hay rake caught her by the ribs and lifted her off the ground. She struggled against it, but another hand grabbed her head, crushing it, and trying to twist it off. She could feel her vertebrae grinding. The pain was impossible. She tore at the huge fingers with her claws, shredding flesh and trying to rip them out at the root, but her assailant's strength was as far beyond hers as hers was beyond a human's. She could not stop it.

'Murnau!' came the fat warlock's voice. 'Behind you!'

She heard the dull chunk of a blade stabbing into flesh, and suddenly the thing that held her shrieked in agony and flung her away. She spun through the air and hit something hard and narrow, snapping it, then landed on what felt like a collapsed bed.

Another stabbing thud, and another inhuman scream battered her ears as she tried to stand.

'I have a claw too,' came Gabriella's ragged cry. 'You see? You see!'

Heavy footsteps thundered away across the floor and there was a tremendous shattering of glass and sudden rush of cold winter wind.

'Damned coward!' rasped the little man, then his footsteps retreated towards the hallway door.

Ulrika regained her feet and ran after the warlock's steps, then tripped on something soft and came down hard on the edge of a table.

'Stop!' she cried, and pushed painfully to her feet.

She clutched her aching shoulder and limped after the fading footsteps. It wasn't until she dodged around a broken table that she realised she could once again see. The unnatural blackness was dissolving. She looked around as she rushed for the door. The room was a shambles. Every stick of furniture was ripped to kindling and the logs from the fire had been scattered across the rug, setting it on fire. The tall windows on the outside wall, which had been so carefully blacked-out and curtained, were smashed and open to the night.

Then she saw Countess Gabriella on her knees beside the toppled wash stand, head down and clutching her arms, her robe shredded and soaked in blood. Ulrika stopped and ran back, the invisible beast and the fat little man forgotten.

'Mistress!' she cried, dropping to her knees beside her. 'Are you hurt?'

'Oh, yes,' said Gabriella weakly. 'Very much so.'

She sank against Ulrika, her arms falling limp in her lap and a thin dagger slipping to the floor.

Ulrika gasped when she saw her wounds through the rents in the countess's tattered silk robe. Her breasts and belly had been shredded to the muscle and the bones of her left arm gleamed through four deep ragged gashes. Splinters of glass and wood pierced her legs and face.

'Please fetch Imma,' she murmured. 'I must feed.'

'Yes, mistress,' said Ulrika, and stood to look for the girl. She saw her in the midst of the debris, lying on the rug and staring up at the ceiling, her face frozen in an expression of almost comic shock.

'Imma, get up.'

The maid did not respond.

Ulrika stepped around a broken chair and crossed to her. 'Imma...'

The girl was not dead, but it wouldn't be long. Both her arms were broken, bent at impossible angles, and a snapped off table leg jutted up through her belly where she had fallen upon it.

She turned blind eyes towards Ulrika as she stepped to her. 'M–mistress?'

Ulrika swore, then bent and lifted the girl off the impaling leg and carried her to Gabriella. Blood ran down her wrists from the wound in Imma's back.

'She is dying, mistress,' said Ulrika, lowering her to the floor.

Imma cried out weakly at the movement, then looked at Gabriella. 'I am sorry, mistress, but it hurts so.'

'It is I who am sorry,' said Gabriella. She smoothed the girl's hair. 'But I will take away the pain. Do you wish that?'

'Oh yes, mistress,' Imma whimpered.

Gabriella motioned to Ulrika to lift Imma into her lap, and then she lowered her fangs to the maid's lacerated neck and drank. Imma gasped, then sighed and closed her eyes, her face growing calm.

Ulrika watched in amazement as Gabriella's wounds slowly began to knit at the edges. Even the worst of them, on her left arm, clotted and grew narrower, though they did not fully close.

After a long moment, Gabriella raised her head again and sighed. She looked almost herself again, despite being smeared with blood and dressed in crimsoned rags. She pushed the unconscious maid towards Ulrika.

'Finish her,' she said. 'You are wounded too.'

'Finish her?' Ulrika asked uncertainly.

'Here, it will be a mercy,' said Gabriella.

'Aye, mistress.'

Ulrika raised the maid into a close embrace, then bit where Gabriella had bitten. Unwished-for emotion welled up in her as she drank the last dregs of her blood. Imma had said she would die for her. Ulrika had not thought the words would ever be more than a sentimental vow, but now they had come true. Imma's blood was healing her as it had Gabriella, while the girl's heart-fire dimmed to a guttering candle flame. At least Ulrika was able to give her a peaceful end in return.

By the time Imma's heartbeat slowed and stopped altogether, and her blood ceased to flow, Ulrika's wounds too were healing, and she let the maid slip gently to the floor.

'The poor child,' said Gabriella. She laid a hand on Imma's cold white forehead. 'Humans are so fragile.'

Ulrika helped the countess to her feet and she crossed to the wash stand, righting it and filling the cracked bowl with water from a pitcher, miraculously whole.

'Find me another robe,' Gabriella said as she took off her shredded garment and began to wash her face and body and clean her wounds.

'Yes, mistress.' Ulrika crossed to the smashed wardrobe and pulled away the shattered doors.

'Did I kill the beast?' Gabriella asked.

'No, mistress,' said Ulrika. 'It fled out the window.' She found another robe and returned to Gabriella. 'What was it?' she asked. 'Did you see it?'

Gabriella dried and bound her crusted wounds with the old robe and held out her arms for Ulrika to dress her. 'I did not. Not in the blackness. But it was a vampire of some kind, of that much I am sure.'

Ulrika helped her into the robe and settled it on her shoulders. 'How do you know this?'

Gabriella turned, wrapping the robe around her nakedness, then crossed to the thin-bladed dagger she had let slip to the floor. She picked it up and showed it to Ulrika. 'My silvered blade,' she said. 'It fled when I stabbed it.'

Ulrika eyed the weapon askance. 'Mistress, I am thankful that it saved your life, but why would you carry such a thing?'

Gabriella smiled as she found its jewelled sheath among the wreckage. 'It is a misericorde – a mercy dagger – a quick end if I am caught by men. It is painful, but quicker by far than burning, or being driven into the sun.' She winced and touched her left arm through the cloth. Blood continued to seep through the dressings and the robe. 'Had I been wearing it, the fight would have gone very differently. Unfortunately it was in my valise, and I had to hunt for it in the dark. I believe I will wear it from now on – even when sleeping. One never knows when one may be attacked here in Nuln.'

She paused then, the dagger halfway into its sheath, then turned to Ulrika. 'But how did they know to attack me here?' she asked. 'We have been here three nights, and have done little to announce our presence. How many people know we are here?'

'Hermione and her household,' said Ulrika, thinking back. 'Madam Dagmar. Rodrik. They were the only ones present when Hermione ordered us here.'

Gabriella frowned. 'Well, I hope it was none of them, but they might have talked incautiously to someone who wishes us ill.'

'Or there might be spies watching Hermione's house,' said Ulrika. 'We might have been followed.'

Gabriella nodded. 'I like that explanation better. It leaves out treachery–'

There was a thunder of boots on the stairs and Ulrika leapt up, grabbing her sabre and going on guard. Gabriella gripped her dagger.

The door flew open and Rodrik ran in, sword in hand. He stopped dead inside the door and stared around at the wreckage, then looked to Countess Gabriella.

'Mistress!' he cried, then shoved through the broken furniture to her. 'What has happened here?' He saw the blood on her sleeve. 'You are hurt!'

'Fear not,' said Gabriella. 'I am much recovered.'

'But who did this?' Rodrik asked.

'It was the killer,' said Ulrika. 'It tried to take another victim.'

Rodrik cursed and stood, glaring at Gabriella. 'This is what comes of making me messenger! I should have been at your side!'

Gabriella smiled at him and caressed his cheek. 'It is better that you were not, beloved,' she said. 'For you would be dead like poor Imma.'

'But I am your champion!' he protested. 'It is my duty to protect you!' He shot a look at Ulrika. 'This is *not* a job for a spy.'

Gabriella took his arm. 'You may yet have your chance,' she said. 'The thing means to kill us all, I think, and its retreat was only temporary.' She looked up at him again. 'In the meantime, you may do me another service. If you would kindly bare your neck, I have wounds remaining.'

Rodrik lifted his hand to his collar, then paused, frowning. 'No, mistress,' he said, and stepped back. 'I should not be weakened while you are still in danger. I will fetch Aldrich's coachman, if he is not dead too.'

Gabriella stiffened, for a moment shocked at being refused, then nodded. 'You are right. I need you sharp. Go then, but be quick.'

'Yes, countess.' He bowed, then started for the corridor.

'Wait,' said Gabriella.

Rodrik stopped at the door. 'Mistress?'

'What news from Hermione?'

Rodrik paused, pursing his lips, then spoke. 'Madam Dagmar was murdered while returning from Mathilda's brothel last night. Torn apart like the others. She was discovered by the watch before dawn, hung from the railing in front of the Silver Lily, just as Alfina was, her fangs extended. The witch hunters are renewing their hunt. Lady Hermione wishes to speak with you about it.'

CHAPTER FIFTEEN
A KNIFE IN THE BACK

IT WAS ONLY a few hours before dawn when Gabriella, Ulrika, Lotte and Rodrik departed for Lady Hermione's in the guildmaster's coach, leaving Guildmaster Aldrich's house blazing like a torch behind them and taking all their belongings with them, strapped to the roof. Gabriella had ordered the burning. Fire hid a multitude of sins – Aldrich's murder, shattered furniture, broken windows, a dead maid and butler, a missing wife – that it would be best the witch hunters never found.

Ulrika was again dressed like a lady, in bodice, skirts and wig. This was as much necessity as it was deference to Gabriella's wishes, for her riding clothes had been shredded, bloodied and begrimed over the course of the evening, and were not just inappropriate for visiting, but actually indecent.

As they travelled through the cold, empty Altestadt streets, Ulrika told Gabriella of her adventures earlier that night, of finding the plague house, and the black robe, and how it led her to the Garden of Morr. In all of it she left out any mention of Templar Holmann, for she knew Gabriella would not approve.

When she reached the part about fighting the ghouls in the graveyard, Rodrik growled under his breath. He had continued stiff and distant since learning of the killer's attack, and this seemed only to add to his anger.

'You see how well your *spy* handles things, mistress?' he said. 'She flees in the face of danger, and has undoubtedly alerted your enemy that we search for him. He will have moved by now, and all chance of finding him again lost.'

'I was overwhelmed,' snapped Ulrika. 'You would have been dead.'

'I would not have gone alone,' Rodrik sneered.

'Children,' said Gabriella. 'Peace. I will not have squabbling. You have both done admirably in difficult circumstances. Now, quiet, if you please. I am still feeling weak.'

Rodrik nodded curtly, and turned to the window, but it was clear his pride was not assuaged. Ulrika shot him a glance of loathing, then she too looked out of the window. They made the rest of the journey in silence.

SILENCE WAITED FOR them at their destination as well. Lady Hermione stood rigid in powder-blue silk and eyed them icily as they entered her drawing room and curtseyed and bowed before her. Around the perimeter, von Zechlin and her other gentlemen lounged in attitudes of studied nonchalance and observed with seemingly sleepy eyes. Famke's eyes, on the other hand, were wide and darting. She stood beside Frau Otilia a few paces behind her mistress, her fingers twisted together in a white-knuckled knot.

Something was most definitely amiss. Ulrika dropped her hand to her hilt, but of course her sabre wasn't there. She looked to Gabriella, but if the countess noticed the tension in the air, she did not betray it.

'Sister,' said Gabriella. 'Rodrik has told me the terrible news. I mourn with you.'

'Liar!' snarled Hermione.

Gabriella looked up, her brows raised. 'I beg your pardon?'

Hermione released her rigid posture and stabbed an angry finger at the countess. 'I know you for what you are now! I know what you've done! You helped kill Madam Dagmar!' She shot a hate-filled glance at Ulrika. 'You and your Kislevite assassin are in league with Mathilda and her butchers!'

Ulrika blinked in surprise. Was Hermione mad?

Gabriella laughed. 'Don't be ridiculous. How did you come by this foolish idea?'

Hermione grinned wolfishly. 'You try to deny it, *von Carstein*?'

Gabriella pulled up, her cool composure cracking. 'What? What did you call me?'

Hermione indicated her housekeeper with a gesture. 'It was Otilia that reminded me of your true heritage – that you are more of Vashanesh's blood than of our queen's.' She sneered. 'I thought at first that you meant only to try and take my position, to climb the ladder of the queen's favour over my corpse, but I know now I was wrong. You have reverted to your true nature. You mean to destroy us all in the name of Sylvania, to kill the Lahmians of Nuln and salt the earth here with such suspicion and fear that our sisterhood will not be able to return. Well, your plot won't succeed, von Carstein. It will end here.'

'Hermione,' said Gabriella. 'This is lunacy. I long ago proved beyond a doubt where my loyalties lay, and I have proved it again many times. You know this. You were there!'

'Loyalties can change, sister,' said Hermione, circling her menacingly. 'Jealousies can stew when one is stuck in the hinterlands for a century or two. And so you conspired secretly with Mathilda to kill us all, and used this "investigation" to turn our suspicions into blind alleys.'

Gabriella frowned. 'Are you saying now that Mathilda is a von Carstein too?'

'She can become a wolf,' said Hermione. 'No *pure* Lahmian has that power!'

Gabriella shook her head, dismayed. 'You are distraught, sister. I understand that. There have been four deaths. It is enough to frighten anyone, but you must calm down and think clearly. Striking out at me will not–'

'Don't try that on me, witch!' hissed Hermione. 'I will not fall again for soothing words! You and Mathilda have been against us from the beginning!'

'But we haven't!' cried Gabriella. 'You have no proof!'

Hermione smiled. 'Haven't I? What did you do when we parted ways here after visiting Mathilda's flea pit?'

'I went home to Herr Aldrich,' said Gabriella. 'I stayed there all evening.'

'You used that excuse before,' said Hermione. 'But what of your Kislevite protégée, who wears dresses and long hair when you bring her to my parlour, but is a mannish, shock-headed spy out of my sight? Did she perhaps let you go home alone, and instead follow poor Dagmar home?'

'She did not,' said Gabriella. 'She was with me the whole night.'

'Was she?' asked Hermione. 'Dagmar was killed before her coach reached the Silver Lily. Who but you and I knew she was out?'

A memory flashed through Ulrika's mind – something black darting quickly in the corner of her eye as she and the others had travelled back from Mathilda's in Hermione's coach. She had looked out the window and seen only Dagmar's coach, and thought she was jumping at shadows, but had there been something there after all?

Gabriella sighed, exasperated. 'You still have presented no proof, Hermione. Well, I have proof you are wrong. Ulrika and I were attacked ourselves this night, by the killer. He nearly killed me. He did kill Herr Aldrich and poor dear Imma.'

Hermione stared, shocked. 'Aldrich is dead?' She recovered herself and bared her teeth. 'Then it was you who killed him! Another blow to our network of spies. You do your work well, traitor.'

'I didn't kill him,' said Gabriella patiently. 'The beast killed him.'

Hermione's eyes blazed. 'And where is *your* proof, sister! Can you prove it was not you?'

'Certainly, I can,' said Gabriella. She turned to Rodrik. 'Beloved, you saw what had occurred at Aldrich's. Tell her.'

Rodrik nodded, and opened his mouth to speak, but then paused. A cunning look came into his eyes. He turned to Hermione. 'I'm afraid I did not see what occurred, m'lady,' he said, stiffly. 'I arrived after the fact. It might have been as the countess says. It might not.'

Gabriella rocked as if struck, and turned on Rodrik. 'What! What do you say? Do you dare lie? You saw the wreckage! You saw the blood, and poor Imma dead!'

Rodrik inclined his head with perfect politeness, but there was a curl to his lip. 'I did indeed see all that, mistress,' he said. 'But I was not there to witness the attack, or the attacker, and cannot be certain there was one. The countess and her new servant could have just as easily caused the damage themselves, as some sort of cover.'

'Ha!' cried Hermione, jubilant.

Gabriella stared at Rodrik as if he had become a stranger. 'Rodrik, I don't understand.'

'Nor can I swear that the Kislevite did not go out on the night Madam Dagmar died,' Rodrik continued as if she had not spoke. 'For all I know, the countess went out too.'

Gabriella snarled. 'What are you saying, villain? You were with us that night. You know we did no such thing!'

Rodrik bowed, looking smug. 'Countess, I do not. As you have so ordered things that I am no longer allowed to stay at your side, and am instead removed to an inn, I do not know what occurs when I leave you at your new home. I cannot therefore say that you are innocent of these crimes.'

Gabriella advanced on him, her eyes blazing with fury. 'You jealous little infant! You will betray me because we were parted for three days? What of your vow to protect me?'

'None of that,' said Hermione primly. She was enjoying herself now. 'Do you deny that he is telling the truth? Can he vouch for any of your tale?'

'No he cannot,' said Gabriella through her teeth, then raised her eyes to meet Rodrik's. 'But he could certainly trust the veracity of what he did see. He could certainly give his mistress the benefit of the doubt.'

'Ha!' said Hermione again. 'You have no witnesses then!'

'And neither do you!' Gabriella shot back. 'Rodrik cannot vouch for us, but neither can he say we did anything other than what we say we did. He wasn't there.' She turned on the knight again. 'But I do know something he can vouch for.' She raised her chin and glared at him. 'Tell the truth, sir. Have I at any time in your hearing spoken of conspiring with Madam Mathilda or with the von Carsteins against Hermione or any of my Lahmian sisters?'

Rodrik hesitated, frowning.

'Come, sir,' Gabriella snapped. 'Speak!'

Rodrik squared his shoulders. 'No, m'lady, you have not, though I am not often in your presence these days.'

Gabriella smirked, and was about to turn on Hermione, but Rodrik continued.

'But I *have* heard you say that you thought Lady Hermione the least suited to lead here in Nuln,' he said evenly. 'And that you wished she had died instead of the others.'

Gabriella froze, like a cat settling to spring, eyes boring into Rodrik's. 'You spoiled child.' She started stalking towards him, shoulders hunched and eyes glaring. 'You petty little–'

Hermione stepped before her, holding out her arms. 'You will not touch him, sister. He is under my protection now. Stand away.'

Gabriella snarled, her fangs and claws extending. 'And you will not tell me what I may do with my swain!'

Hermione jumped back, a look of triumph in her eyes though she was miming fear. 'She attacks me! She is with the killers! Champions, defend me!'

Ulrika went on guard behind Gabriella, watching her back, as all around the room von Zechlin's exquisites jumped from their languid poses and strode forwards to surround them, drawing their rapiers. Famke stepped forwards to stand at Hermione's shoulder, her face troubled, while Otilia backed quickly to the door.

'Rodrik!' called Gabriella. 'Take von Zechlin. Ulrika and I will handle the bitch and her curs.'

But when Rodrik drew his sword, he stepped away from the countess and instead joined the closing circle of Hermione's men.

'I am sorry, my lady,' he said, and pulled down his collar to show his neck, revealing two scabbing puncture wounds. He had been freshly bled. 'But I am no longer yours to command.'

CHAPTER SIXTEEN
THE POWDER KEG

GABRIELLA STARED AT the bite marks then turned towards Hermione. 'How dare you bleed a swain of mine!'

Hermione laughed. 'He is yours no more. You neglected him for too long. I could not bear to see him so forlorn.'

Gabriella swivelled back to Rodrik. 'Traitor!' she growled. 'Oath breaker!'

Rodrik raised his sword and pointed it at her, looking noble. 'I did not turn away from you, m'lady, until you turned away from me.'

Von Zechlin pushed past Rodrik. 'Enough talk! Attack!' He lunged at Gabriella with his rapier. His men followed suit.

Gabriella batted the blade aside and slashed at him with her claws, but he dodged back and the men to either side of him slashed at her.

Ulrika dodged three blades of her own, now desperately wishing she were dressed in her riding clothes, no

matter how bloodied and torn, and had her sabre at
her side. Armed and able to move, the seven men who
surrounded them would have given her few qualms,
but encumbered and bladeless, she wasn't so certain.
She kicked a delicate Tilean table at her opponents,
making two of them stumble. Beyond them, she saw
Hermione dragging Famke back towards the corridor
door.

'Hermione is retreating, mistress,' she said over her
shoulder. 'Should I kill her?'

'No,' grunted Gabriella, clawing the arm of the gentleman next to Rodrik. 'Not without permission from
the queen. We must escape.'

Ulrika grunted with annoyance. 'Very well, mistress.'
Obeying the queen's law might be the death of them.

Her three opponents came in again. They were
indeed fine blades, as Hermione had bragged. Each
stabbed at her in a different place so that she could not
block them all. She blocked none.

She let two of them stab her through an arm and a
leg while twisting away from the one that aimed at her
heart. The pain was excruciating, but what did it matter? A drink of blood and the wounds were soon no
more than a memory. She caught the wrist of the man
who had made the heart thrust and tore it open to the
bone with her claws.

He screeched and crumpled and she had his rapier.
Armed at last! The two others were drawing back for
second thrusts. She stamped into a straight lunge and
ran the first through the heart, then whipped the blade
out again and parried the slash of the second as it whis-
tled towards her head. He fell back, wide-eyed as her
blade snaked for his neck.

The violence and scent of flowing blood made her want to pursue him, but she held back. Gabriella had ordered her to escape, not kill.

'This way, mistress!'

Gabriella leapt back from Rodrik and von Zechlin and another of Hermione's gentlemen. The countess had a blade now too, and a dandy lay across a chair, bleeding on the upholstery.

'Stay back!' she cried.

The gentlemen didn't listen, and came in again.

Ulrika blocked the attack of von Zechlin's man, while Gabriella knocked away Rodrik's and von Zechlin's blades. The countess was no swordswoman, but her inhuman speed made up for any deficiencies of form. She kicked von Zechlin into the man Ulrika had earlier driven back. They went down together, slipping on an Araby rug but, as she faced Rodrik, he dashed the rapier from her hand with his heavier sword, and raised it to strike.

'Mistress!' cried Ulrika, and tried to push to her side, but the other men got in her way.

She hacked at them as Gabriella faced Rodrik and spread her arms.

'Truly, sir knight?' the countess asked, raising her chin. 'Will one bite truly turn you? Will you strike your sworn lady?'

Rodrik hesitated, sword quivering, eyes pained.

Gabriella snarled and struck, a pistol-shot slap across his cheek that slammed him to the floor. He gasped, stunned, staring up at the ceiling as the deep claw marks on the left side of his face welled with blood from ear to chin.

Ulrika pinked her two opponents and dived through them to Gabriella. The countess was reaching for Rodrik to finish him, but from behind came a streak of powder-blue silk.

'Mistress, look out!'

Gabriella turned just as Hermione slammed into her and the two women crashed down through a low table in an explosion of gilded splinters and crinolines. Hermione's claws were digging into Gabriella's throat.

'Mistress!' Ulrika leapt forwards, raising her rapier to run Hermione through.

'No!' gasped Gabriella.

Ulrika cursed and flung the blade away, then grabbed Hermione by her hair and the back of her dress and hauled her up. Hermione twisted in her grasp, spitting and clawing, and scratched Ulrika's face. Ulrika tried to peel her off, but she clung to her head and neck, tearing.

Ulrika wrenched back with her head, leaving Hermione holding nothing but her long wig, then threw her at the harpsichord. Hermione crashed into one of its legs and snapped it. The heavy instrument clanged down on top of her, splintering the parquet floor.

Von Zechlin and the surviving men cried out in alarm and ran for the instrument.

Gabriella laughed and took Ulrika's hand. 'Well done, beloved! Now, come!'

They ran for the door as clangs and sounds of struggle followed them. Only Famke blocked their way. She stood on guard, fangs and claws extended, but her eyes wide with fear.

'Step aside, girl,' said Gabriella calmly.

Famke's gaze twitched from her to Ulrika, then to the confusion behind them.

'Your mistress needs you,' said Ulrika.

Famke shot her a look that might have been gratitude, then ran around them towards the harpsichord. 'Mistress! Are you hurt?' she cried.

Ulrika threw open the door and she and Hermione made to run into the hall. Otilia was scrambling back from them, face white. She had obviously been listening at the key hole.

Gabriella shoved her aside and they ran for the front door. Behind them, Hermione's voice raised, shrill with rage.

'Get them! Leave me! Get them!'

The sounds of pursuit followed them as they burst out into the drive. Ulrika looked back into the house. Von Zechlin and two of his men were pelting down the hall for the door.

Ulrika stopped at the bottom of the steps as Gabriella opened the door to the coach. 'Should I kill them, mistress?' she asked, going on guard.

'In the street?' barked Gabriella. 'Foolish child. Get in!' She shoved back Lotte, who had peered out to see what the trouble was, and plunged into the coach, then rapped on the ceiling for the driver to go before Ulrika had got all the way in. 'Go! Fly!' she shouted.

Ulrika slammed the door as the coach rumbled forwards, then looked out the window and back. Von Zechlin and his men were spilling out of the house and skidding down the stairs after them. Rodrik came last, wheezing and holding his bloody face.

It looked for a moment as if the gentlemen were going to pursue the coach down the street, but von Zechlin looked around at the pre-dawn traffic and called them back. Ulrika smiled as they trudged back into the house with many an angry look. Having to maintain a respectable front must be such a disadvantage.

The last thing Ulrika saw as the house vanished from view around a corner was Otilia, the housekeeper, glaring in her direction, then slowly closing the door.

AFTER A FEW streets, Uwe the coachman's voice came from above. 'Where shall I take you, mistress?'

Gabriella sighed and leaned back against the bench, tidying her dishevelled coiffure. 'A very good question,' she said.

Ulrika turned to her, taking her hand. 'Mistress, let us leave this rat's nest and go back to Sylvania.' She gestured angrily back the way they had come. 'Who among them is worth saving? Rodrik is a vain fool, and Mistress Hermione is so concerned with her standing that she strikes out at those who would help her. While we have been trying to find the killer she has hampered us and thwarted us at every step. Let her die!'

Gabriella brushed dust from her skirts and adjusted her bodice. 'Would that I could,' she said. 'But one does not go against the orders of the queen. I must continue the investigation, with Hermione's help or without it.'

'But how?' Ulrika asked. 'We have no house, no allies. What will we do?'

Gabriella smiled, tired. 'We will have to make new allies.' She raised her voice and rapped on the wall. 'Uwe! South of the river! To the Wolf's Head!'

Ulrika's raised an eyebrow. 'Mathilda?'

Gabriella laughed. 'Hermione was so convinced the she-wolf and I were in collusion when we were not, and now she has driven us together. Her actions make realities of her fears.'

As THEY DROVE through the waking city, it was clear that the discovery of Dagmar's corpse had stirred Nuln's vampire hysteria to new heights. The charm sellers were thicker than ever on the streets, hawking garlic and leather collars and silver pendants in the shape of Sigmar's hammer or the twin-tailed comet. Broadsheet vendors cried their headlines.

'Brothel of Blood in the Handelbezirk!'

'Vampire harlot found dead!'

'Witch hunters close brothel, arrest whores by the dozen!'

Street-corner demagogues shrilled at the men and women trudging to their jobs on the river and in the manufactories.

'They walk among us!' shrieked one. 'From the high to the low! From the rich to the poor! And it is our lust that allows them in! Resist the harlot! Resist the mistress! Be pure in your own heart and ye shall be safe!'

'Can you trust your wife?' cried another, spraying spittle. 'Can you trust your daughter? All women are vampires! All beauty is witchery! All must burn!'

And it seemed that the people were taking the messages to heart, for everywhere she looked, Ulrika saw men and women eyeing each other suspiciously. A group of austerely dressed men watched with distrust as a pretty young apple-seller pushed past them with her barrow. A group of children ran after an old woman in widow's black, pointing and singing, 'Vampire! Vampire! Don't let her catch you!'

The very air seemed tense with fear and suppressed violence. Nuln, the city of cannon and blackpowder, seemed ready to explode.

IT WAS FULL dawn when they at last found their way through the milling slums of the Faulestadt and reached the Wolf's Head Tavern, then turned down the narrow alley between the tottering tenements and waited at the disguised gate that guarded the hidden court.

At their coachman's call, Red, the henna-haired woman who had been their escort on their last visit, peeked over the top of the wall and looked down at them.

'She's having her kip,' she called. 'And ain't t'be disturbed.'

'It is a matter of some urgency,' said Gabriella, leaning out with a veil over her face. 'And touches on her safety.'

Red's head pulled back and Ulrika heard a brief murmur of discussion behind the wall, then she popped back out.

'Y'better come in, then,' she said. 'Hang on.'

Ulrika and Gabriella sat back in their seats and waited as the false wall swung noisily in and the coach rumbled forwards into the muddy yard.

Lotte peered out through the louvres at the ramshackle buildings and rough men that surrounded them, her eyes growing wider by the moment. 'Are we safe here, mistress?' she asked.

'Safe?' said Gabriella. 'I cannot say. But we have so far received more courtesy here than in Hermione's gilded halls. Hopefully we shall also receive a fairer hearing.'

She and Ulrika fixed their veils in place and stepped from the coach, leaving Lotte to wait, then once again followed the red-headed hoyden as she led them down past the wards of misdirection and confusion to the subterranean world below the Wolf's Head, and then through the hidden door into Madam Mathilda's opulently shabby parlour. There was a wait there as their guide disappeared through a further door and had a conversation with Mathilda's maid, but at last the door opened again and Mathilda herself came out, barefoot and spilling out of a belted red satin robe. Her hair, previously a wild black mane, was wound around her head and wrapped in a pink scarf.

'Ladies,' she croaked, coming forwards with a bleary smile. 'I'm afraid y'never catch me at my best.' She sprawled opposite them on the chaise and put a bare leg up. 'What is it? Are y'here to tell me Hermione's coming for me after all?'

'She may indeed be,' said Gabriella. 'But we come seeking refuge and help, for she has decided we are her enemies as well.'

Mathilda's eyes widened at that. 'Do tell. Did y'tread mud on her carpets?'

Gabriella smiled and shook her head. 'She believes that we have conspired with you to kill all our other sisters here, and wants to execute us for it without trial. We had to fight our way out of her house.' She narrowed her lips. 'Madam Dagmar is dead. Have you heard?'

Mathilda nodded. 'Witch hunters closed down her place. We've been getting some of her less discriminating customers. Killed on the way back from our little chat, wasn't she? Did y'do it?'

Gabriella gave her a look. 'If I was going to kill any of my sisters here in Nuln, Dagmar would not be first on my list.'

Mathilda grinned. 'Nor mine. So, do we give Hermione what she's asking for and go to war?'

'No,' said Gabriella. 'It is precisely to prevent a war that I came here.' She sat forwards. 'We must find the true killer as soon as possible, before Hermione can gather her forces. If we can bring her proof of someone else's involvement, I think even this rift can be smoothed over.'

'Forgive me, mistress,' said Ulrika, frowning. 'You wish to smooth this over? She attacked you. I understand you don't want a war, but you should at least tell the queen what she has done. You should get permission to kill her.'

Gabriella patted Ulrika's hand. 'I will indeed tell the queen, beloved, but nothing will come of it. There are too few of us for her to execute her daughters for squabbling.'

'And four fewer just now,' interjected Mathilda.

Gabriella nodded. 'Indeed. Hermione will be reprimanded, perhaps demoted, but nothing else. Had she succeeded in killing me, yes, something would have been done. But she didn't succeed, so...' She shrugged.

Ulrika crossed her arms. She didn't like it. It didn't seem fair.

'So y'want my help finding this killer, then,' said Mathilda, scratching herself. 'Any leads so far?'

Gabriella shuddered. 'Well, he attacked us in our rooms this evening,' she said. 'And he is at least two persons.'

'Who?' said Mathilda, sitting up. 'What does he, er, they, look like?'

'We did not see,' said Gabriella. 'One of them is a warlock of some kind, a necromancer perhaps, and a living man, if his heartbeat was to be believed. He created an unnatural blackness that even our night sight was unable to pierce. The other is a foul, stinking undead monster – enormous and terribly strong, and I believe gifted with flight. It did not speak, however, so I know not if it is beast or man.'

'Attacking vampires in the dark,' muttered Mathilda. 'Clever. We ain't used to that.'

Gabriella turned to Ulrika. 'But though we did not see them, Ulrika believes she has found their lair.'

Mathilda smiled. 'That's better. Where is it?'

'In the Garden of Morr, in the Temple Quarter,' said Ulrika. 'We – I followed some clues there, and found a crypt that reeked of the monster's stench. But I was attacked by ghouls before I could investigate further. If we were to go back–'

'Ghouls?' said Mathilda. 'In Nuln's garden? I thought them raven monks took better care.' She scratched her scalp through her coiled hair with a long painted fingernail. 'Y'might be right about a necromancer being at the back of this. Maybe the big ripper is just his pet – a terror or a varghulf or some giant wight.'

'I have been thinking the same,' said Gabriella. 'The attacks have intelligence. They aren't the work of a mere beast. A cunning warlock with some monster on a leash would explain much. What I don't understand is their intent. Why do they attack us? Such servants of darkness are more often our allies than our enemies.'

'Maybe they're in the pay of some rival,' said Mathilda, then sat up, eyes bright. 'You don't suppose Hermione–?'

'No,' said Gabriella. 'As tempting as the thought is, she would be bringing as much trouble upon herself as the rest of us. The witch hunters are harassing us all, and the citizens are mad with fear, and check every shadow for us.'

'Aye,' said Mathilda, sinking back with a sigh. 'They're even killing girls who ain't vampires. A doxy down the street was burned last night just for being pale and having long dark hair. Dangerous times.'

'Then let us go back to the graveyard and finish it!' said Ulrika. 'Forearmed with what we know, we can kill it this time.'

Gabriella nodded, then looked at Mathilda. 'Will you help? We will need numbers to combat their ghouls, and claws to counter their claws.'

'And their sorcery?' asked Mathilda. 'I ain't quick with incantations and the like.'

'I shall take care of that,' said Gabriella.

Mathilda frowned for a moment, then nodded. 'Right, you'll have your numbers, and your claws. I don't want to be the last Lahmian in Nuln. I meant what I told miss toffy nose. I don't want nothing north of the river.' She stood, grunting. 'Let me find ye a place t'rest for the day. I'll get my lads and lasses together and we'll go have a walk in the garden once the sun goes down.'

She reached for a tarnished bell on a side table, but before she could ring it there was a thunder of footsteps on the stairs. Ulrika and the others went on guard as the door burst open. It was Red, panting with effort and fright.

'Mistress!' she cried. 'Witch hunters! Looking for vampires!'

Mathilda sneered. 'Let 'em look. They'll not find us down here.'

'But, mistress,' said the woman, wild-eyed. 'They've set the place on fire! The Wolf's ablaze!'

Mathilda cursed, then turned to Gabriella. 'You're the cause of this! They followed you!'

'No one followed me,' said Gabriella. 'I am sorceress enough for that, I think.' She looked up at the roof, as if she could see through it to who was behind the attack. 'Someone must have told them we had come.'

'Are you accusing one of my chicks?' asked Mathilda, her voice cold.

'No,' said Gabriella. 'But–'

'Hermione!' cried Ulrika.

Gabriella shook her head, but her face was troubled. 'I would hate to think it. We may kill each other, but to turn a sister over to the witch hunters?'

'Who else could it be?' asked Ulrika. 'Rodrik?'

Gabriella looked up at her with sad eyes. 'That is more likely, curse him.'

'I don't care who it was who done it!' shouted Mathilda. 'They're burning down my house because of you! You're bad luck! The both of you!'

She turned to her servant. 'Red, get everybody out. Through the hidey-holes. Take what you can and leave the rest. We'll meet at Suki's place. Got it?'

'Aye, mistress,' said Red, then turned and ran out the door again.

Gabriella stepped up to Mathilda. 'Your wards won't protect you down here?' she asked.

The madam pulled away from her, starting back towards her bedchamber. 'I told ye. I ain't quick with the incantations. The whole place'll be down around our heads in a minute. Now leave me be.'

'Mistress,' said Gabriella. 'I am truly sorry. I never intended–'

Mathilda turned on her. 'Never mind about that. Just get out. The door's behind you, and good luck with the flames.'

'But, sister,' said Gabriella. 'The graveyard. The killer. We have to work together.'

Mathilda laughed wildly. 'I've got a bit too much on my plate at the moment, dearie, thanks to you. I'm afraid yer on yer own until I get sorted out again. Now go, and don't come back. Yer a damned curse!'

She slammed out of the room, leaving Gabriella and Ulrika standing in the middle of it alone. Ulrika lifted her head. From above came the distinct smell of smoke.

'Merde,' said Gabriella, then held out her hand. 'Come, beloved, put your veil on. We must go.'

Ulrika took the countess's hand and let herself be led to the door. 'But… but the fire,' she said as they passed through into the vestibule and started up the stair.

'We have no other choice,' said Gabriella.

Ulrika moaned with fear. Fire could bring the true death. It was as terrifying an enemy as the sun. 'I hope the coach is still there,' she said.

'Hush, child,' said Gabriella. 'I must concentrate on these wards.'

They continued up the steps which, as before, seemed to branch and shift before them in a way that muddled the senses – at least they muddled Ulrika's senses. With her eyes closed and a hand on Ulrika's arm, the countess went up them slowly, but without faltering.

At every landing the smell of smoke got stronger and the sounds of fear and confusion louder. Shouts and cries of pain came through the walls, as well as the crackling roar and heat of fire. Ulrika tried to remain calm, though visions of being lost in the maze of stairways while they filled with smoke forced themselves upon her like unwanted suitors. She wanted to tear the walls down with her claws, but knew that would only bring her closer to the flames.

Pitiful screams and clangings made her cringe as they passed the level of the black hotel – hostages and kidnap victims shaking the bars of their cells and pleading to be let out. Maniacal laughter and hysterical sobbing came from the poppy den as flaming reality invaded the dreams of the lotus-eaters.

The last flight was just as she'd feared, opaque with smoke and red from reflected flames. She could not see the door at the top of the stairs. It might well be blocked.

'Cover your head with your cloak, my dear,' said Gabriella, as she did the same.

The countess's calm voice steadied her and she did as she asked, then they took hands again and ran up the steps together.

Despite the cloak, the smoke burned her eyes and her throat, and the heat from nearby flames roasted her face and arms. The last treads cracked and fell through as they trod on them and they tumbled forwards onto oven-hot planks. Ulrika scrambled up and pulled Gabriella up with her. They lurched on, entirely blind, then slammed into the door. It flew open, unbarred, and they staggered out into the muddy yard.

Looking out from under the hem of her cloak, Ulrika saw with a gasp of relief that the coach was still there, the coachman struggling to hold the terrified horses still. She and Gabriella ran for it through crowds of bashers and harlots who dashed hither and thither like headless chickens, shouting and weeping. Though it was full daylight now, the square was nearly as dark as night. Huge clouds of black smoke billowed up from the tavern and tenements around them and blacked out the sky, and what light there was came instead from the flames that roared from charred windows like dragon's breath. The entire ring of buildings around the yard was aflame.

'Very thorough, these saviours of humanity,' growled Gabriella as they stumbled on.

Lotte threw the door open as they reached the coach. 'Oh, mistress,' she cried. 'I was so worried!'

But just as they were about to enter, a loud bang from the secret gate made them pause and look out from under their cloaks. A phalanx of booted, long-coated witch hunters was pushing it open and striding

in through the gap, pistols and rapiers drawn. A warrior priest walked with them, a heavy book and
heavier hammer in his hands. The bashers and bawds
cowered back before these interlopers, pleading for
mercy, but the witch hunters paid them no mind.
Ulrika cursed as she saw that their leader was Captain
Meinhart Schenk, who they had previously met in
Hermione's parlour on their first night in Nuln. He
held a smoking pistol in one hand. Gabriella groaned.

Schenk pointed at the countess with the spent
pistol. 'The woman was right!' he called. 'She *is* here!'
He strode towards her. 'Lady, you are under arrest on
suspicion of being a vampire.'

'And you may arrest the other on the certainty of it,
captain,' said another witch hunter, stepping from the
ranks and pointing at Ulrika. 'For she has revealed her
true foul nature to me.'

Ulrika's heart sank as he raised his head and the
wide brim of his hat revealed his piercing grey eyes. It
was Templar Friedrich Holmann.

CHAPTER SEVENTEEN
A FLAME TO THE FUSE

'INTO THE COACH', barked Gabriella, then sprung through the door and rapped on the wall as Ulrika scrabbled in behind her and slammed the door. 'Ride out, Uwe. Ride them down!'

'Yes, countess,' cried the coachman, and with a whip crack and a neighing of horses, the coach jolted forwards and splashed through the muddy, crowded yard.

From outside came the cries of the witch hunters and a tattoo of pistol shots. Ulrika was afraid Uwe would be shot dead before they reached the gate, but somehow they missed and the coach bounced on. Lotte shrieked as a face appeared in Ulrika's window – a witch hunter, trying to open the door. Ulrika punched the man in the nose and he fell away. It hadn't been Holmann. Ulrika wished it had.

A hard crash knocked them all sideways as the coach flew through the half-closed gate, scraping one wall and splintering the woodwork, and then they were in the narrow alley, rocking and pitching, the smoking wooden walls whipping past inches from the windows on both sides. The cries and pounding footsteps of the witch hunters followed behind them. They were not giving up the chase.

Gabriella clutched the sides of the coach, her eyes staring at nothing. '"*The woman was right*",' she said. 'What woman did he mean?'

'Could it be anyone but Hermione?' asked Ulrika.

'She is the one woman it can't be,' said Gabriella shaking her head. 'Could Hermione name me without exposing herself? Did I not call her "cousin" in Schenk's presence? She would be admitting relations with a vampire.'

Sunlight stabbed into the coach as it wheeled wildly into the street and out of the shadows of the narrow walls and the cloud of smoke. Ulrika slammed the windows shut and slapped down the louvres, closing out the horrible light that bit at her through her clothes.

Her brief view of the street before the slats cut it off had shown a scene of chaos. Crowds of shabby slum dwellers surrounded the blazing inn, gaping at the fire, while others ran back and forth with buckets, and people on the roofs opposite tried to wet down their shingles and beat out flying sparks with straw brooms.

Uwe didn't slow, and Ulrika heard a heavy thud as one of the wheels hit a soft body. Cries of surprise and anger blared at them as they bounced on. Then Schenk's bellow came from behind.

'Stop that coach! Stop the vampires! They set the fire!'

A shocked babble rose from the crowd at the command, and the word 'vampire' ricocheted to and fro outside the coach like the buzz of a bee caught in a glass jar.

Gabriella snarled. 'Very clever, witch hunter.'

Fists began to thump on the sides of the coach, and Ulrika heard Uwe's angry shouts and the crack of his whip from above. Gabriella opened the louvres a fraction, just enough for Ulrika to see the milling bodies around them.

'Mistress, I'm frightened,' Lotte whimpered.

'Fear not, dearest,' said the countess. 'We will win free.' She raised her voice to a shout. 'Ride them down, Uwe! Do not stop!'

Ulrika swallowed. The coach was slowing and jarring as it bounced over screaming bumps. If it stopped, they would be overwhelmed. 'Use your power, mistress,' she said. 'Drive them away.'

'I dare not,' said Gabriella. 'They have a priest of Sigmar. He might sense it.'

'Isn't it a bit late for discretion?' Ulrika asked. 'They already know we are vampires!'

Gabriella shook her head. 'No. Until one bares one's fangs there is always a chance to deny it.'

Ulrika shot Gabriella a guilty look at that, but kept silent, afraid to admit exposing herself to Holmann.

The countess drew her bodice dagger and made to open her window. 'So we must fight like frightened ladies, not queens of the night,' she said. 'Ulrika, fix your veil.'

Ulrika adjusted her veil, which had come loose in their flight, then drew her own dagger and threw open her window as Gabriella did the same on her side of the coach.

Wincing in the sun's poisonous glare, Ulrika squinted through the thin black fabric at the knots of angry peasants who were trying to catch the speeding horses and climb up on the running board. Uwe's lash licked among them, striping faces and arms, but they were not deterred.

A man caught the sill of Ulrika's window and she stabbed the back of his hand with her dagger. As he fell away a woman shouted and tried to thrust a torch through the opening. Lotte shrieked. Ulrika kicked the door open and it cracked the woman on the shoulder, sending her careening into a few others.

A young man made a leap for the open door as Ulrika tried to close it again. She slammed it just as he caught the frame, and crushed his fingers. He howled in pain and she released him, then closed the door tight.

The coach broke through the fringe of the crowd and speeded up again. Ulrika breathed a sigh of relief and looked back. The wide-brimmed hats of the witch hunters were caught in the middle of the densely packed street, and she could hear Schenk screaming for them to get out of the way. She grinned. The mob was a double-edged sword, it seemed.

She started to draw her head back in, but then, out of the corner of her eye, she saw a familiar face and looked again. Von Zechlin! He and his men were trotting out from a side street near the Wolf's Head on horseback and spurring after the coach – and Rodrik was with them!

'Mistress!' she cried. 'Hermione's men, and Rodrik!'

Gabriella slid across the bench and looked over Ulrika's shoulder. 'I should have killed him,' she snarled. 'I should have killed them all.' She rapped on the wall. 'Uwe! Beware behind you!'

'I see them, mistress!'

The coach slewed around a tight corner, its iron-shod wheels skidding sideways through the wet mud of the unpaved street and throwing Ulrika and Lotte together, then straightened out and raced down a narrow crooked lane, but it was a slow clumsy thing compared to the mounts of Hermione's gentlemen, and they closed the gap swiftly.

Von Zechlin spurred ahead of the rest, shooting into the narrow gap between the coach and the shops that lined the street. Ulrika tried to slash at him as he passed, but missed. He pulled ahead and raised his sword to strike at the withers of the left-side horse.

'Fool,' cackled Gabriella, then. 'Left, Uwe! Left!'

There came a crack of the whip and the coach swerved abruptly, crushing von Zechlin and his horse against a half-timbered wall. Horse and mount went down together in a pinwheel of limbs and ploughed up a bow-wave of mud as they hit the ground.

Ulrika laughed and looked back. The rest of Hermione's gentlemen were pulling up to see to their fallen captain, but one came on, his horse leaping the wreckage.

'Rodrik is still with us, mistress,' said Ulrika. 'And gaining.'

Gabriella looked out of her window, then nodded. 'Now I think we can use sorcery.'

She closed her eyes and curled her fingers around each other, then tightened them into a white-knuckled grip while muttering under her breath. It looked like she was choking someone.

Ulrika looked back. She was. Though his horse was plunging on, Rodrik was clawing at his neck and turning purple. He could barely keep his seat. Ulrika eagerly waited for him to fall, but he reined in instead, then bowed over his horse's neck, hacking and coughing. The coach lurched as Uwe took it around another corner and she was thrown back into her seat. When she looked out again, Rodrik was out of sight. She cursed.

'Did you kill him?' she asked Gabriella.

'I doubt it,' the countess replied. 'He has dropped back out of my reach.' She smiled. 'Still, he will think twice about following, I believe.' She raised her voice. 'Uwe! Slower now, but keep twisting the trail!'

'Aye, mistress.'

Lotte and Ulrika closed the windows again and the three of them rode in silence for a few moments as Uwe turned the coach left and right and left through the tiny, winding streets of the slums. But then, into that silence came an unsettling noise. At first it sounded like the sea, heard from over a distant hill, then it sounded like the roar of battle, then like some wild orgiastic celebration, the howling of beastmen in the woods, drunk on rage and violence.

The coach jolted to an abrupt stop and Uwe's voice came to them from above. 'You'd better see this, mistress.'

Gabriella opened her window and Ulrika followed suit, looking ahead. They were in a narrow alley, deep in the shadow of tenements that rose five storeys high on either side of them, but twenty paces ahead was a more open street, and parading down it was a throng of maddened humanity.

Ulrika remembered seeing similar mobs when she had been in Praag during the siege – crowds whipped into fearful fury by street-corner firebrands who preached murder and mayhem against anyone who wasn't with them. They seemed rabid with hate, roaring and shaking make-shift weapons over their heads.

'Kill the vampires!' they cried. 'Burn the vampires!'

Ulrika winced as she saw that a quartet of them carried a half-naked girl on their shoulders, tied to a chair and horribly beaten. The rest pelted her with cobbles and muck and spit curses at her. She couldn't have been more than fifteen. At the same time, though she was loath to admit it, she felt a shameful rush of relief. If the mob thought they had caught their quarry, then perhaps they wouldn't pay any attention to Gabriella's coach. Then she saw that such a hope was a foolish fantasy. The mob was too voracious to be satisfied with a single victim.

As she watched, a handful of men pounced on a middle-aged woman trying to go the other way down the street. She struggled, but they pinned her down and pried open her mouth, looking at her teeth then, apparently disappointed at what they found, they left the woman lying there weeping and ran off in search of other prey.

Ulrika swallowed, trying to force down a lump of dread that filled her breast. Nuln had been waiting for this. The rumours of vampires had been the dry wood of a pyre, piling higher and higher in the public square over the last weeks, waiting patiently for someone to burn. Now that fool Captain Schenk, with his cry of

'Vampire!' had set the spark to the tinder, and the pyre was ablaze, but it was rapidly growing out of control. If it went unchecked, she feared all Nuln would burn.

'We can't stay here, mistress,' called Uwe. 'We have to get away.'

'Aye,' said Gabriella, thinking. 'But to where, and how?'

'Out of the city?' asked Ulrika, hopefully.

Gabriella shook her head. 'I must see Hermione again. I cannot imagine that she sent the witch hunters after us, but if she did, I must know. That would be a crime I could take to the queen.' She raised her voice again. 'Uwe. To the bridge. But keep to the side streets.'

'Aye, mistress.'

Ulrika heard him hop down from his bench, and start guiding the horses around in a circle in the tight space.

'Won't the witch hunters be watching the bridge?' she asked. 'Isn't there another?'

'There is,' said Gabriella. 'But the island of the Iron Tower lies midway along it, and the Iron Tower is the witch hunters' garrison. I am not brave enough for that, I'm afraid. We will just have to hope that we reach the main bridge before Schenk does.'

'And if we do not?' Ulrika asked.

Gabriella shook her head, then laughed, an edge of hysteria creeping into her voice. 'We'll cross that bridge when we come to it.'

They sat back in their seats and waited while Uwe backed the coach and made another quarter-turn, the howling of the mob still echoing into the alley. Ulrika prayed to her father's gods that no one would look their way and decide they looked like potential victims. If they did, it would be over. They would be trapped and unable to run.

The countess tapped a nervous foot, her eyes shifting here and there as if chasing fractured thoughts. Then, a moment later, she seemed to grow calmer. She closed the louvres completely, then turned to Lotte, who sat silent and white-faced as she had through the whole chase, her hands knit together in her lap.

'Lotte, my dear,' said Gabriella. 'I want to trade clothes with you. Take off your skirt and bodice.'

Lotte's eyes widened. 'Mistress?'

Gabriella smiled reassuringly and began to unlace her points. 'Come now, darling. All will be well. Be a dear.'

'Y-yes, mistress,' the maid quavered. She began unhooking the eyes that held her neat grey top closed.

Ulrika looked from one to the other as what the countess was asking slowly dawned on her. She meant for Lotte to be mistaken for her if the mob caught them. She was going to give the girl up to the dogs, and Lotte was going along with it.

'Mistress?' she said uneasily.

'Don't worry,' said Gabriella, shrugging out of her beaded velvet bodice. 'I will provide for you if the need arises.'

Ulrika paused. That hadn't been what she was going to ask. But what she would have said died on her lips as well. Arguing for the life of a blood slave was foolish. Nothing would change. She would only anger Gabriella and embarrass Lotte. And given a moment to think about it, she knew she too would happily sacrifice any number of maids to save Gabriella, or herself. They were only animals after all. It was just the premeditated coldness of it that made her wince. She did not like cruelty. When she had hunted with her father she had killed her deer quickly and cleanly. She did not like to see them twitch with pain, or be torn apart by the hounds.

Uwe got the coach turned about at last, and they moved off down the alley to begin their careful side-winding through the slums, always being sure that the mob was not about to cross their path. Ulrika felt like they were caught in some sort of human flood, and were seeking high ground and easy fords across a dangerous river. The panic had spread throughout all the neighbourhoods south of the river, and people seemed to be using the excuse of the vampire hunt for any mischief they could imagine. Shop fronts were being smashed in and looting was rampant. Peering out through the slatted window, Ulrika saw men rolling kegs of beer ahead of them and laughing. Others were dragging old women out of houses and flinging them in the mud, and everywhere was the sweet pork stink of burning flesh.

As they passed a pyre that burned in the middle of a grimy area of forges and manufactories, Ulrika snarled, transferring some of her anger at Gabriella's cold-blooded actions to the villains who had set a pair of men on fire, bound together as if they were embracing. She shivered. Today was a day to hide away if you were odd or beautiful or did not often mix with your fellows. The outcasts were burning in Nuln, branded vampires as a matter of convenience. It made her want to leap out of the coach and butcher the mobs to the last cowardly man and finger-pointing woman.

A street later the change of clothes had been completed, and Gabriella was dressed in Lotte's prim uniform and Lotte wore Gabriella's rich bodice and beaded skirts. Neither looked quite convincing in their parts. Gabriella's eyes were too sharp and aware to be those of a demure maid, and Lotte's were too wide and frightened to be those of an imperturbable aristocrat, but Ulrika doubted the mob would look at their faces.

She glanced down at her own beautiful dresses, and Gabriella's earlier words finally sank home. How would the countess provide for her? What could she do to save her, dressed as she was? A chill ran down her spine as a thought came to her. Perhaps Gabriella had only been soothing her as she had Lotte. Perhaps she meant to throw her to the dogs as well.

The coach slowed and stopped again. All three of them looked up, nervous.

'We are coming to the Brukestrasse, mistress,' came Uwe's voice. 'The bridge is only two streets north, but there is a... a crowd.'

Gabriella bit her lip. 'Go forward on foot and look for witch hunters on the bridge, then report back to me.'

'Aye, mistress.'

They heard Uwe climb down and trot off down the street. Ulrika's jaw clenched as she looked out through the half-closed louvres. Men stood in the doors of the workshops, watching ne'er-do-wells running by towards the fun. So far no one had paid any notice of the coach, but all it would take was a single glance, and if they were discovered before Uwe returned they would be dead – oarless in the flood with the burning light of the sun all around them like a sea of flame.

The seconds crawled by. They could hear shouting and screaming and laughing from the Brukestrasse – the mob at their horrible work. Ulrika wondered if Schenk had any remorse about stirring up the populace as he had. The old witch hunter adage was 'better ten innocent men die than one creature of darkness live'. Well, she was certain that more than ten innocent men had died today, and she doubted Schenk had caught any creatures of darkness – at least not yet.

Quick steps came back to the coach and Uwe stepped up on the running board to speak through the louvres. 'I'm sorry, mistress,' he said, out of breath. 'There are four witch hunters at the bridge, and the area around it is filled with troublemakers.'

Gabriella nodded, her eyes dark. 'Then I suppose we must try the Iron Bridge after all. Turn about.'

'Aye, mistress.'

They heard him climb back up to his bench and then flick the reins at the horses. The coach rumbled forwards and started to arc around in the narrow street but, just as they were sideways to traffic, Ulrika heard shouts and laughing and running boots coming towards them from the direction they wanted to go. She looked through the louvres.

Five young men in apprentices' smocks were sprinting down the street with iron pokers and spit forks in their hands, laughing and looking back over their shoulders. A burly man in a smith's leather apron was puffing behind them, shouting at them to stop.

'Give them things back!' he cried. 'Y'didn't pay for 'em!'

The young men jeered at him and thumbed their noses.

'We need 'em to hunt vampires!' a blond one shouted. 'You're not going to stop us hunting vampires, are you?'

They turned back to find Gabriella's coach in their way.

'Move that snob-wagon!' shouted the blond boy.

'Out of the way,' cried another.

'Sorry, lads,' said Uwe. 'Street's blocked that way. Just trying to turn around.'

'Well, y'picked a good time for it, Ranald curse ye.'

Ulrika heard thuds and gruntings and the whickering of the horses as the boys ran around the back and the front of the coach. Then one of them hopped up on the running board, laughing, and tried to poke his fingers through the window slats.

'Who y'hiding in there, anyway?' he said. 'Is she pretty?'

Ulrika instinctively slapped at his fingers, then shut the louvres with a snap as he jerked back.

'Hoy!' the boy cried, and she heard him backing away. 'Snooty bitch!'

'Come on, Dortman!' called one of his friends. 'Yer laggin'.'

'But she hit me!' he cried, running off. 'She closed the window and…' His voice trailed off and his footsteps slowed, then suddenly sped up again. 'Hey, lads! Wait a moment!'

CHAPTER EIGHTEEN
EXPLOSION AND AFTERMATH

'MERDE,' SAID GABRIELLA, and closed her eyes. Then, 'Uwe! Away! Quickly!'

'Aye, mistress.'

The whip cracked again and the horses pulled the coach through its arc faster, but not fast enough. Too quickly, the boys' footsteps came running back, and more with them. Ulrika's heart sank.

'She closed the window, I tell you!' the one called Dortman was shouting. 'She closed out the sun!'

'The coach from the inn was black, weren't it?' asked another voice.

'Aye,' said a third. 'And they never found it!'

'Hoy, coachman!' shouted the blond boy. 'Hold on a minute!'

Uwe whipped up the horses and the coach lurched ahead, gaining speed. The boys responded like hounds that have flushed the fox. They bayed and hallooed, and called to everyone else on the street.

'Vampires! The coach! Stop them! Kill them!'

'Lock the windows and fix the louvres closed,' said Gabriella.

Ulrika took one last look out before she complied. There were nearly two score people running after the coach now, and more joining from every workshop they passed. She hooked the window latch, then had to catch herself as the coach hurtled around a corner and she was thrown against the wall. Lotte crashed into her, then clung to her, whimpering.

There was a splintering bang outside as they struck something, and angry cries, then another smash from the other side of the coach. Above them, Uwe cursed.

'I'm sorry, mistress,' he called. 'I've gone wrong. It's too tight here.'

The coach slowed drastically, grinding on both sides, and the sounds of the mob grew loud behind them.

'It widens out just ahead,' Uwe said. 'Hang on!'

The coach ploughed forwards, but too slowly. The shouts and boot thuds of the crowd flowed around them, and cries of 'Catch the horses!' and 'Bring him down!' were loud outside of the windows.

'Lotte,' said Gabriella quietly. 'Come here. Bare your neck.'

The maid looked at Gabriella fearfully, then reluctantly let go of Ulrika and crossed to Gabriella's bench, pulling aside the fancy lace that only recently the countess had worn.

The coach shuddered to a stop as Gabriella took the girl in her arms and bit her neck. Lotte moaned and closed her eyes, her arms circling the countess's waist. Outside, Ulrika could hear Uwe shouting at the mob and lashing with his whip.

'Stay back, y'jackals!' he cried. 'Get away or I'll shoot!'

Heavy thumps battered the sides of the coach, and harsh voices screamed for the doors to be opened. The door handles rattled, then broke. Uwe's pistol cracked and a man screamed. Cries of 'Kill him!' welled up all around.

Gabriella stood and eased Lotte back onto Ulrika's bench. The girl was still swooning.

'Feed,' the countess said. 'We may need all our strength.'

Ulrika hesitated unhappily, then extended her fangs and bit where Gabriella had bitten, drinking from Lotte as the girl slumped limp against her, sighing in ecstasy. Gabriella sat down again and began murmuring and weaving her fingers in arcane patterns.

Outside Uwe was shouting. 'Put me down, you bastards! Put me–' His words broke off in a gasp, and then a cry of pain, and the sick thuds of wood and iron on soft flesh battered Ulrika's ears, curdling the warm comfort of Lotte's blood.

'Now the coach!' shouted someone, and the battering on the walls grew even fiercer. A club splintered the louvres. Spearheads of sunlight lanced through the cracks.

'That's enough,' said Gabriella. 'Now give her to me.'

Ulrika looked up and blinked in surprise. Gabriella was almost invisible, little more than a shadow against the leather bench as she stood. She looked down at herself. She too was translucent.

'Give her to me,' Gabriella said. 'And when I say, open the door, then draw your feet up onto the bench and sit very still. Do you understand me?'

Ulrika swallowed, then nodded and lifted the woozy Lotte to her feet. Gabriella took the maid's arm and stood her in front of the left-side door. Another club smashed at the louvres. The splinters sprayed all of them. The coach rocked under them. It felt as if it might tip at any moment.

'Open it,' said Gabriella.

Ulrika reached for the lock, then paused, frightened of what was to come. It was like opening the door to a wolf pack. She steeled herself and gripped the lock.

Gabriella kissed Lotte on the cheek as Ulrika turned the latch. 'Thank you for your service, beloved,' she whispered, then kicked the door open and shoved the girl out into the seething mob. They roared as she landed among them.

Ulrika choked at the suddenness of it, and stared as the crowd pounced upon Lotte and bore her up, tearing at her fancy clothes and beating her with their cudgels and tools.

'Burn her!' shouted the boy called Dortman. 'Burn the vampire!'

The blond boy struck Lotte with his stolen poker, breaking her arm with a snap. The maid shrieked with pain.

'Lotte!' Ulrika cried.

'Sit back, curse you!' hissed Gabriella. 'Feet up, and be still!'

Ulrika clenched her fists but did as she was told, pressing back against the bench and drawing her feet up, then tucking her skirts out of the way. Gabriella mirrored her position on the other bench, and they sat there silent as outside the mob raged around Lotte, kicking and beating her and throwing her around like a rag doll on a storm-tossed sea. Frustrated fury boiled in Ulrika's chest. She wanted to leap out and tear the mob apart as they were tearing apart Lotte. She wanted to push Gabriella out and see her suffer the same fate. It wasn't fair! It wasn't right! No one should have to suffer so before death, and particularly not a girl who had been so loyal and sweet in life.

Those on the edges of the crowd, too far from Lotte to join in the savage sport, quickly looked for other fun. A handful of men and women poked their heads into the open coach door and glanced around inside. One saw Gabriella's fan on the floor and snatched it. Two others seemed to look directly at Ulrika, and she thought for an instant that Gabriella's spell hadn't worked, but then they drew back and started to climb up to the roof.

'Lotsa swag up here!' called one. 'Look at all them trunks!'

'Take the horses!' shouted another.

Gabriella ground her teeth as the coach rocked and her valises and wardrobes were thrown down to smash on the street. 'Thieving dogs,' she growled.

But then came a call that made Ulrika's blood-warmed stomach go cold again.

'Smash the coach! Take its wood for the fire!'

She looked over at the translucent Gabriella as the crowd roared their approval at this suggestion, and saw that she too was alarmed. The countess turned to the right-hand door, which remained locked, and cracked open the louvres to peek through as the mob began to rock the coach back and forth.

'We are against the wall of some sort of workshop,' Gabriella whispered, clutching her seat. 'We will go out and into that. Be sure not to bump anyone.'

'Yes, mistress,' said Ulrika.

'And keep your head covered. The illusion is no protection from sunlight.'

Gabriella turned the lock with diaphanous fingers and opened the door slowly, waiting for a reaction. None came, except for the continued cheering and rocking of the coach. She hopped out. Ulrika threw her cloak over her head and followed right behind her, but the coach lurched under her feet just as she jumped, and she fell heavily against a half-timbered wall. Gabriella pulled her up and they froze, pressed against the plaster. There were rioters to the left and right of them, shoving at the sides of the coach and putting their shoulders to the wheels. Ulrika could have reached out and touched them.

Gabriella whispered in her ear. 'The door is to the right. We will go when it is clear.'

Ulrika nodded. She hoped it would be soon. The sun was gnawing at her through her clothes like she was covered in ants. She looked right. Two wooden steps led up to an open door with a sign in the shape of a stretched cow skin over it – a tannery. A few men in aprons and rolled sleeves stood in the door, staring out at the riot and holding clubs, ready to defend their business if the mob turned its attention their way.

Just then, with a deafening cheer from the crowd, the coach went up and over and smashed down on its side. The rioters ran forwards laughing wildly, and began to smash it and kick it, for all the world like primitive hunters dancing around their kill.

'Now!' hissed Gabriella, and led Ulrika towards the door, tiptoeing around the backs of the rioters.

There was just enough room between the three men who stood in the door for a slim person to slip through, but Gabriella and Ulrika, with the layers of crinolines under their dresses, did not have slim silhouettes. Gabriella paused and looked around for another door. There was none. She cursed under her breath then began to gather her skirts about her as tightly as she could.

Ulrika did the same, edging awkwardly away as two women surged towards her, fighting over a bodice from one of Gabriella's trunks.

Gabriella crept up the steps and edged through the three men, ducking and bending to avoid elbows and the ends of cudgels. Ulrika took a steadying breath and followed. She passed through the first two men without any trouble, but the third stood behind them, peering over their shoulders, and she had to slip sideways almost directly in front of his face. He shifted just as she was about to pass him, and she stepped back, bumping the back of a man she had already passed.

She ducked aside and into the tannery as he turned, scowling at the man behind him.

'Y'want to go out there, do ye?' he snapped.

Ulrika inched to Gabriella and they watched, nervous.

'Not I,' said the man at the back.

'Then quit yer shovin'.'

'I didn't shove ye.'

Gabriella's hand curled around Ulrika's and squeezed, waiting for them to look around, but the man at the front only snorted and turned back to watch the madness outside.

Ulrika and Gabriella let out silent breaths, then Gabriella tugged on Ulrika's hand and pointed to a stair that rose along a side wall to the left.

'We will find a place here to wait out the day,' she said.

Ulrika looked around as they crossed the room to it. The place had a high ceiling with gantries and chains hanging from it, and rows of huge round vats on the floor. From the vats came an overpowering stench of urine and excrement that made Ulrika cringe and gag. She wondered that she hadn't noticed it before, but she supposed her blind panic and fear of imminent death had blocked it out.

Men were stomping around in the vats, their breeches rolled up above the knee, and pushing raw cow hides down into the muck with long poles. Ulrika shuddered. She couldn't imagine a worse job. They must have no sense of smell whatsoever.

Gabriella led her up the stairs to the first floor. This was a large loft with wide open windows. Wooden frames with cured skins stretched across them were stacked to the ceiling. Some workers were stretching more hides in one corner, but most were at the windows, looking down at the street and talking amongst themselves.

Gabriella shook her head. 'This won't do,' she murmured, and turned to a second flight of stairs.

At the top was a dark corridor lined with doors covered with leather curtains. Gabriella and Ulrika crossed to one and looked through it. Inside was a dark room piled high with finished hides. Ulrika looked into another. It was the same, only the hides were dyed a different colour.

'This is better,' said Gabriella, and held aside a curtain. 'Come.'

Ulrika ducked into the room. It was long and narrow, with the skins piled on either side of a narrow path. At the far end was a shuttered window, and from it came the cheers and jeers of the mob. Ulrika walked towards it. She didn't want to look, but she couldn't stop herself. She climbed over a pile of skins at the end of the row and put her eyes to the cracks in the shutter.

Down below her in the street the crowd was swirling like a whirlpool around a bright central vortex. A pyre, made from timber torn from the coach, had been built where the narrow street widened out into a small square, and flame was beginning to lick the edges of the wood. In the centre of it knelt Lotte, bruised and naked, with her arms tied around the circumference of an empty wooden barrel as if she was a drunk hugging a keg of beer, and though she was beaten and helpless, the crowd still pelted her with rocks and filth, and shouted curses at her.

And still through all the noise Ulrika could hear a pitiful little voice moaning over and over, 'Mistress. Mistress, help me. Help me.'

Ulrika turned away as the flames crept closer, wishing for the first time that her inhuman hearing wasn't so acute. Gabriella was looking at her with sad eyes. She had become solid and opaque again.

'I'm sorry, child,' she said.

Ulrika lowered her head. 'Must we be so cruel?'

'We must survive,' said Gabriella, then stepped forwards and took Ulrika in her arms. 'We may try our best to do so without causing unnecessary pain to our swains and servants, but when it is a choice between us and them, there is no question.' She sighed. 'If I could, I would go down there and give Lotte a swift end to her suffering, but I cannot.'

'But is there no spell?' Ulrika asked. 'Surely you could kill her from here.'

Gabriella hesitated then shook her head. 'I could, but I will not. Sorcery is dangerous. I use it only when I myself am in peril. To do otherwise would be to risk mishap or discovery.'

Ulrika tensed and made to speak, but Gabriella shushed her, stroking her hair. 'We must be selfish, beloved. The world wants us dead. Nature itself abhors us. We cannot allow anything to threaten the fragile thread that holds us to this world, not even kindness.'

Ulrika butted her head against Gabriella's shoulder, angry and wishing she could weep. 'I wish you had killed me. This is no way to live.'

Gabriella lifted Ulrika's chin and looked her levelly in the eye. 'I told you once before that you had only to walk in the sun to end it. I will not stop you if you wish to go down and die to spare Lotte her pain.' She stepped back. 'Is that what you wish?'

Ulrika turned towards the window, visions of death and vengeance filling her head. She could kick through the shutters and leap down amongst the mob. She could put Lotte out of her agony with a single blow, then kill as many of that hateful pack of filth as she might before the sun and the flames of the pyre burned her to death. It would be a good end, a grand end, but it would be an end all the same. Was she ready to be done with her life? Was she ready for what was to come after? If what Gabriella had told her about what happened to vampires when they died was true, the pain Lotte was suffering would be nothing compared to that which awaited her. Could she face that, for the life of a maid?

Ulrika dropped to her knees with a sob. 'I am weak,' she rasped. 'I am a coward.'

Gabriella knelt beside her, putting her arms around her. 'You are stronger and braver than most of us, dear heart, and more compassionate. Most wouldn't even consider it. Most would call you a fool, but I love you for it. A vampire must sometimes kill to live. It is our nature. But it is when we do so without regret, without conscience, that we are most a danger to ourselves. If you can hold on to this affection for humanity without letting it rule you, you will live long and grow great among us.'

Ulrika hugged her and nodded against her breast. 'Thank you, mistress,' she mumbled. 'I will try.'

'I know you will,' said Gabriella, then paused before speaking again. 'Though I fear you have already failed at least once.'

Ulrika frowned, confused, then lifted her head. 'What do you mean, mistress?'

Gabriella looked down at her, her face set and cold. 'Tell me of this young witch hunter who singled you out at Mathilda's place. How does he know you? How does he know you are a vampire?'

CHAPTER NINETEEN
MASQUERADE

ULRIKA LOOKED AT Gabriella with widening eyes. All the warmth had gone from her voice, and all the sympathy from her gaze. It was as if a door had closed.

'Don't make me pull it from you,' she said when Ulrika did not speak.

'No, mistress.' Ulrika hung her head. 'I won't. I… I met him while chasing the warlock in the sewers. He was after him too.'

'You didn't mention him before,' said Gabriella.

'I… I didn't think it was important,' Ulrika stammered.

Gabriella raised an eyebrow. 'No?'

'I tricked him,' said Ulrika. 'I made him think I was a vampire hunter, and we parted ways with him none the wiser.'

'He seemed wiser today.'

'Yes, I…' Ulrika dug her nails into her palms. 'We met again. He was at the plague house when I discovered the

275

place of Mistress Alfina's death there. I… I used him. He knew that the robes I found were those of a priest of Morr, and I let him interrogate the priests and lead me to the graveyard and the crypt where I believe the killer hides.'

'How very Lahmian of you,' said Gabriella coolly. 'But your mask must have slipped, yes?'

'We were attacked by ghouls,' said Ulrika. 'They were going to kill him. I… I let my claws out to save him.'

'And he saw this,' said Gabriella.

Ulrika nodded miserably. 'He called me a monster and tried to kill me.'

'Yet you did not kill him.'

Ulrika shook her head. 'I could not. He… he is a good man.'

'And our mortal enemy.' Gabriella sighed and pulled Ulrika close again. 'Beloved, I understand. It has happened before. In this strange instance you find yourself on the same side as this man, and he is stalwart and brave, and from the little I saw of him, not unhandsome. You fight side by side with him and, as you are a warrior born, you are loath to let a comrade die. But he is *not* your comrade, and you cannot think of him that way.'

She lay back against the mound of skins and drew Ulrika down with her. 'You are not human any more, my dear. Though you look it, and sometimes may feel it, you are not. You cannot have normal relations with them. There are only four options when dealing with men: fool them, kill them, enslave them or give them the blood kiss. A human who knows what you are and is not bound to you cannot be trusted – and a witch hunter least of all – as you have learned to your regret today.'

'I'm sorry, mistress,' said Ulrika. 'I won't let it happen again.'

Gabriella squeezed her hand. 'It is a hard lesson to learn, I know, but it must be learned. You will have nothing but misery and pain otherwise. I speak from experience in this.' She curled against Ulrika. 'Now come, rest your head. There is nothing for us to do but wait until dark. Then we will cross the river and speak to Hermione.'

Ulrika closed her eyes, but the shouting of the mob and the crackling of flames from out in the square made it hard for her to sleep.

AFTER THE DAY's mad frenzy, the setting of the sun brought a frightened, unnatural silence to Nuln. As Ulrika and Gabriella crept through them, the chilly streets of the Industrielplatz were dark and deserted except for the blackened debris of the day's excesses. Even the forges, which usually roared day and night, had gone cold and quiet. Everywhere they saw shattered windows and broken tools and clubs, and the sign of Sigmar's hammer painted crudely on the fronts of businesses and workshops as a ward against the undead.

The witch hunters were still on guard at the great bridge, stopping every coach and questioning every woman who crossed it, so they turned about and trudged a weary mile back the way they had come to the bridge of the Iron Tower, but that too was watched.

'They will undoubtedly have our descriptions,' said Gabriella, drawing back into the shadow of a foundry to think. 'And may be carrying silver or garlic or daemonroot to test us. I don't care to risk it. They will not be so polite here as they were in Hermione's parlour.'

'Can we take a boat?' asked Ulrika. 'There must be some fisherman willing to take us across.'

Gabriella shuddered. 'An open boat is too dangerous. Vampires are not partial to running water. No. I have a better way, I think.' She turned south and started walking back towards the Faulestadt, the warren of filthy streets and tottering tenements they had fled only that morning. 'A Lahmian way.'

'SLUMMING, M'LADY?' a leering fellow in printers' sleeves asked Ulrika. 'Tired o' weak Altestadt wine, and lookin' fer strong Faulestadt beer?'

'They wearing it short north of the river?' chimed in his mate, a fisherman by the smell of him, who was grinning at Ulrika's hair. 'We wear it long down here!' he said, and slapped his leg near the knee.

'Her ladyship is waiting for a gentleman of the watch,' said Gabriella in a prim voice that matched the maid's uniform that she still wore, 'who has asked her to come to this establishment and identify the men who stole a necklace and her wig from her.'

The men's eyes widened at this, and they suddenly found they had business elsewhere.

Ulrika let out a sigh of relief.

'Thank you, mistress,' she whispered. 'I did not know what a lady would say.'

'Call me Gabby, here, m'lady,' said Gabriella, still in her maid's voice. 'And a lady would let her maid answer for her. Men of that sort are not to be spoken to by a woman of your stature.'

They were sitting at a corner table in the Pitcher and Ramrod, a tavern of the sort that ladies of quality did not enter, with or without escort, and were therefore garnering their fair share of odd glances and dirty remarks as they watched the vulgar customs of the boisterous clientele.

'This is why the streets are quiet!' said Gabriella, raising her voice to be heard over the din. 'They've all come here!'

Ulrika nodded. It was true. At the trestle tables under the low smoke-blackened beams, jostling crowds of bravos and bashers and begrimed foundry men drank and laughed with feverish energy, while painted strumpets teased money and drink from them and sometimes took them upstairs. Other men babbled loudly about vampires and burnings and bragged of their part in the day's happenings, and with each telling, the fangs got longer and the claws more cruel. Ulrika shook her head, bemused and disgusted. *They huddle together around the fire like savages scared of the dark,* she thought.

Gabriella seemed to pay no attention to the stories or the men who told them. She only watched the comings and goings of the harlots as they sashayed around the room, plying their trade, while Ulrika waited, stiff and ill at ease. It wasn't the place that made her uncomfortable, though the burgeoning panic that bubbled beneath the chatter and cheer did set her teeth on edge. She had been in rougher taverns than this many times – the White Boar in Praag, for instance – and had happily mucked in with soldiers and ruffians all her life. It was what Gabriella meant to have her do that didn't sit well with her.

'Mistress,' she said at last, leaning in to speak in Gabriella's ear. 'I see how this ruse will work for you, but I… I have never played the bawd before. I don't know how to do it. I fear I will ruin your game.'

Gabriella turned to her and looked her up and down, then smiled slyly. 'It's true. Your height and strong bones give you a certain solemn beauty when you are dressed as a lady, but you will look a clown in harlot's fripperies.' She frowned for a moment, then laughed. 'Ah! I have it. You shall wear breeches again – as you are most comfortable that way – and play my drake.'

Ulrika raised her eyebrows. 'What is a drake?'

Gabriella grinned. 'You are not familiar with the term? Strange. A drake is a gentleman of the female sex, a companion and protector of ladies of easy virtue who don't trust men. They watch their backs and make sure they are paid for their work.'

Ulrika blinked, flustered, as she took in the meaning of the words, and Gabriella laughed. 'Fear not, child. The part will require little from you. You must only look sullen and dangerous, and you have accomplished that already.'

Ulrika looked away, embarrassed. *A gentleman of the female sex?* To her, her mannish clothes had always been a matter of pragmatism. She was a warrior, raised by a warrior. Therefore, she wore a warrior's clothes, and had come to find them comfortable. She had never associated them with anything else, or worried what others might construe about her because of them. People could think what they might, for she knew who she was, and what and whom she found attractive. Strange then that the idea of pretending to be what she already appeared was so discomforting, but it was so.

At last she shrugged. She might not care for it, but Gabriella was right. It was a role she could play – certainly better than she could play a flirt.

A little while later, Gabriella put a hand on Ulrika's arm and nodded across the room. 'Here we are,' she said. 'A perfect pair for our necessity.'

Ulrika followed her glance. A tall, thin young basher, roaring drunk, was staggering after a smirking harlot who was leading him by the belt towards the stairs. Ulrika wrinkled her nose. The man might be the right height and build, but his clothes were both garish and grimy, and the grease from his lank, black hair had darkened his collar. She shuddered at the thought of the vermin that no doubt infested him.

The couple stumbled up the stairs to the first floor. Ulrika looked to Gabriella. The countess waited until they were out of sight, then stood.

'Come, m'lady,' she said, sniffing. 'We will wait upstairs for the gentleman. I will not have these ruffians' eyes upon you.'

Ulrika stood and followed her as she started up the steps. A few eyes followed them, and a few knowing grins, but most were too busy with their own debaucheries to notice.

They reached the first floor just in time to see a door closing halfway down the candle-lit corridor. Gabriella padded ahead swiftly and Ulrika hurried behind. From all around them came giggles and amorous moanings and groanings. They stopped at the door and Gabriella began mumbling a spell.

'Do we kill them, mistress?' asked Ulrika.

'Shhh!' said Gabriella, and kept mumbling.

Ulrika looked back down the hall, uneasy, listening while from behind the door came the voices of their quarry.

'Ger it off, then,' slurred a male voice. 'I wanna see da goods.'

'All business, are ye?' replied a coarse female voice. 'Right then, here you are. Don't get many of them to the pound, do ye?'

Gabriella finished mumbling and rolled her eyes. 'Ah, the sweet poetry of seduction.' Her left hand was clenched around a squirming black shadow. She reached out with her right and turned the latch. It was locked. She turned harder and the lock snapped.

The harlot looked up from climbing into a sway-backed bed as the door swung open and Gabriella and Ulrika stepped into the squalid little room.

'Hoy!' she cried. 'Bugger off! I got a customer!'

The bravo grinned, revealing yellow teeth. 'More th' merrier, says I.'

Gabriella closed the door, then extended her left hand and opened her fingers. 'Sleep,' she said.

The squirming shadow dissipated into a cloud of mist that drifted towards the harlot and the bravo. They drew back, frightened, as it came at them, but then smiled and sagged to the pillows as it enveloped them, their eyes closing.

Ulrika hesitated as Gabriella stepped forwards. 'Are they…?'

'Only dreaming, my child,' said Gabriella as she crossed to a trunk at the foot of the bed and began to rummage through the mound of colourful clothes within. 'And having a more pleasant encounter than they would have awake, I'll wager.' She pointed at the slumbering basher. 'Come. Strip him and yourself. Too much of the night has passed already.'

Ulrika crossed to the man and began her unpleasant task. The basher's sword had been of quality once, as had his doublet and breeches – dark red gabardine with black brocade panels – but it looked like he hadn't laundered them for several years, and they smelled strongly of stale food and unwashed flesh. His shirt and small clothes were even worse, and crawled with vermin, just as she had feared.

'Mistress,' she said. 'I… I cannot.'

Gabriella looked over and made a face. 'Very well. Here.' She threw a frilly white blouse at her. 'You must wear the doublet and breeches, but you may wear that underneath. Indeed it will add to your imposture.'

Ulrika took the undergarment with relief. It was threadbare and tattered, but at least marginally cleaner. She stripped out of her lady's clothes and pulled on the harlot's blouse and the bravo's kit. It was tight in the hips and the chest, but fit well enough otherwise. The unfamiliar sword hung oddly at her side, and the boots were loose, but she stuffed them with rags ripped from the harlot's skirts and they were a little better. Finally, to appease her tortured nose, she searched among the harlot's combs and rouges until she found a vial of scent, and doused her new clothes in it. She still reeked, but at least now it was of rose water.

When she was finished, she turned to Gabriella to find the prim lady's maid gone and a saucy wanton standing hip-shot in her place, her breasts nearly spilling from a low-cut yellow bodice, and a leering smile on her painted face.

'Fancy a go, m'lord?' Gabriella drawled in a harsh slum accent.

Ulrika smiled in spite of herself. 'I'm beginning to think you have not always been a countess, countess,' she said.

Gabriella smiled. 'Our queen asks us to play many roles in our service to her.' She stepped to the shuttered window and opened it, then looked down. 'Now gather up your things and put them in that satchel with mine. We must go.'

GABRIELLA PLAYED HER part to the hilt as she and Ulrika walked through the empty streets of the Faulestadt slums, swinging her hips and tossing her hair like a professional though there were precious few passersby to see her show. Ulrika supposed she was playing her part correctly as well, for she strode stiffly behind the countess, looking uncomfortable and wary – which was no act.

'The witch hunters at the bridge will still stop us, mistress,' she said. 'Even dressed as we are.'

'If we are alone they will,' said Gabriella. 'Which is why we must find some company.' She peered down an intersecting street. 'I am only looking for the right sort of tavern, and the right sort of men. Ah! That looks promising.'

She threw back her shoulders, then sauntered towards a building lit from lintel to eaves with red lanterns – a beacon of light in the dark sea of the fear-fraught night. There was a line of rich carriages drawn up near the door, over which hung a sign that proclaimed the name of the place to be the Cannon's Mouth.

'Come, my dashing drake,' Gabriella said, looking back. 'The Altestadt is but a wink away.'

CHAPTER TWENTY
LADY HERMIONE REGRETS

'AND WHAT BRINGS such refined noblemen as yerselves south of the river, m'lords,' asked Gabriella.

The four drunk boys who surrounded the countess laughed. Ulrika, leaning against a shadowed pillar nearby, doubted they were nobles, but rather the sons of wealthy merchants, flaunting their fathers' money in loud clothes and jewellery that true noble sons would disdain as tasteless. The Cannon's Mouth seemed to cater to their ilk. It was an overdone parody of the true squalor of the Pitcher and Ramrod, with the same trestle tables and blackened beams, but with better-looking harlots, dice and cards in a back room, and enormous bouncers to keep the peace. A place for rich boys from across the river to come, drawn by the promise of danger – but not too much – and a little naughty fun. Well, they had been drawn by the score this night. Just like it had been at the Pitcher and Ramrod, the crowd was five deep at the bar, and giddy with edgy laughter and loud talk – huddling around the fire in fear of the dark.

'We came t'hunt vampires,' slurred the drunkest of the merchants' sons, a moonfaced redhead in sky-blue doublet and breeches. 'Drive 'em into the sunshine and watch 'em turn to ash.'

Gabriella raised an amused eyebrow. 'And did you catch any, m'lords?'

'Nah,' said a pudgy boy in orange velvet with his hair plastered across his forehead in an elaborate spitcurl. 'Saw plenty burning, though. That was good sport!'

'Thirsty work, though,' said the third boy, who seemed to be the leader. He was shorter than the others, but more handsome, and with a sharp glint to his eyes. 'And rousing as well.'

'Aye,' said Gabriella, stroking his chin. 'I don't doubt it.' She ran a finger down his velvet-clad chest. 'And what would y'say if I was to tell ye *I* was a vampire?'

The boys laughed again, louder.

'You?' said the fourth, a blond wisp of a boy in an emerald doublet and earrings. 'You ain't pale enough! Nor skinny enough!'

Gabriella kept her eyes on the handsome leader. Her finger trailed lower. 'But if I was? Would y'pound yer wooden stake into me? Would y'make me scream and turn to dust?'

Handsome's eyes glazed with lust, but the others jeered and shoved him.

'And what about us, then?' said Moonface, pulling Gabriella around by the shoulder. 'We're hunters too, you know!'

She smiled slyly at him, then around at the others. 'Oh, it might take more than one stake t'kill me,' she murmured. 'It might take a whole night of pounding to see me dead.' She leaned against Spitcurl's chest, arching her back and pushing out her chest. 'If only we had some quiet place away from all this smoke and villainy t'do the deed.'

There was a quick exchange of looks between the boys as they began to weigh the reality of going through with what Gabriella was suggesting.

The countess seemed to sense the hesitation, for she twisted again, rubbing up between Handsome and the boy with the earrings. 'Haven't ye a place of yer own, then?' she purred. 'Are ye not men of the world?'

Watching the boys' faces, it seemed to Ulrika that Gabriella was using more than words and her beauty on them, for their eyes had the dull look of stunned cattle, and though they obviously had objections and questions, they seemed to find it nearly impossible to voice them.

'What about your carriage house, Sebastian?' asked Handsome, turning to Moonface. 'You've taken girls there before, haven't you?'

'I... I don't know,' Moonface mumbled. 'My father–'

'Your father's face-down in his port by now,' sneered Spitcurl. 'Come on, Sebastian, don't be a woman. Did we not make blood oath together?'

Moonface licked his lips. 'I... oh, very well. But you best remember that blood oath if we get caught.'

They all slapped him on the back and cheered.

'There's a good lad,' said the boy with the earrings.

Handsome linked arms with Gabriella and started for the door of the tavern. 'Come, vampire. We have you under arrest now. You shall face the iron tower.'

'Four iron towers!' crowed Spitcurl.

She laughed merrily, then beckoned to Ulrika as she passed her with the young men. 'This way, Rika. We're going with these gentlemen.'

This brought the boys up short. They turned and stared at Ulrika, angry frowns furrowing their foreheads.

'What's this?' said Spitcurl.

'You didn't say anything about a friend,' said Handsome.

'Is it a man or a woman?' said the boy with the earrings, grimacing.

'I'm not sleeping with that!' said Moonface.

Gabriella smiled and stroked their arms and chests. 'Rika's nothing to worry about, my lords. She only keeps me safe down here in the smoke.'

'Then she can stay here,' said Moonface. 'You're perfectly safe with us.'

'Of course I am,' said Gabriella smoothly. 'But I wouldn't want t'trouble any of you gentlemen fer a ride back in the morning, would I? And it's a long lonely walk through rough quarters ere I get home.' She leaned against Handsome and looked straight in his eyes, her lips inches from his. 'She'll stay out of sight and out of mind, I promise you, but I'm afraid I can't come if she stays behind.'

The four boys exchanged another round of glances, with Handsome pleading and the others uncertain, but at last Spitcurl shrugged.

'Very well,' he said. 'But she can ride with the coachman. She reeks of rose water.'

ULRIKA'S HAND DROPPED to the hilt of her stolen rapier as the coach approached the bridge and the four witch hunters who watched the traffic that crossed it. If Friedrich Holmann was among them, their masquerade was over before it began. She relaxed somewhat when she didn't see his face, but kept her hand where it was. She felt like she was sticking her head in a dragon's mouth.

The head witch hunter stepped forwards and held up a hand, then stepped around to the window, carrying a lantern. He hadn't given Ulrika, huddled beside the coachman, a second glance.

'Show me your faces,' said the witch hunter, lifting his lantern to the window.

There was laughter from inside the coach, then came a shriek from Gabriella and Spitcurl's braying voice. 'Look, templar! We've caught a vampire! She's going to be the death of us!'

'Aye!' came Moonface's cry. 'Show him your teeth, fiend!'

Ulrika tensed and gripped the bench, ready to leap down and kill the witch hunter before he could draw his blade, but then she heard a soft slap and Gabriella's laughter.

'Those aren't my teeth, beloved! Shame on you!'

Looking down from above, Ulrika couldn't see the witch hunter's expression under his broad-brimmed hat, but his rigid posture spoke eloquently of his disgust.

'You young fools,' he growled. 'This is no laughing matter. Death stalks the streets of Nuln and you carouse with strumpets.' He stepped back from the coach and waved it on with a curt hand. 'Away with you, and may Sigmar forgive you your frivolities.'

Ulrika relaxed her grip on her sword as the coachman geed the horses and the coach started forwards again, but she didn't relax entirely until they had crossed the bridge and rattled onto the cobbles of the Neuestadt.

As THEY DROVE through the commercial district, Ulrika saw that, despite the witch hunters' best efforts, some of the day's madness had spread north of the river. There were many shops with broken windows, and hammers of Sigmar were painted on many doors and walls. Though the streets were empty but for a few double-strength watch patrols, the taverns were doing booming business here as well.

Seeing such signs of panic, Ulrika feared another stop at the gate to the Altestadt, but it didn't occur. The guards there seemed to recognise the coach and its occupants. They only saluted, while their captain nodded at its windows.

'A dangerous night to be out, young masters,' he said. 'Best get home.'

'Aye, captain,' came Handsome's voice. 'Home to bed.'

The boys laughed at that, and they rode on.

It was harder to tell if the Altestadt had succumbed to the rest of the city's fright. The streets were always quiet there at night, and the watch always on patrol, but Ulrika thought she felt a more than usual uneasiness in the glances of the guards who patrolled the mansions they passed, and in the faces of the rich merchants who hurried by them on their way home.

A few minutes later, the coach pulled into the carriage yard of a stately townhouse in the Kaufman District, and the boys tumbled out with Gabriella in tow and many a finger to the lips and exaggerated shushings. Ulrika dropped her satchel to the ground then and climbed down from the bench with the coachman as Handsome came towards them.

Ulrika was afraid he was going to say something to her, but he didn't even look at her. Instead, he slipped a crown into the coachman's hand and gave him a wink. 'None the wiser, eh, Ulf?'

'None the wiser, sir,' said the coachman, nodding and pocketing the coin.

As he led the horses to the carriage house stable, Spitcurl and the others brought Gabriella to a door at the back of the structure that apparently led to an apartment above it. Gabriella gave Ulrika a smile and wink as they hurried her inside.

Spitcurl saw this and shot an annoyed look back at Ulrika. 'Stay out of sight of the house, can't you? If my father sees you he'll have the watch in.'

Ulrika nodded respectfully, then picked up the satchel full of clothes and stepped around the far corner of the stable to take a seat on the edge of a stone well. She wondered how long she'd have to wait. Would Gabriella take her masquerade to its conclusion? That seemed a waste of time. The night was nearly half over already. Would she kill the boys? Would she beguile them in some way?

Almost as she thought it there came the sound of a window opening and a hiss from above her. She looked up. Gabriella was looking down at her.

'Bring the clothes!' she whispered.

Ulrika hurried around the carriage house again and slipped into the door. A dog-legged stairway led to a single high-ceilinged apartment with a bed at the far end, and a few chairs around a hearth against one wall. The four boys lay like unstuffed dolls in the centre of the room, snoring peacefully.

Gabriella stepped over them, shuddering, and reached for the bag of clothes. 'If I had had to bear one more pinch or squeeze I would have ripped their hands off. Animals! Every one of them!'

Gabriella pulled out the fancy clothes that Ulrika had worn and Ulrika helped her put them on. They were too long for the countess, but she was going to see Hermione, and refused to do so dressed as a maid or a harlot. Ulrika looked longingly at the clothes of the sleeping boys, which were infinitely cleaner than her stolen rags, but none of them was even remotely her size. The boy with the earrings, however, seemed to have the right-sized feet, so she pulled off his boots and tried them on. They fit almost perfectly. With a sigh of relief she left him the bravo's great galoshes and hurried down the steps with Gabriella.

LADY HERMIONE'S HOUSE was dark as they approached it, and Ulrika and Gabriella slowed uneasily, looking around for a trap. Ulrika strained her hearing to listen for hidden heartbeats or the subtle shifting of things with dead hearts lying in wait. She heard nothing, and apparently Gabriella was satisfied as well, for after a moment she continued to the door and knocked.

An answer was long in coming, but just as she was raising her hand to knock again, they heard the lock turn and the door opened a crack. A timid maid peered out at them through the gap.

'Gebhart, is that–?' she began, then gasped and tried to pull the door shut.

Gabriella stopped the door with a hand, then drew herself up and looked down her nose. 'Countess Gabriella von Nachthafen to see Lady Hermione,' she said.

The maid's eyes widened at this and she shrank back even further behind the door. 'Lady Hermione regrets she is not at home to visitors today,' she said. 'W-would you care to leave a card?'

Gabriella snarled and slammed the door open, knocking the maid back into the entry hall and sending her sprawling. Ulrika drew her stolen rapier and strode in beside the countess, looking for threats. She saw none. The maid was alone and the house quiet. She closed the door as Gabriella crossed to the maid and pulled her up by the front of her bodice.

'Not at home?' Gabriella whispered as the girl tried to draw away. 'Does she cower in her boudoir for fear of my wrath? Fetch her, girl. I would speak to her.'

'But… but, m'lady,' stammered the maid. 'She is truly not at home! She has gone away!'

'Gone away?' Gabriella's eyes flared. 'Gone away where?'

The maid paled and trembled. 'I – I am not to say.'

Gabriella shook the girl until her teeth snapped. 'Will you deny me? I will pull your fingers off, one joint at a time! Where is she?'

The girl wept with fright. 'She has gone to the country, m'lady!' she wailed, hanging limp in Gabriella's grip. 'To Mondthaus, her estate! Frau

Otilia said she must wait there until things calmed down in the city!'

Gabriella paused. 'Did she? And von Zechlin? Lord Rodrik? Mistress Famke? The rest?'

'M'lady took Lord von Zechlin with her,' said the girl. 'He was hurt. The others went too.'

Gabriella nodded, thinking, then looked at the maid again. 'And who is this Gebhart you were expecting?'

The girl hesitated.

Gabriella closed her hand around her neck. 'Answer me.'

'He – he is the footman!' babbled the girl. 'Frau Otilia sent him on an errand before they left.'

'What errand?'

'He was to go to Madam Mathilda,' said the maid. 'He was to invite her to Mondthaus to escape the riots.'

Gabriella stared at the girl. 'What? After all that has passed between them? I don't believe it.'

'That is what Otilia said, m'lady.'

Gabriella frowned, deep in thought, then seemed to remember she had the maid still in her grip. She set her on her feet again and smoothed her clothes. 'I am sorry, dear heart. You are not to blame for betraying your mistress. It is she who did wrong, by telling you to lie.' She patted the girl's hand. 'Now tell me how I may find this Mondthaus.'

'Yes, m'lady.'

Ulrika waited at the door as Gabriella wrote down the directions the maid gave her. The estate was apparently only ten or so miles to the south of Nuln, on the edges of Wissenland's wine country.

Gabriella dismissed the girl with another pat of the hand, then turned to Ulrika and motioned her to the door, her face turning grave.

'We must part here,' she said as she stepped out onto the porch. 'I don't know what game Hermione is playing now, but I fear that Mathilda will accept her invitation at the head of a war party. I must find some proper travelling attire in Hermione's wardrobe, then go and try to keep the peace. *You* must go back to the Garden of Morr and find something – *anything* – that will convince these two harridans that it is not a sister who is killing the Lahmians of Nuln.'

'Forgive me, mistress,' said Ulrika. 'But I would not have you go out to that place unescorted. If you recall, Lady Hermione tried to kill you the last time you paid her a visit.'

'And I do not wish to let you go alone into the lair of that beast,' said Gabriella, sighing. 'It is not something anyone should face alone, but I have no choice. Both things must be done immediately.' She urged Ulrika down the steps, then stopped her again and handed her the directions she had written down. 'Here. Take these. I have them in my head now. When you have found something, speed as quickly as you may to me there.'

'But what if there is nothing to find?' asked Ulrika, turning at the bottom of the steps.

'There must be!' said Gabriella, and Ulrika thought she had never seen her mistress look more haggard and lost. 'I know not what else will stop this war.'

CHAPTER TWENTY-ONE
ILL MET BY MOONLIGHT

Ulrika hurried through the deserted streets of the Altestadt, her mind so full she hardly knew where she went. How precarious things had become in such a short time! Countess Gabriella had rode into this city in a fine coach, with a champion and a maid and a lady in waiting, and with a wagon of beautiful clothes and furnishings rolling behind her. She had wielded influence and commanded respect amongst her peers, and seemed to have the situation well in hand. Yet now, in the space of two days, she had lost nearly everything – her lodgings burned, her maid killed, her fine clothes stolen, her coach destroyed, her champion gone to her chief rival, and worst of all, the mission upon which she had been sent to Nuln, a tattered, insoluble ruin. She had been ordered to find the killer and save the lives and organisation of the Lahmian sisters here, and instead, the killer had struck again and again, and the sisters were at each other's throats, and likely to kill her as well.

It seemed Gabriella had introduced Ulrika to the neat, tidy world of the daughters of the deathless queen just in time for it to collapse into bloody rubble. The life of restraint and court intrigue that the countess had described to her had been replaced by one of hiding in alleys and fighting in graveyards. Ulrika felt sorry more for Gabriella than for herself. It seemed completely unfair that so kind and honourable a woman had been driven nearly to destruction in the pursuit of duty.

Ulrika wished she could give Gabriella some of the comfort that Gabriella had given her in these past weeks. After each trial Ulrika had faced, the countess had been there, holding her in her arms and soothing her wounds. Even Ulrika's most foolish mistakes she had forgiven. Certainly she had been stern at times, even cold, but never for long, and never without cause. As an unwilling, unwanted foundling in a strange new world, Ulrika could not have asked for a kinder, more caring mother, and it pained her to see her lost and hurt. Gabriella needed a mother herself at the moment, but Ulrika knew she was too young and inexperienced to play that role for her. All she could do was try her best to bring her what she needed to convince the others to stop their war.

She ran on, vowing she would not fail.

FREEZING FOG AGAIN muffled the overgrown grounds of the Garden of Morr in its chill embrace, and Ulrika moved through the monuments and mausoleums using her ears as much as her eyes to detect any night-time wanderers. Her sense of direction and sense of smell helped too, guiding her through the maze of grassy hills and dells to the ancient, abandoned quarter of the cemetery where she and Witch Hunter Friedrich Holmann had found the valley of the ghouls.

As she neared the place, the rotting corpse reek began to grow stronger, and she went slower and drew her rapier, not knowing if the scent merely lingered or if the ghouls or their master hid near her in the fog. At last she saw the tall grey silhouettes of the cypress trees that surrounded the valley of the crypts looming out of the fog like slope-shouldered giants in pointed helms.

From there she went forwards at a snail's pace, pushing her senses ahead of her so she wouldn't walk into another ambush, and as she reached the bottom of the cypress rise she heard a single heartbeat ahead of her, and then, almost instantly afterwards, a muttered curse. A twinge ran up her spine at the sounds, for she knew both the heart and the voice. It seemed that she and Templar Holmann had found each other once more.

She almost laughed at the implausibility of it, but then her smile faded. It was no laughing matter. It would have been much better for both of them had she never found him again, for Gabriella had been clear. It was her duty to kill him. But what if they didn't meet? What if she pretended she had missed him in the fog, and instead went around to the far side of the valley and entered it from there? No. That was only cowardice, and it still left him alive with the knowledge of what she was – knowledge that could harm the countess later after all this was over. There wasn't any choice. She would have to face him.

She started slowly up the hill, trying to muster some anger against him in order to make killing him easier. She could not. She had been stung when he had singled her out in Mathilda's coachyard, but she could not call it a betrayal. It was she who had betrayed him by pretending to be something she wasn't. He had only done what he was called to do by his beliefs. She sighed and continued on. She would have to do it in cold blood.

Halfway up, she heard him curse again, apparently frustrated.

'Where is it?' he hissed. 'I know it's here!'

She continued on, and a few paces later she saw his long-coated silhouette. He had his sword in one hand and a pistol in the other, while a lantern hung from his belt, and he was walking backwards and forwards across the side of the hill like a hound sniffing for the scent. After a moment he seemed to find it, and started up towards the top, but just as he reached the cypresses that ringed the valley of the ghouls, he paused and reversed direction, and started back down the hill.

Ulrika frowned, confused. What was he doing? He had only to push through the trees and he would find the place he was looking for.

Holmann stopped abruptly halfway down the hill and looked around him, then stared at a nearby monument and balled his fists. 'Not again! I was just here! Curse this fog!'

Ulrika almost laughed. How could he not see the valley? It was foggy, but no worse than when they had come together to the spot previously. Why had he turned away when he had been right at the boundary?

Then, all at once, Ulrika knew exactly why. There was a spell of confusion laid on the place, made to keep people from finding it. With her inhuman senses, Ulrika had seen through it, and had last time led Holmann into the valley without even knowing it was there. Now he had returned to the spot, but without Ulrika's guidance he could not pierce the enchantment.

A wave of compassion for the templar flooded Ulrika. Here was a man who did not mask his fear of the unknown by boasting around the fire. Here was a man who instead stepped bravely into the night to face the enemies of his kind, and yet, with his limited human senses, he could only stumble around in the darkness, lost and befuddled while his foe, quicker, stronger and blessed with abilities he could only dream of, crept up on him to take his life before he knew it was even threatened. Such seemed the fate of all men in this world of daemons and monsters, and it saddened Ulrika to have to murder one who had the courage to fight that fate – but it had to be done.

She rose and crept towards him as he started up the hill again. But then, with only ten paces between them, she heard another heartbeat in the fog, and then another. The pulses were slow but still strong, and with them came a new gust of corpse stench. More ghouls.

Ulrika paused, her chest constricting. It seemed that Holmann's shuffling and cursing had not gone unnoticed. The undead killer's guard dogs had come sniffing at the gate, and were slinking closer. Ulrika could see the shadow of one lurking in the ring of cypress trees at the top of the hill, waiting as Holmann approached, and the other blurred from one grave-stone to the next off to his right. This was a perfect solution. Holmann would be dead as Gabriella wished, and Ulrika wouldn't have to do the killing. All she had to do was continue up the hill to the line of trees and let the witch hunter be the distraction that allowed her to pass through them unnoticed.

Aye, it was perfect, which did not explain why she found herself padding under the branches of the cypresses towards the closer of the ghouls, rapier poised to strike.

The misshapen thing didn't hear her coming until she was three paces away, and by then it was too late. She sprang as it spun to face her, and she ran it through the neck. It gargled wordlessly and clawed at the blade as it died.

The noise brought Holmann's head up, and he went on guard where he stood, halfway down the hill, sword and pistol at the ready.

'Show yourself!' he barked.

As Ulrika hesitated, the second ghoul leapt from hiding, bounding over a gravestone and launching itself at the witch hunter. Holmann turned and fired and the thing went down in a rolling ball, blood spraying, but then it gathered its limbs under itself and lumbered at the templar again like a charging ape.

A third ghoul, one Ulrika had missed, broke from a clump of rose bushes further down the slope, aiming for Holmann's back as he parried the claws of the second and clubbed it with the butt of his pistol.

Ulrika cursed. She should leave now. Let him die. Forget him. But again she was sprinting to intercept. What was she doing? She suddenly felt just like

Holmann, walking up to the cypresses but unable to push through them into the valley. There was a barrier here, and she could not make herself cross it.

She jumped over Holmann's head and landed in front of the third ghoul. It shrieked and lunged at her, claws extended. She hacked at them, severing half a dozen fingers, but still it came, immune to pain. Its head shot forwards, snarling, jaws distending. She jammed her forearm up under its chin and its filed teeth snapped shut an inch before her face, its corpse breath gagging her.

She ran it through, then shoved it back. It slid off her blade and curled on the ground like a burnt spider. She cut off its head, just to be sure, then turned.

Holmann was levelling his second pistol at her, the other ghoul dead at his feet.

Ulrika froze, knowing he loaded silvered shot. 'Is that any way to greet your rescuer, templar?' she asked.

He glared at her, his hand trembling. 'Why do you torment me so, fiend? Why do you toy with me? Why not kill me and have done?'

Ulrika blinked at him, then lowered her sword. 'I don't know. It is what I must do, and only a moment ago I fully intended to, and then...' She trailed off and gestured around at the dead ghouls. 'I did this.'

'*Why?*' Holmann demanded. 'For what evil design do you keep me alive?'

'None, Herr Holmann,' she sighed. 'None. I... I just can't seem to kill you.' Her mouth twisted with bitterness. 'I seem to have a... a fondness for you.'

'Do not lie to me, monster!' Holmann cried. 'Creatures of the night have no fondnesses! They have no hearts!'

'I heard that too, when I lived,' said Ulrika, as much to herself as to him. 'But I find much to contradict it now I am dead. Would it ache so, if it wasn't there?'

Holmann sneered. 'You seek to cozen me with sentiment. I will not be beguiled into lowering my gun.'

Ulrika looked up at him, frowning, as something dawned on her. 'And why haven't you fired it before now, templar?' she asked. 'Witch hunters are known to be heartless as well.'

Holmann glared at her, and the tremble of his hand became a violent shake. 'Bitch!' he cried. 'Whore!' Then, with a snarl that was as much a sob, he turned the gun and put it to his own head.

'No!' Ulrika cried, and leapt up the hill at him.

The gun went off as she grabbed at his wrist, and she slammed down with him on the grass not knowing if he was alive or dead. She rolled off him and came to her knees, looking down at him. His arm was flung over his face, the spent pistol slack in his hand. She pulled his arm away, then breathed a sigh of relief. His face was black from exploding powder, and his eyebrows singed, but the ball had missed. He lived, though he did not seem grateful for it.

He jerked his arm from her grip and rolled on his side, facing away from her. 'Leave me be!'

'Templar Holmann,' she said. 'Friedrich–'

'I killed my own family because of their sin,' he choked. 'My mother and father! Yet I cannot kill you.' He covered his face with his hands. 'I am not worthy to be called a Templar of Sigmar. I am not worthy of life!'

Ulrika held herself still beside him, wanting to comfort him, but knowing her touch would not be welcome. 'And I cannot kill you,' she said softly. 'Though you denounce me and threaten my kind and burn down a house around me.'

Three slow-burning heart-fires bloomed at the top of the ridge and Ulrika looked up. More ghouls in the cypresses. She stood and took up her rapier to face them.

'Get up, Templar Holmann,' she said. 'There is work yet to be done.'

The ghouls sped down the slope, gibbering and shrieking. Holmann looked up at the sound and groaned, but got to his feet as well.

Ulrika leapt to meet them, hacking one across the shins, then spinning as it stumbled and transfixing a second with her blade. The third crashed into her side and she rolled down the hill with it as it clawed and bit at her.

They slid to a stop on the wet grass and she caught its throat in her left hand, pushing its mouth away from her as it raked her with its talons. She tried to free her sword arm, but it was trapped awkwardly against the ground.

'Foul maggot,' she growled. 'I have claws too.'

She extended her nails and closed her free hand around its neck, then jerked it back, tearing its throat and windpipe out in a red gush. It reared back, clutching at the ruin of its neck and trying to scream. She freed her arm at last and chopped it in the side, shattering ribs and finding organs.

It sank to the side and she extricated herself from its limbs. Up the hill, Holmann was finishing off the one she had lamed earlier. It fell with his sword through its right eye, and the witch hunter turned to face her, breathing heavily. His eyes were full of pain and uncertainty.

Ulrika raised a hand as she stood. 'Let us not go through it again, shall we?' she said, then nodded up the hill. 'Our purposes are the same here. We both seek to discover what is beyond those trees. We both seek to kill it. Let us put what lies between us aside for this common goal.' She sighed. 'Perhaps it will slay us both, and our troubles will be ended.'

Holmann frowned. 'You seek to kill it too?'

'Did we not track it here together?' Ulrika asked.

'But, I thought–'

'That I led you here as a ruse?' Ulrika laughed. 'Herr Holmann, had I wished to kill you, there would have been no better place for it than the plague house, or the sewers where I first discovered you. No. I may have lied in all else, but in this, at least, I spoke the truth. I am a vampire hunter.'

She whipped her rapier through the air to shake the ghoul blood from it, then started up the hill towards the trees. 'Now, will you come? Our prey awaits.'

Holmann stood undecided for a long moment, but then followed at last. As he joined her at the line of cypresses he frowned and sniffed. 'Is it you that smells of rose water?'

Ulrika cringed with shame. 'They are borrowed clothes. Pay it no mind. Now, hurry.'

CHAPTER TWENTY-TWO
INTO THE CRYPT

HOLMANN STOPPED, STUNNED, as he pushed though the row of cypress trees with Ulrika and looked around at the bowl of the misty circular valley.

'Why could I not find this before?' he murmured.

'An enchantment,' said Ulrika. She smiled. 'You see, we help each other. You can speak to priests. I can see what is hidden.'

She pushed her senses ahead of her, hunting heart-fires or footsteps, and found neither. She started stealthily down towards the cluster of crypts that surrounded the dry fountain at the bottom.

Holmann followed behind her, still troubled. 'I understand none of this,' he said. 'Why would a vampire hunt another vampire?'

Ulrika paused behind a statue of a winged saint holding a sword. She raised her head and inhaled. The rotten corpse smell was so overpowering here that it blotted out almost everything else. 'Do you imagine us more united in purpose than humanity?' she asked. 'We have feuds. We have murderers and madmen among us that threaten the rest. And others who work for the common good.' She moved on.

'There are no good vampires,' said Holmann, creeping after her. 'They are all monsters that drink the blood of humans. Even you.'

'And if that blood is freely given?' asked Ulrika.

Holmann grunted angrily. 'Do you say it is freely given when you take it from some beglamoured slave?'

Ulrika was about to snap off an equally angry retort, but she paused. His words aligned uncomfortably with her own feelings about the blood-swains she had drunk from. Quentin and Imma had lost all self will when she had fed from them. And could she say they had been willing before they had fallen under their mistress's influence?

'Then let us just say that some are worse than others,' she said at last, then added to herself, just like witch hunters. The thought raised a question in her head, and she turned to Holmann again. 'Why have you come here alone?' she asked. 'You were overwhelmed the last time. You should have brought reinforcements. Where are your comrades?'

Holmann snorted. 'Captain Schenk is convinced that he already knows who the vampires are, and continues to hunt them in the Faulestadt. We went to the Wolf's Head because a woman told him it was a nest of vampires. And indeed, we found you, but when you vanished, he would not listen to me when I mentioned this crypt. He said that vampires could not live on sanctified ground.' He snorted. 'So I came alone.'

Ulrika hardly heard half of what he said. 'What woman?' she asked, clutching his shoulder. 'Who told him about the Wolf's Head?'

Holmann shrugged and drew away from her. 'I know not. I wasn't there.'

Ulrika cursed under her breath. Had it been Hermione? Who else could it be? And yet, as Gabriella had said, could she have been so stupid as to endanger herself by exposing her 'cousin'?

They continued on, and after a moment reached the flat bottom of the valley. Nothing but a broad swath of grass separated them from the crypts than ringed the fountain. Ulrika paused, looking around, then hurried across the grass to the back of one of the mausoleums with Holmann hunching after her. Burdock and thorny rose vines grew up all around the stone structure, and moss and mould mottled it like mange. Ulrika strained her ears, but heard nothing untoward, either in front or behind. She edged around the tomb and padded down the overgrown alley that ran between it and the next with Holmann coming slowly behind.

As they neared the front they squatted down and peered around at the faces of the crypts. All were in great disrepair, their marble sooty and crumbling, their sculpted figures weathered to ghostly amorphous lumps, and their heavy wood and brass doors rotting and green with verdigris, but one, directly across from them beyond the fountain, was wide open. Its black portal yawned like a mouth, and exhaled the reek of death in a nauseating cloud that seemed to fill the valley and cling to Ulrika's skin like an oily film.

'That… is it,' she said, gagging.

Holmann nodded. He took a handkerchief from his coat and tied it around his nose and mouth, then checked his pistols, drawing back the hammers before settling them back into their holsters. 'Ready,' he said.

They crouched forwards, then circled around the dry fountain and approached the dark opening. Ulrika couldn't hear any movement from within it, nor could she sense any heart-fires, but then a vampire hadn't one, and could be as still as a corpse, if it wished.

They stopped on either side of the portal, then listened again. Still nothing. Ulrika motioned for Holmann to wait, then peeked around the door jamb and looked inside. The interior was square and small, no more than five paces to a side, and the walls were lined with large brass plaques, all with weathered names engraved upon them. In the centre, a flight of marble steps sank into the floor, disappearing into darkness. Ulrika saw no ghouls waiting in ambush, nor any vampire, just drifts of dry leaves in the corners and muddy, clawed footprints leading to the stairs.

Ulrika turned back to Holmann and beckoned him in. They crossed to the stairwell together and looked down. The corpse stink rose from it like heat from a stove. The steps descended straight ahead of them, and ended at an open door that appeared to be directly under the back wall of the mausoleum. The dirty flagstone floor beyond the door flickered with shadows and orange light from some hidden fire.

'It is bigger underneath than above,' said Holmann.

Ulrika nodded and started down the steps. Holmann drew a pistol and followed. Halfway down Ulrika stretched out her senses again. Now she heard

the ghouls. Now she felt the banked fires of their corrupted hearts.

'Five or six,' she murmured. 'Maybe more.'

'Be there a hundred,' said Holmann. 'I will not
flinch.'

As they crept down the last few steps, more of the
room revealed itself, and Ulrika paused to survey it.

It was bigger than the mausoleum but, as above, the
walls were lined with brass plaques that named the
dead buried behind them, and there were a few
grander sarcophagi rising out of the floor in a line
going down the centre of the room as well, stone statues of ancient knights lying on them with hands
clasped over their armoured chests. Two doors on
each of the side walls appeared to open into further
chambers.

She edged forwards to the door for a better look,
Holmann at her shoulder. The flickering yellow light
came from the far end, a rubble-ringed camp fire that
revealed a scene of contradicting elements. Nests of
twigs and leaves were mounded against one wall, and
Ulrika could see ghouls sleeping in them, but on the
other side of the room there was a true bed as well,
with a headboard and blankets and a night cap hung
on one of the bedposts. To the left of this was a writing desk, complete with inkwell, papers and books.
Ulrika found it disorientating to see such domestic
things in such a macabre location. Even more confusing was the wooden coffin that lay open to the right of
the bed. The box was so large it looked like it might
have been built for a beastman or an orc. Ulrika
thought it must be eight feet tall by four feet wide. She
swallowed, remembering the monstrous thing she

and Gabriella had fought in the cloud of unnatural darkness at Guildmaster Aldrich's house. That horror might well have been big enough to require such a coffin. But where was it now? She was too far away and at too low an angle to see inside the coffin. Was it inside?

She turned her gaze to the threats she could see. Huddled close around the fire were the ghouls she had sensed earlier – a handful of them, squatting on their haunches and pulling meat off a human carcass and stuffing it in their mouths. A huge midden heap of stripped and cracked bones was mounded against the wall behind them. Torn and bloodied clothes were buried within it.

Ulrika pointed at them. 'Human bones,' she whispered. 'Is this what became of the vanished?'

'Aye,' growled Holmann, raising his pistol. 'Depraved cannibals. Let us cleanse them.'

Ulrika was tempted to follow his lead, but the risk was too great. She put a hand on his arm. 'Wait,' she said. 'What if the owner of the coffin lies within it?'

'Then I will cleanse it too.'

Ulrika rolled her eyes. 'Your faith in your abilities is inspiring.'

'My faith is in Sigmar,' he said.

'That's all very well,' whispered Ulrika. 'But I have faced this thing before, and it will take more than faith to defeat it. We will need reinforcements. Come. Let us go before it wakes.'

Holmann glared at her. 'Do you protect your own kind?'

Ulrika groaned. 'Have you listened to nothing I have said? This thing is my enemy! Now–'

The slap of naked running feet echoed from the crypt above them. Ulrika and Holmann looked up and back, then rolled left and right out of the doorway to press against the wall of the chamber.

Two ghouls ran down the stairs into the chamber, each carrying a dead comrade in its arms. They threw them down in the middle of the room, croaking to the ghouls at the fire and pointing to the stairs. The ghouls stood and turned, then stared past the newcomers, gape-mouthed. One pointed a clawed finger right at Ulrika and screeched a warning.

Ulrika froze as all eyes turned on her and Holmann. The two ghouls who had run in leapt back in fright and dropped into fighting crouches. Holmann fired his pistol at one and missed.

A small, rational part of Ulrika's brain was shouting at her to run. There was no enemy between her and the stairs, and she needed to get back to Gabriella and tell her what she had found here. But she didn't want to run. The ghouls' fright was like a drug. It enflamed her. It made her hungry and ready to kill. If the horror was in the coffin, so be it. She was ready.

With a joyous howl, Ulrika pounced on the closest ghoul, slashing it with her rapier then smashing it to the ground with a shoulder to the chest. The other dodged aside, yelping, but Holmann's second pistol cracked and this time found its mark. The thing went down with a hole in its chest.

Ulrika tore the throat out of the one that struggled beneath her, then jumped up again and found herself shoulder to shoulder with Holmann between two of the stone sarcophagi. The ghouls from the fire were coming, swarming left and right in an attempt to surround them.

'Abductors of the innocent!' Holman shouted, tearing a glass vial from his bandolier and hurling it at them. 'Come and die!'

It shattered on a sarcophagus and sprayed them all with holy water. They screamed and flinched away but still came on, howling in rage and pain.

One leapt up on a sarcophagus and launched itself at Ulrika. She caught it by the wrist and swung it past her to smash into the sarcophagus behind. Its spine snapped and it dropped to the floor, folded in half. Then the others arrived, all leaping at once to try to drag her and Holmann down by weight of numbers.

Holmann's heavy sword severed a ghoul's arm. He crammed another vial down the throat of a second ghoul as it bit his hand. 'Fiend! This will be your last meal!'

Ulrika blocked two attacks with slashing parries and kicked a third ghoul back into the wall.

The throat of the ghoul that had swallowed the vial disintegrated from the inside out, but the dying thing's fangs were clamped around Holmann's hand and wouldn't let go. He hacked at another with his sword, but missed as he tried to shake free.

Ulrika made to help him, but a third ghoul leapt on her back, sinking its teeth into her shoulder. She hissed and drove herself back against the sarcophagus behind her, crushing it. It gasped and let go with its teeth. She threw an elbow into its jaw then lunged forwards over Holmann's trapped hand to impale the shoulder of the one that threatened him.

The thing fell back, shrieking, then scurried for the stairs as two more leapt in. Ulrika buried her blade to the hilt in the chest of the first one, while Holmann split the last ghoul's mangy, scabrous head down to the teeth.

Ulrika turned, ready for more, but the fight was over. Two more wounded ghouls were scampering through the door to the stairs, wailing with fear. All the rest were dead or dying around them.

'We should go after them,' said Holmann, tugging his hand free from the dead ghoul's maw at last. His glove was torn, as was his flesh beneath it.

Ulrika shook her head and turned towards the out-sized coffin. 'They are only dogs. I want their master.'

She killed the ghouls that still breathed as she stepped over them, then started towards the big wooden box. Holmann joined her, drawing a wooden stake and a hammer from his belt. They gagged and choked as they got closer. The death stench boiled up from the coffin in great reeking waves. Ulrika pinched her nose shut. Holmann winced and held his stake and hammer high, ready to strike.

They looked in. The coffin was empty except for a layer of wet, mouldy earth that covered the bottom, in which was pressed a deep impression of a huge, mis-shapen body.

Panic welled up all at once in Ulrika's breast. If the killer wasn't here, where was it? What was it doing? Who was it after now? She had a sinking suspicion she knew.

'A monster indeed,' said Holmann, coughing as he slipped the wooden stake and hammer back into his belt. 'This is what tore the walls and floor of the plague house.'

Ulrika stepped away too. 'Aye,' she said. 'And rended the bodies of the victims.'

'The vampires, you mean?' said Holmann.

'They were still victims.'

Ulrika turned to the bed that stood near the coffin. It had been neatly made-up, and the juxtaposition with its ruinous surroundings made her head spin. Surely this hadn't been used by the monster? She lowered her head to the pillow and inhaled. Faintly through the all-pervasive corpse stink she could smell the clove scent of the little man, the sorcerer she had chased through the sewers, and who had been in Aldrich's house when the monster had attacked Gabriella.

She stepped around the bed to the little writing desk. This smelled of the sorcerer too, and showed the same neatness as the bed. A tidy row of leather-bound journals were lined up on a shelf at the back, while pens, blotters, sealing wax and a sheaf of parchment sheets were all fit into little pigeon holes below. A stack of heavier tomes, ancient, eldritch and mouldering, was squared up along the left edge of the desk as if with plumb line and rule.

'Those should be burned,' said Holmann, staring at them balefully.

'Be my guest,' said Ulrika, distracted. She sat and took down the right-most journal and flipped through it, hoping for some clue to the whereabouts of the killer, or the plans of the sorcerer, but the precisely written entries were in a language she could not understand. She did not even recognise the letter forms. What she did recognise was the hand that wrote it. The same neat hand had written the blackmail note that had tricked Mistress Alfina into leaving Aldrich's residence and going to the plague house.

She glared at unfathomable words before her. The answer to the mystery of the killings was in these pages, she was sure of it, but the foreign script locked that knowledge away from her as surely as if it had been sealed in a vault. She held the journal out to Holmann, who was gingerly picking up the vile tomes and carrying them to the fire.

'Can you read this?' she asked.

He paused and squinted at the writing, then grimaced. 'It is the arcane script of magicians,' he said, sneering. 'We are taught to recognise it, but not to read it, lest it corrupt us.'

'Very wise,' muttered Ulrika wryly. 'But not very useful.'

She fluttered through the sheaf of parchment, but the sheets were all blank. Then she noticed a drawer under the writing surface. She opened it. A very curious collection of objects lay within it. On the left were three golden pomanders on decorative chains, in the middle, a small pile of folded papers, and on the right, the severed forelegs of an animal – a large dog it looked like, sawed off neatly at the elbow joint and bound with tidy bandages. She stared at the black-furred legs as realisation rocked her. The paw-prints in the mud, outside the Silver Lily – they had been made with these! The warlock had killed some poor dog to set a false trail that led to Mathilda. No doubt the tufts of fur had come from it too.

She shook her head as she turned to look at the pomanders, admiring in spite of herself the depth of planning that had gone into the plot. She lifted one of the latticed golden orbs and smelled it. It was filled with cloves – another piece of the puzzle made clear.

So the warlock didn't care for his companion's smell any more than she did.

She put the pomander back and examined the folded papers. Each had originally been sealed with wax, but no sigil had been pressed into it. She picked up the pile and opened one at random. There was a short note inside it, in plain Reikspiel, but the words made Ulrika's skin prickle with horror.

> *They go to M's. H and G in one coach, D in another. D has only two guards.*

Ulrika read it again. M for Mathilda. H for Hermione. G for Gabriella, and D for Dagmar. Dagmar – this note had been the madam's death warrant. It had told the killers that she would be travelling without the others on her way back from the meeting at Mathilda's. Someone had been spying on them! But who?

Ulrika turned the paper over, looking for a signature or mark. There was none. She looked again at the writing, a graceful looping script. It looked familiar to her. She had seen it somewhere before, but couldn't remember where. She closed her eyes, trying to think. It wouldn't come.

With a curse she put the note aside and opened the one on the top of the stack, hoping it would goad her brain. It certainly did that.

> *No word of G. At your order, H has been convinced to retreat to MH. M has been summoned too. Map enclosed.*

The prickling of Ulrika's skin became a bath of ice. Hermione and Mathilda had been tricked into going to the country, to Mondthaus, Hermione's country estate. The monster and the sorcerer were no doubt lying in wait. And… and Gabriella was going there too!

Ulrika bolted to her feet, knocking over the chair and nearly upsetting the desk. Her mistress was in danger!

Holmann looked up from throwing the arcane books on the fire. 'What is it?'

Ulrika turned and started across the room towards the stairs, stuffing the note in her doublet as she went. 'I must go.'

Holmann started after her. 'Wait! What have you learned?'

She ignored him, dodging around the sarcophagi and the dead ghouls and running through the door to the stairs. He ran after her.

As she reached the top and entered the mausoleum, she saw that the doors were closed. She ran to them and shoved. Her wrists and elbows stung at the impact. The doors didn't move.

She glared at them. Perhaps they swung in instead of out. Unfortunately, there were no handles on the inside. She caught at the heavy brass bosses that studded the weathered wood and pulled with all her might. The doors remained immobile. She stepped back, snarling, as Holmann puffed up the stairs behind her.

'What's happened?' he asked.

'The beasts have locked us in!' she growled. 'We're trapped!'

CHAPTER TWENTY-THREE
A RELUCTANT VOW

HOLMANN STEPPED TO the doors and tried them for himself, then began to look around the frame for a lever or knob, but Ulrika's sensitive eyes had already sought for such a thing and found nothing. She got down on her hands and knees and looked through the gap between the bottom of the door and the threshold.

'Cunning dogs!' she said, and let her forehead sink to the floor with a sigh. 'They have piled gravestones before it.' She closed her eyes, then cursed and rose to her feet again. 'Here. Push with me. We must at least try.'

Holmann nodded and they put their shoulders to the same door; then, on a count of three, heaved as hard as they could. It did not move an inch.

'Again!'

Still nothing. Holmann's considerable strength and her inhuman power were not enough. The marble

floor beneath their feet was too slippery, the gravestones too heavy.

Ulrika shoved away from the door with an angry
growl, then charged it and kicked it. She only hurt her
foot.

'It can't be like this!' she hissed. 'I must get away! I
may already be too late!' She turned to the stairs
again as a hope came to her. 'They must have a back
door! They must have a way to escape in case of trouble!'

She flew down the stairs again and into the fire-lit
crypt, then began pacing its perimeter and examining
the walls. Holmann thudded into the room a
moment after and crossed to her.

'What was in the note, fraulein?' he asked. 'What
has alarmed you?'

Ulrika hesitated. So far she had mentioned the
other Lahmians as little as possible when talking to
Holmann. He was the enemy, after all, and she didn't
want to expose them. On the other hand, he must
know already, and the other witch hunters too.
Schenk had come to find them at Mathilda's, hadn't
he? That thought brought another. Schenk had said a
woman had told him Gabriella would be at the
Wolf's Head. Was it the same traitor who had
informed the sorcerer of their movements? Who was
it? Who would want to turn both the witch hunters
and the undead against them?

'Lady,' rasped Holmann. 'If what you learned is
some threat to Nuln or Sigmar's Empire, then I insist
I be told of it!'

Ulrika cursed with frustration. She had completed
her circuit of the crypt and found nothing – no holes,

no loose marble sheets, no telltale footprints. She turned to the side rooms. 'The woman I serve has walked into a trap,' she said, distracted. 'She has gone unsuspecting to a house outside the city where the monster and the sorcerer wait to kill her. I must go to her.'

The first of the side rooms was dark, but Ulrika could see well enough. Holmann however went to the fire and took a brand from it, then returned to her. She had already moved on to the second room. There was nothing in the first but more beds of twigs and piles of gnawed bones.

'She is a vampire, your mistress?' Holmann asked as she walked the walls.

Ulrika curled her lip. 'Does it matter? The thing which is after her is, and its companion is a follower of the black arts. It is they who are the threat to Sigmar's Empire, not my lady.' She cursed again and flung herself out of the room as she found no signs of a hidden door in it.

Holmann followed her into the third room. 'You must take me with you,' he said. 'I must be sure they are destroyed.'

Ulrika laughed. 'I think not. I would not trust you to stop at killing only the beast and the sorcerer.' Nor would I trust the countess not to kill you, she added silently.

'I'm afraid I must insist,' said Holmann.

Ulrika pushed past him out of the room and crossed to the fourth. 'You are hardly in a position to insist on anything,' she said.

She stalked around the last chamber, punching and kicking the marble sheeting methodically and listening for the hollow boom of a cavity. There was none. She cursed again and turned back to the door.

Holmann stood there, his sword pointed at her heart. 'You will not stay me from my duty.'

She sighed. 'Herr Holmann, the point is moot, I think, for I can find no way out of this place.' She spread her hands. 'Neither of us is going anywhere. We are trapped here.'

He squinted suspiciously at her. 'Is this a trick? Do you seek to keep me from this encounter?'

Ulrika laughed. 'At the cost of keeping away myself? Don't be a fool. If I wanted to leave you behind…' She stepped forwards and caught his wrist before he knew she was moving, then twisted it. He hissed in pain and his sword clattered to the floor. She leaned in to him. 'I would not have to trap myself to do it.'

She pushed him away from her, then stepped out into the central room again and slumped against a sarcophagus, burying her face in her hands. 'I will wait for the return of the monster and the warlock, and then I will take vengeance upon them for what I could not stop.'

She heard the scrape of Holmann's sword as he stooped to pick it up. 'And if they do not return?'

She looked up at him, then paused, thinking what would happen if she remained locked in this place with Holmann for a day or longer. When had she last fed? It had been Lotte, that morning, just before Gabriella had thrown her to the crowd. She could most likely last another day or two, but then…

'If they do not return, then you should reload your pistols with silvered shot,' she said. 'For I will eventually become the thing you think I am.'

A strange look came upon Holmann's face. 'You would have me kill you?'

She shook her head. 'No. I would have us both escape, but should things come to such conclusions, I–' She swallowed, then continued. 'Let us only say that I have more often thought about killing myself than I have killing you.'

Holmann's face grew more troubled, and at the same time more excited. 'You would rather die than take human blood? You cannot live with what you have become?'

Ulrika chuckled. 'Let us not tumble into melodrama, templar. I am not some tragic heroine from a Detlef Sierck play. As I have been told more than once, I have the opportunity to right the situation every day at sunrise.' She shrugged. 'I am a coward, and when it comes to it, I will do what I must to stay alive. I only tell you so that you may prepare yourself to do the same.'

Holmann nodded, and looked away. 'I… I shall.'

Ulrika pushed away from the sarcophagus, grinning and gesturing to the ghoul's campfire, a morbid humour overtaking her. 'And if you succeed, then you can burn me on this fire and make all right with Sigmar. If *I* succeed, I will lay you behind one of these plaques and say what I remember of my father's prayers over your body–' She stopped suddenly, staring at the walls, her eyes going wide.

'What is it?' asked Holmann, looking around uneasily. 'Do you hear them coming back?'

'The plaques!' Ulrika cried. 'I didn't check the plaques!'

She sprang to the wall and pried at the edges of the nearest plaque. The things were slightly more than two feet on a side, and bolted into the marble at chest height. The one she tugged at wouldn't come. She extended her claws and hooked them behind it, then gave a mighty heave. With a screech, the thing came free, its bolts ripping from the wall and clanging to the ground. Ulrika looked behind it. A skeleton dressed in the fashions of half a millennium ago lay inside a deep narrow niche, its arms folded over its chest. She looked at the back wall of the hole. It was solid and undisturbed. She cursed and moved to the next plaque. Holmann stepped to another.

'If it doesn't come easily, it is likely not the one,' he said. 'They would not have bolted shut an escape hatch.'

Ulrika snorted, embarrassed. 'Very true, Templar Holmann. Forgive me. I was carried away.'

They went swiftly around the room, pulling at the plaques one after the other. Ulrika's spine began to tingle with dread when they reached the last one and it was as firm as the others but, at last, in the second of the left-hand side rooms, she found it. The plaque came away with a single tug and she barely caught it before it hit the floor. Inside, the niche was empty but for a smear of dirt, and when she looked at the back she saw a black hole smashed through the marble with a tunnel of raw earth behind.

'Herr Holmann!' she said in a loud whisper, for he was trying the plaques in the next room. 'Here!'

After a second he ran in, torch high, then crossed to the open niche, exhaling with relief. 'Praise Sigmar,' he said. 'I was beginning to doubt.'

Ulrika drew her sword and laid it in the niche. 'I will go in first,' she said. 'So that we will not betray ourselves with light. I'll call for you if it's clear.'

For a moment, Holmann looked as if mistrust was going to get the best of him, but then he just nodded. 'Good luck,' he said.

Ulrika stuck her head and shoulders into the niche, then levered the rest of her in. She pushed her sword ahead of her and went forwards on her elbows and knees. Six feet in, she edged through the hole in the back wall and into a narrow tunnel of moist earth. She had a hard time believing that the monster that slept in that huge coffin could squeeze through such a small space, but perhaps it could change its shape, or maybe it was tall but very skinny.

Clumps of earth came down on her as she pushed on, and she shuddered. The idea of being buried alive but never dying was enough to make her want to scream and tear at the walls. After about two body lengths, the earth tunnel took a sharp left-hand turn, then continued. Now even Ulrika's sight failed her. There was no light at all, just blackness, and the sound of her own movements, too close in her ears. She had no idea how much further the tunnel went, or where it was leading. She had expected it to angle up towards the surface at some point, but so far it hadn't.

Then, another body length beyond the bend, she pushed her rapier forwards again and it struck something hard ahead of her. She poked it. It felt like rock. She clenched her jaw, nervous, then elbow-walked ahead and reached out. It was rock. Smooth and masoned. The fools had run into the foundations of one of the other crypts!

She felt around, hoping to find that the tunnel turned away from the wall, but instead found a jagged edge to the rock. She ran her hand over the rough lip.

It was a hole in the wall. She reached through it. Smooth marble. A narrow square tunnel of it. She sighed with relief, then laughed at herself for not guessing what she would find. She had come to another niche. The ghouls had tunnelled from the basement of one crypt to another, and hid both entrances in grave niches. She pulled herself through the hole and, sure enough, at the end of the niche was a cover of brass.

A tremor of uneasiness rippled through her as she pressed against it. Had the ghouls remembered this back door? Had they blocked this exit too? Were the doors of the mausoleum above locked?

The plaque shifted as she pushed, then fell away all at once. With scrabbling hands she caught the edge of it before it smashed to the floor, then lowered it gently and looked around. There was more light here, filtering through a door to her left. She was in a crypt much like the one she had just left, with plaques on three walls and the door in the fourth, leading to a stairway. There were no ghouls, and no flicker of firelight.

Ulrika eeled out of the hole to the floor, then picked herself up and turned back to the tunnel.

'Holmann!' she whispered. 'Come ahead!'

She waited a moment, wondering if he could hear her around the bend in the tunnel, but then came a rustling and thudding from the far end. Relieved, she took her sword from the niche and padded to the stairs, then crept up them.

The mausoleum above the crypt was in this case round, but in all other particulars much like the other one, except in one important detail. The doors were cracked open. A thrill of excitement went through her. She could see the sky between them. Freedom was near.

She tip-toed back down to the crypt and waited at the open niche. After a minute, torchlight illuminated the insides of the tunnel, then Holmann's face appeared. His eyes were wide and he was sweating, but he relaxed when he saw her, and pressed on.

'The door is open above,' she said as she helped him out. 'We are free. Come.' She started towards the stairs.

'Wait,' he said.

Ulrika turned back to him, impatient. 'What? I must go. Now!'

'And I must go with you.'

Ulrika ground her teeth. 'I told you. I cannot allow that. Were it only the monster we faced, perhaps, but I must protect my mistress, from *all* harm.'

Holmann stepped towards her, brushing the dirt from his knees and long coat. 'How many gates lie between you and this house in the country? How many miles? Can you fly?'

'What are you talking about?' she asked.

He reached up and tapped the brim of his hat. 'A witch hunter opens all gates,' he said. 'And no one will deny him the use of a horse or carriage in the pursuit of his duties. If you want to reach this place swiftly, I am your passport.'

Ulrika paused, considering. She had proved herself able to climb the Altestadt wall, and she might even be able to go over the main city wall, but each passage would take time, and be fraught with danger. And though she was swifter than a human, and had more stamina, she was not swifter than a horse. Holmann was right. It would be an easier journey with him than without him.

She pursed her lips, then nodded. 'You may come, but on one condition.'

It was his turn to pause. 'What is it?'

'You will swear, by Sigmar and your own honour, that you will not harm or attempt to arrest my mistress or any of her companions, tonight or in the future.'

Holmann's face darkened. 'I cannot swear to that.'

'You must,' said Ulrika. 'Come, Holmann. Please. Leave them to Schenk. If he finds them guilty, so be it. Only don't denounce them yourself. That is all I ask.'

'All you ask,' said Holmann, 'is that I renounce my vows and give up being a Templar of Sigmar.'

'No,' said Ulrika. 'Not so much as that. Just... just turn your eyes to other targets – cultists, witches, necromancers, I care not.'

He hesitated, then looked away. 'I... I cannot. A Templar of Sigmar cannot "turn his eyes" from evil. I am sorry.'

Ulrika sighed. 'Then I will leave you here, and good luck to you.' She turned and started for the steps.

She was halfway up them when he called out again. 'Stop!'

She looked back, fully expecting to find him aiming his pistols at her, but he was not. He stood in the door to the crypt, his head lowered, unable to look at her.

'I will swear it,' he said.

She stared at him. 'Truly?'

'Aye. These fiends must be destroyed.'

She walked back down to him. 'Then let me hear it. All of it. And look me in the eye.'

He reluctantly raised his chin and met her gaze. He looked miserable. 'I swear,' he said, 'by Sigmar and my honour, that I will not harm or attempt to arrest your mistress or any of her companions, tonight or in the future.'

She winced at the pain in his voice. Then she gave him a curt military bow. 'Thank you, Herr Holmann. You honour me with this pledge.' She turned for the steps. 'Now hurry, there is no more time to waste.'

CHAPTER TWENTY-FOUR
THE HAND OF THE TRAITOR

THE LAST GHOULS saw Ulrika and Holmann stepping from the second mausoleum and bounded away, shrieking, from where they had sat on the gravestones they had piled in front of the other crypt. Ulrika ignored them and ran with the witch hunter through the hills and valleys of the fog-shrouded graveyard until they came at last to the spike-topped wall. She clambered up this with ease, then gave him a hand and hauled him up as if she was lifting a child. He muttered a curse at this unnatural show of strength, but said nothing out loud, and they hopped down to the street and hurried on.

Holmann knew of an inn just on the far side of the Temple District that kept horses, and when they reached it Ulrika waited outside while he went in and browbeat the landlord into saddling two and giving him the use of them 'on the business of the temple' without a fee.

After that their journey proceeded at a much quicker pace. They galloped through the streets of the Aldig quarter to the Neuestadt Gate and were waved through without even having to slow. She thought there might be some trouble as they reached the river and thundered across the great bridge, where four witch hunters still watched the south end, but Holmann waved a hand at them and raised his voice.

'News for Captain Schenk! Stand clear, brothers!' he cried, and they parted before him.

They pounded down the Brukestrasse through the Faulestadt to the South Gate, and there had to stop for the first time since they had mounted, for the towering main gates were closed for the night, and one of the small doors at the side had to be opened and the horses led through on foot, but then they were off again, spurring down a wide road between moonlit snow-covered fields.

Despite what lay before her, Ulrika revelled in the ride. The snow had melted from the roads and the dirt was packed and firm – perfect for a gallop. How long had it been since she had raced flat out? Had it been that time with Felix on her father's lands? That long? It felt marvellous. She gave the horse its head and let it surge away, topping a low rise and then barrelling down the other side in a spray of mud. The land, with its tidy white fields and its knots of bare winter trees, hadn't the wild austere beauty of the oblast, with its endless vistas and huge skies, but after a week in the hemmed-in labyrinth of Nuln's narrow streets, it felt as wide as all of Kislev.

After a while, when the horse started to flag a bit, she reined up and looked behind her. Holmann was coming doggedly on a hundred paces back.

She grinned as he caught up. 'I'm sorry, Templar Holmann. It has been too long.'

He gave her an odd look. 'You ride well.'

She shrugged. 'I told you. I am the daughter of a march boyar. I grew up on horses, and fought in my father's rota. That part was also not a lie.'

He nodded, then looked away, his jaw set. 'I… I can see that.'

Ulrika frowned. What was troubling him now? Then she remembered how he had looked at her before, on their way to the Temple of Morr the night they had met at the plague house, and how he had all but confessed to finding her attractive. The same fire had shone from his eyes just now, as he watched her ride, and then he had quietly and deliberately ground it out.

She wanted to say something to comfort him, but she refrained. It would only make it worse.

They rode on in silence for a while, but then Holmann spoke up again.

'How long has it been since you became… what you have become?' he asked.

Ulrika closed her eyes. She could almost read his thoughts. He was torturing himself with what might have happened had they met before she had been turned. He was thinking, 'If only I had killed the fiend that seduced her before it found her. If only fate had put me in her path a little sooner.'

'A hundred years, Herr Holmann,' she said without meeting his eyes. 'More than a hundred. Long before you were born.'

The witch hunter nodded sadly, but Ulrika thought he looked slightly more at peace.

As THEY GOT closer to the village that was the last crossroads before Mondthaus, Ulrika began to worry more and more about what Gabriella would do if she brought Holmann into her presence. She might have got a pledge out of the witch hunter not to hurt her, but she would never get a pledge out of the countess not to hurt him – not to mention Hermione. All in all, it would be better if he didn't arrive at the house. If he didn't, he would not die facing the monster, nor would he fall into the clutches of Gabriella or any of the other Lahmians.

The more she thought about the idea, the better she liked it. It would even have the added benefit of making him hate her, and thereby curing him of his painful attraction to her and set him back on the road to being the staunch enemy of evil and corruption he strove to be. She would be doing him a favour.

Her mind made up, she pulled up sharply and waved at Holmann to stop. He drew up next to her, concerned.

'What is it?' he asked.

She edged her horse next to his. 'I'm sorry, Herr Holmann,' she said. 'You won't be coming.'

Holmann frowned, confused, and in that instant she backhanded him across the face, then shoved him sideways as he reeled. He toppled from his saddle and crashed to the road in a splash of mud. Ulrika leaned forwards and caught his horse's reins, then spurred her own. The two horses plunged ahead, leaving Holmann sitting up in the middle of the road, a look of almost comic surprise on his spattered face as he receded quickly behind her.

Ulrika turned her gaze away from him and focused on the road ahead, trying to squash down the bubble of guilt that rose up and tightened her chest.

LESS THAN HALF an hour later, she found the final turning to Mondthaus and angled her horse into it, going at speed. All around, the snow-blanketed farmland rolled away smoothly, but the road she galloped along wound up into a patch of thick pine forest and jutting rocks – an untillable tor in the middle of the fertile plain. The fir trees quickly closed overhead, and the wind, which had had nothing to cry about in the flatlands, now moaned as it was torn by their branches.

In the thick undergrowth on either side of the narrow path she could occasionally see old stone walls, broken and moss-covered, and once, a stone of one of the old races, eerily illuminated by a stray shaft of moonlight that shot down through the close canopy of the trees.

As she got closer to the summit of the tor, a momentary dizziness came upon her, and she felt suddenly convinced that she was going the wrong way. With a curse and an effort of will she focused her mind and stayed on the path. It was another spell like that which had hid the crypt of the beast, but stronger, and seemingly attuned to her kind.

The urge to turn around grew more urgent as she pressed on, and she had to fight the compulsion to rein in with every stride of her horse. Then, ahead of her, she saw an iron gate set in a high sturdy wall. She pushed on towards it, though it felt like she was fighting a strong tide, then jumped down and reached for the gate.

She couldn't even touch it. Some black energy flared from the bars as her fingers neared it and pushed them away. It was like a trick with lode stones she had seen an alchemist do once. The harder she pushed against the force, the harder it pushed back at her. Had the beast and the sorcerer already come and locked the door behind them? Was this their magic? Had they killed everyone and occupied the house?

A growl rumbled in her throat. If that was the case, she would find some way to break their seal and slaughter them all. She would get vengeance for those she was too late to protect. She stepped back and surveyed the top of the wall. She could climb it easily, but would the energy be there too?

A crossbow bolt chimed off the gate and zipped past her ear. She dropped to a crouch and looked past the bars. One of Hermione's gentlemen was coming forwards and laying another bolt in the groove. Ulrika sighed with relief when she saw him, despite his threatening posture. For if the gentlemen were still defending the house, it meant the beast had not yet struck, or – an even more thrilling thought – it had already been defeated!

'Be off!' he shouted. 'They're tipped with silver, and the next one's through your heart!'

'I have urgent news for your mistress!' Ulrika called back. 'I have discovered the lair of the killer!'

The man laughed. 'The killers are captured, hoyden.'

Ulrika's eyes widened at this. Hermione had trapped the beast and the sorcerer? The war was over?

'Your mistress and the she-wolf,' the guard continued, sneering. 'Caught and chained and standing trial.'

Ulrika's momentary hope shattered. She groaned. Could it be true? Could Hermione and her men have over-powered Gabriella and Mathilda? She grimaced. With silvered weapons, she supposed they could.

'Then chain me too!' she cried. She stood and unbuckled her sword belt, then threw it to the side. 'For I have evidence to present in their defence.' She raised her hands over her head.

The man with the crossbow frowned, uncertain, then looked questioningly to his left.

A voice behind the wall answered him. 'Better to have them all in one basket, I suppose.'

The crossbowman nodded, then turned back to Ulrika. 'On your knees. Hands on your head.'

Ulrika did as she was told, then waited as the gate creaked open of its own accord and the crossbowman covered her with the silvered bolt. Three more men came out from behind the wall. One Ulrika recognised as another of Hermione's gentlemen, but the other two were dressed in huntsmen's garb, and looked to be retainers of the estate. One of these came forwards with heavy manacles and pulled Ulrika's hands down behind her back, while the other two put swords to her throat.

When the manacles were fastened, the huntsman hoisted her to her feet then shoved her forwards through the gate. It closed behind them, and he and the other huntsman led her up the path while the two gentlemen remained there on guard.

Ulrika surreptitiously tested the manacles as they walked on, straining at the chain that linked them. It was strong indeed. She felt she would be able to break them given opportunity and time, but it wouldn't be quick. She sighed. If Lady Hermione was willing to look at the note she had found and listen to what she had to say, all would be well but, if she were blind and deaf to even that evidence, then Ulrika was walking meekly to her death, for she would not be able to defend herself, bound as she was.

The path twisted up through overgrown shrubbery and overhanging trees until, as the slope began to level off, a hulking, slate-roofed manor house was revealed among them, shouldering up from the crest of the tor to rise silhouetted against the clear night sky. The left end of the manse appeared to be an old keep, its raw stone and tiny, slotted windows a reminder of a brutal bygone era, but newer additions showed a more open face. The front door had grand marble steps leading up to it, and a portico topped with a balcony while, on the far right, a stately section made in the Tilean manner displayed a magnificent stained-glass window that was easily twice Ulrika's height. And yet, despite the rugged beauty of the place, and the warm light that glowed from its many windows, it did not appear welcoming. No. That was wrong. Really it appeared too welcoming – unsettlingly so – like a giant jewelled snake waiting in its lair and mesmerising intruders with its glittering eyes and iridescent scales as it wrapped them uncomplaining in its coils, then swallowed them whole.

Another retainer on the steps opened the door and Ulrika's huntsman guards prodded her through it into a small entry way. There was a high-ceilinged corridor ahead of her with richly-panelled double doors at the end. From behind these, she could hear the sounds of argument.

The huntsmen led her to the doors, then knocked quietly upon them. They cracked open and Otilia the housekeeper looked out.

'Yes?'

'Countess Gabriella's ward, Frau Otilia,' said the first.

Otilia looked Ulrika up and down with a cool eye, then smiled, which was even colder.

'Put her with the others,' she said, then stepped aside and opened the doors.

The huntsmen pushed Ulrika into a sumptuous panelled room, set about with gilded furniture and lit by a huge gold and crystal chandelier that hung from the coffered ceiling. Ahead of her, tall windows and leaded-glass doors looked out into a moonlit garden, while to her left, a fire roared in a marble fireplace decorated with carved dragons and knights.

It was to the fire that her guards led her. Countess Gabriella and Madam Mathilda knelt before it, hands chained behind them like her own, and their backs uncomfortably close to the flames. Glaring down at them with her Cathay fan white-knuckled in one delicate hand was Lady Hermione, all in white, her gentlemen in a half-circle behind her and von Zechlin at her right, his left arm wrapped in bandages and his face a mess of scabbed-over lacerations. Rodrik stood at her left, also bandaged. Famke fidgeted off to one side, chewing the nails of her long, slender fingers.

Gabriella shot Ulrika a sad smirk as the crossbowmen forced her to kneel beside her, but she said nothing. Mathilda was speaking, and not softly.

'I didn't come t'kill ye, y'daft bitch!' she was braying. 'Y'invited me here! Y'said we was to talk peace!'

Hermione slapped her with her closed fan. 'I did no such thing! There can be no peace between us! Not after you killed Dagmar and the others!'

'But I didn't!' insisted Mathilda. 'Why would I?'

'I thought you said *I* killed Dagmar,' said Gabriella dryly. 'You should make up your mind.'

'You both did it!' Hermione shrilled. 'You have conspired against me from the first!'

Ulrika had had enough. 'Mistresses!' she cried, in a voice she had last used when addressing cavalry troops in the field. 'I have proof that the killer is none of us! And that he is on his way here.'

Everyone turned to look at her, staring.

'How dare you interrupt your betters, girl!' snapped Hermione, but Gabriella cut her off.

'Who is it then?' she asked. 'And what is this proof?'

Ulrika looked around at them, waiting to be shouted down, but even Hermione seemed willing to hear.

'The killer is a great undead beast that resides in a crypt within the Garden of Morr in the Temple District,' she said. 'Its companion, or master, or servant – I know not which – is a warlock capable of hiding the beast even from our eyes. I found the beast's coffin and the necromancer's books in the crypt.'

'Are we expected to believe this story because you tell it?' sneered Hermione. 'You are your mistress's creature after all.'

'I said I have proof!' Ulrika cried, then continued before Hermione could draw a breath. 'In the necromancer's desk I found notes from a spy.' She looked around at them all. 'Someone among us who has told him our every move. Someone who knew Madam Dagmar would be alone in her coach the night she died. Someone who knew that Mathilda would come here even though she was not invited.'

Hermione and her gentlemen all began to look around at each other, frowning suspiciously.

'The note is in my doublet,' said Ulrika to Hermione. 'I would give it to you except my hands are bound.'

'I will get it for you, mistress,' said Otilia, coming forwards from where she stood at the door.

Ulrika turned towards her, nodding to where the note was tucked, then froze, all at once remembering where she had seen the graceful script of the note before. It had been on the directions that Otilia had given Gabriella when Hermione had sent them to stay at Aldrich's house – directions written in Otilia's own hand!

Suddenly other things flashed back to her – things that had seemed inconsequential at the time. It had been Otilia who had suggested that the Lahmians look for clues in front of the Silver Lily, where the little warlock had planted the fur and the paw prints that had led them erroneously to suspect Mathilda. It had been Otilia who had poisoned Hermione against Gabriella by reminding her of the countess's von Carstein blood. It had been Otilia who had urged Hermione to retreat to Mondthaus and who had tricked Mathilda into following her here with the false promise of peace talks.

'No!' Ulrika barked. 'Not her! No one but Lady Hermione! I trust no one else!'

Otilia paused, her face going pale, but Hermione rolled her eyes.

'Don't be ridiculous,' she said. 'I'm not touching you. You stink of rose water and corpses. Otilia, fetch me the note.'

'No!' snarled Ulrika. 'I will bite her throat out if she comes near me!'

Von Zechlin snorted and drew his sword. 'Stay back, Frau Otilia. I will deal with this tatterdemalion.'

Otilia continued forwards. 'No, no,' she said. 'It is no trouble, m'lord. I am not afraid.'

'Nonsense,' said von Zechlin, laying his sword against Ulrika's neck. 'A gentleman allows no woman to be exposed to danger, regardless of her station. Now stay still, filth.'

With fastidious fingers he pulled aside the grimy edge of Ulrika's doublet and withdrew the note which she had tucked between it and her shirt. Ulrika shot a glance at Otilia and saw that she was backing quietly but quickly towards the door.

'Stop her!' Ulrika shouted. 'She's going to run!'

Otilia froze as everyone turned to look at her. 'I was merely retiring to my place, mistress,' she said with a curtsey to Hermione and a dagger glare at Ulrika.

Von Zechlin waved the note open, then held it up so that Hermione could read it. 'I would not have you touch it, m'lady,' he said. 'It is as filthy as the wretch herself.'

Hermione peered sceptically at the little piece of paper, but then her face fell and she snatched it from von Zechlin to read it again. 'Otilia!' she cried. 'This is in your hand!'

Everyone turned again to Otilia, and saw that she was halfway out of the door.

'Seize her!' shrieked Hermione.

Two of her gentlemen leapt to do her bidding as Otilia ran out of the door and slammed it behind her. They threw it open again and raced out after her. Everyone in the room waited, listening to the sounds of a scuffle from the hall, and then the door opened again and the men dragged Otilia back in, her perfectly coifed hair now awry, and her face white except for two spots of livid red on her cheeks. They brought her before Hermione and forced her down, holding onto her shoulders.

'Explain yourself, Otilia,' said Hermione, holding out the note. 'What have you done?'

'There is little to explain, mistress,' the housekeeper said. 'I have betrayed you.'

'But... but why?' said Hermione, looking distraught. 'Haven't I always cared for you? Haven't I loved you? You were my most loyal servant!'

'Aye,' said Otilia, her voice suddenly sharpening. 'And what has that loyalty won me? Nothing!' She raised her chin defiantly and looked Hermione in the eye. 'For ten years you have dangled the blood kiss before me, always promising it, but always next year, next year.' She shot a dark look at Famke. 'And then you take in this gutter slut, this peasant with no manners, and give her what you have denied me! Look at me!' she spat, pointing to her face. 'I will be forty this year. Already I am old! I do not want to be made immortal when I am a hag!'

Hermione gaped at her, unstrung. 'Oh, but beloved, I was going to give it to you. I only–'

'No more lies!' snarled Otilia. 'You knew you'd not hold my loyalty once you turned me. You only used the promise of it as a carrot. Well I saw through it at last! I am done with you!' She laughed wildly, her eyes fever-bright. 'I found someone willing to give me the gift now! And all that was required was your destruction!'

'Who?' asked Gabriella, straining forwards on her knees. 'To whom have you betrayed us?'

But Hermione stepped to Otilia before she could answer, and lifted her off the floor by the neck, her claws extending. 'Traitorous bitch!' she hissed. 'Do you want my kiss? You shall have it!'

'No, Hermione,' called Gabriella. 'Don't kill her yet! Ask her who–'

A silent thunderclap concussion staggered Ulrika and cut off Gabriella's words. Ulrika felt as if she had been struck by lightning, or knocked down by a towering wave. At the same time, a pressure she hadn't realised was there seemed to have lifted from her chest. Her ears popped and she felt dizzy and light. She looked around. Gabriella and Mathilda were writhing on the ground, thrashing their heads around on the rug, and Hermione had dropped Otilia and fallen against von Zechlin, clutching her temples and hissing in pain. In the corner, Famke was slumped unconscious against the wall.

Strangely, none of the humans seemed to have felt a thing. They were staring at their stricken mistresses in utter befuddlement.

'My lady,' said von Zechlin, trying to support Hermione with his one unwounded arm. 'What has happened? Are you well?'

Hermione winced and shook her head, then found her feet and looked around, her eyes wide, and paler than Ulrika had ever seen her. 'My wards. The defences of the house,' she said. 'They are all broken. Something has shattered them.'

Rodrik and von Zechlin and the rest of the gentlemen drew their swords and turned in uneasy circles, not sure where the threat would come from.

On the floor at their feet, Otilia laughed, high and harsh. 'He is coming!' she cried. 'He is bringing your doom, mistress!'

Hermione snarled and wrenched her up off the floor again. 'Who!' she croaked. 'Who has done this?'

With a deafening crash, the glass doors to the garden exploded inwards and a huge form erupted through them, flaring enormous bat wings as it landed in the middle of the room. It glared at them with hooded red eyes and dropped into a hunch-backed crouch, wet, crimsoned claws extending like scythe blades from its massive hands as its wings shrank and shrivelled into the skin of its long, dead-white arms.

'Vengeance!' it rasped in a voice like gravel between mill stones. 'Vengeance on my tormentors!'

CHAPTER TWENTY-FIVE
THE BEAST

THE WHOLE ROOM stared, frozen, as the thing stepped forwards and roared. Ulrika had thought it frightening when she had fought it blind. It was even more horrifying revealed – a twisted, towering, misshapen thing, both hulking and gaunt, powerful and crippled, terrifying and pitiful at the same time.

Its naked arms and legs were striated with muscle, but also bent and deformed, as if broken and poorly set, and its chest was sunken and scarred with a thousand old wounds. But hardest to look at was its head, which looked like a broken egg – bald and white and shattered. The left half of its hollow-cheeked face was lower than the right, and the left sphere of its skull was crushed and flat and thinly covered in a lumpy network of scar-tissue. Its jaw too had been broken at some point, and angled off to the right so that its teeth did not meet neatly with each other when it closed its mouth.

'A Strigoi,' murmured Gabriella from where she lay. 'I should have guessed.'

Hermione choked and dropped Otilia to clap her hands over her mouth and nose as the monster's rancid corpse stench enveloped them all. Famke choked awake, sputtering and retching at the smell. Von Zechlin and Rodrik and the other gentlemen coughed and cursed and staggered back, and Ulrika, Gabriella and Mathilda, who could not bring their hands to their faces because of their chains, tried to bury their noses against their shoulders.

'What do you want with us, monster!' cried Hermione, grimacing and edging backwards as she waved her men forwards. 'Why do you prey upon us!'

'You know why!' roared the beast. 'It was you who sent the soldiers! It was you who made them break me!'

'What?' Hermione said as her men spread out to encircle the thing. 'What soldiers? What are you talking about!'

'A hundred years!' it bellowed, stepping forwards and gusting more stench at them. 'A hundred years I lay in that pit, broken with the boulders the soldiers threw down on me! A hundred years without knowing who had sent them. Now I know. It was you! The bitches of Nuln! You are my tormentors!'

'Who has been telling you these lies!' cried Hermione. 'I never sent soldiers against you. I don't know you! I've never seen you before!'

'The voice does not lie!' cried the Strigoi. 'The voice said it was you! It said I would be renewed when I killed you! Reformed!'

'A voice?' Mathilda barked a laugh. 'You hear voices? You're mad!'

'Mad?' the Strigoi shrieked. 'Yes, I am mad! You broke my head!'

And with that it pounced, smashing through Hermione's gentlemen as if they weren't there to lunge at her, its bloody claws slashing.

Hermione shrieked and ducked away from it to flee for the heavy door which led to the stone keep – the oldest and strongest part of the house.

'Protect me!' she screamed over her shoulder. 'Don't let it get me!'

Von Zechlin and Rodrik and the others recovered themselves and charged it as it turned after her. It back-handed them, hooked claws extended, and three flew back, chests crushed and guts spilling onto the carpet, but the others hemmed it in within a circle of flashing blades.

Otilia backed away as the battle raged, clutching her bruised throat and laughing at Hermione. 'Here is your killer, mistress!' she cried. 'And even if you kill him, you still die, for there is more doom to come! I go to fetch it!' And with that, she turned and fled out the door.

'This is doom enough, I think,' Gabriella muttered, lying on her side and struggling to break her chains.

Ulrika did the same, knowing the Strigoi was coming for them as soon as it finished with the men, but with her arms behind her it was impossible. She dropped onto her back and started pulling them up under her legs.

'Sister, wait! Gabriella shouted as Hermione unlocked the heavy door. 'Don't leave us chained! Free us!'

Hermione ignored her and threw open the door. She turned and held out a hand to Famke. 'Famke! Come quickly!'

'No, Famke!' called Ulrika, wrenching her chained arms past her feet. 'Help us! Help us break our chains!'

Famke looked from Hermione to Ulrika and back, frozen with indecision, as two more men died and the Strigoi threw a third across the room to crash through a table.

'What you two need is thinner arms,' laughed Mathilda, then with a howl of pain and a grinding of bone on bone, her form twisted and changed and fur sprouted from her skin. Her jaw and nose extended into a long, fanged snout, and the hair on her head shrank down to thick black fur, revealing pointed ears. The shackles dropped from her skinny forelegs as her wolfish transformation became complete, and she bounded towards the Strigoi, snarling and snapping, her human clothes bagging around her.

'Famke!' Hermione shrilled. 'Come here this minute!'

But Famke had made up her mind the other way. She dodged around the swirling melee in the centre of the room just as Ulrika lurched to her knees again.

'Thank you,' Ulrika said.

Famke said nothing, only knelt beside her and pushed against one of her manacles while pulling the other towards her. Ulrika added her strength too, pulling her arms apart as hard as she could. The iron of the manacles cut into her flesh and bruised her bones, but she only pulled harder. She would be no one's sitting duck.

Over Famke's heaving shoulders, Ulrika saw the Strigoi knock Rodrik over a chair and backhand Mathilda's wolf form into a wall, then pick up von Zechlin in one huge hand. The wounded champion struggled in its grip and stabbed into its shoulder with his sword. The Strigoi howled and tore von Zechlin's sword arm off at the shoulder, flinging it across the room, then crushed his chest like it was a bird's nest.

The huge she-wolf leapt on the Strigoi's back and bit the scruff of its neck. It roared and caught her with both hands then threw her off, slamming her into a wall.

The Strigoi's angry red eyes turned on Ulrika, Famke and Gabriella, and it stepped towards them through the bodies of the gentlemen that all lay broken and dying at his feet.

'Hurry, children,' said Gabriella quietly.

Ulrika looked down. The links between her manacles were stretching, but were not yet broken. She strained harder.

'Famke!' shrieked Hermione from the door. 'Get away!'

'You,' rumbled the Strigoi, pointing at Gabriella. 'You burned me with silver. You die first.'

It shambled forwards, lurching with each step, and reached out for her.

With a snap like a whip-crack, the chain between Ulrika's manacles broke. She lunged forwards and pulled Gabriella away just as the Strigoi's claws started to close around her, then snatched up a poker from the fireplace and stabbed it into the beast's right eye.

The Strigoi fell back, screaming and clutching at its face, wrenching the poker from Ulrika's hands. She cursed the loss of the weapon, then hauled Famke up and pushed her in the direction of the door.

'Go!' she shouted. 'Go!'

But as the girl galumphed for Hermione, the Strigoi tore the poker from its broken socket and flung it blindly. By sheer accident, it cracked Famke on the back of the head and she crashed face-first to the floor.

From the door, Hermione shrieked. 'No!' and ran out to help her.

By the fireplace, Ulrika turned to Gabriella, sprawled beside her on the rug, and grabbed her manacles, which were still behind her back. In front of them, the Strigoi was getting to its knees and mewling as it pawed at its ruined eye.

'Sorry, mistress,' she said. 'This will hurt.'

'Just do it,' hissed Gabriella.

Ulrika knelt on one manacle, pressing it hard against the floor, then jerked up on the other using both hands. Gabriella grunted with pain as her arms twisted in her sockets, but did not otherwise complain.

The Strigoi felt around it, then caught up one of the wounded gentlemen. With a roar, it bit into the man's neck and shoulder, crushing his clavicle with its powerful jaws and drinking deep. The man screamed in pain. Beyond the beast, Hermione was carrying the unconscious Famke back towards the heavy door.

Ulrika jerked on the chain once more and it popped, slapping her in the face with a broken link. She staggered up, pulling Gabriella with her, then both immediately dived aside, for the Strigoi was charging them, its eye half-restored beneath a mask of blood.

'That way!' shouted Gabriella, pointing to where Hermione was carrying Famke through the heavy door.

Ulrika ran with the countess as the Strigoi skidded to a stop, inches from the fire, then reversed course. Rodrik and Mathilda — back to human form and mostly naked — lurched up from where the beast had thrown them and stumbled after them. But just as they reached the door, Hermione heaved Famke through it, then turned and slammed it in their faces.

Gabriella crashed into the thick oak planks, then pounded on them. 'Hermione! Open the door!'

'M'lady, please!' cried Rodrik.

They heard the lock clack shut.

Mathilda kicked it. 'Selfish bitch!'

Gabriella sneered at Rodrik as they turned to face the oncoming Strigoi. 'Such concern your new mistress shows for you.'

She clutched Ulrika's arm. 'Up the stairs! Quick!'

Ulrika dodged around the newel post and started up the stairs with the countess as Mathilda and Rodrik scrambled behind. The Strigoi thundered after them, bawling slurred curses. Halfway up the first flight, Ulrika almost tripped over von Zechlin's unsocketed arm, which still held his exquisite rapier. She grabbed for the sword as she ran. The arm came with it. She took both. There was no time to separate them.

There was another heavy door to the right of the stairs at the top, and Ulrika realised that it too must lead to the stone keep. It was ajar! She and Gabriella ran for it but, as they reached it, it slammed shut and the lock shot home, just as had happened below.

'You commit murder, sister!' shouted Gabriella. 'The queen will hear of this!'

'Unless *we're* murdered,' growled Mathilda.

They turned to the stairs, which shook and boomed under the Strigoi's heavy tread. It was clambering up from the turning on its hands and feet, so huge that it couldn't stand upright in the well.

'Come,' said Gabriella. 'We can hold it here!'

Ulrika pried the dead fingers of von Zechlin's arm from his rapier and threw the grisly thing at the monster, then joined Rodrik and Mathilda as they lined up at the top of the stairs. They rained blows down upon the Strigoi as it lashed up at them with its claws and tried to catch their legs.

'Brother, please! Sheath your claws!' called Gabriella. 'We are not your enemies! We did not hurt you!'

'Liar!' it roared. 'You broke my bones! Now I will mend them with your blood!'

The thing caught Mathilda's foot and she fell, but Ulrika slashed down at its wrist and it let go before it could pull her down the stairs. Mathilda jumped back to her feet, hissing and barking.

'Fool!' Gabriella cried. 'Our blood will not heal you! You have been tricked!'

'No!' the Strigoi bellowed. 'It is true! The voice told me so! The voice does not lie!'

It surged up, tearing the railing from the stairs and swinging it at them like a pole arm. Ulrika and the others danced back as the length of rail swept at their knees. The monster charged up behind it, its words becoming a gibbering, incomprehensible screech.

'Run!' cried Gabriella.

They turned and fled down the hall. There were two doors on the left, and one on the right. Ulrika tried the left-hand ones, but they were both locked. Gabriella turned the latch of the right-hand one and it opened.

'In! In!' she cried, then dashed through it.

Mathilda and Rodrik dived after her. Ulrika looked back, then ducked as the Strigoi hurled the length of rail at her like a bolt from a ballista. It glanced off her shoulder and clattered down the hall. She threw herself through the door, wincing in pain. Gabriella slammed and locked it behind her.

Almost instantly they heard the Strigoi beating and clawing at it.

'That won't hold him for long,' said Gabriella.

'Don't worry,' said Mathilda. 'We'll get the ungainly bastard as he squeezes through.'

Ulrika got to her feet and looked around. They were in a small, powder-blue boudoir, filled with curved-back chairs, lace pillows and delicate little tables set with porcelain vases from Cathay. There were doors on the side walls and a painted sun on the ceiling. She grimaced. Hermione really did have the most execrable taste.

Gabriella drew a dagger from her bodice and handed it to Ulrika. It was the one with the silvered blade. 'Use this,' she said. 'My hands will be busy with spells.'

Ulrika took the thing warily in her off hand. 'Y-yes, mistress.'

'Give it to me!' said Rodrik, raising his voice to be heard over the Strigoi's thumping. 'I don't fear it.'

'No,' sniffed Gabriella. 'I don't give silver to those I don't trust.'

Rodrik's face fell, but he said nothing, only turned to the door and readied himself as Gabriella started murmuring incantations behind him.

Ulrika went on guard as well, then looked over at Mathilda, a sudden thought coming to her. 'Where is your gang? Surely you didn't come here unescorted.'

Mathilda curled her lip. 'They're locked in the cellar, and a fat lot of good they're doing down there.' She shot a look at Rodrik. 'Sir knight and the other "gentlemen" ambushed us as they waved us through the gate. Pistols and bolts of silver.'

Ulrika nodded. 'They had me the same way.'

A crack appeared in the door, and it bent inwards in the centre. Mathilda growled and tore off the remains of her clothes, then dropped to all fours, a wolf again before her front paws touched the ground.

Another shattering impact and the Strigoi's malformed head, shoulders and arms burst through into the room in an explosion of splinters and flying timber. Ulrika, Rodrik and Mathilda leapt at it as one, swords and claws and teeth flashing, while from behind them, a column of black flames hit it in the chest and enveloped it.

The Strigoi roared in pain and frustration, flailing blindly. It blocked Ulrika's rapier with a hardened forearm, but she jabbed it in the shoulder with the silvered dagger. Its roar turned into a shriek, and it jerked back violently, trying to retreat out of the door.

'Good!' called Gabriella. 'Press him! Kill him!'

Ulrika pushed forwards, looking for another opening for the dagger. Mathilda hung from its left arm by her teeth, trying to hold it in the door, while Rodrik stabbed over her head, aiming for the Strigoi's eyes.

Then a sharp voice in the hallway cried out strange, barbaric words and, like black waves surging around a rock, a flood of writhing shadows poured over the retreating Strigoi's shoulders and around its sides. The shadows splashed over Ulrika and the others, and where they touched they burned, a stinging, biting pain, like bathing in lye. Ulrika staggered back, covering her face as her eyes burned and dried. She crashed against a chair and fell across it. Mathilda yelped and rolled on the floor, while Rodrik slashed dangerously around with his sword, shouting, 'Get them off! Get them off!'

Gabriella rasped out a new incantation and the shadows lessened, as did the burning, but they had done their job. The Strigoi was through the door, and a round little man in black robes followed it, more weird words spilling from his lips. Ulrika snarled at the sight of him. Her nemesis! The warlock!

Gabriella hauled her up and pulled her towards the door on the left-hand wall. 'Back!' she cried. 'Hurry!'

She threw open the door and pushed Ulrika through it as the Strigoi advanced and an unnatural blackness began to spread from the warlock's pudgy hands and filled the boudoir. Rodrik rushed through with them, cursing, and the she-wolf bounded after him, inches ahead of the monster's claws.

Gabriella slammed the door in the Strigoi's face and threw the lock. The door shook and splintered as it slammed into it, but stayed closed.

'I wondered where his keeper was,' said the countess, backing away. 'Well, I am prepared this time.'

There came another smash on the door, and black tendrils began to snake around the edges of it. Ulrika looked behind her, seeking escape or advantage. They were in a huge and lavish bedroom – Hermione's, without a doubt – with curtained windows on two walls, and a pair of tall, glass-panelled doors that led out to a balcony to her right. A swagged and canopied four-poster bed sat against the left wall like some elephantine duchess, while a scattering of frilly chairs and tables and chests of drawers served it for courtiers. Above them, the curving arms of an enormous chandelier spread like a gold and crystal jellyfish, and there was a circular tower room in the far corner in which hung a delicately made golden birdcage, big enough to hold a man. Ulrika sighed sadly when she saw it. If only it had been silver, and big enough to hold a monster.

Another smash and the door buckled. The black tendrils poured through the cracks.

'I will hold back that infernal darkness,' said Gabriella as she began to move her hands in arcane patterns, 'and keep the sorcerer in check. But it will take all my concentration. You will have to deal with the Strigoi.'

'Aye, mistress,' said Ulrika, not taking her eyes from the door.

'Don't worry,' said Rodrik. 'I have his measure now.'

The she-wolf only growled and lowered her shaggy black head.

Then from behind them came the bright tinkle of breaking glass. Ulrika shot a glance over her shoulder. A clawed white hand was tearing the pane out of a broken window. Another hand punched through another window, a foot kicked through a third.

Rodrik turned. 'What is that?'

The glass in the balcony doors smashed in and three hunched, half-naked forms crawled through the gaps. Ghouls! More were climbing through every window in the room.

'Ursun's teeth and claws,' cursed Ulrika.

Rodrik and the she-wolf edged back towards the left-hand wall, trying to keep all threats in front of them. Ulrika took Gabriella's arm and drew her back with them.

'Mistress,' she said. 'Come away from the–'

With a final shattering crash, the door from the boudoir exploded inwards and the huge Strigoi bulled through it, surrounded by a spreading fog of impenetrable black. It came forwards, splinters raining from its sloping shoulders, as its deformed followers pulled themselves through the broken windows and closed in from every corner of the room.

CHAPTER TWENTY-SIX
CRIMSON AND SILVER

WITH A FINAL tearing syllable, Gabriella completed her incantation and shot out her hands. The black billows of sorcerous darkness retreated like smoke before a strong wind, but the ghouls and the Strigoi came on, and in the broken door appeared the sorcerer, his bland round face a mask of concentration as he struggled against the countess's wards.

'Murnau! Kill the sorceress!' he rasped. 'The others will be blind without her spells.'

'Kill the Strigoi!' hissed Gabriella through clenched teeth. 'The ghouls will flee with its death.'

'I'll kill it!' barked Ulrika, waving Rodrik and the she-wolf back. 'You two keep the ghouls at bay!'

'But–' began Rodrik, but Gabriella cut him off.

'Do as she says!' she snapped. 'She has the silver!'

There was no more time for argument. The ghouls surged in from all sides, and the Strigoi launched itself at Gabriella, claws raised. As the she-wolf and Rodrik met the scabrous horde head on, Ulrika leapt into the monster's path, slashing wildly with her rapier while cupping the silvered dagger for a hidden strike. But the thing the sorcerer had called Murnau had learned its lesson. It ignored her sword, letting it chop into its hip to the bone though its knees buckled in agony, and struck instead only at her off hand.

Its blow hurt like a hammer fall, knocking the dagger from Ulrika's grasp and tearing red trenches in her wrist. She tried to snatch the little blade as it skittered across the wooden floor, but Murnau's other hand smashed her between the shoulders, sending her flying across the room to slam headfirst into the wall.

Her skull dented the plaster as she hit, and she crumpled to the floor, her vision dimming and the room spinning in dizzy circles. The Strigoi was down too, struggling to rise as it clutched its bloody, butchered hip. If she could find the dagger again she could finish it. She searched the floor. There. It had come to rest at the sorcerer's feet. But as she started to crawl for it, the little man snatched it up, laughing in triumph.

His laugh became a shriek of pain as Gabriella made him pay for his break in concentration and blasted him with a column of black fire. He staggered back into the doorway, his clothes smoking, but then recovered and thrust out his hands in a shielding gesture. Gabriella's flames stopped as if they had struck a wall, then turned back towards her, reaching for her with licking fingers. She held them off with difficulty, murmuring furiously under her breath.

The Strigoi rose and limped towards her again but, frozen in her duel with the warlock, she could do nothing except inch back towards the wall.

'Mistress!'

Ulrika flailed to her feet, and almost fell over again as her head spun. She wasn't going to reach the Strigoi in time, and Rodrik and the she-wolf were surrounded by ghouls. They could not break away. Murnau limped under the chandelier, slashing at Gabriella as she stumbled back, still trying to hold the warlock's spells at bay.

The death of her blood father, Adolphus Krieger, suddenly flashed through Ulrika's mind. The troll-slayer Snorri Nosebiter had killed the vampire by dropping a massive iron chandelier on him! Ulrika's eyes followed the chain that raised and lowered the chandelier, and saw that its winch was bolted to the wall only two steps from her. She threw herself towards it, raising her rapier and swung a clumsy blow at the chain.

It was enough. With a ringing clash, the chain parted and whirred through its pulleys. The heavy gold chandelier dropped like a stone, smashing down on the Strigoi in an explosion of crystal and flying candles, and crushing it to the floor. Unfortunately, it also knocked the she-wolf flat, and sent Rodrik and Countess Gabriella staggering.

The ghouls pounced on them.

Ulrika shouted in dismay and staggered forwards, weaving like a drunk, and hacked around at the hunched fiends, stabbing their sunken eyes and chopping through their albino fingers and wrists to drive them away. The horde shrank back at the fury of her onslaught, but before she could reach Gabriella, Murnau surged up, lifting the heavy golden wheel of the chandelier over its bloody head and roaring with rage.

Ulrika cursed. So much for killing the Strigoi the way Krieger had died. It wasn't even stunned.

The ghouls scattered for the corners of the room as Murnau turned blazing red eyes on Ulrika and made to hurl the chandelier at her. She turned and ran, then dived through the curtains of Hermione's four-poster bed and bounced down on the far side as the massive metal fixture sailed over her head, crashing through the canopy and smashing into the fireplace behind her, dragging bunting and curtains and broken bed-posts with it.

'Pesky fly!' bellowed the Strigoi. 'Stand and face me!'

Ulrika looked over the edge of the bed and saw it limping towards her. Could nothing stop the monster? Its scalp was split to the bone, it had deep gashes in its arms and neck, jagged crystal shards buried in its shoulders, and still it came. At least she had distracted it from Gabriella, who was recovering and resuming her duel with the warlock, while Rodrik and the she-wolf were up and cutting down ghouls again, but how could she kill it without the silvered dagger?

The smell of smoke made her look behind her. The curtains and canopy that had snagged on the chande-lier were starting to burn in the fireplace. Fire! That was the way! Fire could stop it!

The Strigoi lurched around the bed, reaching for her. She tore off the sheets and blankets and hurled them at it, covering its head. It snarled and clutched at them, trying to pull them off. Ulrika rolled to the hearth and yanked out a broken bedpost, trailing with flaming curtains, then swung them at the monster like a flail. The curtains slapped across its back, setting the sheets that covered him to smouldering, but not fast enough. It would have them off before the flames really caught.

She looked around, desperate, and saw an oil-lamp on a little table by the bed. She grabbed it and hurled it at Murnau. It shattered on its bony shoulder and the oil splashed everywhere. Instantly, flames erupted from the sheets and the Strigoi howled in pain.

Ulrika charged in, laughing with relief and slashing at its legs with her rapier as it staggered around, trying to pull the burning mantle from its head. She had done it! It was as good as dead! But then, from across the room, the sorcerer shrieked a strange phrase and the flames shrank to nothing and went out, replaced by a cloud of smoke that stank of burnt hair.

The Strigoi ripped the blackened sheets from its head and grabbed for her, its face and neck covered in blisters.

'Burn me, will you?' it roared. 'I'll burn you!'

Ulrika hopped back, slashing at its arms, but it slapped her blade aside and kicked her in the chest with one huge, clawed foot. She flew back and crashed down on the wreckage of the curtain-shrouded chandelier, falling between two of its golden arms and getting tangled in the mess of bunting. She struggled to pull herself out as the Strigoi limped closer, but could get no purchase on the loose cloth. She felt like she had been thrown in a barrel, posterior first, and was folded in half, arms and legs flailing. It was ridiculous, an embarrassing way to die.

Then she felt heat on her head and shoulders. The flames that were consuming the curtains were creeping towards her. With a cry she tried to pull away from them, but only slipped further between the two arms of the chandelier. She was trapped, and the Strigoi and the fire were both closing in.

'Leave her, fool!' came the sorcerer's voice. 'Get the witch! The witch!'

The Strigoi snarled, reluctant, but started back towards Gabriella, glaring over its shoulder at Ulrika. 'Don't burn too fast, little fly,' it rasped. 'You are mine to finish.'

Ulrika dropped her rapier and struggled harder to pull herself free of the chandelier. She had to protect the countess. Her thrashing only sank her deeper into the pocket of drapery. The fire singed the hair on the back of her head. Its crackle was loud in her ears.

As she slipped lower, she could just see the Strigoi closing in on Gabriella from behind. Rodrik and the she-wolf were busy fighting back to back in the seething circle of ghouls. They didn't see it coming!

'Mistress, look out!' Ulrika cried. 'Mathilda! Rodrik! Stop him!'

Gabriella was still locked in frozen combat with the sorcerer, but Rodrik and the she-wolf cried out, fear in his eyes, and tried to fight free of the ghouls.

The view vanished as Ulrika dropped deeper into the pocket of bunting. A coil of flaming fabric slithered down on top of her, burning her face. She shrieked and scrabbled wildly at the yielding cloth and tore through it with her claws to thud on the floor. Chagrin stung her, painful as the blisters on her cheeks, as she rolled away from the blazing cloth. She could have cut herself out of the pocket at any time! She had forgotten her claws! She had been thinking like a human!

A scream from Gabriella brought her head up and she looked around. In the centre of the room, Murnau was raising the struggling countess over its head in one hand while the she-wolf dragged at the other with her jaws and Rodrik fought towards them through the last few ghouls.

'Mistress,' gasped Ulrika, pushing unsteadily to her feet. 'I'm coming!'

As Ulrika stumbled forwards, Murnau flung the she-wolf through the shattered balcony doors. She smashed into the balustrade, then tumbled over it and fell to the yard, just as Rodrik broke free of the ghouls and chopped Murnau in the ribs. The monster howled and swung Gabriella at him like a club, smashing him flat and stomping on his ribs.

'No, beast!' cried Ulrika, hacking down the last remaining ghouls to reach it. 'Fight me!'

Murnau roared and flung Gabriella at her. Ulrika ducked instinctively as the countess sailed over her head, then ran the Strigoi through the gut with her rapier and tried to claw its eyes with her free hand. It clubbed her in the face with a bone-knuckled fist, and she crashed to the floor, leaving the sword sticking out of its stomach. The monster collapsed in agony, clawing at it.

As her consciousness wavered, a shadow in black robes caught the corner of Ulrika's eye. It was the warlock, the silvered dagger in his hand, creeping towards Gabriella, who lay slumped unconscious on the ruin of the bed.

'No!' Ulrika gasped, but the Strigoi's sledgehammer fist had stunned her and her limbs wouldn't answer.

Rodrik staggered back to his feet, echoing her cry, and stumbled for the sorcerer, bent double over his shattered ribs and dragging his heavy sword behind him. He swung wildly just as the little man stabbed down at Gabriella, striking him a glancing blow, then crashed headlong into him.

The silvered dagger tore the mattress an inch from Gabriella's arm as Rodrik and the warlock tumbled together to the floor. Rodrik elbowed the little man in the face, then pushed to his knees, straddling him, and raised his sword.

The warlock stabbed Rodrik under the ribs with the silvered dagger, and the knight grunted and toppled sideways, his sword slipping from his grip. The little man shoved him off and struggled to his feet.

In a panic, Ulrika fought again to stand, but the Strigoi recovered first, and grabbed her from behind, picking her up by the neck.

'Now, you burn!' it roared, then raised her over its head and turned towards the fire.

As she struggled weakly in the Strigoi's grip, Ulrika saw the sorcerer leaning over Gabriella, laughing, the silvered dagger held high.

'Mistress,' she cried, 'Mistress, wake up.' But she knew it would be too late.

A thunderclap bang punched her in the ears, and the Strigoi squealed and staggered beneath her. She slipped from its suddenly slack fingers and crashed to the ground head first.

Through a fog of pain she saw the sorcerer turn, eyes wide, then another thunderclap rang through the room and he jerked back, the silvered dagger flying from his hand as his head exploded in a shower of gore and he sank to the floor.

Ulrika rolled onto her back and looked up. A tall figure in a broad hat stood in the bedroom door, a smoking pistol in each hand. Ulrika blinked in surprise.

It was witch hunter Templar Friedrich Holmann.

CHAPTER TWENTY-SEVEN
THE UNKINDEST CUT

THE STRIGOI ROARED and stepped over Ulrika, limping unsteadily towards the witch hunter. She could see a smoking, black-edged hole in its back where the silvered pistol ball had struck it, and also the bloodied point of her rapier, still piercing it from front to back. Holmann tossed his pistols aside as it came towards him. He ripped a glass vial from his bandolier and drew his sword, his grey eyes blazing with righteous fury.

'Foul fiend of darkness,' he cried, hurling the globe. 'In Sigmar's name, I shall destroy thee!'

The Strigoi knocked the vial away, shattering it, and the water splashed its hand and arm. It snarled as its skin bubbled and hissed, but it did not slow. Holmann dodged its swipes and cut its arms with his sword, but the beast hardly seemed to feel it.

Ulrika shook her head, trying to clear her dizziness, then forced herself to her feet. Steel and blessed water would not be enough to stop Murnau, even wounded as it was. Without silver or fire, Holmann didn't stand a chance.

Bright metal winked at her from the floor – the silvered dagger! It lay where the sorcerer had dropped it when he had died. She staggered towards it as Murnau knocked Holmann into the bed beside the still unconscious Gabriella, stunning him, then raised its claws for a final strike. Ulrika snatched up the dagger and fell towards the Strigoi, stabbing for its bullet wound. She fell short. The shining blade only scored its flank.

It was enough to get its attention. The Strigoi howled as its flesh blackened, and flailed a maddened backhand at her. The barrel-sized fist hit her in the chest and sent her skidding on her back across the polished floor to crash into the remains of the balcony doors.

'No more silver!' it cried, stomping after her. 'No more pain!'

Ulrika struggled to get to her feet as the thing lumbered closer, but the shock of so many impacts had made her limbs numb and clumsy. The room kept tilting to the left.

Holmann picked himself up from the bed and threw another vial at Murnau. The Strigoi roared as the glass shattered and blessed water splashed across its back, raising blisters and steam.

'Sigmar grant me strength!' cried Holmann, charging in and aiming a cut at its neck.

Murnau turned and caught his sword arm, and flung him at Ulrika just as she made it to her feet. They slammed backwards together through the shattered doors to crash down on the stone flags of the balcony. The silvered dagger bounced from Ulrika's grasp and disappeared over the edge to fall to the yard below.

Holmann groaned on top of her, clutching his wrenched and mangled arm. Inside, the Strigoi was limping towards them, its hideous face contorted in pain and Ulrika's rapier still sticking from its belly.

'Get off,' she said. 'It's coming.'

'I should let it kill you for your treachery,' he growled, but rolled aside.

'I left you behind to keep you safe.' She grabbed the balustrade and pulled herself upright.

He rose beside her, wincing, and switched his sword to his left hand while he pressed his right against his side. 'My safety is not your concern.'

The Strigoi smashed through the door, snarling and swiping at them both. Holmann dived left, slashing behind him, left-handed and awkward. Ulrika sprang up onto the balustrade and looked down. In the yard below Mathilda, still in her she-wolf guise, was fighting a handful of ghouls, while more craned their necks towards the balcony and bayed their hunger. No escape there.

The Strigoi lashed out at Ulrika's legs, trying to sweep her off the railing. She leapt over its arm and grabbed at a gargoyle that held a lantern in its granite jaws beside the doors. Her battered skull throbbed and she nearly lost her grip to dizziness, but then pulled herself up and caught the edge of the slanted snow-patched roof.

The Strigoi's claws grabbed her right leg, but Holmann hacked at it from behind and its grip loosened as it turned to swipe at him.

Ulrika heaved herself up onto the snowy roof and shouted down at it. 'Not him, cracked-pate! Me! Up here!'

She tore slate shingles from the roof and flung them down at Murnau's head. It snarled and shielded itself with an upraised arm, but she skimmed a slate past it and cracked it in the teeth. It roared, furious, and reached for the roof with its massive hands.

This was a good idea, she thought as she crabbed backwards through the snow towards the ridge line. A slippery, uneven surface was just the thing to even the odds. Here the Strigoi's clumsiness and terrible wounds would cancel out its strength, while her agility would give her an advantage. Murnau would be slipping on the icy slates while she danced on them.

She saw her mistake as soon as it started after her. Murnau's claws did not skid on the stone shingles, they smashed through them and bit into the wood lathing beneath. It pulled itself up by main force and crawled towards her like some starved albino ape, its clawed feet digging into the roof the same way its hands did.

'Svoloch!' she swore in her native tongue.

'Ha!' it laughed. 'You've trapped yourself, little fly! And you've lost your silver fang!'

Ulrika backed down the ridge line as Murnau rose up and snatched at her with its claws. Without a weapon she couldn't hope to fight it. Its reach was too great. She shot a glance behind her. The end of the roof was fast approaching.

Its right claw raked her shoulder and knocked her on her back on the narrow roof peak. She started to slide down the snowy slates and caught herself, arms flung wide. The Strigoi roared in triumph and raised its fists to smash down at her. She looked up. The hilt of her rapier was still sticking out of its gut, right above her. She reached up and yanked it out, twisting as she pulled.

The Strigoi screeched in pain and staggered back. She slashed at it and tried to get to her feet again. It batted the blade aside with one claw and slapped her with the other, knocking her back towards the end of the roof and sending her sliding down the slant. She threw out her sword arm and stopped herself. Her head was hanging over the end of the roof. There was no more room to run.

The Strigoi climbed down the slope towards her, crushing slates with every step. Beyond it, Ulrika saw Holmann struggling to pull himself up from the balcony with his almost useless right arm. She had to give the templar credit for not giving up, but he was going to be far too late.

The Strigoi grabbed for her legs. She slashed at its hands, but started sliding again and missed. The monster caught her ankle and picked her up, holding her upside down over a sheer, three-storey drop. The scene spun dizzyingly beneath her – a small cobbled service yard between the old keep and the new wing of the house, with a quaint covered well in its centre.

'So, little fly,' rasped the Strigoi. 'Can you fly?'

Ulrika arched around like a cat in a trap, hacking at the Strigoi's left leg with all her might. The blade bit deep, finding bone, and it grunted and dropped her, stumbling back. With a desperate twist she caught the edge of the roof, letting the rapier bounce away down the slant. Her claws carved shrieking lines in the slate as her weight pulled her down and she slipped towards the edge.

The Strigoi stumped forwards again to stomp on her fingers, blood running down its leg like a red waterfall. She hooked its left foot and pulled herself up. It grabbed her, its claws crushing her ribs as it tried to tear her free, but she held on, sinking her fangs into the back of his ankle. It howled and pulled harder. She clung tighter, clamping down with her jaw like a pit dog killing a rat. Then, with a final mighty heave, it pulled her free – and she ripped its tendons out with her teeth.

As blood sprayed in a wide arc, the Strigoi fell sideways, its leg suddenly unable to support it. Ulrika scrabbled at the edge of the roof as the monster hit the slanting slates, but its claws held her tight. It bounced once, then plummeted down into the yard, clutching Ulrika to its shoulder like a favourite doll.

There was a frozen moment of horrible vertigo – just enough time to know that she would die – and then a jaw-snapping impact, a deafening crash, a second impact, more painful than the first, and then…

'Fraulein Magdova!'

The voice was loud, but far away, strange but familiar. She wished it weren't so dark so she could see who was speaking. She wished she would stop falling so the world would stop spinning.

'Fraulein!'

The pain came back. It felt like she had been plunged into a tub of ice water and beaten with sticks. All her body hurt. All of it – head to toe and inside and out. It was with difficulty that she sorted out all the sensations screaming for her attention and realised she was lying on something hard and cold.

She opened her eyes, then shut them again. The world was still spinning, much too fast. She tried again. Still spinning, but she was ready for it this time. The first thing she saw was the night sky, greying a little in one corner. Next she saw a high white wall, rising up to a peak, and then a man in a broad hat, standing at the peak, looking down at her.

'Fraulein,' he said. 'Do you live?'

'It…' she said haltingly. 'It seems so.'

The man's shoulders slumped, though whether in relief or disappointment she could not tell.

'Don't move,' he said. 'I will come to you.' Then he vanished.

Ulrika nodded absently, then frowned as she noticed dust and snow settling all around her. It felt to her jumbled brain that a week had past since she had fallen from the roof, but if the dust was still settling it must have been only seconds. Seconds! That meant Murnau might still be trying to kill her!

She tried to sit up, and all her pain hit her again, as fresh as the first time. She groaned, and sank back, using only her head to look around, and found the Strigoi.

From the vantage of the ground, it was for a moment hard to tell what had happened to it. The monster's long, scrawny body was above her, blocking out a good portion of the sky, and seeming to hang in the air. She wasn't sure how that could be, but then tipping her head further she saw that it seemed to be lying on its back on the roof of the covered well.

She still didn't quite understand, so she rolled over onto her stomach and pushed herself to her knees. Every muscle in her body shrieked at this torture but amazingly, Ulrika could feel no broken bones. How had she fallen three storeys onto cobbles without breaking a bone? Even being what she was it seemed impossible.

She sat back and looked up at the Strigoi again, and all became clearer. It was indeed lying on the well, but not precisely on the roof. It had smashed through the roof as it had fallen, and impaled itself on one of the thick oak uprights that held the roof aloft. Two feet of splintered beam stuck up through its shattered chest like a giant white tooth running with blood, and it lay splayed like some unimaginably ugly butterfly pierced by a pin.

'The beast broke my fall,' she murmured, wonderingly. What a miracle that she had bounced away and missed the impalement it had suffered.

Running footsteps brought her head up, and she tried and failed to stand. Holmann raced into the yard, sword drawn, and hurried to her.

'Fraulein,' he said, kneeling beside her. 'You should not move.'

She waved a dismissive hand at him, then leaned against the lip of the well and levered herself to her feet. The world swayed around her and her ribs and limbs and wounds throbbed with pain, but she was standing. She turned stiffly to the witch hunter.

'May I trouble you for your sword, Templar Holmann?' she asked. 'I seem to have misplaced mine.'

He looked warily at her. 'What do you intend?'

'I intend to be certain,' she said, and looked at the Strigoi.

Holmann hesitated, then reversed his heavy sword and held it out to her. She took the hilt, then stepped to the Strigoi's head, which hung off the edge of the well's roof and stared up at the sky. She raised the sword high, then stepped back, startled, as the monster's eyes blinked open and it turned to look at her, all the anger gone from its gaze, to be replaced by a sad confusion.

'The voice,' it rattled. 'The voice lied.'

The voice again. 'What voice?' asked Ulrika. 'Who told you to do this?'

'The… voice,' it replied, and then its eyes went blank and it sagged back.

Ulrika brought Holmann's sword down with a sharp snap of her wrists and severed the Strigoi's head from its shoulders in a single blow. It thudded to the cobbles and rolled to Holmann's legs.

He smiled grimly. 'It seems you were right to be certain,' he said, then held out his hand to take the sword back.

It was Ulrika's turn to hesitate. Now that he was here, she was presented again with the dilemma of what to do with him. It remained her duty to kill him, as Gabriella had ordered, and she could do it here. She had a sword and he was defenceless, his right arm torn and twisted. But how could she? He had saved her life. He had saved *Gabriella's* life, and he had trusted her with his sword even though she had tricked him on the road.

She wiped the blade clean, then reversed it and offered it back to him. He looked at her strangely as he took it back, as if he too had wondered if she would return it.

'You should go now,' she said. 'The killer is dead. Your job is done. Be off before things get… difficult.'

Holmann frowned. 'I… I would not leave you if there is to be more trouble.'

'No trouble for me,' she said. 'Just you.' She picked up the Strigoi's head by one of its outsized ears, then held it out to him. 'Here. Take this and go. Show it to your captain and claim your glory. But hurry.'

Holmann reached out for the hideous thing with his left hand but, before he could take it, Ulrika heard soft footsteps at the opening to the yard.

Madam Mathilda stood there, stark naked, her ample curves covered in scratches and bite marks, some bone deep. Ulrika groaned. Another minute and Holmann would have been away. Now it was too late.

Mathilda smiled approvingly, showing still-sharp teeth. 'Well done, dearie,' she said. 'His cowardly corpse-eaters ran off as soon as he fell.' She beckoned them forwards. 'Now bring his ugly head and yer little sweetheart, and we'll have a nice chat inside by the fire.'

Holmann shot a questioning glance at Ulrika.

She hung her head. 'Don't try it,' she murmured. 'You could not outrun her.'

'Witch hunters do not run,' he said, then set his jaw and bowed her forwards.

They walked together out of the yard, then around to the front door as Mathilda padded naked behind them, watching their every step.

As they neared the porch, Ulrika saw the silvered dagger which had fallen from the balcony above. She stooped and picked it up, then looked back at Mathilda.

The madam smiled broadly. 'Best return that to yer mistress, dearie, and don't get any ideas.'

Ulrika nodded, cowed, and tucked the dagger into her torn and bloodied doublet.

GABRIELLA WAS CARRYING Rodrik down the stairs as Mathilda herded Ulrika and Holmann into the morning room. Ulrika almost laughed at the incongruousness of the image, the delicate lady with the powerful knight in her arms, but Rodrik was deathly pale, and the countess was limping so badly she nearly dropped him.

Ulrika dropped the Strigoi's head and ran to her, taking some of Rodrik's weight. His chest was concave inside his doublet, and soaked in blood, and his sword arm was bent back the wrong way.

They lay him on a chaise as Mathilda and Templar Holmann watched from a respectful distance. As his head touched the cushions his eyes fluttered open and he looked up at Gabriella. Blood bubbled from his lips as he spoke. 'Mistress,' he said. 'Forgive me. Forgive my jealousy. I should never have left you.'

Gabriella took his hand in hers. 'And I should never have made you jealous, beloved.' She kissed his cheek. 'You are forgiven.'

Rodrik lifted her hand to his crimson lips and kissed her fingers. 'Thank you, mistress. I am proud to have died in your defence.' He took a ragged breath. 'It is all I have ever lived for.'

The breath rattled out of his throat and his head sank back, his eyes staring sightlessly at the ceiling. Gabriella looked at him for a long moment, then reached out and closed his eyelids.

'Poor besotted Rodrik,' she said sadly. 'His devotion drove him from me, then brought him back to die.'

'I'm sorry, mistress,' said Ulrika. 'I feel as if my presence pushed him away.'

Gabriella shook her head. 'You are not to blame. I could have found a way to give you your glory without denying him his. I was as petty in my way as he.' She looked at the back of her hand and saw the blood from his lips. 'He was a vain, prideful fool, but a true heart. I will miss him.'

She sighed, then licked her fingers and looked up. Her eyes focused on Holmann, standing stiff and uncomfortable a few paces behind Ulrika.

'So,' she said. 'So this is your witch hunter.'

Ulrika nodded, fearful of what was to come. 'Templar Friedrich Holmann, countess.'

Gabriella stood unsteadily, then curtseyed to Holmann. 'I am in your debt, templar,' she said. 'Your timely shots saved my life, and very likely the life of Mistress Ulrika.'

Holmann inclined his head. 'I did my duty, lady. That is all.'

Gabriella smiled at him coolly. 'And is your duty done? Or will you now arrest me?'

Holmann hesitated, his hands clenched at his side. 'I have vowed to Lady Ulrika that I would not,' he said.

'Did you?' said Gabriella. 'And you mean to honour this vow?'

Holmann stiffened even further. 'I... I have never broken my word, lady.'

'How very noble of you,' said Gabriella.

'I told ye he was her sweetheart,' chuckled Mathilda.

Holmann flushed. 'She promised me I would be in at the death of the monster. That I should have the credit of it.'

'Ah, I see,' said Gabriella, smiling slyly. 'That explains it.' She looked like she was going to say more, but at that moment, the heavy door to the old keep creaked open and Hermione and Famke peeked out, like two frightened rabbits looking from their hole.

'Is it dead?' asked Hermione.

Gabriella and Mathilda turned on her with cold eyes.

'No thanks to you,' said Gabriella.

'Left us t'die while she hid in her rookery,' sneered Mathilda. 'We'd have lost half what we lost had ye and yer ungainly get lent a hand.'

'I must protect my own!' Hermione protested, stepping out with Famke behind her.

Gabriella stepped towards her. 'Are we not your own? We are your sisters. You closed the door in our faces.'

'I panicked!' said Hermione. 'Fear overwhelmed me.'

Gabriella snorted. 'Surely the mark of a great leader. No wonder you worry for your position.'

Hermione's eyes flared at this. 'So you *do* conspire against me! You will use this tragedy to poison the queen's opinion of me.'

Mathilda laughed. 'Yer doin' just fine with that all by yer lonesome.'

As the argument continued, Ulrika edged back towards Holmann. 'Take the monster's head and go,' she whispered. 'Before they remember you are here.'

Holmann looked at the Strigoi's head, which was bleeding into the carpet where Ulrika had dropped it, but still he hesitated.

'Will you come to harm for letting me go?' he asked.

She smirked and pressed his arm. 'My safety is not your concern.'

He smiled wryly at that, then frowned again, his eyes troubled. 'I–'

The door to the front hall opened, cutting off his words, and Frau Otilia stepped in, looking flushed, but otherwise as neat and prim as she always had. 'Your pardon, mistresses,' she said, curtseying.

Hermione's argument with Gabriella and Mathilda trailed off as they noticed her.

Hermione's eyes went wide. 'You dare to show your face again, traitor? I shall have your head for what you have done!'

Gabriella started towards her, claws extending. 'Your plot failed, wretch. We have destroyed the doom you wished upon us.'

'Oh, but you have not,' she said, then curtseyed again and smiled at Hermione. 'Captain Meinhart Schenk to see you, mistress.'

CHAPTER TWENTY-EIGHT
THE TESTING OF A VOW

MATHILDA YELPED LIKE a dog and bolted out the smashed-in garden doors at Otilia's words, but the others seemed too stunned to react. They only stared as the housekeeper stepped to the side and bowed the tall, broad figure of the witch hunter captain and six of his dour lieutenants into the room. The templars strode in booted and spurred, long coats flaring, and hands on the hilts of their long swords as they glared around.

Beside Ulrika, Templar Holmann grunted with what sounded like dismay, and she heard Famke and Hermione growling, but before the Lahmians could betray themselves, Gabriella strode forwards and spread her arms in welcome.

'Captain Schenk!' she cried. 'I'm so glad you've come!'

The witch hunter stopped foursquare in the centre of the room and gave her a level look. 'Are you now?'

he asked dryly. 'So you are looking forward to your arrest?'

Gabriella put a hand to her breast and looked surprised. 'Arrest me? I don't understand. Are you not here to save us from the horrible fiends that attacked us?'

'Don't talk nonsense,' said Schenk. '*You* are the fiends.'

Gabriella's eyes widened. 'Captain, what strange misapprehension are you under? Look around you! We have been the victims of a terrible attack!'

Schenk glared at her scornfully. 'You shall be victims of Sigmar's justice soon enough, seducer. You–' He paused as he saw Holmann standing beside Ulrika. 'Templar Holmann? What are you doing here?' he asked sharply.

Holmann looked to Ulrika, his jaw working, and she was afraid that he was going to betray her then and there, but after an endless second, he stepped aside to reveal the Strigoi's head on the carpet behind him.

'I… I came to slay the vampire, captain,' he said.

Schenk stared at the huge, ugly head, making the sign of the hammer on his chest. 'Sigmar's golden beard, what foul beast is this?'

'Have you not been listening, captain?' asked Gabriella, stepping forwards. 'We have been besieged here. This vampire and its hideous servants broke in and tried to kill us!'

'And why would a vampire kill other vampires?' asked Schenk.

Gabriella stared at him, then looked around at Hermione, Famke and Ulrika. 'You still believe us vampires? I thought we cleared up all that silliness before.' She rolled her eyes. 'To think so many innocent women died because you were amusing yourselves invading ladies' parlours and questioning their virtue when you should have been out in the streets hunting for that!'

'Innocent women!' sneered Schenk. 'Lady, you will have to do better than that to cozen me! I saw the corpses of the others with my own eyes – beautiful highborn ladies like yourself, hiding their monstrous nature with honeyed words and witchy wiles, just as you do.' He glared around at them all. 'You are a foul sisterhood of fiends, seducing others to a fate worse than death, and you shall burn for it!' He turned to his men. 'Arrest them!'

Gabriella stepped forwards, hands outstretched in supplication. 'Captain, please! Listen! You don't understand! Those women were good servants of Sigmar and the Empire until that monster attacked them! It was he that made them as you saw them! And it was he that killed them when they refused, even in their corrupted state, to go against their nature and be his brides!'

Schenk stopped and stared at Gabriella, and Ulrika did too. From the moment they had walked in the door, she'd thought it inevitable that they would have to kill Schenk and his men, but somehow, impossibly, the countess seemed to have found an explanation that might appease the witch hunters and save their places in society – that is, she had if Schenk believed her. Her admiration for the countess rose even higher. Never had she seen so quick and clever a speaker.

Captain Schenk waved back his men, then stood before Gabriella, his hands on his hips. 'What is this you say? How do you know this? If I remember correctly, you arrived in Nuln only a few days ago. And *you…*' He turned to point at Hermione. 'You said you hardly knew the other women at all.'

'I do not *know*, captain,' Gabriella said. 'Not for certain, for I never met the other ladies who were the beast's victims, but I can infer from what it said to us when it attacked us. It said it wanted us for its brides. It said it wanted a queen.' She raised her chin. 'And if you do not believe that we repelled its advances to the best of our abilities, look upon our dead.' She indicated Rodrik's corpse, limp and white upon the chaise, and then those of the other gentlemen sprawled across the floor. 'My champion, Lady Hermione's guards, all killed while defending us. And still they were not enough.' She turned to Holmann. 'Were it not for the intervention of this brave young templar, you would indeed have found a house of vampire women here, for it would have infected us all. Instead, he saved us, and perhaps all the women of Nuln. We are forever in his debt.'

Schenk swung his heavy head to look at Holmann as Gabriella curtseyed to him. 'Templar, is this true?' he growled. 'Did you save these women from becoming vampires?'

Ulrika's jaw clenched as Holmann hesitated. This was the moment of truth – or untruth. He had not had to lie yet. Would he do so now and honour his vow to her, or would his vow to his god and his order take precedence? She shot him a pleading look. He did not look at her.

'I… I shot the beast, captain,' he said. 'And it was my sword that slew it.'

Ulrika had to fight to hide a smile. Well done, Herr Holmann, she thought. Neither a lie nor the whole truth.

'And the women?' Schenk pressed.

'I saw no evidence that they are anything other than what they appear,' said Holmann.

And he has the makings of a lawyer, thought Ulrika.

'But, but you denounced them before!' sputtered Schenk. He pointed at Ulrika. 'You called that one vampire in my presence!'

Ulrika's stomach dropped. She had forgotten about that. Holmann and Schenk had seen them in the yard of the Wolf's Head. The ruse was going to collapse. They would have to fight after all.

Holmann swallowed. 'At the time… I thought she was, for I saw her fight with a strength and agility that I could not credit a natural woman possessing.' He grimaced, and Ulrika thought he was close to tears. 'But she has proved herself no fiend. She is the daughter of a boyar, a noble warrior who twice saved my life from this monster's minions, and who fought by my side against it.'

'Are you beglamoured, boy?' barked Schenk. 'We saw them together. You pointed her out! You said you had seen her fangs!'

'When was this?' broke in Gabriella quickly. 'I do not recall meeting Templar Holmann before this night.'

Schenk turned on her. 'Ha! Do you lie now? You were at that hellish brothel, the Wolf's Head, in the Faulestadt. You ran us down in your coach!'

Gabriella drew herself up disdainfully. 'A brothel? South of the river? Ridiculous! No lady of quality or upright character would go to such a place.'

'You make my point for me,' said Schenk dryly. 'But there's no use denying it, countess. I saw you. My men saw you.'

'Truly?' said Gabriella, haughty. 'Or do you dislike me so much that you saw only what you wished to see?' She reached up and smoothed her mussed coiffeur. 'Tell me, then. How did I wear my hair? And Ulrika, did she wear her wig, or was she showing her blonde locks as now?'

Schenk snorted. 'Do not seek to trick me, countess. You wore a veil and your ward had her cloak over her head against the daylight. Proof of your vampirism, if any other was needed.'

Gabriella stopped dead and stared at him in apparent disbelief. 'You saw a woman with a veil over her face, and another woman hiding beneath a cloak and you decided they were Ulrika and I? Really, captain, perhaps it is you who is beglamoured.' She turned to Schenk's men, holding out an imperious hand. 'Did any of you see these women's faces? Any of you?' She looked to Holmann when they stayed silent. 'Templar?'

Holmann shook his head, looking befuddled. 'In truth I did not, m'lady. Not clearly.'

'But the woman told us you would be there!' said Schenk, his face red and flustered.

'What woman?' demanded Gabriella. 'Who gave you this lie?'

'The same as brought us here!' said Schenk, turning back towards the door to the front hall. 'Frau Krohner, Lady Hermione's housekeeper.'

Everyone turned with him, but Otilia was not there. It appeared she had slipped away sometime during the proceedings. Captain Schenk paused, confused.

Gabriella smiled to herself. 'Captain, I would not believe the word of that woman. I know not what madness possessed her, but I believe that she was in league with the fiend from the beginning. I believe it was her that led the thing to the women it killed, for she certainly led it here tonight.'

'What?' said Schenk. 'You have proof of this?'

'Her absence would seem proof enough,' said Gabriella. 'But there is indeed more.' She turned to Hermione. 'Cousin, have you the note we found?'

Hermione blinked, for a moment confused, then remembered. 'Yes!' she said. 'I have it.'

She reached into her sleeve and drew out the note, then handed it to Schenk. 'You will find that it is written in Otilia's hand,' she said.

'We found it upon one of the monster's minions,' added Gabriella as Schenk unfolded it.

"No word of G," murmured Schenk, reading aloud. "At your order, H has been convinced to retreat to MH. M has been summoned too. Map enclosed." He looked up, his brow clouded, then looked from Gabriella to Hermione. 'G for Countess Gabriella. H for Lady Hermione. Who is M?'

Ulrika tensed, shooting a nervous look at Gabriella. What lie could she tell to cover that? If she mentioned Mathilda, it would link them to the Wolf's Head and all would collapse again. But if she made up a name, Schenk would be able to check it and find it false.

'I know not,' said Gabriella smoothly. 'But is your first name not Meinhart, captain?'

Schenk's mouth fell open. His men looked at each other – the first human reaction Ulrika had seen from them.

'But – but why would she summon us if she conspired with the fiend?' Schenk asked, as much to himself as to the others.

Gabriella shrugged. 'A trap?' she asked. 'Perhaps she thought it would slay you after it murdered us. Or that you would arrest us if it failed.'

Schenk crumpled the note in his hand, then turned away with a curse and chewed his lip.

'She cannot have got far, captain,' said Gabriella, speaking to his back. 'Catch her and you will know all.'

Schenk turned back to her, glaring. 'You are right,' he said. 'And I will compare her story with yours in minute detail. Sigmar shall have his reckoning!' he spun for the door, his long coat flaring, and beckoned for his men. 'Come. To the horses. Holmann, you too, and bring that head.'

His men started after him, and Holmann turned to Ulrika and gave her a sad look of farewell, but before Schenk had reached the hall, Gabriella stepped after him.

'Captain Schenk,' she cried. 'Please, must you all go? The fiend's minions are still at large in the woods. We would fear for our lives alone in this broken house, just four defenceless women.'

Schenk turned, angry at being delayed, and she sidled towards him, hands clasped.

'Could you not leave at least Templar Holmann,' she pleaded. 'who has protected us so well already?'

Ulrika's skin prickled at the words, fearing the countess's true reason for wanting Holmann to stay behind, and she silently prayed to Ursun for Schenk to deny her request.

'Very well,' said Schenk. 'He will escort you to the city. I will find you again there.' And with that he strode out into the hallway and away with his men behind them, one of them gathering up the Strigoi's head.

As soon as they were gone, Hermione and Famke let out sighs of relief, while Gabriella sagged and stumbled to a chair, clutching her side.

Ulrika gasped and hurried to her. 'Mistress, are you so badly hurt?'

'I will recover,' said Gabriella, easing back in the chair. 'But there is much to be done before that.' She smiled up at Ulrika. 'First, you shall take our brave hero upstairs and see to his wounds, and your own. Let him rest in one of the guest rooms and return to me. I would speak with you.'

Ulrika blinked at her, fearing to hope. *See to his wounds?* Did that mean that Gabriella didn't intend to kill him? Would she trust his vow enough to let him go? Ulrika bowed quickly to her, wanting to be away before she changed her mind. 'Yes, mistress,' she said. 'I will bind his wounds and return.'

She turned and crossed back to Holmann. He was staring at the floor with a pained expression on his face, as he had since he had last spoken. He hadn't seemed to hear Gabriella. He didn't seem aware of anything at all.

Ulrika took his arm and led him to the stairs, wondering as she did if any amount of bandaging would heal the wound he had suffered this evening.

* * *

ULRIKA BROUGHT HOLMANN to a guest room, then found water and needle and thread in what must have been Famke's room, and clean linen in an armoire. The witch hunter did not complain as she helped him off with his coat and doublet and shirt, nor did he flinch as she washed his wounds and sewed the bigger ones closed but, as she tied off the last thread, he let out a sigh that was more than half a sob.

She looked up, concerned. 'Have I hurt you, Herr Holmann?' she asked.

'More than you can ever know,' he said.

'Friedrich–' she said, but he cut her off.

'In keeping my vow to you I have foresworn the vow I made to Sigmar,' he rasped. 'And the vow I made over my parents' graves.'

'I'm sorry,' she said. 'I should not have bound you to it. I should have left you behind at the graveyard and gone without you. Forgive me.'

He shook his head. 'It is I who should ask forgiveness – from my parents, from Sigmar, and from you – for I should not have made the vow.'

'You were under duress,' said Ulrika. 'I put you in an impossible situation. You–'

'No,' he said, his voice rising. 'You don't understand. I made the vow without intending to keep it! I meant to betray you!'

Ulrika stared at him, shocked. She hadn't suspected it, even for a second.

'A vow made to a monster is not binding,' he continued. 'It is not dishonourable to cheat a fiend. Indeed, it is policy.'

'But… but you didn't betray me,' said Ulrika.

Holmann hung his head. His voice, when it came, was rough and broken. 'Because… you are not a monster.'

Emotion constricted Ulrika's throat. 'Friedrich…'

'Even as we fought the Strigoi, I was planning to finish your mistress and the others,' he said. 'And you as well. Your betrayal on the road had hardened me to it. But–' He swallowed, then went on. 'But then you returned my sword to me.'

Ulrika frowned. 'I don't understand.'

'After you beheaded the Strigoi,' said Holmann. 'I saw it in your eyes that you were contemplating killing me, but you did not, though I could not have stopped you if you'd tried. You told me to go, though you would have faced the wrath of the others for doing so. A fiend would not have done these things, and so…'

'And so you kept the vow you meant to break,' she said.

He nodded. 'And broke the vows I thought I would keep forever.' He closed his eyes. 'And because of that, I cannot go back. I can no longer be a witch hunter. I… I will have to go somewhere – somewhere out of the Empire.'

Ulrika's chest tightened unbearably. 'Herr Holmann, don't say that!' she pleaded. 'You did a great thing here this night – a thing any templar would be proud to have done. You helped slay an evil horror that had abducted and killed countless innocents. You are still good. You can still be the man you were!'

'I killed the man I was!' Holmann cried. 'I broke my vow to my god! I lied to Captain Schenk! I protected you and your mistress against Sigmar's law!'

'But surely the good you did counter-balances that!' insisted Ulrika. 'Surely one tiny slip cannot wipe out a whole lifetime of valour!'

Holmann hung his head, his jaw tight. 'The Templars of Sigmar recognise no spectrum of morality. Evil is evil, and good is good. An ocean of good with but a single drop of evil in it is evil, and must be destroyed. If I–' He faltered, closing his eyes. 'If I find that I can see such a spectrum, then I can no longer be a templar, no matter that I cannot imagine being anything else.'

Ulrika stared at him, wanting to shout at him, wanting to beat him until he saw sense. He was a better, smarter man than Schenk or any of the other witch hunters she had ever met. He was precisely the sort of man who should be a templar, and he was running from it. She wanted to slap him. But no, it was really herself she wanted to slap and beat. It was she who had done this to him. She had put the worm of doubt in his mind. She had made his eyes, which had before seen only in black and white, suddenly see in shades of grey. She had, because of a fondness for him she would never have acted upon, and her foolish, misguided mercy, destroyed his life and his image of himself. She felt like some giant child who breaks her toys without realising her strength. She would have been more merciful if she had killed him when first they had met.

She stood suddenly, her face feeling as hard as stone. 'Rest,' she said. 'I must go to her.' Then she swept out of the room without waiting for him to reply.

* * *

THE MORNING ROOM was empty when Ulrika returned to it. Curtains had been drawn over the shattered windows, but the sun was streaming through the broken doors and the room was too light for a vampire to stay in. She followed the muffled sound of raised voices to an adjacent room, much darker, which revealed itself to be a music room, with a harpsichord in one corner and a harp in another.

Mathilda had returned, and found clothes, and she and Gabriella and Hermione stood in three corners of the room, looking as if they might start another battle at any moment, while Famke cowered in a chair to one side and watched with nervous eyes.

'Y'tried t'kill us!' Mathilda was shouting at Hermione. 'Y'ordered my death!'

'I was tricked!' cried Hermione. 'That vile conspirator Otilia whispered poison in my ear!'

'Well, y'needn't have listened!'

'Sisters, please,' said Gabriella, holding up her hands. 'Let us leave the past to the past. We know who the real killers were now, and how cunning their plan was – to turn us against each other and expose us to all of Nuln. What we still must discover is why they did it, and who was behind it. I refuse to believe that addle-pated monstrosity was anything but a sad dupe. He was manipulated as much as any of us. A "voice" told him that our blood would restore him?' she raised an eyebrow. 'So who was the voice? Who would benefit from our destruction?'

'I fear there is a more pressing question, sister,' said Hermione, stepping to a chair and sinking into it.

Gabriella raised an eyebrow. 'Oh?'

'Schenk,' said Hermione. 'You may have cooled his suspicions for the moment, but he will not be appeased for long. Even if he doesn't attack, he will always have an eye turned towards us. It will be impossible to operate.'

Gabriella nodded, her brow furrowed. 'You are right, sister. I fear it may be time to bid farewell to our current incarnations and find new guises under which to live.' She looked around. 'Perhaps we should all die here after all, savaged by ghouls.'

As the three Lahmians began to discuss the merits of this plan, Ulrika felt a hand on her arm and turned. Famke was standing beside her, a look of concern on her beautiful face.

'You look troubled, sister,' she murmured. 'Has the man hurt you?'

Ulrika turned her head to hide the pain that twisted her face at the girl's words. 'No, sister,' she said. 'I have hurt the man.'

Famke stroked her shoulder. 'Well, he most likely deserved it. They all do.'

'Not this one, I fear,' said Ulrika. She pressed Famke's hand and smiled at her. 'But thank you for your concern.'

Famke grinned shyly. 'I am just glad that we all seem to be on the same side again. Perhaps we will see more of each other now.'

'I hope so,' said Ulrika.

She turned back to the three sisters as Gabriella's voice rose again.

'Then it's decided,' she was saying. 'We will make our demise here, then wait in hiding while we consult with the queen as to our new places.'

Hermione sighed, looking around. 'I wish it weren't so. I have put so much into this place.'

Gabriella smiled. 'There will be new places, and new opportunities to decorate.' She stood as Hermione laughed. 'I will return in a moment to help with the preparations, but I have a few things I must attend to first.' She curtseyed, then limped towards Ulrika.

Ulrika hurried forwards and lent her her arm, and supported her out of the room.

'How badly are you hurt, mistress?' asked Ulrika as they entered the demolished morning room.

'Broken ribs,' said Gabriella, wincing. 'Broken leg. It matters not. All will be well when I feed.' She stopped as they reached the bottom of the stair and turned to Ulrika, looking grave. 'But first, I must speak with you, and I believe you know the subject.'

Ulrika froze, her chest tightening with dread. 'Templar Holmann?'

Gabriella nodded. 'You have two options,' she said. 'Bleed him and make him your swain, or kill him. I leave the choice to you.'

CHAPTER TWENTY-NINE
CHILDHOOD'S END

Ulrika lowered her eyes. She could not meet Gabriella's gaze. 'I choose neither,' she said. 'I want to let him go.'

'I'm sorry, beloved,' said Gabriella quietly. 'But that you cannot do.'

'But why not?' Ulrika asked, her voice rising. 'Did he not save your life and mine? Did he not honour his pledge? He lied to Schenk and broke his vow to his god rather than break it!'

'I know,' Gabriella replied. 'And it nearly killed him. A man so tortured will not long remain silent. His anguish will break him and he will speak, and we will be exposed.'

'He won't speak,' said Ulrika. 'He told me. He is going to go away. He will no longer be a witch hunter. I... cured him of that. He means to leave the Empire.'

Gabriella shook her head. 'It is still too great a risk. He might change his mind.'

Ulrika stepped back, struggling not to shout. 'But, but what does that matter? We are going to vanish, are we not? Did you not just agree with Hermione that we would pretend to die here and find new identities? What does it matter what he says?'

'Because no one must know we were vampires even after our "death",' said Gabriella patiently. 'Nuln and the world must think that there was only ever one vampire – a huge, hideous monster that preyed on innocent women. The suspicion that some of those women were also creatures of the night must fade so that we may live in peace when we enter our new roles. We cannot have Templar Holmann speaking of dead Lahmians, because we want the world to believe that there are no Lahmians at all.'

'Mistress, please,' Ulrika begged. 'I know you for a good and honourable woman. How can you not deal fairly with him when he has dealt more than fairly with us?'

Gabriella raised her chin. 'I am as good and honourable as it is within my power to be. And I deal as fairly as is possible with the living. But I must protect myself and my kind first, and when it is a choice between the death of a vampire and the death of a man, who do you suggest I allow to die?'

Ulrika stood rigid, searching an argument against the countess's cold logic, but finding none.

Gabriella sighed and stepped to her, taking her arm. 'I am sorry, my dear. But if you love him so, then make him your swain. He can be a replacement for Rodrik if you like. Then he will always be with you.'

Ulrika pulled free of her, angry. 'It is because I love him so that I won't make a swain of him!' she cried. 'I

love him for what he is – for all his hardness and honour and pain. He is a good man, a man with a mind
of his own. I won't make some fawning, hem-kissing
lapdog of him! It… it would sicken me! I do not want
slaves for lovers, I want equals!'

Gabriella nodded, and some painful memory
seemed to pass behind her eyes. 'Aye,' she said. 'I
understand. This is why we are wisest when we love
among our own kind, or not at all.' She looked up at
Ulrika, her eyes sad. 'Then I'm afraid you must kill
him. It is really the most merciful choice.'

Ulrika met her glance, her breast boiling with anger.
'You command me to kill? You promised my friends
you would teach me to do no harm!'

Gabriella did not flinch from her glare. Instead she
held it, her eyes growing as cold as winter stars. 'You
have already done the harm, girl,' she said. 'The
moment you revealed yourself to him. He was dead
then, and you only tortured him by dragging out his
death throes until now. If you wish to honour my vow
to your friends, then kill him and repair the harm, and
don't do it again. Consider it a lesson learned.' She
held out her arm. 'Now come, help me up the stairs.'

Ulrika took Gabriella's arm and started up the steps
with her, all the while her mind whirling like water
going down a drain. Every argument the countess had
put forward made sense. For her protection and the
protection of the Lahmian sisterhood, Templar Holmann must die. For his own sanity and the peace of
his soul, Templar Holmann must die. For Ulrika's own
guilt and pain, Templar Holmann must die, but still,
all she could think of was running ahead and lowering him out of a window and telling him to flee.

They came at last to the door of the guest room where Ulrika had left the witch hunter, and stopped before it. Gabriella turned to Ulrika and gave her a questioning look. Ulrika hesitated then shook her head.

'I'm sorry, mistress,' she said. 'I cannot.'

Gabriella's face grew closed and still, a blank mask. 'You disappoint me, child,' she said. 'But very well, then I will do it.'

Ulrika stepped in front of the door. 'Mistress, please.'

Gabriella shoved her aside with surprising strength, then opened the door and stepped in. Ulrika prayed that she would find the room empty and the window open, but her hope was denied. Holmann lay on the bed, bare to the waist and clutching his wounded arm, eyes closed in pain. Ulrika stopped in the door, paralysed, as Gabriella continued towards him.

Holmann opened his eyes and looked up as she approached. 'Lady?'

Gabriella smiled at him and sat beside him on the bed. 'Templar Holmann,' she said. 'Your wounds plague you?'

'Only a little,' he said. 'If you wish me to leave, I will be on my way.'

'Not at all,' said Gabriella. 'You must rest. Tonight will be soon enough for you to go. Will your pain let you sleep?'

'I will manage,' said Holmann. 'Though if you have some brandy?'

Gabriella stroked his forehead. 'I have something better than that,' she said. 'Something that will ease your pain, and my own. Now, close your eyes.'

Holmann pulled back, suddenly wary. He shot a questioning look over Gabriella's shoulder to Ulrika. 'Close my eyes?' he asked. 'What will you do?'

Ulrika lowered her head, unable to meet his gaze.

'I only want to help you sleep, Herr Templar,' said Gabriella, taking his chin and turning his face back to hers. 'Now close your eyes.'

Holmann struggled to sit up. 'Lady, I do not like this. Please. Fetch me brandy or leave me be.'

'Close your eyes,' Gabriella repeated, her voice like warm honey. 'Close your eyes.'

'Lady…' Holmann murmured, his eyelids drooping. 'Ulrika, tell… her…'

Ulrika sobbed as the templar's head fell back against the pillow and Gabriella lowered her lips to his bare neck. Ulrika was unable to watch. She clutched her arms to her chest and pressed her face to the door frame, closing her eyes and wishing for tears.

There was something hard under her left elbow – something inside her doublet. Her eyes flashed open. The silvered dagger. She held still as a terrible thought came to her, then turned and looked at Gabriella, bent over Holmann and entirely defenceless.

Ulrika's hand slipped inside her doublet and closed around the hilt of the dagger. The countess wouldn't even know it was coming. She would be dead before she could turn. Ulrika could save Holmann and run away with him – leave the Empire, have adventures in foreign lands, live outside any society except their own.

But as quick as the daydreams came, the realities overran them like Kossar cavalry – Holmann growing old, hating her for feeding, trying to kill her as he had his parents. Could she kill Gabriella for that? Could she murder the woman who had saved her and raised her, who had protected her and comforted her when she had made some childish mistake? Without Gabriella, Ulrika would be dead.

The thought made her look up. The curtains over the window were only partially closed, and a sword blade of sunlight stabbed through into the dimness. If she could not kill Gabriella, perhaps she could kill herself. She had silver in her hand and sunlight only steps away. But though visions of stabbing herself in the neck, or crashing through the leaded window into the daylight flashed through her mind, they remained only visions. She could move neither her hand nor her feet.

Gabriella sat back with a sigh of relief, then turned to Ulrika. 'Will you feed, beloved?'

Ulrika closed her eyes and shook her head – and let go of the dagger, a coward once again. 'Not from him,' she said. 'I couldn't.'

'Of course,' said Gabriella. 'I understand.' She turned back to Holmann, who lay now in blissful slumber, took his rugged head in her delicate hands, and snapped his neck as if it were a twig.

Ulrika choked and turned away, eyes closing tight, sobbing without tears. Behind her she heard Gabriella stand and cross to her. The countess's arms slipped around her and held her close.

'I am sorry, beloved,' she whispered. 'But it had to be.'

Ulrika struggled in her embrace, but Gabriella only held her tighter.

'I know the pain is terrible,' she said. 'But it will pass, I promise you. And the sooner you put humans and human emotions behind you, the sooner it will go.'

She kissed Ulrika on the cheek, then released her and stepped to the door. 'Now come,' she said. 'We have much to do.'

Ulrika hesitated as Gabriella passed into the hall. She looked back at Holmann, his hard, handsome face made weak and childish by the insipid smile Lahmian mercy had painted upon it, then she shot a last glance at the blade of sunlight streaming through the half-covered window.

Someday, she thought as she turned and followed the countess, someday I will have the courage.

ABOUT THE AUTHOR

Nathan Long was a struggling screenwriter for fifteen years, during which time he had three movies made and a handful of live-action and animated TV episodes produced. Now he is a novelist, and is enjoying it much more. For Black Library he has written three Warhammer novels featuring the Blackhearts, and has taken over the Gotrek and Felix series, starting with the eighth installment, *Orcslayer*. He lives in Hollywood.

THE GOTREK & FELIX SERIES

ISBN 978-1-84416-374-8

ISBN 978-1-84416-417-2

UK ISBN 978-1-84416-732-6   US ISBN 978-1-84416-733-3

WARHAMMER

GREY SEER

BY C·L·WERNER

A THANQUOL & BONERIPPER NOVEL

UK ISBN 978-1-84416-738-8   US ISBN 978-1-84416-739-5